FOR THE LOVE OF THE DEVIL

SHAUN STAFFORD

STREAK OF GENIUS PUBLICATIONS
127 Essex Road, Stamford, Lincs PE9 1LA

FOR THE LOVE OF THE DEVIL

First published in Great Britain in 2010 by Streak Of Genius Publications

www.streakofgenius.co.uk

Set in Palatino Linotype 10pt

Printed and bound in Great Britain by Lulu, Inc

ISBN 978-0-9561583-3-8

1 3 5 7 9 0 8 6 4 2

For Deanna

For loving me
and the demon inside …

Shaun Stafford lives in Stamford, Lincs. He has two sons. By day, he leads a mundane, wholly non-Bohemian, existence, but we can't tell you what he does. By night, he writes fiction. He has written numerous books, and has written and starred in a number of short films. Written in 1999, *For The Love Of The Devil* is from his back catalogue of work.

Also available by Shaun Stafford

The Journal

die Stunde X

Blood Money

Email: shaun.stafford@streakofgenius.co.uk

Acknowledgements

Being a writer, albeit a distinctively average one, is a lonely and sometimes terrifying existence, full of feelings of insecurity, self-deprecation and shame. All of us writers need our egos constantly massaging, lest we swallow a bottle of pills, slit our wrists or blow our brains out in a desperate and unsuccessful attempt to seek fame. Fortunately, I do have a number of people willing to massage that part of me (the ego, that is), giving me the confidence to keep on writing and, hopefully, like a fine wine, improving with time. It would be wrong of me not to thank them, even if they're all fully aware of my insincerity.

So, a shout out to Tom *(you're still a complete and utter bastard, even more so now that you have a pub),* Jez *(one of the few people to have actually read all of my books),* Carol *(who, bizarrely, seemed to hero-worship me when I first started writing (according to Barry)),* Deano *(the next one's for you!),* Dicko, *and my main writing competitor, the humorous* Mr Wright. *You didn't all tell me what a wonderful writer I was, but I sense that was because, unlike me, you don't have the ability to sound sincere when you're not. But you did provide me with criticism (some of it constructive), which has helped me to hone my talent! A special thanks also to* Lexi, *for letting me use her photograph for the cover of this book – she's an awesome photographer!*

As is the going trend, I'd also like to take this opportunity to thank my friend (though I fear he is less of a friend after taking on the onerous task of editing this book than he was before) and editor, Barry Warburton, *the only man who is even more stubborn and opinionated than I am. He took on the diabolically onerous task of editing this book. One day, Barry, I will actually listen to you, but only if you manage to spot the typos that litter all of my books* ***before*** *they are actually published!*

PROLOGUE

As his Mercedes-Benz wound along the country lanes leading away from London, Michael Bartholomew still wasn't certain what had made him decide he was no longer safe where he was. But something had. Some niggling little voice at the back of his mind had been growing louder all through the last week, until today it had become a shout, so loud and fearsome that he could no longer ignore it.

"You have to leave," the voice had told him. "They know. *They* know."

He fumbled around in his pocket for his cigarettes, opening the pack with the thumb of one hand and tapping the pack on the wrist of his other, until the last cigarette popped out. He took it between his lips, at the same time pushing in the cigarette lighter. He tossed the empty packet onto the top of the dashboard, where it fell upon the inside of the heated windscreen.

Just a guilty conscience, he had told himself when the voice had first manifested itself. Everyone suffered from a guilty conscience, even those supposedly without one. Hell, even Hitler must've wondered about all of the kids his men had butchered in the concentration camps at some time in his life. Perhaps when he was all alone in the bunker in Berlin, Luger pistol in his hand, moments from his death. Perhaps, Bartholomew wondered, that was what had finally driven Hitler to suicide.

The cigarette lighter popped out and immediately he pounced on it, holding the glowing tip to the cigarette in his mouth and puffing it into life. He replaced the lighter and pulled up at a T-junction, glancing left and right, deciding which was the best route to take. But he had no idea where he was going, so what the hell difference did it make?

Left, and the sign before him told him that he would be on his way to Dunstable. Right, and he could pay Leighton Buzzard, amongst others, a visit. It all amounted to the same thing. Whichever direction he chose, he was on the road to nowhere.

He chose left, and accelerated harshly, the fat tyres of the Mercedes chirping as the traction control system fought to prevent wheel spin. The empty cigarette packet flew first to the right, then back to the left as the car straightened out on the narrow, deserted B-road. It hit the door pillar on the far side, and then bounced upwards, landing on the knees of the woman sitting beside him.

Cathy Bartholomew awoke with a start, first looking down at the cigarette packet in confusion, and then turning to look at her husband.

"Where are we now?" she asked quietly, her expression unable to hide her concern. That was hardly surprising, seeing as how he'd told her virtually nothing about why he'd dragged her from their second home in London's city centre.

Michael Bartholomew couldn't really answer. To tell her the truth – that he didn't know precisely where they were, because he had no idea where they were going – would only confuse and worry her even more.

But didn't she have a right to know? A right to know why they had deserted their two children, leaving them behind to face – as only Michael knew – an uncertain future? A right to know that all of this might ultimately turn out to be the product of nothing more than an overactive guilt complex? But that inner voice had sounded so lucid, so real, as though someone were standing right behind him.

"Michael?"

"Go back to sleep, darling," he told her, his tone devoid of life. He couldn't even muster up any encouragement.

"Sleep? How can you expect me to sleep?"

"You *were* asleep," he reminded her.

"It's been a long day," she countered. "And then the minute I get back from that meeting, you're demanding that I pack a suitcase and get in the car. And for what? God only knows, because I certainly don't."

"It's nothing to worry about," Bartholomew tried to reassure her, again in a bland monotone.

"Isn't it?" Cathy fished in her handbag for her mobile. "Let me call the girls, see how they are, let them know we're okay."

Bartholomew wanted to scream, "We're not okay! We're far from fucking okay!" but that would've meant having to let Cathy in on the whole secret. And she would certainly have made him turn back for the girls then. Perhaps, he wondered, they should. Were the girls safe? Surely they wouldn't harm his daughters. After all, they'd done nothing wrong. They hadn't ...

Bartholomew shook his head.

It was as though if he admitted his crimes to himself, somehow Cathy would hear that admission.

He wasn't ready for that.

Not yet.

"Michael, you know I've always supported you in the past ... but what the hell are we doing here? Are we running from someone? And if we are, then who?"

Bartholomew shuddered. It was as though someone had walked over his grave, that odd sensation that shook his insides. Cathy was no fool. She might well have been a walkover, and maybe she was the obedient wife – but she never did anything without wanting to know why. So far, he'd managed to avoid answering her questions. He had the feeling that he wouldn't be able to avoid answering them for much longer.

She was holding her phone, its backlit face illuminating the interior of the car. "I should let them know what's happening," she said. "We're supposed to be going home this weekend, Michael."

"I know that, honey," he said. "But just leave it for the moment, hey? Please?"

Cathy sighed heavily. She tossed the phone into the glove compartment. "Is it something to do with the business?"

"Cathy, you know I'd never do anything to hurt you," Bartholomew said. "I'd never cheat on you, would I?"

"I'd like to think that."

"Well, just trust me on this. I can't tell you anything. Not yet."

Bartholomew looked up to the rear-view mirror. A set of headlights had appeared.

They were being followed!

He brushed the thought aside.

They weren't being followed. That was impossible. He almost laughed.

But the lights were still there, expensive Xenon lamps, like a pair of blue eyes. A BMW, perhaps, something vulgar but not cheap.

His attention to what was behind them didn't go unnoticed by Cathy, who swung her head around. "What is it? Are we being followed?"

"I don't know," he said quietly, following it up with a stern, "No! Look, why would anybody want to follow us?"

"You tell me," she snapped. "You're the man of mystery with all of this crap!"

Bartholomew eased the accelerator slightly. He wanted the car behind to get closer, give it the opportunity to overtake. Glancing ahead, he saw the sharp deviation signs, the road disappearing to the left. He positioned the Mercedes towards the centre of the road. The car behind wouldn't be overtaking yet, and he wanted to adopt an easy line into the corner.

When he turned his gaze back to the mirror, he saw something that made his eyes widen.

He blinked, looked from the mirror, rubbed his eyes.

"Michael!"

His focus snapped back to the road ahead, the black and white chevrons glowing in the light from the Mercedes' headlights. Yanking the wheel sharply to the left, he turned into the corner, only marginally too late, the back end flipping out momentarily, before he corrected. He rounded the bend on the wrong side of the road, pulling back inwards as they exited.

"Jesus, Michael, what the hell do you think you're doing?"

Bartholomew mopped his sweaty brow with the cuff of his shirt, and glanced back up at the mirror. Nothing there – nothing except for the headlights of the car following them.

Perhaps he'd just imagined it.

"Michael?"

"I just lost my concentration for a second," he told her. "Nothing to worry about. I'm tired, that's all."

"Do you want me to take over?" Cathy asked.

Bartholomew didn't answer. He watched as the headlights in the rear-view mirror moved to the right, disappearing from view, before dazzling him in the side mirror. The car was overtaking. He looked to the side, watched as a light coloured BMW swished past, the occupant in the passenger seat looking into the Mercedes. He tried to reassure himself that its occupants were probably just wondering what the hell had caused the luxury saloon in front of them to swerve violently across the road.

The BMW overtook quickly, its rear lights rapidly shrinking as it accelerated away from the Mercedes.

"Honey?"

Bartholomew looked at Cathy. "Huh?"

"I said, do you want me to take over?"

He quickly shook his head. "No." That would mean having to think of a destination. It would also mean handing over the control of their destiny to a woman who wasn't in possession of the full facts.

"Then tell her," a growling voice said.

"What the fuck?"

"Michael?"

Michael Bartholomew looked up in the rear-view mirror.

And this time, he knew he wasn't mistaken.

Here was the owner of the voice that had encouraged him to run away, a voice that had, at first, whispered that encouragement, before shouting out a command he could no longer ignore.

Bartholomew's jaw dropped.

The thing sitting in the rear of the car smiled.

"Glad to see you took my advice, Mikey," it said.

"Who are you?" Bartholomew demanded.

"Michael, who are you talking to?"

"Don't you see?" Bartholomew shouted hysterically, jabbing a finger to the rear of the car. "Don't you fucking see?"

"She doesn't see," the thing told him. "Only people like you can see."

The thing moved quickly, darting between the front seats and grabbing the steering wheel, pulling it out of Bartholomew's hands. The car slew sideways, spinning down the road at a velocity of more than seventy miles per hour. In a panic, and with the sound of Cathy's screams fighting with that of the tyres squealing in his ears, Bartholomew jammed his foot hard on the brakes, but that only made the car spin more violently.

The thing was laughing.

Its face was inches from Bartholomew's, its bright white eyes open, its mouth agape, the brilliant white, sharp teeth dazzling even in the dim illumination from the dashboard. And its laugh was a piercing belly roar that mocked him, terrified him, and unnerved him.

"Fuck you, you bastard!"

Bartholomew lashed out, but the thing was gone, and his fist connected with Cathy's temple. It was a blow full of vehemence, combined with the centrifugal effect of the car being spun around, and it made a sickening crack as it connected. Bartholomew had time to regret his actions, but only for a split second. Looking beyond his wife's stunned face, he saw a telegraph pole, flying towards the car.

It was like being on a fairground waltzer, watching the scenery spin out of view. Only this waltzer came to a bone-crunching halt as the Mercedes slammed into the telegraph pole with a terrific bang and the howl of twisting metal. The car bounced over to one side, and then curled around the telegraph pole, crashing down on the other side in a deep ditch.

Then there was only silence.

It was a few moments before Michael Bartholomew realized that he was still alive.

It was perhaps half a minute before his scrambled mind pulled itself back into something resembling coherence, and attempted to make sense out of what had just happened.

Immediately, his eyes turned to Cathy.

It was easy to see her face, because somehow the interior light had switched itself on, illuminating the whole inside of the car.

Bartholomew traced his eyes across the crumpled ceiling, which was now a glossy crimson in colour, the blood dripping down onto the floor of the car. The car lay in the ditch at an angle, tilted over to the driver's side, with the front pointing slightly skywards. As a result, Cathy's head was lolling backwards, but facing him. The bruise on her face where he had punched her was evident, but there was no open wound, certainly nothing that could explain the massive quantities of blood that had showered the Mercedes' interior.

"Cathy," he said softly.

He tried to move, but as he did, a violent pain shot up his arm and through his shoulder. He screamed in agony.

When he opened his eyes, the thing was there.

"Mikey, what have you done?"

In the light, Bartholomew could see the creature's face more clearly now. It was inhuman, a dark, blood red in colour, with black hair that was slicked back between two protrusions, a little over an inch in length on either side of its head, that were not unlike horns. The teeth were impossibly white, the canines fearsomely long, like those of a savage wolf.

"Well, Mikey boy?"

"Who are you?" Bartholomew asked, his voice hoarse, afraid.

The creature let out another laugh. "Ah, well, you know how some people have got that whole guardian angel shit going on? Well, I am south to the north, west to the east, night to the day. I am darkness to the light, fire to the water, yang to the yin. I am evil ... to the good." The creature moved its face so close to Bartholomew's that he could smell its fetid breath. "Does that make things clearer to you? No? Perhaps this will." It leant back, swung Cathy's face around, and said, "I am death to the life."

Bartholomew stared at his wife's head, all crushed and split open on the left side, her brain exposed, her face soaked in thick lumpy blood.

"Cathy?"

"She's dead, Mikey."

"Cathy?" Bartholomew didn't want to believe what he was seeing. The thing most precious to him, the most important person in his life was gone. All that was left was this bloody, shattered corpse, signifying the horrific and painful way that she had left this earth.

"It's terrible when someone so undeserving dies in so terrible a way, isn't it?" the creature said. "All of that pain ... my God, the pain!"

Bartholomew felt the tears coming, but couldn't wipe them away from his face. His shoulder was broken, and his right hand was trapped between the door and the steering wheel. "This isn't happening," was all he could think of to say.

"Oh, but it is," the creature said, bobbing its head between the seats again, blocking out the horrifying vision of Cathy. "It's very much happening. Your wife is dead, killed by your reckless driving, and you ...

well, your heart *is* weak, isn't it? Isn't that what the consultant told you three weeks ago? A walking infarction, aren't you, Mikey? Your death is but a heartbeat away. Well, not a heartbeat," the creature said with an impish smile, "because your heart is stopping ... right about now."

Bartholomew felt the contractions in his chest, a pain like nothing he'd ever experienced before, like the weight of an elephant sitting on him, forcing the air from his lungs, crushing his ribcage. He felt a strangling sensation in his throat, and moved his left arm, ignorant of the pain as cracked bone ground against cracked bone. He tried to scream out in pain, but the sound wouldn't come. All he could think of was Cathy.

Why hadn't he told her? Why hadn't he just fucking told her?

At least then she wouldn't have gone to her death without knowing why. At least then it would've made sense to her.

He turned to his left, expecting to see the creature, whoever, *whatever*, that might've been.

Instead, he saw Cathy's face. Not the beautiful face of the woman he'd married, but the twisted wreckage of a woman he'd killed.

That image was imprinted onto his retinas as he died.

1

The day was as grey as such a sombre occasion dictated, and Sadie Bartholomew, a black veil pulled over her face, stared blankly out of the window of the black limousine following the two hearses. Beside her, her sixteen-year-old sister was crying. Sadie felt only guilt, because she was still numb from shock, too dumbstruck to offer Jodie any support. She needed that herself – she was only twenty-one, after all.

Aside from Jodie's sobs, the only sound was that of the windscreen wipers squeaking across the wet glass, a noise that easily drowned out that of the car's eerily almost-silent engine. The two black-suited gentlemen sitting in the front of the car neither spoke nor looked at one another. It was a typical funeral procession, something these men probably experienced two or three times a day, five, maybe six days a week, probably fifty-two weeks of the year. Death to them was not only expected, but was familiar, a routine employment that probably became just as tedious to them as any other job did to most of the working population. A way to earn money.

Money.

It all came down to that, didn't it?

In spite of the situation she found herself in, Sadie couldn't help but allow a wry smile to creep across her face. For the last four or five years, her father had given her an allowance. It was a significant amount by anybody else's standards, but considering the amount of wealth Michael Bartholomew had access to, it was nothing more than a drop in the ocean. Now her father was dead, however, she would be more financially secure than he had ever been. The endowment policies on the mortgages for the two houses would ensure that both she and Jodie would have a home each. The insurance policies for both her parents' lives would provide the two sisters with wealth that neither could previously have imagined. And all of this on top of the savings that Michael Bartholomew had in numerous bank accounts.

According to the family's solicitor – who also stood to benefit by taking a considerably substantial percentage for managing the estate – the two sisters would be millionaires many times over.

Sadie let out a sigh. Not a big one, but loud enough for Jodie to glance in her direction, a frown on her face. Sadie looked at her sister, took in her long, black hair, her dark eyes that were now red and puffy, her moist cheeks glistening as they caught the light from outside, and she realized that Jodie had rarely stopped crying since the accident.

Sadie, on the other hand, hadn't even started.

She felt so ashamed, so callous, but she just couldn't force the tears out. She lay in bed, recalling all of the funny moments she had shared with her parents, the jokes her father used to tell, including some offensive and self-deprecating Jewish ones. The way her mother used to say, "We'll keep this our little secret," every time Sadie used to go out on a Friday night when her father was still working in the city centre. She felt as though she was really going to miss her parents, but still the tears wouldn't come.

"Are you okay?" Jodie asked her, her American accent corrupted by four years of British schooling. Jodie couldn't understand why Sadie wasn't as distraught as she was, couldn't comprehend that Sadie was so shell-shocked that she just couldn't really come to terms with what had happened. And Sadie couldn't come to terms with the family's solicitor telling her that, being the eldest, she now had a lot of responsibility. Her father's business, for a start but, more importantly, Jodie who, at only sixteen, wasn't at all ready for a lifetime without parental guidance. At twenty-one, Sadie wasn't sure that she herself was entirely ready either.

Sadie reached across the wide expanse of the back seat of the limousine and grabbed her sister's hand. It felt cold, clammy, horrible to touch.

But it gave her some comfort.

"I'm fine," she told Jodie. She threw her head back and let out another sigh, dropping it back down and pinching the bridge of her nose with her fingers. She wasn't sure why. She didn't have a headache, her sinuses weren't playing up. She supposed she was doing it purely for effect, putting on a performance. She looked at Jodie and kissed her lightly on the temple. "How about you? How are you feeling?"

Jodie shrugged, covered her face with her damp handkerchief, one that had belonged to their mother, and let out another sob.

Sadie instantly embraced her. She may not have felt much emotion herself, but she was determined to be there for her sister when she needed support. She knew that she always would be, no matter what.

As they approached the cemetery, the rain began to pound down on the roof of the car, and the windscreen wipers swept back and forth at a hypnotic pace. The cortege, some twenty cars in length, including two hearses and four black limousines, crawled along at little more than walking pace, and Sadie was willing this ordeal to be over as quickly as possible. She wanted to throw off these depressing black clothes, have as much to drink as possible, and perhaps jump on stage and sing a few songs.

Would that be ever so disrespectful? she wondered.

As the procession turned into the cemetery, Sadie's eyes fell upon the myriad headstones that she could see between each sweep of the windscreen wipers. Then her eyes drifted directly ahead to the nearest hearse, the one that contained their mother's polished black ash casket, with a beautiful wreath fixed to the top. She shuddered as she recalled that her mother's corpse was inside that wooden box, the blood drained away, to be replaced by a chemical supposed to ward off putrefaction. But essentially, nature was breaking down her mother's body into waste elements. And it was all happening within that box.

Jodie kept her eyes covered, which was fortunate, Sadie thought as she saw the black-suited men standing around the freshly dug, open graves, the mounds of earth easily distinguishing them from the other graves in the cemetery. The cortege came to a halt some fifty metres from the graves, and the undertaker sitting alongside the driver hopped out to hold open the door for Sadie. The driver did likewise for Jodie, both men standing with their backs to the open doors.

Sadie climbed out, beneath the shelter of the umbrella the man was holding. He handed it to her, and then closed the door, clasping his hands in front of him. And there, thought Sadie, he would stand, in the rain, until the funeral was over, until they were ready to return to the cars. Probably he would have an umbrella of his own, that he would hold aloft for the duration of the burial service, only to hide away as it concluded. More likely, she thought as she stepped up to the front of the car to meet Jodie, the two men would wait in the warmth of the car itself, stepping out at the last minute, their movements going unnoticed by the mourners.

The two sisters locked their arms around one another as an undertaker led them gently up to the rear of the first hearse, where four pallbearers were carefully lifting out their father's casket.

The walk to the graves was slow, the two girls on show to the whole of the mourning party, and even to a seasoned professional like Sadie, used to standing on stage in front of scores of people, it was a daunting experience, knowing that everyone present was observing their reactions.

The rabbi read the sermon, but to Sadie – whose father was a lapsed Jew, and whose mother hadn't even been christened in any religion – it simply went in one ear and out the other. What was the point in believing in God? Where did it ever get anyone? She watched as the coffins were lowered down to the regulatory six feet under, and shook her head. Well, her parents were non-believers, and they had died in a tragic accident – perhaps, Sadie thought, had they believed in God, they'd still be alive now.

She looked up at the rabbi – that's what he'd believe anyway.

She hugged Jodie closer to her body, holding the umbrella over the both of them. Her younger sister was all cried out, wiping away the residue of tears from her face. Sadie kissed her on the forehead again, and at that moment, felt herself sob, the first time since the accident. But that was all it was – a single, solitary sob. All the same, it was enough for Jodie to look up at her, to squeeze her reassuringly.

Eventually, the rabbi closed his sermon, and one of the undertakers handed a shovel to Sadie, which she took over to the edge of her mother's grave. She used it to throw three shovelfuls of earth into the grave, and then stuck the shovel into the pile of earth. Jodie picked it up, and did likewise, and then gulping back more tears – she didn't want to cry, not here, not on show before a hundred mourners – she moved over to her father's grave and did the same there with a second shovel.

The rest of the mourners started to queue up to do the same, and Sadie heard the thud of earth on wood. Overhead, thunder cracked loudly, and Sadie could sense the uncertainty of the undertakers, the mourners, and even the rabbi. Surely he wouldn't believe that his God would strike lightning down upon a religious service?

"Miss Bartholomew?"

Sadie turned. It was the chief undertaker, his dark suit, long black overcoat, white shirt and black tie contrasting with his pale, gaunt features.

"We should go now," he said, smiling a smile that wouldn't have looked out of place in a horror film. "I don't really want to rush you, but ..." He looked skyward. "It's probably not safe out here," he added, as another crash of thunder rumbled through Sadie's body.

Sadie nodded.

Yes, she thought, let's get out of this place.

As she climbed back in the car, she looked and saw the grave diggers moving in, spades in their hands, ready to finish what the mourners had started. As the rain began to throw itself down up on the roof of the car, massive drops the size of marbles, the thunder once again rocked the cemetery, and Sadie watched as the grave diggers turned and went back the way they'd come.

Life carried on, she thought soberly as the procession, *sans* hearses, returned to the family home in Harrow. Along the way, she saw people carrying on as normal, working, shopping, playing, gossiping, some of them turning and looking at the procession, before going back to their own lives.

Soon, thought Sadie, they'd have to deal with death. Everybody did at least once in their lifetime. Everybody. Whether it be a parent, a grandparent, a child, a partner, or even a pet, somebody's life was touched by death every second of every day. Sadie could only wonder what kind of God designed humanity in such a way that every person found themselves mourning the loss of somebody.

No, she thought as the car pulled into the courtyard of the mansion, there was no God. There were no guardian angels, no one to watch over you when you went about your daily business. You had to look out for yourself.

Because whilst there might not have been a God or angels, there certainly was such a thing as the devil. The devil gave you cancer, took your unborn child away, threw you beneath the wheels of a bus.

Sadie shook that thought away. Negativity would get her nowhere, and she was no theologian, had no desire to discuss religion with anyone, least of all with herself. Once again, the doors to the car were opened, and Sadie and Jodie stepped out, walking up to the front door, which was already being opened by the funeral director.

Sadie thanked the man, who nodded slowly, deferentially, as she passed him and stepped into the warm house. Jodie came in behind her, and the two girls prepared to greet the rest of the mourners, here to pay their last respects to people they were either related to, or else knew very well. Most of the faces, Sadie thought as they shook hands, offered condolences, and kissed cheeks, she didn't know. Even those who claimed they were family members were little more than strangers, over from the United States.

She did recognize her aunt and uncle, and kissed them both. Her aunt was crying, and once more Sadie found herself having to be the strong one. She recalled her uncle saying to her when he'd arrived in the UK yesterday, "You've got to look after your sister now. And that's a great burden for such young shoulders to bear. If you ever need anything ..."

And it had been left at that, as it always was. Most of the guests had said that to Sadie as they passed through into the sitting room, where food and drink had been prepared. "If you ever need any help ..." They never went any further, never concluded with, "just come and ask." What they really meant was, "If you need any help, well, I can't give it to you, but I have to say it – it's protocol, see."

Her uncle, though, was different. He *would* help them – she could trust him. He didn't bother saying more than that, because she knew that she could depend on him.

And now here he was, standing before her now.

"*Shalom*," he said, kissing her tenderly on the cheek. "How are you bearing up?"

Sadie shrugged, a wry smile crossing her face. "I feel like I should be reacting in a different way," she said.

Her uncle frowned and said seriously, "Honey, you don't have to act in any way just to please others. It's been a big shock for you, and it may take weeks for you to fully grasp what's happened here." He led her carefully away from Jodie, as their aunt once again embraced her. "You've got a lot of responsibility towards Jodie now, and that's probably what's playing on your mind. You haven't been given the time to come to terms with what has happened – it only happened yesterday. So don't worry. I know you loved your mom, *aleha ha-shalom* and dad, *alav ha-shalom*. And anyone here who knows you, they know it too." He smiled. "You're a performer, Sadie, but this isn't a performance. This is real life. Just be yourself. Okay?"

Sadie nodded.

"You want me to take charge in there?" he asked, nodding towards the sitting room.

"Please."

He patted her on the shoulder and nodded his head, before disappearing to do his duty.

"Sadie."

Sadie looked up to see the last of the mourners stepping up to her. He was a tall man, thickset, with a friendly face and a head of thick, dark brown hair. He wore spectacles, the kind that tinted with the sun – today, however, they were clear. Dressed in a beige suit, he wasn't exactly in the proper attire for such an occasion, but the black tie marked his respect. Doubtless he would rip it off and replace it with something more jovial the moment he left the wake.

"Alexander," Sadie greeted. "Good of you to come."

"It was the least I could do," Alexander Bartek said, stepping up to her. "Michael was a good business partner. The best. More than that, he was like a father to me."

"I know," Sadie said. There was a silence for perhaps half a minute, but not an embarrassing one. They were alone in the massive hallway now, but the sounds of mourning revellers could be heard coming from the sitting room.

"You know, it's amazing, isn't it? People die, and what's the first thing everyone does? Throw a party!"

Sadie nodded her head. "It's kinda funny," she said. But she wasn't smiling.

"How are you, anyway?"

"Holding up," she answered. "Better than I thought I would be."

"You have a lot of responsibility," Alexander said. "Perhaps it's good that you're not in pieces."

"Everyone keeps telling me I have a lot of responsibilities now."

Alexander was going to say something – she could tell that by looking at him – but he seemed to pause momentarily. "The business," he said. "What are you going to do with it?"

"You mean, our half?"

"Oh, I was never a partner in anything more than name, Sadie," Alexander said. "Michael made me a very wealthy man, and for that I'll be eternally grateful, but the business was always his. He allowed me to make decisions, but I took a pay cheque home, like everyone else. A substantial one, admittedly, but a pay cheque nevertheless."

"I never knew."

Alexander smiled tightly. "There were a lot of things you never knew about your father," he said mysteriously, and Sadie was intrigued.

"Such as?" she asked, but at that moment, her uncle came into the hallway.

"Good morning, Alexander."

"Mr Bartholomew." The two men shook hands.

"Sadie, the natives are getting restless," he said. There was some reluctance in his voice. "I think you're going to have to come in, show your face. I know it's going to be an ordeal, but ..."

"I'll be right there," Sadie said, and her uncle, sensing that she wasn't finished talking with Alexander, nodded and walked off.

Alexander kissed Sadie on the cheek. "I'm going," he said.

"But–"

"Duty calls," he told her. "I've got a flight to catch."

"You're leaving the country?" Sadie's original question was forgotten.

"Well, I guess you could say I'm out of work now," he said. "I've been offered a position back in the US."

"But what about dad's business?"

Alexander smiled. "Sadie, you don't know the first thing about your father's business, do you?"

"I ..." She grinned and shook her head. "I don't even know what it is."

"Exactly. Which is why Anthony Schildt is going to advise you to sell the business, if he hasn't done so already."

Alexander was talking about the family's solicitor. She nodded her head. "That was mentioned," she said.

"I could work for you until you sell up," Alexander said, "but the thought of losing the top position to the son of a new owner doesn't really appeal to me. And I've got lucky – this opportunity just fell into my lap. I have to take it."

"I guess what you're saying makes sense," Sadie conceded. "You'll stay in touch?"

Alexander smiled. "I'll write you with my address the moment I sort one out," he assured her.

"I'm gonna miss you, Alex."

"Me too."

"You know," Sadie said, wondering whether she really should reveal this secret to Alexander. "Dad always tried to get us together. I think he always wanted a son."

"Well, I guess I was the next best thing," Alexander said. "I suppose it was only natural for him to want me as a son-in-law." He said it with his tongue in his cheek. "I'd better be off," he said abruptly. My flight's in a couple of hours."

"Bye, Alex."

Alexander smiled coyly, and then leaned forwards and kissed her gently on the lips. "Another time, another place ... maybe if I was ten years younger." Sadie laughed.

They both knew that no matter what the circumstances, they'd never have got together. There was friendship there, maybe even the kind of love siblings share, but there was never attraction – at least, Sadie wasn't attracted to Alexander.

As he left the house, she wondered if he was attracted to her.

Another regretfully trivial thought on such a disconsolate day.

2

In the two days since the funeral, Sadie was attempting to regain some of the normality in her life. She knew that at some point in the future, she was going to have to sort through her parents' belongings; the clothes, the personal items, her father's extensive library of contemporary novels, and vast CD, DVD and vinyl collection. Some of the things would be thrown out; others, such as clothes, she had decided would be given to charity. But right now, she couldn't bring herself to even enter her parents' bedroom, let alone rifle through their personal effects.

Jodie was, at this moment in time, either upstairs in bed or taking a bath. Sadie had arranged with her school for her to have the next fortnight off. With the Bartholomews being such generous contributors to the school's fund, they were only too happy to oblige, even assuring Sadie that Jodie would be given extra tuition upon her return, something that Sadie knew Jodie wouldn't be at all happy to hear.

The television in the kitchen was on, and Sadie sat at the breakfast bar ignoring it, as the breakfast news presenters shared a few private jokes in between the serious articles. She wasn't in the mood to watch the news, or listen to idle banter. It was only on because it was like company, and that was something she was kind of short of at the moment. The relatives and family friends had long since departed, and she hadn't seen any of her own friends in a week. They were keeping their distance, probably because they weren't sure how she'd react.

The last person she'd spoken to – other than those at the funeral, and of course Jodie – had been Billy, the guitarist and her song-writing partner in *Darcy's Box*. He'd called her up last night to ask how she was doing – but Sadie knew he had an ulterior motive. Not that she could've blamed him –

she knew that if the situation was reversed, she'd be just as anxious to speak to him, with what the band had coming up.

She'd agreed to meet him on Thursday – it was Wednesday today, which gave her some time to think about what she had to say. She wasn't entirely certain whether she could go through with the gig on Friday. Not only was she not in the proper frame of mind to perform to the best of her ability to do the rest of the band justice, she was extremely nervous. Who wouldn't have been? Three A&R men, a handful of local producers, some club booking agents, and a whole host of local talent would be there at the Billabong, some of them wanting to see firsthand the band they'd been hearing so much about, others hoping to see their rivals fail, or maybe even succeed, depending on the type of person they were.

The pressure was on, and at this precise moment in time, Sadie wasn't ready for that kind of responsibility. After all, the band would just be the band, banging away on their instruments – not that she wished to put down their talent – but it was her voice that would stand out the most. And if her voice wasn't up to scratch, then it didn't matter how well the rest of the band performed, their careers would effectively be over before they'd begun.

Sadie put down her toast as Jodie came into the kitchen, her dressing gown pulled tight around her body. Sadie looked at her sister – she was growing up now, physically, if not mentally. Soon, she'd be bringing her boyfriends home, and that was one more thing for Sadie to worry about. She knew what boys were like. More to the point, she knew what teenage girls were like. She had been one once, after all. A pot of hormones, bubbling over.

"What's for breakfast," Jodie asked. At least she wasn't constantly in tears any more, though Sadie had an idea that the slightest thing would set her off again.

"Whatever you make," Sadie replied, standing up and taking the plate of toast across the kitchen to the bin. She tipped in the half eaten round, and then put the plate back on the draining board. "And it's your turn to do the dishes," she added. It was about time things started to get back to normal.

Jodie raised an eyebrow. "I don't believe you cleared those from last night."

Sadie looked at the large pile on the draining board. "That's because it's your turn."

"I don't think so."

"Well, I'm not doing them."

"Me neither."

Sadie smiled. "You'll think differently when you open the cupboard. There are no dishes left."

"You know, I should swear at this point."

"No," Sadie said, walking from the kitchen, "you shouldn't."

As she passed through the hallway, the doorbell rang, and she stopped in her tracks. She was still in her dressing gown, her short hair was unkempt, she hadn't checked her face for spots, or even had a wash that morning – she was in no condition to receive visitors. But neither was Jodie. She considered not answering, but decided it was probably important. They rarely received visitors, and it was unlikely that it was just a parcel.

Maybe it was her uncle, or Alexander back from the US, or Anthony Schildt, here to discuss financial matters.

All the same, it was only eight in the morning – it was a little early for any of those.

Curious, she stepped up to the mirror in the hallway, ran a hand through her hair, did a quick check for any spots, found none, and then ensured that her dressing gown wasn't too revealing. It wasn't – it came down to her ankles, was tied tightly around her waist, and revealed only slightly the bulges of her breasts. Nothing more revealing than a long dress, in fact. Jodie's, on the other hand, didn't even come down to her knees.

"I'll get the door!" Sadie shouted. "You stay in the kitchen!"

She stepped up to the front door, unlocked it, and opened it.

The first thing she saw were the two police officers standing a few feet from the door, their black and white uniforms immediately bringing back disturbing memories of the night her parents were killed, when two officers, one a woman, had visited the house to give them the news.

Then her eyes focused on the two men standing closer to the door.

One of them, a balding man, in his forties, with a friendly face that she never in a million years would have thought belonged to a policeman, was holding up his warrant card. His tone was cheerful – too cheerful for such an ungodly hour – as he said, "Miss Bartholomew? Miss Sadie Bartholomew?"

"That's right," Sadie said, frowning, a little confused.

"Detective Superintendant Saddington," he said. "Economic and Specialist Crime Division, Metropolitan Police. May we come in, Miss Bartholomew?"

"What's this about?" Sadie asked, instantly going on the defensive. She felt weak again, as weak as she had when they'd come to tell her about her parents' deaths.

Saddington smiled. "It really would be better if we came in."

"Just you," she said.

"I really would like my DI to come in as well," Saddington said. He turned to the uniformed officers. "Wait in the car. DI Egan will come out and get you when we're ready." And with that, the two detectives stepped into the house, the DI, a tall, handsome man, with a goatee and long, but neatly brushed hair, closing the door behind him.

"What is this about?" Sadie repeated the question. "What's the Economic and Specialist Crime Division?"

"Fraud squad," Egan said. "In layman's terms."

"Miss Bartholomew, I don't know where to begin, but ..." Saddington dropped his head, sighed, then looked up again. "Yesterday, a gentleman from the Federal Bureau of Investigation came to New Scotland Yard, along with a briefcase full of documents concerning your father's business activities in the United States."

"The FBI?"

"The FBI, yes."

"What kind of business activities?"

"Specifically, fraud and tax evasion," Saddington said. "There really was no easy way to tell you, so I thought I'd just come out and say it. I hope you appreciate my honesty and directness."

Sadie didn't. "Well, I might've done, if you weren't here telling me my father was a crook. You know, we only buried him two days ago. Show some respect, will you?"

Saddington looked at Egan, who simply stared at Sadie impassively. "I don't want to do this, Miss Bartholomew, but we have a warrant here to search these premises, and any other premises owned either by your parents, or by you and your sister, and any vehicles thereon."

"What?"

"We're looking for documents relating to this matter," Egan said. He spoke with a Northern Irish accent. Sadie knew, because she'd once dated a man from Ulster, until she found that, in spite of his wealthy background, he was somehow involved with the Loyalist paramilitaries.

"My father was no criminal," Sadie snapped.

"Miss Bartholomew, I might be a police officer, but I can distinguish between lowlifes and men like your father," Saddington said. "He didn't pay his taxes for a few years, and that makes him a tax evader rather than a child molester. All the same, he *is* a criminal."

"Innocent until proven guilty."

"Not in this case," Egan said. Sadie was now starting to positively dislike the Irishman, but she had an idea that the feeling was mutual.

"Why don't you either shut the fuck up or get out of my house," Sadie hissed.

Egan just smirked.

And when Saddington spoke again, she understood why. "Well, therein lies the problem," he said. "You see, until this matter is resolved, all the Bartholomew assets will have to be frozen."

Sadie couldn't really grasp the precise meaning of that statement. She looked carefully at Saddington. "Which means what?"

"Which means," Egan said, "you will not have access to any of the Bartholomew bank accounts, insurance payments, trust funds or properties."

"You're throwing us out of our home?"

"Homes," corrected Egan. Sadie scowled at him, and even Saddington appeared pissed off with his junior officer.

"It's a temporary measure," he said. "Hopefully, the funds in the accounts owned by your father will be sufficient to pay the taxes owed."

"But what about this fraud?" Sadie enquired. "What kind of fraud?"

"Corporate fraud," Saddington said. "And a number of large American companies were taken in, some to the tune of more than a hundred million dollars. Your father owed a lot of people a lot of money. But Uncle Sam wants his money back first. I believe that our colleagues from the FBI will be visiting your family's solicitor this morning to serve the relevant notices. Doubtless he'll be in touch with you as soon as that happens."

"What kind of debts are we talking about here?" Sadie wanted to know.

"An estimate from the FBI states that the taxes and resultant fines owed to the US Treasury is in excess of a hundred million dollars, and there will more than likely be fines to pay with regards to the fraud charges. Maybe the same again, in addition to the compensation for the monies obtained by deception. It could be five or six hundred million." At that, Sadie almost collapsed. "Perhaps we should be speaking to your solicitor ourselves? He can explain the intricacies of the case to you in simpler terms."

"You're telling me that all of the money my father wanted to leave to my sister and me is being taken from us," Sadie said. "How much more simpler than that can it get?" Saddington raised his eyebrows – Sadie half-expected him to shrug like a naughty schoolboy caught cheating, but he didn't. "How long do we have?"

"We'd like to search the properties immediately," Saddington said. "We'll give you the opportunity to get dressed. I'm sure that you've got nothing to hide."

"And even if you did have," Egan added, "I'm sure we'd find it."

Sadie ignored him. "I mean, how long do we have before we have to leave the house?"

"Sometime today will be fine," Saddington said. His expression changed the moment he said it, and Sadie was given the feeling that he instantly regretted his bluntness. "I'm sorry about this, Miss Bartholomew. It would appear that you're being punished for your father's crimes."

"Yeah, well, I guess you're just doing your job, aren't you?"

"That's all it is," Saddington said. "Nothing personal, really."

Sadie looked at Egan, and knew that for him, this *was* personal. He was clearly a working class boy – the British were more obsessed with class than Americans – and he was making it plain that he viewed Sadie as little more than a spoilt rich kid. She turned back to Saddington. "Can you give us an hour? I have to tell my sister, and we both have to get ready."

Saddington smiled warmly and nodded his head. "Sure," he said. He made a move to leave, then turned back to Sadie. "There was one other thing."

"Yes?" Sadie said, thinking now that the detective was behaving more like a bald Columbo than a real police officer.

"Alexander Bartek," he said. "Would you know how we could get in touch with him?"

"Is he involved in this as well?" Sadie asked. That would explain his urgency to leave the country. She closed her eyes in disbelief as Saddington nodded his head.

"Do you know where he is? Only we can't get an answer at his address."

"He left the country."

"When?" Saddington asked. He didn't seem surprised.

"He came to the funeral, came back to the house, then told me he was leaving that day."

"Did he tell you where he was going?"

"Back to the States."

"Thanks for your help."

"Did my father know he was being investigated?" Sadie blurted out. After all, Alexander must've had an inkling something was going down.

Saddington was momentarily fazed by the question. He shook his head. "Unlikely. As I said, I only found out about it yesterday. Why do you ask?"

"Because nobody knows why my parents were on their way to Leighton Buzzard with a suitcase full of clothes in the boot," Sadie said. "Are you sure that they didn't know?"

Saddington looked at Egan, then back at Sadie. "As I said, Miss Bartholomew, it's highly unlikely. You've been helpful, but we'll leave you to get yourselves ready. You can either stay here while we search the house, or get your solicitor to come out – but somebody has to be present."

Sadie nodded. "I'll get Mr Schildt out," she said.

The two police officers let themselves out of the house, and Sadie was left standing in the hallway, wondering how she was going to break the news to Jodie.

She didn't have to worry.

Jodie came up beside her and held her hand.

"What does this all mean, Say?" she asked. Sadie was momentarily startled, and still stunned by what the police officers had revealed to her. She tried to smile, but her mouth wouldn't move.

Eventually, she said, "It means we have to find somewhere else to live."

3

Detective Superintendant Derek Saddington could scarcely conceal his annoyance with his junior officer at the way he'd spoke to Sadie Bartholomew. He was an old school policeman, respectful, honest and decent, and could distinguish between types and severity of crimes without prejudice. And Sadie Bartholomew had done nothing wrong. It was her father who had broken the law, though as far as Saddington was concerned, corporate fraud and tax evasion were hardly the crimes of the century, much as it was his job to investigate them.

As he sat in the rear of the car, with Egan beside him, and two DCs in the front, he felt as though he had to say something, even if they were within earshot of Egan's own juniors.

"I thought you were a little bit out of order back there, Gerry," he said quietly, noting that the driver of the car glanced in his rear view mirror.

"Oh aye, sir?" The ex-RUC officer lit a cigarette, another thing about him that annoyed Saddington. "In what way?"

"Sadie Bartholomew has been through a lot," Saddington said.

Egan looked at him. "That's right," he admitted, "but she's also been living off that dirty money for the last eight or nine years."

"We'll talk about this later," Saddington said. He had no desire to continue with something that would turn into a reprimand, not in the presence of other, more junior, officers. He wasn't in the habit of making fools of those beneath him. That wasn't the way you earned respect. That was the way you got people to fear you, and eventually, to hate you. Saddington didn't want that, even with an officer like Gerry Egan, who was more used to dealing with terrorists than middle-class kids.

So he left the reprimand for when they'd arrived back at New

Scotland Yard, calling Gerry straight into his office and closing the door firmly behind him. He gestured for Gerry to be seated, and then took a seat behind his own desk.

"I'm not going to argue about this, Gerry," he began, "because I'm your superior, and I don't take bullshit from my men. You understand that? I take advice, suggestions, but never bullshit." Egan shifted position in his seat, like so many men Saddington had interviewed before. "Now, those two kids back there have lost their parents, and we're taking away their lifeline, their wealth, their homes. Irrespective of the fact that you probably don't like middle-class people, Gerry, and irrespective of the fact that you probably believe that Sadie Bartholomew should be working for a living like everyone else, you do not have the right to piss people off like that. It's not your place to stand in judgement, and it certainly isn't your place to adopt such an insulting attitude with innocent people."

Egan frowned. "Sir, if I might speak out of turn here – if I might 'offer some advice' – we don't know whether Sadie Bartholomew was aware of her father's criminal activities."

"Oh, come on, Gerry, that's hardly bloody likely."

"Well, there is also the small matter of the amount of money in Bartholomew's accounts," Egan said. "That money, and all of his assets, doesn't add even add up to the amount the US Treasury want to take in taxes and fines. If Bartholomew owed almost a hundred million dollars in taxes, he must've earned a significant amount."

"Your point being?"

"Where the hell is that money?"

"Where indeed?"

"Swiss bank accounts," Egan said.

"In all probability," Saddington said as his telephone rang. He picked it up. "Saddington."

"Special Agent Rothschild is here to see you, sir," the voice on the other end told him.

"I'll send someone down to get him," Saddington said, cradling the handset. "Are you going somewhere with this line of defence, Gerry?" he asked Egan.

"Aye. What if Sadie Bartholomew knows about these Swiss bank accounts?"

"Unlikely."

"Why ... if you don't mind me asking, sir?"

"Because Bartholomew was a secretive man, with a secret life," Saddington said. "When you're involved with the Mafia, for certain you will need to hide your wealth. But you don't tell anybody about your Swiss bank accounts – not your wife and certainly not your children. Not until you're ready to. And Bartholomew wasn't ready to. He wasn't ready to die."

"He was running," Egan said.

Saddington had to concede that point. He stood up and walked to the door, opening it. "Stuart, could you nip downstairs, find Special Agent Rothschild, and bring him up to my office?"

"Sure, sir," one of the DCs said. Saddington closed the door and returned to his seat. "Well, he probably was, Gerry. And we'll probably never know who from, or why, or indeed where he was running to. But he didn't tell his kids about it. That much is obvious. So the chances are that he also didn't feel the need to tell them about his Swiss bank accounts, if indeed they exist. His wife, maybe, his solicitor, in all likelihood, but never his kids."

"So, you're saying lay off Sadie Bartholomew?"

"I'm saying, Gerry, that we have more important things to consider," Saddington said. "For example, were any acts of fraud perpetrated in the UK? Did Bartholomew's company bend any of our laws, and can we have them for it?"

"Recover some cash for ourselves?"

"The Yanks are going to get a sack load of cash from this," Saddington said. "And it's going to cost the UK maybe a quarter of that to administer everything. We deserve to get something back. And there's a very good chance that if Bartholomew broke the law in the US all those years ago, he was doing the same thing here, particularly with Bartek on his side. And that's another thing. Get as many bods as you can looking into when and to where Bartek flew from this country."

Gerry Egan stood up as there was a knock at the door. "I'll get right on it," he said.

Fine, thought Saddington, *and stay out of my fucking hair while you're at it!*

Egan opened the door and allowed Special Agent Rothschild to step into the office. He then left, closing the door behind him. Saddington sprang to his feet and shook the American's hand.

"Paul," he greeted.

"Derek."

"Take a seat." The two men sat. "So, what brings you here?"

"I've spoken with Schildt, the Bartholomew's lawyer," the American said. "He says he'll do everything he can to help us."

"Did he mention where we can find details of Michael Bartholomew's Swiss bank accounts?" Saddington asked with a smirk.

The American smiled tightly. "What do you think?"

"The Bartholomew girls are moving out of the Harrow property," Saddington said.

Rothschild nodded. "In a way, I feel sorry for the kids, but it has to be done."

Yes, thought Saddington, *because Uncle Sam is demanding repayment of a debt.* But he knew that the Inland Revenue would do just the same. All governments would, because they couldn't survive without money.

"It just seems a shame," Saddington said, finishing his thought aloud, "that those girls are paying for their father's crimes. In all probability, they're going to end up penniless."

"Paying for the sins of their father," the American said. "Sounds very biblical."

"I've never been much of a religious type," Saddington said.

"Well, with the father dead, the key to all of this is probably Bartek," Rothschild said. "Any luck finding him?"

"Afraid not. He apparently left for the United States on the day of the funeral."

"Who told you that?"

"Sadie Bartholomew – the eldest girl."

"You believe her? It wouldn't be the first time that the right-hand man has got into bed with the boss's daughter."

"I don't think for a moment that's the case."

"Well, I've never spoken to the girl. I'm just asking your opinion."

"And in my opinion, she's telling the truth, and she knows no more than that."

"You'll be able to find out what flight he was booked on?"

"We're already working on that," Saddington assured him. "We're putting all of our resources into this, Paul, I hope you can see that. And I hope that you appreciate it, because one day, we might need this favour repaying."

"I will tell you this much," Rothschild said. "If Scaliano doesn't get some of his money back, he's gonna come looking for it. And you don't see the Sicilian Mafia in the UK that often, do you? Bloodthirsty motherfuckers, they'd kill their own grandmother if she crossed them."

"We've dealt with the IRA in this country for years, Paul," Saddington said. "The Mafia are nothing compared to them."

Special Agent Paul Rothschild smiled at that. "The difference being, the Mafia kill only their targets and those who get in the way, and they do it efficiently. Scaliano has half a dozen of the top hitmen in the States on his books. He'd only need to send one over here to get the job done – if he sends more than one, then we know he's pissed."

"How will you know if he's sent anyone?"

"We know three of the faces," Rothschild said. "We just can't prove their involvement in any murders. As for the other three, we know them by reputation and their aliases. If he sends those over, we'll get the information from our undercover agents. None of them are high enough up the chain of command to hear directly what Scaliano is up to, but when hitmen are sent out, that kind of information usually filters down to the troops, even if they don't know who the targets are."

"If we know hitmen are on the way, we can put CO-19 on the case. They can keep a watch on the two girls."

"I don't want those girls to end up dead any more than you do," Rothschild assured him. He stood up. "I've got to report back. When you find out where Bartek's disappeared to, you'll let me know?"

"Of course," Saddington said, getting to his feet. "Do you really think he'd go back to the US? With the Mafia after him?"

"Who knows?" Rothschild said. "But there are scores of international airports he could fly to, and Scaliano doesn't have the resources to watch every airport twenty-four hours a day. In spite of what Hollywood would have you believe, it's actually quite easy to hide in the US. So long as you don't shout about who you are or get yourself known to the local press. Scaliano's a New Yorker – he won't know what the hell's happening in Pissant, Texas. But Bartholomew and Bartek are on the radar again, thanks to Bartholomew getting himself killed."

"Well, Bartek's the key, as you say," Saddington said. "He probably knows the numbers for Bartholomew's accounts."

"We estimate that Bartholomew must have more than five hundred million squirreled away somewhere, with Bartek probably having half that amount. That's three quarters of a billion dollars."

"More money than most people can imagine."

"Exactly. Anyway, I'd better be on my way. You know, Derek, I really do appreciate the help you're giving us."

"And so you should," Saddington said with mock bitterness. "We're doing all of the legwork here."

Rothschild gave a half-smile. "Well, in that case, I'd better let you get on with it."

Saddington was left with most of the rest of the day to contemplate the case. The Bartholomew girls would definitely end up penniless, because unless they could actually locate those Swiss bank accounts, and also do a deal with the Swiss government, every single penny and asset that Michael Bartholomew had owned would be seized to pay off his debts.

He took a liquid lunch in one of the pubs close to New Scotland Yard, mostly frequented by local detectives with their ears to the ground. Not that they could have any information Saddington would be interested in – he dealt with major fraud cases, whereas they dealt with burglaries, bag-snatchings, the occasional armed robbery. In other words, they moved in entirely different circles.

But those local detectives were real men, officers who had worked their way up through the ranks, who hadn't been fast-tracked straight from university. And as such, they both thought like him and spoke his language, and he found himself able to have friendly chats with them about all manner of things not connected with police work. Even conversations about police work – few and far between though they were – were more entertaining, because of the way the detectives told their stories.

Downing his second large Scotch, Saddington said his goodbyes and hailed a taxi to take him back to New Scotland Yard. His superiors might not have been happy with his lunchtime drinking – although he never drank to excess, and never embarrassed himself or his colleagues – but they put up with it. They certainly would not, however, have put up with him being stopped for drinking and driving. That would finish his career, and Saddington was close to retirement age, and stood to leave the force with a great pension. He could never do anything to throw that away, because he'd already thrown enough of his life away.

The afternoon was spent, as usual for post-drinking sessions, in melancholy reflections of his wife and children. His wife had walked out on him twenty years ago, taking their two children, aged one and three, with her. He hadn't even tried to stop her. His work, at that time, seemed more important.

Now, however, he often wondered what his children looked like. They were probably married, maybe he was a grandfather. Christ, he didn't even know if his wife – his ex-wife – had remarried. He, unfortunately, was still married to his work, and there was no chance of him ever getting divorced from that. Not until the Force threw him out.

Then, he thought miserably, he really would have time on his hands to reflect upon his loss, and the life altering decisions made when he was in his early thirties.

There was a knock at the door that jerked him back to the here and now, and he looked up to see Egan stepping into his office.

"Sir, about Alexander Bartek."

"Yes?"

"He didn't fly to the US."

"He didn't?" Saddington said, sitting up straight, his mind totally clear, the alcohol already gone from his system. "So, where did he go? Do we know?"

"Brazil," Egan said, handing over a sheet of paper and sitting down opposite the superintendant. "Rio de Janeiro, on British Airways Flight FS Two Nine Six. That's a passenger list. Bartek flew in seat number one hundred and seventy-two."

Saddington let out a sigh and leaned back in his chair. "Bloody hell. If he'd flown to the US, we could've handed this information over to the FBI, and forgot about the case. Now we're going to have to get the embassies involved."

"You're sending someone out there?"

"If the budget allows," Saddington said. "I'll go. I could do with a holiday."

"Wise decision, sir," Egan said, with not even a hint of jealously.

"Though how I'll find him when I get there, Christ only knows."

"The Brazilians are a wee bit basic when it comes to police work, ain't they, sir?"

Saddington looked up. "You know, that's not a very diplomatic approach, Gerry."

"Speaking my mind and the truth."

"Yes, well," Saddington said, picking up the telephone. "I'll be sure not to relay that opinion to the chief when I go crawling to him for a ticket to Rio de Janeiro."

Egan just smirked and stood up. He was out of the office by the time Saddington's call was connected.

4

Sadie cursed her father for two things as she threaded the sporty Volvo C30 T5, registered in her name, through the heavy traffic that afternoon. Firstly, she cursed him for getting her and Jodie in this mess. How could he do that to his own children? Didn't he know that he was sure to be caught, and that his family would take the brunt of the punishment?

Secondly, she cursed him for moving the family out to the UK all those years ago, away from all their relatives in the United States. Oh, her uncle had told her that if she needed anything, she only had to ask, but she wasn't about to go to him and ask for money so she could continue with her life of leisure. If they'd been back in the US, she could've at least asked him for a place to stay until she got herself and Jodie sorted out with somewhere. As it was, she had £10,000 in her personal savings account, Jodie had maybe half of that, and it was all they had to fund their accommodation and living requirements until Sadie found a job – a proper job, not just singing in a band, arranging their gigs and promotion, and generally earning very little, if anything, for it.

That was a hobby, and her father had supported her.

Now he wasn't here, and she not only had to look after herself, but her sister as well.

Jodie sat beside her, dressed in an FCUK top and a pair of Calvin Klein jeans. She would have to give up that side of her lifestyle, Sadie thought ruefully, and fashion had always been important to her sister. Everything she wore was a designer label, even her underwear.

She stopped at another set of traffic lights and sighed heavily. She seemed to be doing that a lot lately, and it hadn't gone unnoticed.

"Would you stop doing that?" Jodie snapped impatiently, as she inspected her made-up face in the vanity mirror fixed to the back of the sun visor.

"You could always walk, you know."

"Well, I probably would, if I knew where we were going," her sister said with a sarcastic smile.

Sadie couldn't blame her for that. They were on their way to the fifth flat they'd looked at that day, the first four having been either too expensive, or not fit for rats to live in. Curiously, one of them fitted into both categories. Sadie shuddered as she remembered the mould on the walls, the mouse droppings on the windowsills, and the funny smell of decay. So she wasn't exactly holding out much hope for this last flat.

"If this place sucks, we'll just stay in a hotel for tonight."

"We can't afford it," Jodie said.

"Between us, we have fifteen thousand pounds, Jo," Sadie said. "I think we can afford one night of luxury. Or would you rather sleep in a cardboard box?"

"Okay, okay!" Jodie said, turning her attentions back to the mirror. The lights changed, and Sadie moved off.

"Found that zit, huh?"

"Shut up!"

"There is one thing I want you to realize, Jo," Sadie said. "All joking aside, don't just turn up your nose at this place because it only has two bedrooms, one front room and one bathroom. We can't be too choosey, you know. Not anymore."

"I know, I know."

"And hopefully, it'll only be temporary."

"You mean, until they unfreeze Dad's assets?"

"Something like that."

Jodie turned to Sadie, having given up looking in the mirror. "You really think that's gonna happen?"

"It has to happen," Sadie said, though she didn't know whether she was trying to convince Jodie or herself. "

"This is just great," Jodie said. "Fucking Hell! We lose Mom and Dad, and then this has to happen."

Sadie almost smiled. At least Jodie seemed to be over the worst – for the moment, anyway. She was kind of volatile, and Sadie knew that her temperament could change at any moment. Which was why, she kept telling herself, she should be treading carefully. But she couldn't help it. She wanted to get back to normal, and bickering with her younger sister was normal.

After making slow progress through the heavy traffic for twenty minutes, and with the sat nav guiding them, they pulled up outside Lambeth House, where the last flat on their list was located.

Once in the small car park both girls looked up at the ugly pre-war building. Sadie knew exactly what Jodie was going to say, and it wouldn't be for the first time that day.

"Well, I hope it's better on the inside."

She gave her a disparaging look.

"You know, some rich kids actually enjoy making a life for themselves," Sadie said, parking up alongside a three-year-old Renault Laguna. "They see it as something of a challenge. They don't like to live off their parents."

"Well, isn't that commendable," Jodie said sarcastically.

"Look upon it as an adventure," Sadie said.

"I'm not Ray fucking Mears, Say."

They looked up now at the rear of the building, its dark orange brickwork even more hideous than the mock Tudor frontage. There were four storeys to the building, with four tall, narrow windows on each floor, either side of a rear entrance on the ground floor.

"Well, I suppose we'd better take a look," Sadie said, switching off the engine. She turned to look at her sister just in time to catch her rolling her eyes.

The two of them left the car and made their way to the rear entrance, which was locked. There was also no sign of a doorbell. Impatiently, Sadie led the way around to the front of the building, which was also locked. This door, however, possessed an intercom system, and Sadie found the landlord's name amongst the list of tenants, and rang the bell.

"Yes?" a harsh voice answered, almost immediately, as though the owner was already waiting for them.

"Mr Simpson? I'm Sadie Bartholomew. I rang earlier about the flat?"

"Come in," the voice instructed, not softening up at all. A buzzer sounded, and Sadie opened the door, stepping into an old fashioned, but clean, entrance hall. Sadie turned and looked at Jodie, who was already casting a disparaging look around the hallway.

A door to the left opened and a short man, wearing a grubby shirt stepped out. Instantly, Sadie's heart sank. So this was the landlord, Edward Simpson?

"Miss Bartholomew?"

Sadie nodded, and took his outstretched hand. "Pleased to meet you." His shake was firm, rehearsed.

"Yeah," Simpson grunted. "The flat's on the second floor," he added, fumbling with a set of keys. "Sorry, no lift – not a regulatory requirement, thank God!" He led the two girls up the stairs to the second floor, and then pointed to a door situated on the right of the corridor. "Number five," he announced. "Your neighbour there, in number four, is a quiet woman, estate agent, no trouble at all. Your neighbours above – on the third floor – are quiet too. A married couple, no kids, in their forties. But they do have a dog, which I understand is kept quiet."

Sadie nodded. He was clearly already under the impression that they were going to take the flat. And she had to admit that her first impression of the flat – though obviously only from the outside – was good.

"Over there," Simpson said, pointing to the far end of the corridor, where a door marked "Fire Exit" was situated, "is the fire escape." Sadie nodded again. "I don't appreciate it being used as a quick route to the car park." He unlocked the door to the flat. "We had one set of tenants who used to use it more often than the front entrance. A couple of times, they didn't close it properly behind them, and we had a thief in one night, cleared out one of the flats." Simpson swung the door open and stepped into the hallway of the flat. Sadie and Jodie followed.

"You said the flat was unfurnished," Sadie said, noticing that the hallway was devoid of anything other than a crimson carpet.

"I could furnish it for you if you want me to," Simpson said, "but we'd have to renegotiate the deposit and the rent."

"We have our own furniture," Sadie assured him – though they'd taken the barest minimum from the house in Harrow, and that had all been thoroughly searched and then catalogued by the police.

"Let me give you a quick tour," Simpson said. He led them into the first door on the left. "This is the second bedroom. Looks out onto the rear of the building – the car park." Although it was the second bedroom, it was of a considerable size – large enough that Sadie decided that she would claim it for herself.

Simpson led them into the room directly opposite. "And here's the master bedroom. As you can see, there's very little difference in size." Sadie was quite amazed to see that her younger sister wasn't turning her nose up at the flat – not yet, anyway.

Simpson took them along the corridor, showing them the bathroom and kitchen diner. The taps on the sink gleamed, and it was apparent that in spite of the fact that he didn't take much pride in his personal appearance, Simpson liked to keep his flats in pristine condition.

Finally, he took them into the front room, which was the largest room in the flat, stretching from the front of the building to the rear, with a window on both sides, one overlooking the main road, the other overlooking the car park. Against the far wall was a wide gas fireplace, with an inspection label dangling from the front grill.

Simpson made a point of referring to it. "I know someone who lost one of his tenants to carbon monoxide poisoning," he said. "Won't happen to me. I don't take risks with people's lives." He pointed to the device that was fixed to the ceiling above the fireplace. It resembled a smoke alarm, but there was already one of those in the centre of the ceiling. "Carbon monoxide alarm," he explained. "You hear it go off, come and get me. If I'm not here, open all the windows and leave the flat."

"You're very conscientious," Sadie said.

Simpson just shrugged. "The flat's yours if you want it. Seven hundred a month, with the rent in advance, and a fourteen hundred pound deposit."

Sadie looked at Jodie, who was inspecting the walls of the front room. What was she making of this place? She looked back at Simpson. "Could you leave us alone for a few minutes? I'd like to discuss this with my sister."

Simpson nodded. He walked to the door of the room. "I'll be downstairs in my flat," he said. "I'd like an answer today, if possible. I don't want to miss out on any further enquiries." And with that, he was gone.

"Well?"

Jodie looked at her. "It's okay," she said. "I mean, it's grody, for sure, but it's not grody to the max, like some of the places we've looked at today." Sadie thought that was about as much commitment as she was likely to get from her little sister, but Jodie surprised her by continuing. "We have to make sacrifices, and this place ... well, it'll be like our own place, won't it?"

Sadie smiled. "You know, you've had to do a lot of growing up over the last few days, Jo. We both have. And now ... well, we're gonna be flatmates instead of sisters. Well, not instead of, but you know what I mean. And I think this place will be just great." And for the first time in a long while, Sadie actually felt good.

A new start.

She grinned at Jodie and opened her arms, and her little sister threw herself into them.

And she felt closer to her than she had ever done before.

5

The move had gone remarkably well, Sadie thought, as she surveyed the front room of the flat in Lambeth House. The 37" LCD TV from her room back at the house in Harlow was now fixed to the wall. The three-piece suite – comfortable orange leather – which had once been located in the conservatory of the house in Harrow now had pride of place in the large front room of the flat. Along the rear wall, next to the window that looked out onto the car park, was the dining table from the house, though they'd only brought four of the eight chairs with them. Jodie had said that it was unlikely that they'd be holding dinner parties.

Sadie looked at her watch as the removals men left the hallway for the last time, and she thanked them, giving them a twenty pound note as a tip. They were probably expecting a lot more, particularly as they'd collected the furniture from the mansion in Harrow.

As she closed the door, and silence descended upon their new home, Sadie leant back against the wall of the hallway. The removals men had done most of the heavy work, but boxes and suitcases still had to be unpacked, things to be stowed away.

At that moment, her sister came into the hallway.

"That everything?"

"Yeah," Sadie said, stepping up to her bedroom and pushing open the door. Inside were the bed – double, of course, if for no other reason than they were just more comfortable – a set of wardrobes from Ikea, and a matching dressing table and bedside cabinets.

On the floor alongside the bed were three large packing cases, and four suitcases, all of which had to be unpacked. What the hell, Sadie thought, had she brought with her?! She couldn't remember packing away this much stuff back at the mansion. But then, she had grabbed all of her personal effects – her CDs, DVDs, books, a few old copies of NME and Q Magazine that she couldn't bear to part with, in addition to a hell of a lot of clothes, though not even a quarter of what she possessed.

Jodie stepped into the room behind her. "You know, Say, you better make a start here. Looks like it's gonna take you all night!"

"Thanks for the vote of confidence, Jo," Sadie said, glancing over to the empty bookcase the men had put on the wall opposite the bed. Her CDs and DVDs, she thought, should go in the front room. Perhaps some of her books also – the showy ones, the ones that boasted of her intellect. The trashy airport novels she loved so much, but which betrayed her literary ignorance, she would keep in her bedroom.

She looked at her watch. It was a little after seven in the evening. No wonder the removals guys were so pissed off. It was late!

"I'll order us a pizza," Jodie suggested.

"Better than nothing," Sadie said, flopping down on the bed. "But you're doing the dishes!"

"No way! There's not even a goddamned dishwasher in this place!"

So began the Bartholomew girls' first night in their new home. The fact that they were sleeping in their own beds, comfortable and familiar thought they were, could not detract from the unease they felt at their unfamiliar surroundings. Waking up in the middle of the night, Sadie was momentarily confused, because the window was not where it was supposed to be, and besides which, it was way too small. And didn't the walls seem strangely claustrophobic, she thought, as the sun began to pour through the crack in the curtains?

Oh well, she told herself as she showered in the miniature bathroom, they'd get used to it. You couldn't expect to leave home and move into a penthouse, even if your father was reputed to be worth somewhere in the region of a quarter of a billion.

Sadie cursed again as she towel-dried her short, black hair. Oh well, she had a few things planned for today. There was the meeting with the band for a start, to discuss the gig on Friday, the *very important gig*, she reminded herself. And then, after that, there was the interview at

McDonald's, arranged by one of Sadie's old school chums, Melissa. Like Sadie, Melissa had been reasonably intelligent, had achieved high markings in her GCSEs, but she'd taken them no further. Lacking a fabulously wealthy father, Melissa had been forced to fend for herself, and her lack of interest in anything remotely attached to work meant that she certainly was not a career-minded girl. She didn't want to work in a stuffy office, certainly didn't want to get her hands dirty in a factory, and had no desire to either take her education further. Instead, she opted for McDonald's. She'd started at seventeen, and now, four years later, she was an assistant manager, a rather grandiose title for someone who "managed", in the loosest sense of the word, new trainees, mostly Eastern Europeans, in addition to walking around the restaurant wearing a skirt and blouse, with a brush in her hand. A glorified bloody scrubber was how she'd once described herself to Sadie – the salary was shit, she was the first to admit, but it paid the rent. Besides, she'd warned Sadie the previous day, it was nowhere near as shit as the pay for the new trainees. But Melissa was in with the manager – they were good friends, nothing more, mainly because he was gay – and he'd created a position for Sadie, which Sadie thought showed touching loyalty.

Melissa assured her that in spite of the shit pay and the crappy working conditions, the restaurant was actually quite a pleasant place to work. Twenty-five members of staff, all getting along with one another, great banter, and minimal backbiting.

All the same, Sadie wasn't looking forward to working at McDonald's. The stigma attached to such a position was almost as bad as that attached to homeless person. She was dreading answering the question, "Where do you work?" Still, as Jodie had pointed out to her, it was still one step up from KFC!

Jodie was making herself at home in the front room, watching Tricia on the TV. She was still in her dressing gown, and probably would be until after lunch, though Sadie couldn't blame her. Fully dressed herself, wearing a baggy dress, high-heeled sneakers, and the merest hint of CK Be, she strolled into the room and looked down at her sister.

"You will be okay to go back to school next week, won't you?"

Jodie looked up from her bowl of Coco Pops. "I guess," she muttered. "I thought you said I'd have next week off as well though."

"Well, it's just that I won't be here, what with this new job–"

"The mega-exciting position at Ronald's?"

Sadie rolled her eyes. "Yes," she said, barely concealing her mock annoyance. "But it means I won't be here during the day."

"And you don't want to leave me alone?"

Sadie sat down on the sofa next to her sister. "Listen, no one's gonna force you to go back to school, not until you're completely ready. Okay? But if you could manage to go back next week, it would be great for me, and it might do you some good. If you can't do that – and I mean, if you *really* can't do that – then you can have next week off as well, and we'll look at it again."

Jodie nodded. "I am getting kinda bored," she confessed. "You know, there's only so much Tricia and Jerry a girl can take." Sadie hugged her sister and then stood up.

"You off to see the band?"

"Well, we have this gig on Friday," Sadie said. "I didn't know whether I'd be up to it, but I can't really let the guys down. It's gonna be a big night."

"And I can't even be there."

Sadie smiled. "Oh, I don't know, you could pass for eighteen when you're all dressed up. Hell, you look older than me sometimes!"

"You know, Say, when I'm thirty, I might take that as an insult, but I think when you're sixteen, that just about passes as a compliment."

"Yeah, it does, doesn't it?" Sadie said, giving her sister a kiss on the forehead. "See you later, kid."

"Not if I see you first," Jodie assured her.

And with that, Sadie left the flat.

She was meeting the other members of Darcy's Box in one of the classier gastro-pubs in the town centre, the Knife and Fork, at eleven-thirty, and after leaving her Volvo in the nearest car park, she strolled into the bar, nodding a greeting to two of the bar staff she knew by name. Their expressions appeared genuinely sympathetic, and although it annoyed her slightly – she didn't want to be the centre of attention over something like this – she smiled at them as sincerely as she could.

Somebody called her name, and she turned to see Billy McColl, the band's guitarist, waving at her. He pointed to the vodka and Red Bull on the table in front of him, and she figured he must've already got the drinks in.

"Good job I wasn't late," she said, sitting down.

"You are," Mark Spicer, the band's bass player, remarked laconically, as he took a sip from his Guinness.

"Ignore him," Billy said. "Listen, how are you doing?"

"Oh you know ..." Sadie looked at Billy. He was a short man, in his early twenties, with bleached hair styled in that 'just got out of bed' look, an earring in his left ear, and a stud in his right eyebrow. Other than the body modifications, he was quite attractive, and Sadie had always got on with him. Today, he wore baggy jeans – as always – and a tee-shirt that displayed a piece of Banksy graffiti. Billy had always been political, and definitely a conspiracy theorist, though thankfully neither rarely came out in his songs. He was the band's musical genius, the man responsible for writing the music and arranging the songs. Sadie wrote most of the lyrics, with some help from Mark.

Billy and Mark had been the front men for the original band when it had been just a three-piece, but Billy had always had some difficulty in playing the guitar and singing at the same time, and Mark simply was no good as a singer. In fact, Sadie thought as she looked at Mark, with his spiky hair and chiselled, pockmarked features, Mark probably wasn't any good at anything musical. He certainly wasn't Flea on the bass – he was just capable of banging out a regular beat.

She stopped herself. No, she was being mean. Mark could be a handful, certainly, and he had this very high opinion of himself that probably wasn't justified, but he was an integral part of the band, because some of the band's best material had elements of his writing within them. He'd written some of the best lyrics – though not all – and had, on a couple of occasions, come up with a kicking bass riff that always seemed to get the fans shuffling and jumping.

It was just that she couldn't bring herself to like him that much.

"Where's Davey?" she asked, after taking a sip from the vodka and Red Bull. She was referring to the final member of the band, Davey Smith, the drummer.

"Bog," Mark muttered, looking up from the copy of NME he was browsing through.

Sadie glanced at Billy. She was the first to admit that she didn't want any undue sympathy, but she was feeling that Mark was showing a distinct lack of respect for her feelings. She didn't say anything – Billy, she thought, would do that for her when she'd gone.

"How's Jo bearing up?" Billy asked.

"She's doing better than I would've expected," Sadie replied. "So am I, for that matter."

"Heard any more from the police?" Mark asked.

"No, not yet."

Mark shook his head grimly. "You guys must be going through hell." It was as close as she was going to get to sympathy from him. Sadie nodded, then shrugged.

"Well, it's not been easy," she admitted. "But we've finally moved into our new place."

"It's gonna take some getting used to though," Mark said. It was his way of rubbing her nose in it – after all, he was very much a socialist, more so than Billy, and he'd undergone a difficult upbringing. And because of that, Sadie had always allowed him to pick on her, as a way of assuaging her guilt for having a better upbringing than him. She didn't know, however, how much longer she'd allow it to continue.

"We'll get there in the end," she assured him.

"Wah hey!" a voice shouted from behind, and Sadie couldn't help but smile. That was the effect Davey had on people, with his fake Geordie accent – his father came from Newcastle, but his mother was a Londoner, and he'd been born and raised in the capital – and his mad hairstyle, long and fuzzy, the ultimate in puff/mullet combos. He was the band's joker, and excellent drummer, with absolutely no interest in writing songs whatsoever. He provided the back beat to the band's music, and without him and his mad style of playing, the band would be nothing more than a pale imitation of itself ... if that wasn't some kind of paradox.

"Morning, Davey," she greeted. Davey gave her a peck on the cheek and then sat down.

"So, how are you?" he asked, frowning seriously. Sadie grinned and shrugged again.

"I'm doing fine."

"Goodo," Davey said. "So, what are we here to talk about? Cause I'm not particularly happy about drinking at this hour, man. Damn those twenty-four hour drinking rules." He picked up his bottle of beer and supped down a few mouthfuls. Mark scowled in disgust.

"We need to get this gig sorted out," Billy said. "Now, Sadie, are you up to it?"

"Yeah, of course," Sadie replied, though she wasn't entirely convinced.

Billy picked up on it. "You sure?"

"We can't cancel this, no matter what," she said.

"But if you're not up to it," Mark said, "you could screw it up for the rest of us." Billy rolled his eyes.

"Howway, man!"

"Nice to know you have confidence in me, Mark," Sadie snapped.

"You know what I mean. I've got every sympathy with you, Sadie, but this gig is important."

"Oh, and I don't know that? For Christ's sake, Mark, I organized this whole fucking thing, didn't I? Jesus, I should know what this means. And I will be up to it, believe you me. If nothing else, I have even more of an incentive now, don't I? I don't have daddy's money to rely on any more. And more to the point, neither does the fucking band."

Mark scowled again.

"Let's cool it, guys," Billy said. "Now we've agreed that we're all up to it, are we gonna make any changes to the set?"

"Why should we?" Mark asked. "It's going fine, isn't it?"

"I'm concerned about the opener."

"We've always opened with 'Welcome To Your Life'," Mark said. It was the song that he'd contributed the most to, including almost all of the lyrics. In fact, the band were rehearsing an earlier version of the song when Sadie first joined them. "It has a good beat, gets the crowd on their feet ..."

"You're a poet and you don't even know it," Davey said.

"What about 'Serious Hell'?" Billy asked. "It's newer, it starts in a great way, has some great riffs, and Sadie can sing it really well."

"Are you saying I can't do 'Welcome' that good?" Sadie asked with a smile.

"I'm saying that it's time for a change. 'Welcome' is two years old. 'Serious Hell' is three months old, and the crowd love it. Plus, it's more indicative of our style now, ain't it?" Sadie nodded in agreement, and all eyes turned to Mark.

"I suppose so," he admitted. "But I really like 'Welcome'. It's the best song we do." Nobody agreed with that, Sadie thought. Not the rest of the band, not the small fan base they'd built up, nobody. Maybe a year ago, it was a crowd pleaser, but Sadie thought that they shouldn't be so predictable as to keep opening with the same song. Openers changed with every passing year. If they became famous, hit the big time, and if they were still around in twenty years, Sadie didn't want to be opening with 'Welcome To Your Life' or 'Serious Hell'. She wanted to open with the freshest song they had, a song that rocked, certainly, but was an example of their current work. And at the moment, 'Serious Hell' was the freshest opener they had.

"It has to be a majority consensus," Billy said. "All those in favour?" Sadie raised her hand, so did Billy. All eyes turned to Davey – it wouldn't be the first time that the vote was split with no deciding vote. On those occasions, a toss of the coin had decided the debate. This time, however, Davey raised his hand, smiling ruefully at Mark.

"Sorry, man."

"Hey, that's democracy," Mark said with a shrug. "I'll get used to it, won't I?"

"Well, now onto the next business," Billy said, consulting a scruffy sheet of paper. "Rehearsals for the gig, which take place tonight. Everybody can make it, I assume?" There were nods all round. They'd all known about the rehearsals, just as they'd all known about the gig itself. Tonight, they'd practice in a church hall, with perhaps a handful of friends watching, as they argued out arrangements and tried new solos. Tomorrow afternoon, they'd do the sound check at the Billabong, before the gig itself, which was due to start at eight-thirty.

Which posed a slight problem.

"Uh, guys, I have a bit of a dilemma."

"You can't make the rehearsal?" Billy asked anxiously.

"No, I can make the rehearsal," Sadie promised. "But the sound check tomorrow night might be a bit difficult."

"Don't tell us," Mark said, sipping from his pint. "You're getting your hair done?"

"It's a bit more important than that," Sadie said, smiling tightly.

"With respect, Sadie, what could be more important than this sound check?"

"How about work?"

Mark scoffed noisily, making a show of almost spitting out his drink. "Work? I didn't think you knew the meaning of the word."

"That was uncalled for," Billy said softly. "Besides, selling TVs and computers isn't exactly brain surgery, is it?" He was referring to Mark's job at Curry's.

Sadie smiled. "No, I've got a job now."

Billy raised an eyebrow. "Where?"

Sadie closed her eyes and sighed before answering. "McDonald's."

Davey laughed loudly, but not maliciously. Mark smirked and Billy kept a straight face. "Well, there are worse places to work."

"Yeah, like a massage parlour," Mark said.

"No, seriously, I was reading this thing on the Internet," Billy went on. "It's about how they changed the name of Kentucky Fried Chicken to KFC. Apparently, they don't use real chickens anymore."

"Get the fuck out of here," Mark said.

"Howway, man!"

"No, listen, apparently, they genetically engineered this chicken-type thing. It has four legs and four breasts, doesn't have any feet, and it practically has no head. It's to reduce the amount of shit they have to throw away. They can essentially use everything. But here's the thing, they can't have 'chicken' in their name, because it's not actually biologically a chicken anymore."

"Four breasts and four legs? Sounds perfect," Dave said.

"Don't encourage him," Mark said. "Listen, Bill, shut up, yeah. It's bad enough that Sadie's had to take a job in a shit-hole like McDonald's, without you spreading your Internet bullshit!"

"Hey, I needed a job, and Melissa came up with this, which I thought was one hell of a favour."

"So, Melissa's gonna be your boss?" Mark asked.

"What's wrong with that?" Sadie said defensively.

"Nothing," Mark said. "It's just that she's a mate – might put a strain on your friendship, having her telling you to mop up birthday kids' vomit."

"Look, can we get off the subject of my new job, and onto the subject of the problem it causes?"

"Well, we don't *need* you for a sound check. I mean, I can sound check the vocals, and we can tweak it just before the set. That'd work." Billy shrugged at his own suggestion.

"This is important," Mark emphasized. "We don't want screw this up, for fuck's sake."

"It's not gonna get screwed up, Mark. Just chill, man."

"Yeah, chill, dogg, don't have a fucking heart attack," Davey said – at which point, everyone fell silent. Sadie glanced at him, saw the colour literally draining from his face. He'd said the wrong thing – at least, that's what he thought, considering that was how her father had died.

"Davey, it's not a problem," she assured him, patting his hand. "Listen, guys, I've got to go. Believe me, we're gonna do the best set we've ever done. I won't let you down, and I expect none of you to neither."

"You'll be at the rehearsals?" Billy asked.

"Sure, don't worry. And I won't be late." And with that, she walked from the bar and climbed back into her car, with one less problem in her life. Now all she had to worry about was money. She wasn't even considering the possibility that they'd be getting their father's money back. That, as far as she was concerned, was long gone. She was going to have to work for a living, and if that meant wearing a stupid uniform, frying fries and torching burgers for a living, so be it.

At least she'd be able to let her hair down at the rehearsal session tonight. More importantly, Jodie would be able to watch, which Sadie thought would do her good, considering that she wouldn't be able to come to the actual gig.

All in all, she thought as she fired up the Volvo's engine, things could've been a lot worse.

When you got fucked over, you have to learn to make the best of it. And with that, she tugged on her shades, and screeched out of the car park.

6

Alexander Bartek could remember a time when things were better. Okay, so he was just weeks away from accessing a cool three-quarters of a billion dollars in Swiss numbered accounts, but he was on the run. And not just on the run from the police and the FBI, but from the Mafia also. If any of those chasing him should track him down, he was dead. It was as simple as that. The police and FBI would arrest him, put him in prison, and the Mafia would get to him from inside – if the Mafia got to him first, it would just be a case of cutting out the middle man and saving the tax-payer some of the costs of his eventual demise.

Either way, he was dead if he was caught.

Which meant that he was going to be on the run for the rest of his life.

He glanced in the mirror at his reflection as he shaved, and wondered what kind of face he would have in a couple of weeks, after the Brazilian plastic surgeon had finished with him. Hopefully, one more attractive than he possessed now, he told himself with a wry smile. Then perhaps he'd stand a chance with the Sadie Bartholomews of the world. His mind wandered back to a few days ago, to the last time he'd seen here. God, she was so attractive, a delicate little thing, with the body of a goddess ...

He stopped himself.

Sadie was in his past, a fond – but distant – memory. He had to think of the future, of the things that lay ahead. Wealth, a life of leisure, but also a life of constant worry, fear of being tracked down. But that fear shouldn't really have much justification, he tried to reassure himself. After all, the world was a big place, and it was easy to disappear into obscurity, particularly if you had the money to back yourself up. The Mafia only tracked people down in the movies. In real life, it was a little different. The FBI were his real concern, but even that obstacle could be overcome, once he had the million dollars safely here in Rio De Janeiro with him.

So far, four hundred thousand dollars had turned up. One hundred thousand of that would buy him a new face and a new identity to go with it. The remainder would see him safely over the ocean to Switzerland, where he would be able to access both his funds and those belonging to Michael Bartholomew. These were funds that the FBI didn't know about – they must've known that both he and Bartholomew had Swiss accounts, but without those vital numbers, there was no way of tracing them.

Alex smirked at himself in the mirror. His bravado was taking over now. He'd effectively defeated the FBI and the Mafia. There was no way they could get to him now. No way at all. He was almost home and dry. All he had to do today was meet the forger, taking along one hundred thousand US dollars. The thought of carrying that much cash made him slightly nervous, especially as he was going to be visiting one of the less salubrious parts of the city. But he trusted the forger, Mirabela. He'd had dealings with him on previous occasions. The forger was – in spite of his trade – an honest man. He was someone you could rely upon not to stab you in the back.

All the same, the location he'd given Alex had been some cause for concern. Right in the ghetto, some abandoned office block, on the fifth floor. It wasn't where Mirabela conducted his business, where he put together the fake documents – passports, driver licences, National Insurance cards of almost every country in the world – but it was where he wanted to meet Alex to exchange the cash. And Alex couldn't get a satisfactory answer out of him as to why he should choose to meet in such a treacherous area, where the locals would kill you for your Nikes, let alone for one hundred thousand US dollars.

But it wasn't the first time in his life that Alex had felt uneasy going into a deal.

The first time had been some ten years ago, when he was just into his twenties, a young accountant working in Bartholomew's company, who had been approached by the Mafia in New York with a business proposition. He could've cut the deal himself, without involving Bartholomew, but the risks were great, the gamble too high for him to take alone. Besides, Bartholomew knew the stock markets better than Alex, knew all the rules that could be safely broken, and those that couldn't, under any circumstances, be circumnavigated.

Alex needed Bartholomew, and it was with much trepidation that he had approached the man who was his boss, and showed him the deal that the Mafia had proposed.

Bartholomew liked money.

No, that was too soft a phrase. Bartholomew *adored* money. To him, there was nothing more important. Not his wife, who in spite of her age was an attractive woman, and not even his daughters.

And that was how their partnership with the Mafia began. Money laundering through the stock market, somewhere in the region of a million bucks a week. For two years, with Bartholomew playing with the Mafia's money to cut deals on the stock market himself. Deals that saw his own profits rise to previously unimaginable heights.

And it wasn't until the final deal – the one that the Mafia discovered – that things began to go wrong. Bartholomew gambled with some of the profits he should've paid to the Mafia. More than fifty million dollars. He'd done it before, and netted a cool quarter of a billion. This deal should've doubled that. Instead, the deal went sour, and the Mafia's fifty million disappeared. Bartholomew could've paid them back out of his own money, but he didn't see it that way. Things were starting to go bad for the corporation. Alex had projected profit figures in preparation for the tax returns a couple of years in the future, and things didn't look too rosy.

So Bartholomew sold the company, practically overnight, for a hundred million. The company itself had already cut a number of deals with large US corporations, deals that had yet to come to fruition. To be honest, they never would, but Bartholomew was a canny businessman and a superb salesman. He'd sold an idea, and people had bought into it, but he had no intention of seeing it through, because the idea was practically unworkable.

And so he'd cut his losses, left the country with a tidy profit, and had taken Alex with him. He'd taken Alex not only because the Mafia would be after Alex's blood, but because he was a very able right-hand man. And Bartholomew wanted to set up a new business.

He also wanted the two of them to have new identities. They weren't known as Michael Bartholomew and Alexander Bartek on the new company's records. They were Matthew Cartwright and Alec Johnson. It didn't stop them from being their real personas at all other times, but at work, they were Cartwright and Johnson. And in spite of the fact that the new firm still had the Bartholomew name, and that it quickly grew in size and recognition, Cartwright and Johnson were faceless directors, who never sought publicity. Bartholomew still sorted out the deals, with Alex right behind him, but they were made in the imaginary names of two people whose names had been dreamt up by Mirabela, the Brazilian forgery expert he was now in Rio to see.

For eight years, the business had prospered, and through the shortcuts and tax-dodging schemes that Alex had learnt, the two of them had vastly increased their own wealth, amassed though it was in the faceless, nameless Swiss numbered accounts that nobody else knew about.

Bartholomew was working on a ten-year plan – he already had half a billion dollars – and intended to have a billion in his accounts within the next couple of years.

But of course, that never happened.

Because for some reason, Bartholomew had bolted – that much was evident – and had given himself a coronary in the process. The FBI hadn't caught up with them, because Alex had covered their tracks well, and indeed, the FBI only became involved when news of Bartholomew's death leaked back to them.

Thankfully, Alex had found that out after leaving the country, when he'd called the company's secretary to enquire after the business. Which meant that the Mafia was in all likelihood also in the UK somewhere.

And Alex didn't want to hang around and wait for them.

The thing that pissed Alex off, he thought miserably as he wiped the remnants of the shaving foam from his face with a hotel towel, was that Bartholomew hadn't warned him that the Mafia were in the country. It was the least the old Jewish bastard could've done.

Well, he was paying for that omission now, because he was dead, probably rotting away in Hell now, and Alex was just a few weeks away from getting his hands on the Bartholomew fortune – the fortune that mattered, the fortune that nobody else could touch; not the substantial, but in the scheme of things, trifling amount left back in the United Kingdom.

Alex smiled at himself and left the bathroom, returning to the bedroom suite, where on the bed sat eight parcels, each one containing fifty thousand US dollars, mailed into Brazil a few days earlier. They were now just starting to turn up. With cash, his movements would be untraceable. It might be possible for his pursuers to trace him to Brazil. But with a new passport and this cash, he could travel anywhere in the world he chose, and there would be nothing anyone could do to find him.

First, he reminded himself, he had to buy himself that new identity.

He dressed casually – a suit would certainly be out of place in the ghetto to which he was travelling – choosing worn jeans and a faded tee-shirt as his clothes. The weather was mild, but Bartek took a jacket all the same. He stuffed a hundred thousand dollars – two of the packets from the UK – into a beaten-up old Adidas sports bag, and zipped it up tightly. Finally, he removed all items of jewellery, leaving the gold necklace he always wore on the bedside cabinet. His TAG Heuer watch was replaced with one less ostentatious, a scratched, undesirable Sekonda. Now he didn't look like a tourist, and with his dark complexion, he might even pass for Brazilian. His size – he was tall, moderately well built – would deter most muggers, and the fact that he didn't look particularly wealthy meant that he really didn't pose an attractive target. Few people would venture into the ghetto with a hundred grand in cash bundled into an old hold-all.

He was given a strange look by the girl on the reception desk, but he simply smiled at her as he stepped out into the South American sunshine. Glancing at his watch, he saw that he still had an hour before the meeting, and Mirabela would wait for a couple of hours after that before leaving. Mirabela wasn't the kind of man who stuck to schedules. He fully understood that the people who relied upon his services could not always be punctual – he'd told Alex that at a previous meeting, after putting down the Tom Clancy novel he'd been reading – but he joked that he always added waiting time onto the cost of his services.

All the same, Alex didn't want to be late.

The walk across town would be a lengthy one, what with the street urchins begging for money. On previous visits to Rio, he'd simply told them to fuck off, but on this occasion, he was loath to do anything that would draw any attention to himself. The fact that everyone else – tourists excepted – told the urchins to fuck off as well probably meant that he would draw more attention to himself by not doing so. But that didn't alter the fact that one of the little bastards could snatch the hold-all out of his hands and be away with one hundred thousand dollars.

He decided to take a taxi the majority of the way, and walk the last half a mile or so.

The taxi journey was tiresome, more so it seemed for him than the driver, who jabbered away continually in his native Portuguese, a language that Alex had only the barest command of, so that he could only nod in what he considered to be the right places after picking out the odd word. The driver also continually swore at other drivers as he threaded his way through the thick traffic.

Finally, they pulled up in a street that was a few blocks from the abandoned building. The driver gave Alex an odd look, but said nothing. Alex gave him a standard tip, and thanked him in his native tongue. The driver, clearly not expecting more from someone so attired, simply waved and continued complaining to himself, probably about the weather, probably about the state of the economy, probably about the politicians.

Whatever, Alex didn't care.

He'd be walking home from this meeting anyway – the risks weren't so great then.

He walked up an alleyway strewn with litter, feeling the palms of his hands go clammy. He reminded himself that in the pocket of his jacket, he had a flick-knife with a seven-inch blade, but the fact that he'd never used one in anger before, whereas muggers invariably had, also shot to the forefront of his thoughts. He had this image of them taking the knife from him and opening up his belly as though they were gutting a fish.

He shuddered, and at that precise moment, a young boy, no older than six, jumped in front of him, startling him. Like the taxi-driver, he too shouted in Portuguese, but Alex waved him away, giving him the Portuguese equivalent of "Fuck off". The boy lashed out, thumping him in the thigh, at which point, Alex kicked out, catching the boy on the back of the knee and dropping him like a stone. Alex heard a laugh and turned to see some older boys pointing in his direction, clearly amused at the spectacle. The young boy swore vehemently at him, before running back to his friends.

Alex tried not to imagine what would've happened had the older boys decided to react differently.

The graffiti on the walls as he made his way through a seemingly endless maze of alleys overgrown with weeds and bushes was mainly in Portuguese, but there was the occasional scribe in English. But Alex wasn't interested in the writing on the wall – by looking at a street-map, he'd memorized the route through these alleys, and now he was trying to recall which way to go. Left, along another alley that curved off to the right – or right, where the alley intersected a road.

He visualised the road on his map back at the hotel, and turned right.

At the end of the road, he turned left and walked up a street lined on either side by buildings that had long since been abandoned, and which had definitely seen better days. On either side of the street were a handful of cars, some totally trashed, their wheels gone, others little more than burned-out hulks. He spied one car that looked like a Mercedes, and was once again reminded of his partner in crime, the late Michael Bartholomew. If things had gone according to plan, the two of them would now be threading their way through Rio De Janeiro to find the elusive Mirabela.

But now Alex had to do it all by himself.

His memory informed him that the building coming up on the other side of the street was the one where he was supposed to meet the skilled forger. Not many men could command a hundred thousand dollars for probably a day's work, and certainly not every forger – there were plenty of them about, Alexander knew – but Mirabela was different. His passports looked real, looked as though they'd actually been used. He could create any passport, any driver's licence, any ID card, from any country in the world. Iraq, China, the now-defunct USSR, the USA, the UK, they'd all succumbed to his ability. In fact, it was even rumoured that he did work for the CIA and the British Secret Intelligence Service.

He was worth the money, Alex reminded himself, and he was certainly worth the risk.

He paused outside the building, which was a grey concrete affair, with huge windows on every floor, some of which were shattered. He looked up to the top floor, where Mirabela would be waiting, and then his eyes dropped down to an entrance that even in this building's glory days could never have been considered impressive. A set of double-doors, steel framed, very 1960s, and very dull, presented themselves.

Hitching the bag into his other hand – it was heavier than he'd expected – he pushed at one of the doors. It was either locked or jammed, so he tried the other. It swung inwards easily, and Alex stepped into the foyer of the building. An old desk, its surface smeared with what appeared to be dog excrement – at least, he hoped it had come from a dog – stood as a testament to its previous occupants, most probably lawyers, he thought as he strolled past.

A set of elevators were located against the back wall of the small lobby, with an open plan office to his right and a series of doors to his left. Alongside the two elevators were the stairs, and Alex made his way to them. He didn't fancy using the elevator – this building probably hadn't been serviced in years, and there was no telling whether or not they worked, or whether they were safe if they did. Alex didn't want to take the risk.

The stairs echoed beneath his feet as he climbed, windows lining the wall all the way to the top, giving a view of an overgrown garden that was squashed in between this office block and one to the rear. Alex continued to climb cautiously, his ears trying to listen over the sound of his own footsteps for anything that didn't sound natural. But he was no soldier, and had somebody wanted to take him, they could easily have done so.

A shudder ran down his spine, and he stopped for a brief instant, feeling the most sensational and overwhelming sense of fear. He couldn't explain it, but something was telling him to turn and leave the building. It was a strong sensation, but he fought it, and continued to climb, eventually reaching the top floor, where he found himself in a smaller lobby, with doors running off on either side. This, he told himself, was the penthouse suite, where everyone had their own room, and nobody shared an open plan office.

He opened each door in turn, preparing himself for an attack that never came – not that he really expected one. He'd come this far, and Mirabela had to be here, and here alone. That was the way he worked. But as each door was opened, and there was no sign of the forger, he was beginning to feel as though he'd been stood up. A quick check of his watch told him that he wasn't early, and he wasn't overly late. Surely, he thought to himself, Mirabela couldn't have let him down?

He opened the final door, and flinched instinctively as he saw a figure sitting at a desk against the far wall, his back to Alex. Dressed as he was in a brown suit, his long, grey hair in its usual windswept style, Mirabela seemed to be working over a document, probably a passport for somebody else, for he was one of those men who always had to be doing something.

"Mirabela?" Alex didn't know the Brazilian's first name, and Mirabela had never shown any dislike of being addressed in this way.

"You're late," the Brazilian said, his voice hoarse, as though he were getting over a cold.

"I'm sorry, but you did want to meet here, out in the middle of nowhere."

Mirabela sat bolt upright, as though somebody had just shot two thousand volts of electricity through him. "Yes," he said, "I did, didn't I?"

Alex felt slightly ill at ease. There was something odd about the Brazilian. He had never been much of a chatty person, but his job meant that he had to mix with people. He was usually courteous, but today, he seemed strangely distant.

"I've got the money," Alex said.

"You have?"

"The sum we agreed."

"Good," Mirabela said. "And I have your passport."

The door behind Alex slammed shut, but he was almost too confused by Mirabela's answer to notice. How could he possibly have the passport? Nothing had been agreed, and he didn't have a recent photograph. He spun to see that nobody was standing in the doorway. Must've been the wind, he told himself. He didn't want to acknowledge that there had been no wind in the building as he'd climbed the stairs. Maybe somebody had come in through the front doors.

He wanted to get this over as quickly as possible. This was giving him the fucking creeps.

"My passport?"

Mirabela turned around. "Your passport, Alexander," he said, "to Hell."

And the face didn't belong to Mirabela. In fact, the face didn't belong to anything on Earth, so inhuman was it.

Alex felt his knees go weak, and he stumbled back into the wall behind him as the figure who clearly wasn't Mirabela stood up. The face was a blood red in colour, glistening with sweat, the hair – now black – was slicked back, and two protrusions that could only be described as horns seemed to sprout up right before his eyes.

The thing that most definitely wasn't Mirabela threw its head back and let out a howl that seemed to signify pain.

As Alex watched, the thing shed Mirabela's cloths by simply ripping them apart with muscles that seemed to grow on demand, and he could see that the creature the Brazilian had become had a chest that was as red as its face. His eyes were drawn downwards, to the creature's lower body, and here he saw something that was so horrifying, it almost made him lose consciousness.

The creature did not possess legs, not in the proper sense of the word. The two limbs upon which it stood were those of some animal, hairy, crooked, and bent inhumanly, tapering into cloven hooves. As he felt his knees almost buckle once more, he caught a glimpse of something long and red whipping around from behind the creature. A tail, its tip like that of an arrowhead.

"My God," Alex muttered under his breath.

It was clear what this creature was, but that just wasn't possible. The Devil did not exist. The Devil was merely the figment of some religious nut's imagination. There was no such thing as the Devil.

"Keep telling yourself that," the creature hissed, "and you might eventually believe it, in spite of all the evidence to the contrary." It stepped up to him, its gait unnatural on those goat-like limbs. "But that won't change what I am."

"You're the Devil?" Alexander said, the absurdity of the question not actually hitting him.

The creature laughed heartily. "I am not the Devil," it said. "Satan is the Devil. I am Kobold, and I am merely one of Satan's demons. But I am real, Alexander, and I am not the figment of anybody's imagination." It reached out with a hand, and Alex saw the bony fingers, the sharp nails, as they pinched his cheek. "Did that feel real?"

There was little in the way of pain, but the sensation of being touched was real enough.

This was no dream.

Alex collapsed in a heap on the floor, sobbing into his folded arms. "Go away!" he screamed. "Go away!"

The creature, Kobold, stood over him. Alex could feel the heat from its body, as though the once fictional fires of Hell were burning into him. Then it all went cold ...

Alex looked up, to see Kobold standing by the desk.

The creature was picking up the chair upon which it had, moments earlier when in the guise of Mirabela, been sitting.

It brought the chair over to where Alex sat in a confused heap.

It raised the chair over its head.

Alex felt the first blow as it struck the top of his skull, and remarkably, he heard the crack of bone splintering. It felt as painful and as shocking as he had always imagined a vicious blow to the head would feel. He fell forwards onto the floor with a grunt. He tried to open his mouth, to ask the creature why he was doing this, but his lips wouldn't move, and he couldn't voluntarily produce any sound, other than mindless, breathless grunts of pain with each blow from the chair.

There was more splintering, though Alex, barely conscious now, thought that the sounds had to be coming from the chair rather than from his skull. His skull, his shocked, traumatized mind was telling him, was already beaten into little more than pulp.

He was dying.

He was being beaten to death.

And he didn't know why, and he couldn't really comprehend by whose hand his death was being delivered.

7

Returning to Hell was always a daunting prospect, even for a demon of Kobold's calibre, for Hell was an unwelcoming place. But to those souls sent down from Earth, it was the place that lived only in the very worst of nightmares.

Kobold stood on the vast, seemingly endless plain of red soil, beneath a blood red sky out of which cascaded millions of human beings, their limbs flailing helplessly. Their bodies were naked – for you took nothing from the mortal world that you didn't take into it – and for the most part, they were all over the age of ten, for those under that age who had committed unspeakable acts that would condemn them to eternal damnation – few and far between, as far as Kobold had ever witnessed – spent the first hundred years in purgatory, a place where their sins could be purged, before they were judged by the highest angels of Heaven. Those fortunate few who had successfully expunged their sins were allowed up to Heaven. The many who were truly evil were sent down to Hell, where they would be punished for eternity.

The stench of brimstone filled Kobold's nostrils. It was a smell that he had never got used to, even though he'd spent four hundred years in Hell. The three hundred years he'd spent here as a demon – and prior to that, the hundred years as an imp – hadn't dulled his senses to the horror. He felt like a just man walking through a battlefield, witnessing the bloodshed and carnage before him. That was what it was like every day – no, not every day, for there were no days in Hell. There were no seconds, no minutes, no hours, no days, nor were there any weeks, months, years, decades, centuries or millennia. Time meant very little in Hell, as those souls who were being punished beyond the gates of Hell behind him would testify.

Why, some theologians might ask were they given access to the truth, had Kobold been transformed into an imp, then a demon, after just a hundred or so years, when some of the souls in Hell had been languishing within its blood red walls for thousands of years? Some of them, Kobold reflected, had been here longer than Satan himself. And that was a long time.

Well, the simple answer was that demons were the angels of Hell, those souls who weren't truly evil, who, under different circumstances, might've gone to Heaven and become angels. Demons weren't malevolent creatures, they didn't attack people needlessly, no matter what religious myths would have everyone believe. Demons simply brought about the early demise of those whose lives had condemned them to an eternity in Hell, while at the same time doing everything in their power to prevent harm coming to those with righteous souls.

And so only those souls with more than an ounce of goodness in them were transformed, first into imps – creatures with the power to return to Earth invisibly if required, or to show themselves in all their glory, to directly interact with humans and their surroundings – and then into demons, either of the winged variety, whose very image struck terror into all who saw them, or the regular variety – of which Kobold was one.

Demons also had the power to return to Earth, both in their demonic, Hellish form, and in the guise of a human. But their powers were more than tenfold that of imps – they could use their supernatural ability to start fires, to create objects out of nothing, to influence those around them and, of course, to kill.

And with that great power came responsibility, for there was always the temptation to abuse that power, to become as corrupt as those souls who were condemned to an eternity of suffering in Hell. Kobold had seen more than his fair share of corrupted demons, and he had seen the fate that had befallen those who had been captured by Satan himself. They were tortured even more mercilessly than the unfortunate souls – it wasn't a pretty sight.

Kobold folded his arms as he watched wave upon wave of bodies falling from the red sky above, each one of them representing a person who had died on Earth at that precise moment in time, a person who had probably left behind family, friends, all mourners who would grieve the loss.

Some of those souls that fell before him were truly evil, but certainly not all. How many truly evil people were there on Earth at any given moment in time? Just a few hundred, at most, and some of them were still alive, despite every effort to the contrary, because they were protected – not by demons from Hell, but by the Corrupted, demons uncontrolled by the laws of Heaven and Hell, demons who had escaped the clutches of Satan and his soldiers, demons who lived predominantly on Earth, but returned to the nether reaches of Hell periodically to recharge their powers. The Corrupted fought with the demons whenever one was sent to claim a life, protecting only those corrupted souls whose Earthly influence enabled them to murder and maim and wreak havoc – twisted dictators, serial killers, those who had the power to cause as much misery to their fellow human beings as possible.

The battles with the Corrupted were legendary, and demons on either side lost their lives, because it *was* possible for demons to die. And for a demon to die was the worst thing that could ever happen, because it was so final. There was no soul left to roam the Earth, to walk amongst the clouds of Heaven, or the fiery plains of Hell, because the soul was destroyed. Completely and utterly obliterated. So instead of dying, and finding yourself in the afterlife, as everyone eventually did, Kobold included, there was just nothing.

That thought stuck with Kobold. The memory of dying, the memory of being slowly strangled by a noose. Back in the sixteenth century, they hadn't perfected the art of execution and there was no such thing as human rights. If you broke the law in those days, then you were summarily killed for it. Trials were over in a matter of minutes, trials that in the twentieth century would've lasted for months. You spent a night in gaol, if you were lucky, and then you were hanged – if you were lucky. There were worse fates that befell those guilty of more heinous crimes. To be hung, drawn and quartered, to be burnt alive, to be tortured to death ...

It was justice, a kind of justice that still existed in some of the dictatorships across the globe. And Kobold had witnessed the changes – he had seen capital punishment abolished throughout most of the civilized world, though it still existed in some of the more right-wing western countries, the United States included. Still, Kobold thought with a smirk, those who perpetrated acts of violence against other human beings – even those who committed those acts in the name of the state, such as government executioners – were condemning themselves to Hell. You couldn't alter that, no matter what you did with your life after. To murder in cold blood was considered evil by the angels and demons who sat in judgement over those souls on Earth. Repentance was one way out, but it had to be genuine.

And even Kobold was amazed at the number of people who cried out to God as their souls fell down to Hell, who begged for forgiveness. They were the quasi-believers, the ones who said they believed in God, but who never prayed, only when in dire straits. The atheists, at least, weren't hypocrites. When they saw that they'd been wrong all their lives, when they either fell down to Hell or rose to Heaven – for belief in God was no prerequisite to getting into Heaven – the amazement on their faces was a sight to behold. And then there were some who never shouted out to God to save them as they fell to the plains of Hell. They were too dumbstruck by it all to do that.

Just as he had been.

He remembered that day, in 1527, when he had discovered the truth about his wife – that she was an adulteress, that she had slept with no less than fifteen different men in the five years they'd been married. He remembered it well, for the powers of Hell would not allow those who had sinned to forget their sins, nor what drove them to commit them in the first place. He had loved Miriam, for she had been the most beautiful girl in the village, chaste and unspoiled, and she had always looked up to him.

He had been destined to marry her, for their fathers were the best of friends, and so it was, when Miriam was fifteen, that he had asked for her hand, at the insistence of his father – not that needed any persuasion – and she had obliged, at the insistence of her own father. For the next five years, Kobold, who had been called Jordan Weaver in those days, toiled hard in the fields on his father's farm, while Miriam worked in her father's inn. They were going to be wealthy people when both their fathers retired, for they stood to inherit not just one business, but two, both being the only children of their parents. But unbeknown to Jordan, Miriam had been doing more than pouring the ale and preparing the meals for the weary travellers who stopped in her father's inn. She had been offering them all the comforts of home, including a warm bed. Jordan had been too busy to notice, too tired to care for his wife ...

No, he couldn't make excuses for her. She was here, he thought, somewhere amongst the souls being tortured. But that was the thing, wasn't it? In Hell, you recognized nobody – only the demons recognized people, and then only the people they had been allotted to torture. So Kobold had never met Miriam, even though he himself had sent her to Hell where she belonged.

He had cut through her throat so violently with the scythe that he had almost completely severed her head – the man he had found her in bed with was sprayed with the blood that spouted from her wound, and he desperately tried to pull himself from beneath her, exposing his still erect penis as he did so. Jordon had pounced onto the man, pulling a large blade from a sheath attached to his trousers. With the blade, he severed the penis, the man screaming in agony and disbelief at the monstrous act that had been perpetrated against him. And then Jordan had set about killing the man, stabbing him more than thirty times in the chest and abdomen. He could actually remember the precise number of strikes – thirty-seven – because he had received the same amount day after day upon his arrival in Hell. Thirty-seven stab wounds, each one no more than a seemingly innocuous thin slit in the naked flesh of the man who had been sleeping with Miriam. But those wounds had been deep, had severed thick veins and arteries, sliced open vital organs, and the man had been unable to survive.

They came for Jordan an hour later, as he lay in a bloody patch of hay in the barn.

The trial had been brief, and although some had defended his actions as those of a passionate man driven to murder by an adulterous wife, there really was no defence for the double murder, and really no other punishment than execution. He'd been held captive in a gaol in the village that night, in a cell that had seen more than its fair share of condemned men and women. The next day, the gallows had been prepared for him, and he'd been dragged out of a bed that had given him no sleep, and offered the chance to pray with a priest. But Jordan was a non-believer, though he had never previously admitted it – that was a dangerous thing to do in that day and age – and he had spat in the priest's face.

The priest? A hypocrite, Kobold thought, snarling as he did so.

The soldiers had dragged him, hands bound behind his back, to the gallows, which was little more than two posts buried into the soil, with a crossbar between them, from which was suspended the noose. The noose was placed around Jordan's neck, and two men pulled on the other end of the rope, lifting him off the ground. He kicked and lashed out with his feet, his eyes popping out of his head, as the life was strangled from him. A wealthy man could've paid the executioner to pull down on his legs, to expedite the process, but Jordan didn't have any money, and his father had already disowned him. So Jordan was subjected to slow strangulation, in front of the eyes of more than two hundred people from the village, some who probably thought that what he'd done was the proper thing, others who were glad to see him die in such agony.

As the life ebbed from him, he at last felt something pulling on his feet, and thought that somebody – his father perhaps – had paid the executioner to end the suffering.

Then he felt the rush of being dropped, and he began to fall.

This was not the fall he'd been expecting, not the four foot drop to the ground. This was something altogether different. He was falling, falling endlessly, his eyes seeing nothing but black, his ears hearing nothing at all, not even the chants and cries from the baying crowd that had witnessed his execution. It was as though he had been sucked right out of his body.

And as he fell, his eyesight eventually returned, and he looked up to see a blood red sky unlike any he had ever seen before. This wasn't the sky of a beautiful sunset. This was something so unnatural that Jordan was afraid. More afraid than he had been as he'd been dragged to the gallows. Then, he'd been expecting death, been expecting the blackness of nothing as it overcame him.

But he was dead now, of that he was certain, and this wasn't the blackness of nothing that he'd been expecting. This was ...

He looked down, saw the ground beneath him – far, far beneath him, so far that he could see an horizon that stretched for many miles. A rocky ridge was to his left and right, and ahead of him was what appeared to be a huge city, lit by furious fires, a city that spread right over the horizon, that stretched as far as he could see – which had to be more than a hundred miles from this altitude. And Jordan knew that it didn't end there, that it stretched for even further.

He knew, because he knew that this place into which he was falling was Hell.

He knew, because he could see thousands of other people falling downwards, just like him, some of them screaming, some of them praying and crying out to God, others wearing the serene expression of resignation.

He looked down again, but the thousands of people that were falling beneath him became dots the further down he looked, until they were so small that he couldn't see them. This fall, Jordan thought, was breathtakingly awesome – Kobold could remember thinking that, imagining that he were flying.

The fall lasted an eternity, or so it seemed, though it might've been over in a matter of seconds, because time didn't seem to matter anymore. He hit the ground with a force unlike anything he had ever experienced. It blew the wind right out of his body, and he lay naked on the rocky surface, every bone, every muscle, every fibre of his body aching and stinging. He was a broken man, gasping for air, the sounds of the screaming from those around him filling his ears. He heard and even felt more thuds as yet more people landed on the dusty, red surface of this nether world, and that was his only consolation – that he wasn't the only person here. That others – many more than he would ever have thought – had committed acts of evil that had condemned them to this place of suffering.

Then he'd heard the flapping sound of wings – large wings, and lots of them, beating slowly, as they carried whatever was suspended between them through the stinking air of Hell. Looking up, he saw that there were creatures coming from the direction of the city, that an enormous set of gates, probably half a mile high and twice as wide, had opened up in the vast rocky wall, and that a great outpouring of bodies was heading towards those who had fallen. Thousands upon thousands of them, demons, he now knew them to be, some running across the flat dune, others flying through the air, their huge wings keeping them aloft. As they neared the bodies of the fallen souls, the winged demons swooped down, grasping people seemingly at random between huge pairs of talons, before turning round and heading back to the city.

It wasn't a winged demon that had come for Jordan.

It was the regular kind, a sight that Kobold was now used to, but which had struck terror in Jordan's heart.

He help up his hands, and tried to speak, but nothing more than a terrified scream came out from between his lips.

Kobold closed his eyes.

He didn't want to remember the torture, but even now, he could still feel every single knife wound, could still feel the hot burning between his legs as his penis was hacked from his body and tossed to a wild pack of succubi, who fed grotesquely on it. He'd been killed more than a million times, had his head torn from his body in more ways that he'd knew existed, and had returned to consciousness with his entire body intact, only for the torture to begin again.

A never-ending cycle of complete agony.

That was Hell, Kobold told himself, as the winged demons began to beat their wings and start their journey across the plain to the fallen souls for the hourly collection. It didn't matter how much time was left between collections – there was nowhere for the souls to run. They could continue running for the rest of eternity and they would still get nowhere, because even if they managed to climb the vast mountains that walled the plain in on every side, and even if they managed to descend the other side, they'd find themselves in another plain equally as vast, with mountains ringing it.

And the further they got from the gates of Hell, the angrier the demons who had to bring them back became.

There was no escape.

It was just a case of delaying the inevitable.

And Kobold had never known anyone to cross the mountain ranges.

The winged demons screamed out their battle cries as they plucked their chosen souls from the surface of the plain, and the regular demons grabbed theirs and dragged them roughly back to the gates.

One of them, Kobold thought, was Alexander Bartek.

It would be the only soul that he would recognize. None of the others would appeal to him.

That was how demons recognized those they'd chosen.

And as Kobold's powerful eyes scanned the plain, they eventually fell upon the familiar features, easy to spot in the sea of faceless souls.

And he smiled.

Soon, the torture would begin, and he would supervise the imps and succubi as they wrought havoc on Bartek's immortal body. He already had the eternal torture figured out. Usually, it had something to do with the crimes committed by the human form.

This time, however, Bartek hadn't used physical violence on anybody. So Kobold could choose a torture from Bartek's mind. Everyone had fears and everyone had fantasies, and some of those fantasies were evil – and it was easy to juxtapose the fears and fantasies and come up with something so incredibly heinous that no one on Earth could commit such an evil atrocity.

Kobold rushed forwards, diving between the bodies of those souls who were still in a daze, pulling themselves to their feet. He brushed them all aside in his haste to reach Bartek as quickly as possible. He could chase Bartek for the equivalent of many Earth weeks before his powers began to subside, before he needed to recharge them, but in this instance, he didn't think that would be necessary. Only the very determined even attempted to fight their captors – and Bartek certainly wasn't one of them.

So Bartek fell before him quickly.

He looked up into Kobold's face, and immediately a look of recognition shot across his features.

"You!"

Kobold grinned. "Yes, I rather think it is."

Bartek looked around him, at the souls that were either being dragged off screaming or catatonic, or were just walking around in a stupor, awaiting their turn, then turned back to Kobold. "This place?"

"Welcome to Hell," Kobold said, and grabbed Bartek tightly. "We do hope you enjoy your stay." He pulled the accountant's face close to his. "It's going to be a long, long one." And with that, he laughed and dragged Bartek back to the mammoth gates that kept the souls within Hell. He looked up at them as he always did, at their height, at their breadth. On either side of the gateposts, which were a mile apart, were vast torches, burning flames that flickered more than two hundred feet high. The illumination they gave off was immense, but like everywhere in Hell, they gave everything an eerie orange-red hue.

The noise from within the city of Hell was tremendous, overpowering to those who were visiting for the first time. It was as though you could hear everyone within, all the voices, all the screams, from every single torture chamber – and there were quadrillions upon quadrillions of them. The number was astronomical, so large as to outnumber the stars in the universe. And with every day that passed, so the number of chambers increased. The city of Hell was forever growing, sections multiplying in size like some huge body undergoing cell division. It was fortunate that in the afterworlds, there was an infinite amount of space. The supernatural beings who constructed the chambers of Hell did not have to consider where the next piece of land came from – they had the power to create it out of nothing, pushing back the walls of Hell so that there was sufficient space for another hundred thousand chambers.

The only problem was, with every new soul that fell down to Hell, there had to be more imps and occasionally a demon created to deal with them. As it was, Kobold had many hundreds of souls to deal with, managing the imps, succubi and incubi who administered the torture. His time was spread evenly amongst them, but he could not manage many more before his powers became stretched. In time, some of the imps were promoted to demons, and they would take over some of the souls. Fortunately, after a couple of years in Hell the torture slipped into some kind of routine that required no management. The souls were tortured to death many times a day, and for the imps, it was just like going through the motions.

At first, they might enjoy it, delivering pain to those evil souls who had doubtless tortured many human beings during their time on Earth, but it soon became monotonous. They would torture one soul to death, move onto another, then another, then another, before finally returning to the first, who had probably just been rejuvenated, ready for the next bout of torture. Occasionally, the imps added their own fiendish ideas to the torture, but that was frowned upon. The idea was that the soul knew what was going to happen, would feel the same pain each and every time, and would come to fear that pain. The dying was a release that lasted no more than an hour or so. When they came to, occasionally they would remain unmolested for a couple of hours, while the imps completed their rounds. Then the imps would return, and it would start all over again.

Perpetual torture, for all eternity, with no escape.

Unless you were truly remorseful, under which circumstances, you were given a chance to prove yourself by being transformed into an imp.

But only a small percentage of the quadrillions upon quadrillions of souls within Hell ever achieved such a promotion.

Bartek, thought Kobold as he dragged the unfortunate bastard to a vacant chamber, was a pathetic individual, without the necessary abilities to ever achieve promotion. He was weak-willed, a coward, an unrepentant coward – because cowards only repented because they were afraid, not because they truly wanted to, and it was difficult to break that vicious circle.

Kobold would be seeing Bartek for a long time to come, for all eternity maybe, unless one of Kobold's imps was made up to demon, and took this particular sinner off his hands, which in all likelihood was what would happen. Old demons like Kobold – well, in time served, Kobold was still a junior, really – rarely kept the low-level chaff like Bartek. They kept the mass murderers, the child killers, the dictators, those who were almost too powerful for even the demons to handle.

Bartek didn't struggle, not as much as some of them did. It was as though he were in awe of his surroundings – and it really was an awesome sight for the first-time visitor to Hell. The chambers were little more than rocky huts, some single story, others towering many floors over the ground. It was a city that sprawled on and on. Indeed, for a mere mortal to walk through the city, from the gates to the wall on the opposite side, would take many, many centuries. Even a demon wouldn't attempt to walk, not when they had the power to transport themselves to any location, on Earth, in Heaven or in Hell. The vision of the multitude of chambers, with their single doorway and solitary window out of which shone an orange glow from the fire within stayed with every unfortunate soul who paid Hell a visit. Most stayed for all eternity, never seeing beyond the chamber, the prison cell, the four walls carved out of the red rock, the stench of brimstone and sulphur forever in their nostrils, as they experienced firsthand the sins they'd committed on Earth.

Kobold found the empty chamber easily, and tossed Bartek inside, pausing only momentarily as he witnessed the faceless souls around him being dragged or thrown into their respective chambers. How many of those individuals had achieved notoriety on Earth, how many were known by millions for the crimes they'd committed? He would never know, not unless one of them passed his way.

He turned and looked back inside the chamber, where Bartek was dragging his naked form up against the wall on the far side.

"There is no escape," he told him. "Not now. Take a good look, Alexander, because these four walls will be your home for all eternity." And with that pronouncement, he stepped into the chamber.

"What are you going to do?" Bartek demanded to know.

"Do you have any concept what perpetual torture is like, Alexander? Can you conceive the true horror of Hell, of undergoing pain that is relentless?" Kobold took a couple of steps in Bartek's direction. "Usually, your crimes against humanity are returned to you, but in your case, that wouldn't be painful, would it? Juggling figures, cheating people out of their savings, well, that's no punishment for a man like you, is it?"

"Leave me alone," Bartek said. Kobold grabbed the man's face and stared into his eyes. "Leave me alone!"

"Don't fight me, Alexander," the demon said. "Don't fight me, don't fight my imps, don't fight what you cannot change, Alexander, because you're just wasting energy. Does that make sense?"

"Please, leave me alone," Bartek pleaded.

"Ah, now that's touching," Kobold said. "But I've heard it all before. Many, many times. So many times, that I have become desensitized to it. Now, as I was saying, we have to come up with a suitable punishment, one that it fitting for a period of eternity. And for yours, I had to take a journey inside your mind, Alexander, and fish around in the filth and degradation I found there." Bartek stared at Kobold with wide, terrified eyes. "Do these ring any bells?" Kobold asked, turning to the imps that had materialized behind him. But these imps had been transformed from the large-eared, red-skinned creatures they usually were into small boys of no more than ten or eleven. "We all of us have fantasies, do we not? And fantasies are harmless, so long as they remain only fantasies." Bartek looked at the boys, naked as they were, their eyes drifting seductively over his body.

"I have never touched a child in my life!" he shouted. "Never!"

"No," Kobold said. "But here in Hell, if you have to be punished, then that punishment has to be worthy of your crimes. And in a different time, a different place, this may well have been your crime. In your dreams, you abused these young boys. Look at their faces – they are faces you will recognize. The children of neighbours, of friends." Bartek squeezed his eyes shut. "Come now, Alexander, and enjoy them, for they will surely entertain you. But you will have to pay for that entertainment."

"No, no, no! I don't want this!"

Kobold threw his face into Alexander's. "Do you fucking think that the people you cheated out of money wanted that?" He leant back. "It doesn't matter what you want or what you do now," he said, as the imps descended upon Alexander Bartek. To the demon, they were imps, mature yet sexless, their skin as crimson as his own. To Bartek, they appeared as the boys in his sexual fantasies. They stroked him, brought him to a state of arousal, in spite of his protests. Kobold watched the look of pleasure that appeared on his face, heard his soft moans as the imps performed oral sex on him.

He smiled.

Soon, Bartek would be moaning not in pleasure, but in agony.

That was the part Kobold enjoyed the most – seeing those who had sinned getting their just desserts.

It was as one of the imps ripped Bartek's penis from him with its sharp teeth that Kobold felt the pull of the devil calling him. It was an irresistible feeling, and demons were compelled to transport themselves to the devil's chamber immediately. If they delayed, if they were otherwise engaged, as Kobold was now, then the devil himself would transport them instantly to face his wrath.

Kobold paused momentarily before he disappeared from the chamber – for some reason, the urge to do the devil's bidding wasn't as strong as it usually was. It was a thought he dismissed as he materialized in the devil's chamber, which was a mile high and a mile in diameter, with a large pedestal in the centre upon which sat the devil.

Kobold appeared a hundred feet away, and looked upwards at the rocky outcrop that was the devil's throne, standing erect like some mighty stalagmite more than two hundred feet tall. Even from this distance, the devil seemed huge.

The pillar of rock seemed to descend into the ground as the devil's throne lowered down so that his feet were level with Kobold's head. Kobold instantly dropped to his knees as though in supplication, but looked up with fascination into the face of the creature who ruled Hell, who had ruled for thousands of years in fact.

Satan was perhaps twenty feet tall, broadly-built, his inhuman lower torso like that of an animal, in accordance with the legend that had existed on Earth for countless years. He sat with his hairy goat-like legs apart, his glowing red arms resting on the sides of the massive stone throne. His face was as individual as that of any of the demons in Hell, but retained the same red skin. He possessed a long, black goatee beard, and short hair, cropped close to his uneven red skull. The two horns that protruded above either eye were probably a foot in length and tapered to a fine point that could easily disembowel a human, should he choose to use physical as opposed to supernatural force.

His eyes were bestial, the pupils completely dilated, so that they appeared totally black, with the barest minimum of white visible. There were no emotions to be read behind those eyes, not fear, nor loathing, nor hatred or anger. Only the frown on Satan's face gave away his emotional state.

"Kobold," he muttered, his voice deep, grating, rumbling throughout the vast chamber.

"My Lord," Kobold said, lowering his head so that no longer disrespected the devil by looking into his face.

"I am disturbed," Satan continued.

Kobold felt uneasy. Still he didn't look into Satan's face. "Disturbed, my Lord?"

"The Corrupted have great powers of persuasion," Satan said cryptically.

"I don't understand," Kobold said, now risking a look upwards into Satan's face. "I know nothing of the Corrupted."

"You know the story of the Fallen Angel, do you not?" Satan asked.

"Of course, my Lord," Kobold said. "It is legendary."

"Indeed," Satan said, rising off his pedestal and stepping down onto the ground before Kobold. "And totally untrue."

Kobold didn't know what to say. Still on his knees, he watched as Satan clasped his hands behind his back, and walked away from him, stopping fifty feet away.

"The story of the Fallen Angel, as I am sure you are aware, Kobold, is the story of Satan," the devil said. "Not the story of the devil, for that is an altogether different tale. It is my story, and like every tale, it has been exaggerated beyond all boundaries of the truth."

"I don't understand, my Lord."

Satan turned and faced Kobold. "Tell me the story of the Fallen Angel."

Now Kobold was embarrassed. "But my Lord, it is your story."

"Tell it to me as if I have never heard it before, as if you are telling it to somebody other than me."

Kobold took a deep breath. "Well, Satan was the most glorious angel in Heaven, a Seraph, who sat at God's right hand." Satan nodded and arched an eyebrow. "Satan was so close to the seat of power that he himself became corrupted. He began to abuse his power, to abuse his subjects for his own gratification. When God discovered the truth, He sent Satan out of Heaven and into Hell, where he was subjected to the tortures of Purgatory." Satan took a few steps closer to Kobold.

"Go on," he said.

"After a period of Purgatory, Satan became the devil," Kobold said. "It was his place in the hierarchy of Hell. A Seraph is too powerful a being to be transformed into a mere soul, too powerful for even God to destroy completely without a mighty battle."

Satan nodded. "Do you know who the devil was before I came to power?"

"Beelzebub, my Lord," Kobold answered.

"And what do you think made Beelzebub give up his seat of power? The second most powerful seat of power in the Universe? Why do you suppose he simply stepped aside to allow me, Satan, to step into his shoes?"

"I don't know."

"I was no angel, Kobold, no Seraph," Satan said. "Like you, as a mortal, I committed a sinful act, for which I did indeed serve out my time in

Purgatory, because I repented. But there was a power within me that could never be contained in Heaven. Every day humans are born with the power to become to become Angels, Archangels, Principalities, Powers, Virtues, Dominions, Thrones, and Cherubim. That power is within them, within their souls, but it does not alone shape their destiny. How they live their lives, that it what shapes that destiny. But some of them, they bring that power down to Hell, because of the sins they committed. If they repent, if they show remorse, then they are instantly turned into demons, so that they may punish those who have sinned. That is what happened to me."

"So you were never a Seraph?" Kobold asked. Here was Satan, destroying his own legend.

"Never," Satan said. "And do you think that if I were, I would be allowed to roam free, to take over Hell as the devil? Do you really think God would allow that? For me to commit a sin, and instantly be transformed into the devil? The power that role would give me?" Satan strolled across the ground of his chamber and turned away from Kobold. "God would've struck me down, destroyed me ... you know, Kobold, only the Corrupted, the true fallen angels and demons, ever stand a chance of survival, and even then they forever remain the hunted, forever watching their backs for the death that will surely come to them one day."

"My Lord, forgive me," Kobold said uneasily, "but I do not know where you are going with this conversation."

"I instantly became a demon, Kobold," Satan continued. "But even the powers of a demon were not enough to contain what I held inside. For every millennium, a force is born with a power second only to God Himself. Sometimes, that power ends up in Heaven, and out of it, a new Seraph is born. Occasionally, however, one who holds that immense power falls to Hell. If that soul is truly evil ..." Satan paused, clasped his hands behind his back, and looked up at the ceiling high overhead. "Then it is summarily destroyed. Think what should happen if a soul with that power should become one of the Corrupted. The Earth as we know it would become a place full of evil and sin, and it would be destroyed. And Heaven and Hell would be fighting the greatest battle of all."

"You are saying, my Lord, that one of these powerful beings is here ... in Hell?" Satan didn't answer. "One of the Corrupted?" Satan laughed.

"My Lord?"

"I remind you, Kobold, of what I said. The truly evil ones are destroyed, before they ever achieve the kind of power to seize Heaven and Hell." Satan turned to face Kobold. "But there is one with that immense power here in Hell. He walks among us. I know not exactly who. His powers are still immature, and I ... I cannot find him." The expression on Satan's face was one of bewilderment. "But I sense ... I sense that there will be a fight for supremacy here in Hell, as I once fought and destroyed Beelzebub himself." Satan looked back up at the ceiling again.

Kobold didn't know how to react. He just shook his head in puzzlement. "My Lord, why are you speaking to me about this?"

Satan turned and looked at him. "I need the strongest of my demons by my side, Kobold. I need the support of my adjutants. I need you."

"My Lord, surely this is a battle only you can fight ..."

Satan smirked. "In Hell, Kobold, there are rules, yes ... but some of those rules can be broken. My reign as the devil has been a success, has it not? Have the Corrupted taken over Earth, as was threatened by God himself two millennia ago, when I seized power?" Kobold shook his head. "Hell needs me, Kobold. Heaven needs me too. And Earth, it certainly needs me. For do I not take the sick and twisted minds before they reach maturity? Do I not instruct my imps to take the souls of children destined to become monsters, before they wreak havoc on mankind?" Kobold didn't answer. He could not reconcile the deaths of innocent babies with those of the future monsters. "My rule as the devil has been a fair one, Kobold, surely you can see that."

Kobold nodded his head. "I see that, my Lord," he answered, trying not to tell himself that he had never served under any other devil than Satan.

"Then you will fight by my side?"

Kobold considered the request, then nodded his head slowly. "I cannot deny you, my Lord," he said, "for I will always remain your loyal servant."

Satan smiled again. "Yes," he said, "you are, aren't you?"

And with that, he turned away from Kobold.

And Kobold found himself back in the torture chamber, where the imps were hungrily feeding on the lower portion of Alexander Bartek's body.

8

It was the first time Detective Superintendent Saddington had ever left the shores of the United Kingdom, and to find himself in an exotic city such as Rio De Janeiro for his first ever international excursion certainly was an overwhelming sensation. The jet lag still addled his mind as he strolled out of the terminal and up to a man holding a placard with his name written upon it in block capitals, and all he could think of was sleep as he held out his hand and introduced himself.

"Good morning, Detective Superintendent," the Brazilian said as he shook Saddington's hand. He spoke with an obvious accent, but his grasp of the English language appeared almost perfect. "I am Lieutenant Francisco. I will be taking you to meet Captain Sobral."

Saddington nodded. "My accommodation?"

"We have arranged that, as per the agreement with your Scotland Yard," Francisco assured him, taking the suitcase from Saddington's weary hand. "Your flight was pleasant?"

"Long," Saddington said, following the Brazilian as he walked through the sliding doors and out into the South American sunshine. "And tiresome."

"You are tired?"

"Very," Saddington said. "I could've done with a few hours sleep before I got down to work."

"Ah, but unfortunately that is not possible," Francisco said, opening the door of a large, grey car. "Captain Sobral has some news regarding your missing accountant."

"He does?"

"I will let him tell you," Francisco said mysteriously.

Saddington was now intrigued, as he slipped into the worn, yet extremely comfortable, passenger seat, but he figured that was the general idea. Keep him interested enough for him to stay awake. As Francisco climbed in beside him, Saddington said, "How about a hint?"

The Brazilian just smirked and fired up the engine.

His driving wasn't bad, but there were a few moments throughout the journey where Saddington stamped on an imaginary brake pedal in the passenger footwell. He figured that too was a deliberate ploy, lots of abrupt braking and sharp acceleration, designed to jolt his mind awake.

By the time the car pulled up in the car park of Rio's main police headquarters, Saddington was alert, if not totally rested. Francisco left his suitcase in the car and led Saddington inside the police station, where life seemed even more hectic than it was at an inner city nick back home. There were scores of skimpily-clad women – some of whom suspiciously resembled young men – handcuffed to one another. Francisco offered no explanation, and Saddington didn't really need one. The Brazilians were doing what they could to fight prostitution, in particular the "ladyboys", but they were of much interest and value to the tourist trade, so any operations were kept to a minimum, and only occurred when an upstanding member of society complained.

Today, thought Saddington, somebody must've complained.

As they paused at the elevator, one of the hookers looked in his direction, looked him up and down, and smiled. Saddington, polite as ever, was tempted to smile back, until the whore licked her lips and lifted her short, tight skirt to show him she wasn't wearing any panties. She also wasn't a she.

Saddington quickly looked away, to find Francisco smiling at him. "Welcome to Rio," he said.

The upper floors of the building, whilst poorly decorated and with a horrible smell seeming to emanate from the very walls surrounding them, were somewhat less chaotic, with uniformed and plain-clothed officers darting about, documents and files in their hands. None of them seemed to pay Saddington any attention, not until they reached the offices closest to where Captain Sobral sat. There, the police officers took a good look, obviously aware as to the reason behind his visit, and probably with more information about Alexander Bartek than he at this moment in time had.

Francisco led him up to a goldfish bowl of an office, marked with Sobral's name and rank on the door, and he knocked and entered, with Saddington following.

Captain Sobral sat behind a desk piled high with weighty books and thick files in a helter-skelter fashion. A few dusty, framed photographs of Sobral sucking up to local dignitaries were home to spiders who had woven their silky webs over the tops of the frames, and now hid behind them awaiting the arrival of their prey. The glass walls were hidden behind venetian blinds, as dusty as the photographs, most probably rarely opened. The smell of cigars accompanied the acrid smog that hung in the confined space of the office, and Saddington looked around until he found the source – a cigar burning away in a large ashtray full of myriad stubs, sending up a plume of thick tobacco smoke.

Sitting behind the desk, a fat hand with many rings and an expensive gold watch resting on the table before the ashtray, was Captain Sobral, of the Rio De Janeiro police.

He was a big man, with thinning but incredibly curly black hair. His face was round, his chins many, and his eyes were small, his big cheeks squashing them upwards. Dressed in his khaki uniform, he leaned back in his chair as Saddington's eyes fell upon him, and tapped the cigar on the side of the ashtray.

"Detective Superintendent Saddington, I presume," he said, struggling to his feet and extending a clammy hand, which the British detective shook. "Take a seat, please."

"First let me thank you for your assistance, Captain Sobral–"

"Enough," Sobral said, "please, let us dispense with the bullshit protocol. We are in the same field, you and I, and we should offer assistance because it is right, not merely because it is good diplomacy."

"You're right, of course," Saddington agreed. Already, he could see that the outwardly offensive Sobral was sincere, in spite of resembling some South American dictator. "So, let me move onto my second point of order – I would like to apologize in advance should I appear not to be giving you my fullest attention."

"Certainly – you are tired, this much we understand," Sobral said, taking a drag from his cigar. He relaxed in his comfortable leather chair and nodded to Francisco, who left the office. "Now, you are looking for a man by the name of Alexander Bartek, yes?"

"That's right," Saddington answered, as Sobral grabbed something from his desk and tossed it onto his lap. It was a passport – a US passport, because Bartek had never applied for, nor been granted, UK citizenship. Saddington opened it, took a look at the photograph inside. It was Bartek – a few years younger, but certainly there was no mistaking. "You've found him?"

Sobral smirked. "Well, we have, and we haven't." Saddington raised a questioning eyebrow as there was a knock at the door. Francisco entered moments later with a tray upon which were two cups of steaming coffee. He found a space on Sobral's desk, put the tray down, and left the office again. Sobral picked up one of the cups and offered it Saddington.

"What do you mean, you have and you haven't?" he asked curiously. Sobral poured some cream in his coffee and stirred gently. He offered first the cream and then the sugar to the Briton, who shook his head. Now he felt wide awake, and he wanted to get down to business.

"We got lucky," Sobral said. "Twice. The same, this can't be said about Mr Bartek."

Saddington watched as the Brazilian opened a thick file and scanned through some notes, though he doubted whether the Captain really needed to refresh his memory. "First, one of our city's fine hotels contacted us, because one of their guests hadn't returned to his room for the night. As I'm sure you're aware, we have a few problems with crime here. It is not unknown for a tourist to ... shall we say, go missing for a few days. Some are never seen again. The officers who attended the scene found a considerable sum of money, and that passport, but no sign of Alexander Bartek."

"So, he was in the city."

"He was. And more packages containing money – US dollars – have arrived in his absence. It would appear," Sobral said, sipping his coffee, "that Mr Bartek was expecting a lot of money to be coming his way."

"So, he disappeared?"

Sobral smirked again. "Not quite. You see, that very same day, some of my officers responded to a report of a disturbance in an abandoned part of the city. A derelict office block. There, they found two corpses."

Saddington's heart sank. "One of them was Bartek?"

Sobral nodded. "Of course, at the time, my officers weren't aware of that. Subsequent investigation led them to the conclusion that the corpse belonged to Alexander Bartek."

"The other person?"

"The second corpse belonged to a well-known forger by the name of Jesus Mirabela," Sobral answered. "Also known as Marcus Rubela. He was in his mid-seventies, had been working for most of his life as a forger. Excellent abilities in that field. It is obvious that Bartek went to see Mirabela with the intention of buying himself a new identity."

"So what went wrong?"

"Well, as far as we can deduce, Bartek was beaten to death with a chair."

"A chair?"

"The curious thing is that the murderer appears to have been Mirabela."

"But you said he was dead."

"He was – but he was holding the chair, and the only fingerprints on it were his."

Saddington shook his head. "Well, it's a strange case, certainly. But unfortunately, Captain, the investigation is yours."

"Yes," Sobral said with a scowl. "Yes, it is." He took another sip of coffee, then sat back in his chair with his cigar. "I was hoping, however, that you could offer some insight."

Saddington took a deep breath. He was given the opinion that Sobral rarely sought advice from anyone else, because he believed that no one else could match his own analytical mind. But he had confidence in his own abilities, so he responded to the Captain's request. "Well, I suppose we should first ascertain as to why this Mirabela should want to kill Bartek. You say that there was money found in his hotel room. Was any found at the scene of the murder?"

Sobral shook his head. "But in that part of the city, that is not unusual. I would say that some of the ghetto residents will be walking around in Gucci suits for the next couple of years, because it's not inconceivable that Bartek had more than a hundred thousand dollars on him when he left the hotel."

"What makes you say that?"

"Each package posted to the hotel room had fifty thousand dollars inside," Sobral explained. "And we found two empty packages in his room."

Saddington nodded. It was a logical assumption. "Well, there are two possible murderers. One is Mirabela – for whom we have no motive as yet, but we can assume that the exertion of the murder probably killed him, taking into account his age." Sobral made no comment. "The second suspect is unknown, but does have a motive. The money that Bartek was carrying with him. He killed Bartek and then killed Mirabela. I'm presuming we don't yet know how either of them died?"

Sobral shook his head. "Post-mortem reports are due in tomorrow."

"Well, we can assume that this second, unnamed suspect framed Mirabela."

"As you say, the second suspect does seem the more likely of the two," Sobral said. "And as for how he could've known about Bartek's wealth, well, my men have been questioning the hotel staff. We believe that one of them may have opened one of Bartek's packages and discovered the money." Saddington was impressed, although he really shouldn't have been. It was a logical deduction, the proper course of investigation, and back home, he would've expected it from every junior officer working for him. But this was Brazil and he was expecting every police official to be corrupt and incompetent.

Sobral was clearly the exception to that stereotyping.

"Well, whatever the outcome of this investigation, Bartek got what he deserved," Saddington said uncharitably. "But as for our investigation into his finances, I suppose that leaves us with yet another dead end."

"You were hoping for more?"

"Well, it's clear that Bartek had a numbered account in Switzerland," Saddington said. "I mean, we had no proof, but the funds available to him and his partner must've been somewhere in the region of almost a billion US dollars." Sobral raised his eyebrows, then sipped from his coffee. "There's every chance that he came here first to buy himself a new identity with the features he possessed, and then pay a visit elsewhere to buy himself a new face, and a fresh identity. Shifting identities like that in a short space of time would've made it very difficult for us to trace him."

Sobral nodded. "I can understand your frustration," he said. "but I'm sure you will want to wait and see what the post-mortems reveal. If I were in your place, Superintendent, I might be tempted to take advantage of my government's generosity – which must be as rare in the United Kingdom as it is in Brazil – and enjoy myself in this beautiful city of ours."

Saddington smiled. "You know," he said, taking a gulp of coffee, "I might just do that."

9

The day had been as tedious and tiresome as Sadie had expected it would have been. In between sweeping the floors, collecting litter from outside the restaurant, and cleaning up kiddie puke, she was being shown how to operate the overly-complicated – to her, at least – till system. It was then that she realized why she was never charged the same price for the same meal twice – it was because the goddamned tills were so ridiculous. Meant to simplify the purchasing process, they only served to confuse Sadie. And remember, always take the money from the customer *before* you prepare their meal – that way, they don't get the opportunity to see the food before they pay for it. Not that the crap McDonald's served could be called food, Sadie thought grimly. Well, that wasn't fair, she admonished herself. Just because she didn't like fast food – apart from pizza, that was. And what the hell did they put on pizzas, apart from unrecognizable crap? She recalled one of those urban myths – it was Billy who'd told her – where a disgruntled Pizza Hut employed had masturbated all over a pizza before cooking it. In fact, he'd done it a number of times before he was caught out, whereupon he told the police that it aroused him to imagine some strange woman eating his freshly-cooked semen.

Sadie shrugged that thought away as she grabbed another McDonald's bag containing a half-eaten burger, a few cold fries, and a cup with half an iceberg still inside. Why the hell, she thought for not the first time that day, couldn't these fucking assholes learn to use the litter bins provided? They rammed all of their rubbish inside the brown paper bag, but couldn't be assed to ram that inside a McDonald's bin. Bastards!

But the fact that she was performing one of the most menial jobs known to man wasn't all that was getting her down. The uniform, she thought, catching her reflection in the restaurant window, was enough to send shivers down her spine. It was hideous – shapeless pants, a baggy blouse, a stupid goddamned cap, for Christ's sake! Then her eyes shifted across the street to the Disney Store, where its 'cast members' stood greeting the customers, dressed in their blue cardigans, ankle socks and trainers – now that, she corrected herself, was hideous.

And to call them 'cast members'? Who the hell were they trying to kid? Jesus, she half-expected them to come out dressed as Minnie fucking Mouse and sing a song!

So yes, she assured herself, there were worse jobs than this one.

Well, she corrected herself yet again as she spotted yet another pile of vomit, maybe not worse jobs, but certainly worse uniforms.

"Time for a break," a familiar voice said, and Sadie swung around. All day, she'd been dreading seeing someone she knew, letting them see her in this uniform, sweeping the floor like a brainless nerd. But it hadn't happened so far.

Melissa, she was relieved to see, looking every bit as pathetic as she did, her assistant manager's position affording her no better uniform than that which Sadie herself wore, albeit with a few more of those gold stars on her name-badge, and the title 'Assistant Manager' emblazoned above her name. She was a tall girl, which made Sadie, at five-foot-three, feel even more tiny, with a pretty face, angular cheekbones, a pair of the longest legs Sadie had ever seen on a girl – though today, they were covered in pants that were way too short for her – and a huge bosom. Melissa, with all of that, and her long, fair hair, was the archetypal male fantasy, and she knew it. In spite of that, however, she was a good friend, with an instantly likeable personality. Men were attracted to her, and women loved hearing her talk.

Because Melissa could definitely talk.

"I thought you'd never ask," Sadie said, leaning on her brush.

Melissa took off her cap. "Let's go off duty," she said, "grab ourselves something to eat."

"Fancy a McDonald's?"

"Well, we can eat shit for free, or get out of these glad rags and go to the Ragamuffin and have a pub lunch," Melissa said. "We've got an hour."

"What are we waiting for?"

The Ragamuffin was the closest pub to McDonald's, and also one of eight in the town centre. As such, it received a lot of custom, particularly during the weekly lunch time period of midday to two. As Sadie, now wearing jeans and a tee-shirt, followed Melissa – similarly attired – to the pub, she glanced at her watch, saw that it was one-thirty. One thing Melissa had assured her – and Sadie listened to her on this one, because she'd worked a lot more than Sadie had – was that the later you took your lunch, the quicker the day went, because when you came back from lunch, you only had a couple of hours to work before the day was over. Another tip, Melissa had said, was to leave your alarm switched on at the weekend. That way, when it woke you up at seven o'clock on a Saturday morning, you could take great satisfaction in first realizing that it was the weekend, and that you didn't have to work, and then switching the bloody thing off and rolling over for some extra kip. Sadie had no doubt that this worked, because Melissa always seemed in a good mood, in spite of her depressing career choice.

Inside the crowded pub, they managed to find a table, and after ordering some chips, they waited for their meal, Diet-Cokes keeping them cool. Sadie glanced around at the people in the pub, most of them dressed for office work, some in power suits, others in crumpled shirts, trousers, skirts and blouses. She also noticed that a couple of men were already eyeing up Melissa.

Melissa appeared not to have noticed, but Sadie knew that she had.

"Doesn't that get on your nerves?"

"What?"

"All those guys looking at you," Sadie replied, taking a sip of Coke.

"Why should it? God, I'm flattered, even if they do look like freaks."

"Well, I wouldn't fancy being some freak's wet dream," Sadie muttered.

"God, Sadie, you really do know how to lower the tone!"

"Ladies," a man said. Sadie looked up to see a tall man in a suit, bottle of beer in his hand, staring at Melissa, with puppy dog eyes, in spite of his confident exterior. "My friend and I were just wondering whether you'd mind us sharing this table."

Melissa looked at Sadie – they were both single girls, so there wasn't any harm in it. Not that Sadie was particularly attracted to the suited man, nor his friend, who was a little bit on the heavy side. If he lost a few pounds, she thought, then perhaps he might pass for moderately handsome. All the same, Sadie shrugged her shoulders indifferently, and Melissa invited the two of them over.

"So," Melissa asked immediately, "what do you two do?"

"We're civil service," the fat one explained.

"Really, what agency?"

"We could tell you," the confident one said, "but then we'd have to kill you."

"Right," Melissa said with an aloof nod, "you work in the Job Centre then." The fat man blushed, and Sadie rolled her eyes. Great, she thought, a pair of goddamned government pen-pushers.

"What about you?" the confident man asked, before taking a swig of beer.

"I'm in catering," Melissa said. "Management. Sadie, here, is a pop star."

"Now you expect us to believe that?" the confident man said with a smug expression.

"I'm the lead singer with Darcy's Box," Sadie explained. "We're an Indie band. I doubt whether you guys are into Indie music, are you?" Her American accent clearly threw the confident man. He arched an eyebrow, and it was clear that he didn't know whether to believe or disbelieve it.

"So, where do you work?" he asked Melissa.

"She works at some flash restaurant in the city," Sadie said. "She could tell you, but then she'd have to kill you."

"So, McDonald's then?" the fat man said with a smirk. Nobody else smiled, and he resorted to taking a slurp from his pint to hide his blushes and embarrassment.

There were a few moments of silence, then the confident man said, "I'm Paul, by the way."

"Melissa – and this is Sadie."

"This is Stephen," Paul introduced his fat friend, who waved a hand and mouthed a greeting. "So, you ladies are on a lunch break from your executive and celebrity lifestyle?"

"That's right," Melissa said. "Life in catering can be tough."

"Well, that's the nature of fast food, isn't it? Poor pay, long hours, rushed off your feet."

"Well, you know, maybe if assholes like you didn't push so hard," Sadie said, "then people wouldn't have to accept such cruddy jobs, would they?"

Paul frowned. "You know, we do a service to the taxpayer, Sadie. We prevent scrounging bastards from leeching off the public."

"Don't try and justify your right-wing politics," Sadie snapped. She'd been listening to the guys in the band for too long, she told herself, but she just couldn't help it. Confidence was all very well in a person, but you had to be likeable too. And this asshole had an attitude problem. So, he wasn't bad looking, but he seemed to be aware of that, and expected everybody else to be aware of it too.

"A socialist pop star," Paul said, smiling smugly. "What a surprise."

"You know," Melissa said, as the chips were brought over to the table in two large bowls, "I was gonna ask whether you wanted to share our food, but I think there might possibly be a clash of politics here."

"We can work around that," Paul said, turning his attentions back to Melissa. It was clear he had the hots for her, and he would probably change his political views for as long as it took to screw her. "Because there are two things you shouldn't discuss with those you don't know intimately – politics and religion."

"Well," Melissa said, "I guess that means you'll never get to know what religion I am or where my political opinions lie."

"Melissa, come on," Paul said. "How about you meeting me for dinner tonight. I'll take you to a real posh restaurant – somewhere a little bit more impressive than McDonald's."

"I don't think you realize how insulting you're being," Melissa said, casting an incredulous look in Sadie's direction.

"You know, do you practice at being obnoxious, or is it a requirement for working in the Job Centre?" Sadie asked Paul, before shoving a chip in her mouth. She looked at Stephen, whose expression told her that he just wanted the ground to open up and swallow him.

"Why don't we leave these two lovebirds?" Paul said to Melissa. "I'm sure Sadie and Stephen would like to get to know each other better."

"Well, I know I don't want to get to know you any better, so what makes you think Sadie wants to get to know your fat friend any better?" Sadie could see that the moment she'd opened her mouth, Melissa had instantly regretted saying what she'd said. The fat one, Stephen, wasn't to blame for any of this. And the expression on his face told both girls that Melissa had overstepped the mark.

Paul, probably for the first time in his life, thought of somebody else, and nodded his head. "Come on, Stephen, I think we were mistaken when we thought these two were ladies." And with that, the two of them left the table.

"Probably think we're lesbians now," Melissa said.

"You know, you probably went too far there," Sadie told her.

"I know, I know," Melissa said. "It's just ... well, that idiot just really got to me. I mean, who the fuck did he think he was?"

Sadie chomped on a few more chips and took a sip from the Diet-Coke, her eyes scanning the bar for any of Paul or Stephen's friends. She was feeling rather paranoid, concerned that a rumour would spread about the two girls. Not that many men would believe it, particularly of Melissa, who couldn't look any less the stereotypical lesbian.

As she looked at the people sitting at the bar, her eyes fell upon one of the most handsome men she'd ever seen in her life. He was smartly dressed, mobile phone resting on the bar alongside a drink – a whiskey, by the look of it – with a sharply handsome face, and black hair that flopped across his forehead. His eyes were the most startling feature, dark as pools of oil. At that moment, they weren't looking in her direction, which was good, because it gave Sadie even longer to allow her own to linger over him.

Her attention to this stranger didn't go unnoticed by Melissa, who gave her a sharp nudge.

"Found your soul mate at last?" she asked.

"Huh?"

"That bloke at the bar," Melissa said. "Only I couldn't help but notice you've been undressing him in your mind."

"I'm not that kind of girl," Sadie said coyly. "But he is a hunk."

"Well, I won't argue with you there."

Sadie looked back at the stranger, who chose that precise moment to look at her. Immediately, she felt her face flush, and turned away. "God, he saw me looking," she said, nonchalantly picking up a chip and eating it.

"Well, that's normally the way you meet men, Say," Melissa said. "You look at him, he looks at you, your hearts connect across a crowded room, and bingo!"

"Why can't guys like that ever come over?" Sadie said.

"Look on the bright side," Melissa said, "he'd probably be a complete arsehole too."

"More likely he'd fancy you instead."

"You've got a very low self-esteem, Say."

Sadie moved her eyes around the room again, as though looking at nothing in particular. Her eyes switched past the stranger – was he still looking at her? She couldn't tell in that brief instant. She moved them back to where he was standing.

Only he wasn't standing there anymore.

"Shit." She thought she'd just said the word in her head, but it came out loud.

"He's gone!" Melissa said. "God, what the hell did you do to him? Did you have a bogey on your nose, or something?"

"That's my luck," Sadie said, the image of the stranger still burned onto her mind. "I see someone who's an absolute hunk, and he does a goddamned disappearing act." She shook her head. "You know, I'll never get the chance to see him again, will I?"

"Well, there are sixty million people in this country, maybe twenty million men of consenting age," Melissa said, slipping a chip into her mouth. "I'd say that it's probably unlikely you'll ever see him again. I mean, I come in here most lunch times, and I've never seen him before."

"Maybe he's just started working in this area."

"I hate to say this, Say, but you're starting to sound really desperate."

"I am," Sadie said. "You know, I haven't had a guy in months."

"You haven't had a guy, or you haven't *had* a guy?" Melissa asked with a cheeky smile.

"Neither," Sadie said bluntly. "Do you think I'd sound like a whore if I said I was missing sex?"

"Depends on who you said it to," Melissa answered. "Look, Say, you've got to get out there, find yourself a decent man, one who'll look after you."

"One like the guy who just walked out of here?" Sadie asked, her eyes dreamily half-closed.

"Oh, forget him!" Melissa said, tossing a chip at her. "Look, you've got that gig tonight, haven't you?"

"Did you have to remind me?" Sadie said, her forehead creasing up.

"Why?"

"Melissa, you know I don't like to think about gigs, not until they're just about to happen. It's like going to the dentist or going for a smear – you try to put it to the back of your mind until you're just about to get to the embarrassing or painful part. No, forget that, it isn't like going for a smear. I get a buzz on stage – well, after I've sang a couple of songs. I don't get a buzz going for a smear." Sadie chose that moment to take a sip of Coke, which was a big mistake, especially as she'd just fed Melissa a perfect line.

"Not unless the nurse inserts a vibrator instead of a ..."

That was as far as she got before both girls burst out laughing again, Sadie spraying the two bowls of chips with Diet Coke and saliva.

"God, Sadie, you know, I do have saliva of my own, thank you very much!"

Sadie laughed again until she almost peed herself. It was always the same – Melissa had that effect on her. Now, why couldn't she find a guy with Melissa's personality?

And she instantly wondered what kind of personality that stranger standing at the bar had. There was something about him – she just couldn't get him out of her mind.

It was kind of spooky.

10

Detective Superintendent Saddington had been enjoying himself sightseeing in the city when his mobile phone rang unexpectedly. He walked across the plaza to a railing overlooking the *Baia de Guanabra,* taking in its beautiful views as he retrieved the phone from his pocket.

"Saddington," he said gruffly.

"Ah, Superintendent, this is Captain Sobral."

Saddington immediately stood upright, resting one hand on the railing as tourists passed by and admired the magnificent vista. "What is it?"

Sobral didn't answer at first. Then he said, "There's been a slight discrepancy revealed with the post-mortem reports."

"Serious?"

"Well, not so much serious, as peculiar," Sobral responded.

Saddington watched as an American family snapped off a few frames with an expensive digital camera. By their side, a young Japanese couple were using their camcorder to capture moving images of what was probably their honeymoon. "You need me there immediately?"

Sobral, "Well, there's no particular rush – but we do have an eyewitness account of the incident."

Saddington closed his eyes and shook his head. Christ, this wasn't even his bloody case! It had nothing to do with him. Unless, of course, the Mafia had taken Bartek down. "Are we talking about a hit here?"

"I don't think so," Sobral said coolly. "Not unless the Mafia have taken to wearing devil masks."

Saddington frowned and turned away from the tourists. "Devil masks?"

"It would be better if you could interview the witness yourself," Sobral told him.

Resigned to the fact that his vacation was effectively over – well, it was never intended to be a vacation in the first place, he reminded himself – he said, "I'll be right over – as soon as I find a bloody taxi-driver who understands English."

"No need," Sobral assured him. "I can get Francisco to collect you. Where are you?"

Saddington grimaced and looked at his surroundings. Where the hell was he? "Listen, I'm gonna have to get back to you on that," he said, switching off the phone and stepping up to the tourists.

Surely they must know what this place was called.

An hour later, he was sitting in Sobral's office, the fan blowing fresh cigar smoke across the room and evaporating the sweat from his body, cooling him rather more rapidly than he would've liked. The post-mortem report was laid on the desk in front of him, and he skimmed through the text. Mirabela, as he'd suspected, had died of a coronary infarction. Nothing unusual there. He shifted to Bartek's report. Multiple blows to the head, skull fractures, massive haemorrhaging, expired from serious brain trauma and shock.

He looked up. "I don't get it," he said. "I can't see anything abnormal in these reports – other than Bartek was beaten to death. They're just routine—"

Sobral held up a hand as he puffed on his cigar. "Take a look at the time of death on both reports."

Saddington looked at Mirabela's – approximate time of death, seven-forty-five AM. He looked at Bartek's – approximate time of death, midday. He frowned thoughtfully and looked up at Sobral again. "That's a big difference."

"Well, it's probable that your as yet unidentified suspect arrived at the abandoned building early, killed Mirabela, and waited more than four hours for Bartek to arrive," the Brazilian said, "although I can't really see that myself."

"It's probably just a discrepancy," Saddington suggested. "Timing death can be tricky. A couple of hours each way for both of them, and they'd meet in the middle."

"Hmm, but if they died within a few minutes of one another, there wouldn't be that much of a difference in their estimated times of death."

Saddington couldn't argue with that reasoning. "But what does it mean?"

Sobral shrugged. "Who knows? It certainly makes things more confusing." He opened a drawer in his desk and took out a bottle of whiskey and two tumblers. "I only have Jim Beam," he said. "Fancy a drink?"

Saddington shook his head. Habit took over. He was on duty, after all.

"I think," Sobral said, pouring out two generous measures, "you might want one, after you hear what the eyewitness said." He leaned forwards and gave one of the tumblers to Saddington.

"Now I'm intrigued."

"You should be," Sobral said, nodding to Francisco, who left the office. "The witness, he can't speak a word of English, but I will translate."

Saddington frowned. "Is this necessary? I mean, can't you just tell me?"

"I could, but you probably wouldn't believe me."

Francisco came back into the office with a short man in tow. The clothes he was wearing had certainly seen better days. The jeans were covered in oil and dirt, the tee-shirt torn at the seams in a couple of places. His jacket had probably once graced the shoulders of a young American tourist – now, it was torn and grubby. The man's face was coated in a few days' growth, his skin filthy and greasy. He looked at Saddington with wary eyes, and it seemed apparent that he had probably seen better days himself.

"This is Pablo Porecatu," Sobral introduced. "He lives in the ghettos. He doesn't work ..." He gestured for the tramp to be seated. "... but he makes money by fleecing the locals and the tourists. His house is a tin hovel the likes of which you have probably never seen before in your life. This is all the background you need to know about Porecatu. From that, you can clearly see that he is probably not the most credible of witnesses. But he is all we have."

Saddington nodded his head and looked down at the whiskey in his hand. What did this man have to say that was so bizarre, so extraordinary, that he had to have a drink? He turned to Sobral. "I've seen some strange things in my time," he said, "and believe me, I've had to rely on some outlandish sources of information. Whatever this man has to say, I can judge it on its own merit, not on how he looks."

"That's just it," Sobral said grimly. "If you should judge his information on its merit, you will simply disregard it out of hand. But the people in this country, they are superstitious, religious even. Christ himself looks down upon Rio De Janeiro."

"Why do I get the feeling that this is going to sound ridiculous?"

Sobral turned to the tramp and spoke to him in Portuguese, asking him some kind of question by the tone of his voice. Porecatu responded excitedly, directing his answer at Saddington, who had absolutely no idea what he was jabbering on about. The British detective turned to Sobral.

"You know, this is going to get tiresome."

"You might not understand him," the Brazilian said, puffing on his cigar and blowing a smoke ring in the direction of the fan, where the cool, brisk air tore it apart, "that's why I'm here. I'll tell you what he told us. But I wanted you to hear the conviction in his voice. Does he sound like a liar to you? Does he look like a liar?"

"First impression, he looks like he's seen something disturbing," Saddington said, eyeing up the drunk again. He looked back at Sobral. "So, what exactly *did* he see?"

"Porecatu was spending his days in the derelict block opposite that where the two bodies were found," Sobral said. "So he had an ideal view of the office where the murder, or murders, took place. This has all been checked out by Francisco and his men. From the room where he was staying, they could see right inside that office." Saddington nodded his head, and looked back at Porecatu, who babbled something else. Francisco patted him on the shoulder, and said something to him. "He claims he was looking out of the window when something in the building opposite caught his eye. A man, matching Bartek's description, was standing upright in full view of the window."

Saddington looked at the tramp again. Okay, so he may well have been a drunk, but it was unlikely he would make this story up. Exaggerate it, yes, but not invent it entirely. "Go on."

Sobral took a gulp of his whiskey, and Saddington watched his face flush as the heat from the spirit engulfed him. "He claims to have actually witnessed the murder. And here's where it goes strange." Saddington was on the edge of his seat. "He claims ..." Sobral drained his whiskey. "He claims the murderer was the devil himself."

It was something of an anticlimax for Saddington. He'd been expecting something a little bit out of the ordinary, but not so far from the mainstream as to belong in a horror story, and therefore be of no use whatsoever. He shook his head. "The devil?"

Sobral nodded. "It sounds ridiculous, yes, but ... there was the discrepancy concerning the times of death."

Saddington stopped himself from insulting the Brazilian outright. Here he was, captain of the Rio De Janeiro police department, and he was behaving like some superstitious tribesman out in the rain forest. "There will be a logical explanation for this, naturally."

"Like the old bastard is nothing more than a drunken bum," Francisco muttered. Sobral glared at him.

"Francisco does not share my religious convictions."

"I'm sorry, Captain, but religion doesn't come into this," Saddington said. "Now I know I come from a country where religion isn't exactly encouraged, but nevertheless, there really has to be a more logical explanation. I think Francisco may be right. Porecatu has clearly inflated the truth. He's obviously a drunk, he's obviously under the influence right now, and he's dressed up what actually happened. I don't doubt for a minute that he witnessed the murder, but it appears to have profoundly affected his judgment." He looked at Sobral again.

The Brazilian seemed deep in thought. "His description was quite emphatic," he said. "Here's what he said, translated for you. *'The devil rose up and struck the foreigner. His skin was a deep red in colour, like the fires of Hell. He was hitting the foreigner, beating him with a chair.'* Now, we know that Bartek was beaten to death with the chair in that room. And the only fingerprints on that chair belonged to Mirabela. Here, he finishes with this. *'The devil opened out his arms like this—'* and he opened out his arms," Sobral said, performing the action himself, "*'—and he disappeared in a brilliant flame that burnt my eyes.'* He was quite insistent that it happened like that."

Saddington let out a sigh. "This is your investigation, Captain, but you asked me for my advice, and I am more than happy to give it. Under the circumstances, I have just this one piece of advice. Disregard this man's statement, and continue questioning the hotel staff. Somebody had inside information, and that person could only have come from the hotel – or maybe from the courier service who delivered the packages of money."

Sobral was looking at Porecatu. "If you could hear him, understand the words that came out of his mouth, you would believe him."

Saddington didn't argue. Instead, he said, "Mirabela died of a heart attack, which was probably induced by the fear of being attacked by the killer. You could probably squeeze something supernatural in there, granted, but Bartek was savagely beaten to death. Now, I'm no theologian, but I would say that the devil has the power to kill without resorting to physical force. Why would he beat Bartek to death when he could just send out a thunderbolt and disintegrate him?"

Francisco chortled, but Sobral, an insulted look on his face, was undeterred. "I don't think you realize how religious we are in this country, Superintendent."

"I apologize for any offence caused," Saddington said, getting to his feet. "Let us put it down to a clash of cultures, and part as professional colleagues." He extended a hand. Sobral paused, took a drag from his cigar, then stood up himself. He shook Saddington's hand.

"A clash of cultures," he agreed.

"Thank you for your assistance, Captain."

"It was our pleasure," Sobral assured him.

And with that, Saddington left the office.

It was amazing, he thought as he hailed a taxi to take him back to his hotel. He'd come to Brazil with this preconception about how backward the police force and the people were going to be, only to be proven wrong when he'd first met Sobral, who'd come across as immaculately professional and competent. Now, he was leaving the country with that view completely overturned, and the bigoted preconceptions had proven to be absolutely correct after all.

Devils indeed!

Whatever next?
Guardian angels?

11

Sadie stared across the dressing room to where the rest of the band was sitting. Billy had his guitar in his lap, and was casually strumming a few chords, practicing shifting between some of the more difficult ones, and making plenty of mistakes. Mark was anxiously biting his nails, which was something he did prior to every gig – by the end of the night, he had no nails left, and his fingers hurt like hell whenever they got wet. Davey was the least troubled of the lot of them. He was tapping out a beat with his drumsticks on the coffee table in front of him. He put his lack of anxiety down to the fact that he was hidden behind his drum kit, and that he was confident of being able to hold a beat, and that was all that mattered to him.

Sadie, for her own part, was sipping on a bottle of beer. Alcohol, she found, was the best relaxant, and it only took a couple of bottles for her nerves to be replaced by eagerness. It was something that most of the lead singers in all of the local bands did. Musicians needed to be able to think straight, so alcohol wasn't a good idea – singers needed to lose their inhibitions, and alcohol was perfect for that.

She took another gulp of beer and closed her eyes, trying to imagine what the gig was going to be like. The Billabong was packed, but then it always was on a Friday night – band night. Darcy's Box had performed here on maybe a dozen previous occasions, trying to add at least two new songs to the set on each visit, and chopping the older ones. They'd built up a fairly solid fan base, who had each bought a copy of their first demo, the cost of producing which was paid for by Sadie – or rather, by her father. All the same, if they'd organized their own gig, and only the faithful turned up, they'd probably sell no more than a hundred tickets. They needed thousands to ensure interest from the record companies. In fact, an insider had already advised the boys – before Sadie had joined the band – that they should tour the country, get themselves known by the public. Oh, those who happened to be in the Billabong, or in any one of the half a dozen places where they'd played, were clearly interested in what they heard, what they saw, but they only bagged a couple of demos sales after each gig, and that just wasn't enough.

Sadie considered her future. Now, this seemed like the only chance she had to get back her lifestyle, to live in a nice house, to continue driving a luxury car, and in all reality, it was nothing more than a pipe dream. Some people wanted to be actors, and never made it because the competition was intense; others wanted to be writers, but their lack of insider knowledge and contacts seemed to prevent that from ever happening; and then there were those like Sadie, like the boys in the band, like the people in the dozens of other bands in the locality, who all wanted to be pop stars.

Oh, some of them might've baulked at the word 'pop', may well have considered it beneath them, because they had delusions of superior creativity, but that was what it all came down to. You could be a big fish in the rock chart, in the Indie chart, in the dance chart, but you would probably still be a small fish in the one that really mattered – the pop chart. It was what all *pop-star-wannabes* aspired to, and Sadie was no exception, but now there really was an urgency there to succeed, to prove that she really hadn't needed her father's financial backing or network of contacts, which incidentally, she had never used.

Sadie, like the rest of the band, had a dream, and had the determination, but what it really boiled down to was not how good you were, but who you knew. And at the moment, they knew nobody.

Then Billy said, "I didn't want to mention this to you guys, but ..." All eyes turned to him, anxiety on their faces, Sadie's included. "Well, we all know that Sadie put this gig together, put out the word to some local faces, but we don't know how many will definitely arrive."

"Somebody's gotta turn up," Sadie said, somewhat insulted that her organizational skills were being questioned and doubted. "Jesus, I sent out dozens of demo discs, and those publicity packs. I thought it was very professional." She looked around the dressing room to see the other two nodding, even Mark, which was surprising.

"I'm not saying you did a crap job, Say," Billy assured her. "But we know what these arseholes are like. Cocaine parties hold more appeal than unsigned bands. But that wasn't where I was heading with this conversation. I was stopped on the way in by this geezer."

"Who?" Mark asked, taking his nails from his mouth for a moment, which was a merciful release because the sound of splintering nails echoing in an open mouth was starting to get on Sadie's nerves.

"You ever heard of Martin Walsh?"

Sadie shook her head. So did Davey.

Mark frowned. "Walsh. He's a local producer, ain't he?"

Billy nodded. "That's him. He wished us luck, said he liked our stuff. I mean, he's not exactly the most famous producer in the world, but he's got a few contacts, and if he backs us, well, it's a foot in the door, ain't it?"

Sadie had to agree. "That's pretty good news. At least we know somebody turned up. Can't remember sending a disc out to him."

"You concentrated on the record labels," Billy reminded her. "Walsh isn't affiliated to any label. He produces independently. I think he's had a couple of recent hits. Top tens, I think they were, but I couldn't swear on it. There was that band from around here that had that hit a few months back."

"And then disappeared without a trace," Mark said. "I remember them. Methadone, weren't they?"

"The name vaguely rings a bell," Sadie said.

"Well, he worked on their album," Billy said. "He heard about us by word of mouth. By the way he was talking, he's seen us a couple of times before. He said that he'd put in a word for us if there was anyone here to talk to."

The band fell silent again, now all a little bit more nervous than they were before, thanks to the information Billy had given them. They'd now be working under more pressure, because they now knew that a record producer was in the audience, a producer who had expressed an interest in them, who would probably agree to work with them in the future if they put on a good show.

Sadie finished off her bottle of beer and looked at her watch. Another fifteen minutes to go. She stood up and walked over to the dressing table, upon which had been placed a six-pack of bottles. Two of the bottles were gone – Sadie and Davey had seen to that. Sadie pulled another bottle from the pack, cracked off the lid, and turned to Davey.

"You want another?"

Davey stopped beating out a rhythm, and swirled his drumsticks. "Well, I don't mind if I do, Miss Bartholomew."

Sadie opened another bottle and handed it to him on the way back to her seat. She sat down and sighed loudly. Mark was reading through the set's playlist. They'd decided on the different opener, and he had admitted – at Thursday night's rehearsal – that it was probably a good decision. That reminded Sadie that she hadn't performed the sound check for her vocals, that it had all been handled by Billy, who'd assured her that he'd attempt to reproduce her vocal volume.

But you could never get that right, the doubt in Sadie's mind told her. Her vocals were going to sound like shit. She just knew it. Here was their chance. At least one producer in the audience, possibly some reps from the independent record labels, and she hadn't even been able to sort out her vocals, thanks to that cruddy job at McDonald's, which thankfully none of the band had mentioned.

There was a knock at the door, and the club's owner stepped into the dressing room. He was in his forties, an immigrant from Australia, who'd come over before the wave of Aussie soap stars had familiarized the British public with their nasally accents. He wore a black jacket, with matching trousers, and a black silk shirt that was undone to a point midway down his chest, revealing possibly a little bit too much of the copious greying hair. The hair on his head was dark, probably dyed, Sadie had always thought, and his olive complexion wasn't so much faked as not actually caused by the weak British sun. It was clearly a sunbed tan, utilizing those artificial carcinogenic UV rays. Surgery had rectified a prominent nose some years before and, more recently, had taken away the crow's feet from around his eyes and the wrinkles from around his mouth.

All the same, for all his plastic appearance, Jeff Phillips was a friendly enough guy to work for. He enjoyed listening to the local talent, gave them the opportunity to perform in his club – at first for nothing, but later paying them more than the going rate should they prove to be a popular draw – and never pushed his luck with any of the young female singers.

As he stepped into the middle of the room, he clapped his jewel-encrusted hands together. "Right, you little beauties, we've got a packed house out there, and most of them are here to see you. And I just want you guys to know, it's been a pleasure having you play here."

"Thanks, Jeff," Billy said.

"I just want you guys to remember me, you know, if you make it big."

"Hey, we'll never forget you, Jeff," Davey said. "You gave us our first gig, didn't you?"

Jeff grinned and sat down on the dressing table next to the beers. He cracked open a bottle for himself and said, "You know, if I'd have been a shrewder businessman, I would've signed up as your manager."

"Well, you live and learn, don't you?" Billy said with a smile.

"I'd trust you more than those goddamned sharks that are out there," Sadie said, adding, "I don't mean out there, as in, out in the club, but out there, you know, in the general meaning of the word ... uh, phrase ... listen, I'm gonna shut up, okay?" She swigged from her bottle.

"Sadie always gets like that before a gig," Billy said quietly. The band laughed, Sadie included.

"It's the drink," she said. "I need to lose my inhibitions before I can perform."

"I'd watch what I was saying, if I were you," Jeff said, "or people might misconstrue." There were more laughs, most of them nervous. Then Jeff's face turned all serious. "Though speaking of sharks, I did hear that Martin Walsh was here."

"You know him?" Billy said with a frown. Clearly the use of the word 'shark' in the same sentence had thrown him.

Jeff smiled tightly and took a sip of the beer. "Far be it from me to tell tales, but ... listen guys, I'd watch him if I were you. That's the solitary piece of advice that I have that's worth giving to you."

"Watch him?" Mark enquired. "Why?"

"I don't wanna get into some kind of slandering situation."

"Come on, Jeff, you can't give us half the information here," Sadie said. Now she was curious. If Martin Walsh was probably their best hope of securing a recording contract, they had to know what the problem was with him. They had to know what kind of business deals he pulled.

Jeff said quietly, "I wouldn't trust him as far as I could throw him. You heard of that band, Methadone?"

"We were just talking about them," Billy said.

"You know they had a female keyboard player?" Sadie shook her head, but Mark and Billy nodded. Davey sat in the corner, listening intently. "Well, Martin took a fancy to her. There are a few dodgy tales about Martin's sexual peccadilloes, but I don't know the facts, and I really don't want to indulge in idle gossip. Anyway, the keyboard player turned him down. That's why Methadone failed."

"You're joking?" Billy said in astonishment. "Fucking hell!"

"Well, Sadie, you know what you've got to do for the band," Mark said with a smirk.

"Fuck you, Spicer," Sadie snapped, flipping him the finger.

"It's no laughing matter," Jeff said soberly. "You've got to watch out with this guy. He's into all kinds – drugs, sex, any kind of vice. The guy's a bloody party animal. And I hear he's got a party on for tomorrow night."

"You going?" Mark asked.

"Hey, I've got to network, and Martin's hardly likely to try and fuck me, now is he?" Jeff said, holding out his arms. "But remember what I said, guys. Watch him. I mean, a few bands have worked well with him – mainly all male bands – because he keeps it all professional. But if he starts to take a liking to you," he said, looking at Sadie, "you guys could be in trouble. You could be in way over your depth, because he's quite powerful and influential with the indie labels. He could put it about that you're awkward to work with, that you lack professionalism, even that you're just plain crap."

Sadie began to feel nervous. Now there was even more pressure on her. There was no saying that Martin Walsh was actually going to find her attractive, but if he was, she had to handle it delicately, or ruin any chance they had of ever making it. But there was no way she would prostitute herself just to assure the band of getting a record deal. No way!

She had a feeling that Billy and Davey would certainly side with her. Mark, on the other hand, was a little less scrupulous, and would probably never forgive her for ruining their chances.

Perhaps, she thought with a smile as she took another swig from the bottle, she should make herself a little more ugly, a little less attractive. That way, the music would sell the band to Martin Walsh. But then, he was probably a marketer, like the rest of them, and faces who didn't fit with a band, no matter how talented, were quickly thrown aside, particularly if they were the lead singer.

Sex appeal sold records.

It was a sad fact of life, but it was true.

Jeff stood up and looked at his watch. "Well, I think it's time you guys were hitting the stage." Sadie drained the bottle of lager and put it on the floor next to her chair. Davey was the first of the band to stand, with Billy second. Mark dragged himself to his feet reluctantly, and continued biting his nails. Sadie, dressed in her stage gear, which consisted of a long skirt, a baggy tee-shirt and trainers – much the same as the clothes she wore off-stage – got to her feet and stretched noisily.

Twenty seconds later, they were standing on the stage, the lights dim as the band readied their instruments, and Sadie could see the audience. There had to be more than two hundred people in the club, all of them ready to listen to the band. Grabbing the microphone, because she didn't really have anything else to do until the band kicked off with the intro, she looked around at the faces that were staring up at the stage.

Some of them, to the left and right, were sitting at tables, while those in the centre of the large hall were standing, ready to dance if so persuaded by the music. Sadie's eyes skipped over them, and moved to the tables to the left, which were about thirty feet away.

And her eyes fell upon a familiar face.

The stranger from the pub that lunch time.

The handsome man she thought she'd never see again was sitting all alone at a table, a glass of whiskey in front of him, staring impassively at the stage, at her.

She turned to look at Billy.

Surely this guy had to be one of the scouts from a record label. It couldn't have been a coincidence. And he seemed to be maintain a professional air, not appearing too interested in what the band were about to do.

Billy strummed his guitar softly, and the sound echoed through the club. Mark thumbed out a basic riff on his bass, just readying his fingers, as Davey tapped out a jazz beat on his cymbals. Then the stage lights came on, and the audience disappeared into blackness beyond. Their shouts of encouragement could be heard as the band looked to Sadie to introduce them.

"How you doing?" she asked, her voice bouncing around the walls of the club. She didn't know what the audience said back to her, didn't really care. She was in performance mode now, and soon she'd be dancing and singing.

She shuddered one last time as the enormity of it all hit her.

Then she said, "You wanna have a good time?" There was a cheer from more than a hundred voices. "Well, get up and dance, 'cause we're Darcy's Box and we're here to give you a good time!" And as she finished speaking, Billy began to thrash out the riff for the first song.

And the gig began.

12

Kobold picked up the glass of whiskey and took a sip. His human form warmed to the taste, his throat burning, his belly on fire. But it was nothing like the burning from the infernos of Hell, and he found himself liking the sensation. There was something pleasingly sinful in it, something that reminded him of breaking the rules of mankind when he was human. He grinned and turned his attentions back to the stage, where the vision of beauty was singing.

He didn't know why he was here, just as he didn't know what had drawn him to the public house earlier that day, but there was something about this woman that he found attractive, a sensation that perturbed him, because as a demon, love and any other emotion were meaningless, and humans could never be more than annoyances that had to be punished.

And that was all she was. A human, probably a sinner – though he wasn't aware of any sins she'd committed that would condemn her to Hell. Worse than that, she was the daughter of one of his charges, Michael Bartholomew, who at that precise moment in time was enduring the vilest torture possible at the hands of Kobold's small group of imps.

Kobold considered Bartholomew's torture for a moment, taking another sip from the whiskey. The man's torture was more mental than physical, though with every torturous act in Hell, there was always an element of pain. Bartholomew had to witness his wife's head being crushed by a heavy rock – not his real wife, for she was with the multitude of righteous souls in Heaven, a nameless creature who would live out all eternity in everlasting bliss. Oh, she'd sinned in her time, but God was merciful. In simple terms, you had to be truly evil, a habitual criminal, to be condemned to Hell. And the vast majority of people weren't. Some served out time in purgatory, only to be finally accepted in Heaven by the angels, and on the whole, there were far more souls in Heaven than in Hell.

So it wasn't Cathy Bartholomew who was being killed before Michael Bartholomew. It was a vision, a nightmarish image conjured up by the imps, but so realistic that Bartholomew didn't guess that it wasn't really her. She could hold a conversation with him, reminisce about their past, remind him of the times they had together, of the good things he had thrown away and destroyed.

Every time the rock was raised, he let out a tormented wail. And as soon as she was dead, as soon as her body was torn to pieces by the imps, Bartholomew was then beaten about the head with the same rock that killed his wife. And he couldn't move, because he was chained to the wall.

He was powerless.

And that was what Hell was all about. Taking away the power from those who had it, who abused it, who used the power they had to destroy the lives of others. Taking it away from them, and making them pay.

Kobold looked at the stage once more.

That sweet creature could not be blamed for her father's sins. She was a creature of beauty, and she had the voice—

"Of an angel?"

Kobold swung his head around in the direction of the voice, his eyes finding its owner.

The woman was young, probably the same age as the human body he had created for himself. Her long hair was blond, her eyes blue, her features immediately pleasing to the eye. She was smartly dressed, and she looked at Kobold with eyes that seemed to understand, that seemed to fully comprehend what he was.

That thought scared him.

It was, he noted, the first time anyone other than Satan had had that effect on him for hundreds of years.

Kobold frowned.

"Who are you?" he asked, the tone of his voice gruff, distinctly inhuman.

The woman smiled. "My name is Reizend," she said.

"Well, I'm not interested in company," Kobold told her, turning back to the girl on stage.

"You have to stop thinking of her as merely a girl," Reizend told him.

Once more, Kobold shot her a mystified look. "What are you talking about?"

"She has a name, you know," Reizend said. "When you're dressed like that, you have to think in a certain way."

Kobold took another swig from the whiskey. Something about this woman was disturbing him, and he had never before been disturbed by any human – not since becoming a demon. "You're not making any sense," he said harshly.

"That's because you're not broadening your mind," the woman said with a smile. She ran a hand through her hair in a way that Kobold found intriguing. "You're thinking one-dimensionally. I mean, I can understand why – don't get me wrong, it's not a criticism. Believe me, I know what you're going through. I went through it myself."

Kobold paused for a second. "Elucidate," he commanded.

Reizend let out a quiet laugh. "That's precisely what I mean, Kobold," she said.

"How do you know my name?" Kobold demanded to know.

"When you're wearing the human form, Kobold, you must act like a human," Reizend advised him. "If you don't, people are going to get suspicious. And you cannot afford to have any kind of suspicion levelled at you."

Kobold finished the whiskey. "You seem to know something that you shouldn't."

Reizend smiled again and closed her eyes. Kobold watched her perform the action, saw her open them again. When she did, the whole world went quiet. Frowning, he looked around the bar, at the band on the stage – they were frozen in place. Time no longer existed.

Only one kind of creature could do that.

Kobold's jaw dropped. "You're an angel?"

Reizend grinned. "Finally!"

Kobold jumped slightly as the world began again, and the band continued thrashing out the song they'd been playing before Reizend had halted time. "What are you doing here?"

"I could ask you the same thing," Reizend said. "Surely one of Satan's right-hand men shouldn't be cavorting about the Earth for no good reason." She took a sip from the glass of Coke she was holding. "You aren't here for a purpose, are you?"

Kobold looked at the girl on stage again. No, he wasn't here for any legitimate purpose, nothing that would be approved by Satan. He was breaking the rules, and he could find himself being punished. And Satan's punishments were legendary.

But he couldn't lie, especially not to an angel.

Instead, he chose not to answer her question. "What about you?"

"My purpose here?" Reizend smirked. "Oh, Kobold, I couldn't possibly tell you, could I?"

"Then why did you speak with me? Why did you reveal yourself? Surely you had no need. After all, you appear to know everything about me, do you not?"

"I possess powers that you do not," she said. "Just as you possess powers that I do not."

"Then why are you here?"

"You are worried, aren't you?"

Kobold looked up as a waitress came over to the table. He ordered another whiskey, this time a double, as he'd seen many humans ask for.

"You have to get rid of that attitude, Kobold," Reizend told him. "Please, just listen to me. If you want to be received as a human, if you want to sit here in bars, admiring her from afar, then you have to know how to act." Kobold looked again at the girl, and wondered why she had such a hold over him. "Her name is Sadie."

"I know," Kobold said.

"Then think of her as Sadie," Reizend said. "Think of her as your equal."

"But she is not," Kobold said.

"No, she isn't. You are a demon, and she is merely a human. But if you want her to accept you as a human, you have to think of her as an equal."

"Why would I want that?"

Reizend paused as the waitress returned with the drink. When they were alone again, she continued. "I know exactly what you're thinking, Kobold."

"You're here to protect her?" Kobold asked indignantly. "You must know that I am not one of the Corrupted. I would never harm her. It's against the laws of Hell to knowingly harm someone who has not sinned."

Reizend took another sip of Coke, but she couldn't conceal the knowing smile. "I'm not here to protect her, Kobold. I came here looking for you."

"Why?"

"You know all about Satan, don't you?"

"Satan is our Lord," Kobold said.

"*Your* Lord, Kobold, not mine."

"I do not question Satan's authority."

"Because he is the devil?"

"Precisely."

"In human terminology, Kobold, the devil is purely an administrative post," Reizend said. "God, *our* Lord, rules the kingdoms of Heaven, Earth and Hell. The holder of the position of the devil merely acts on the Lord's behalf."

"Your point being?"

"My point being, Kobold, that Satan is one of the Lord's servants, just as you and I are."

"That much I have already figured out for myself."

"Satan can also be corrupted."

"Satan is incorruptible," Kobold growled.

"Is he? What did he ask of you earlier today?"

"There are no days in Hell," Kobold said, taking a mouthful of whiskey. It tasted excellent, and made the body in which he was lounging feel loose, light-headed – the effects of alcohol, which he could easily overcome if he chose to. But the sensation was relaxing him – he needed to relax.

"He asked for your support, didn't he? Because he fears that a battle for his supremacy may be about to take place."

"You have all the answers."

"I do, yes," Reizend said, getting to her feet. "And I can't give them to you. I can only point you in the right direction, and hope that you work them out for yourself. Before it's too late."

"You cannot leave," Kobold said.

"We are equals, Kobold," Reizend reminded him. "Your powers cannot hold me."

Kobold looked at the girl – Sadie, he corrected himself – on the stage, and then closed his eyes. "I need your help," he said meekly. When he opened his eyes, Reizend was sitting again. "I have these feelings – I have never before felt them for anyone."

"You did once," Reizend assured him. "When you were human."

"That was a long time ago."

"You're feeling attraction, perhaps even love ... certainly, you are feeling lust."

"I am feeling all of those things," confessed Kobold. "And yet, that is surely impossible for a demon?"

Reizend smiled. "You will have it all worked out soon, Kobold. For now, enjoy yourself. And if you truly want to enjoy yourself with Sadie, you will need to recall what it is like to be a human once more. More to the point, you will have to recall that, and then update the memory. Things are different now, Kobold. People speak differently."

"I had noticed," Kobold said. It was a totally different world, and although he'd witnessed all of the changes, and knew what people meant in the way they spoke, he had had little opportunity to practice that new knowledge by interacting with humans.

"Just mellow out, Kobold," Reizend said. "For a start, you'll have to think of a name – a human name."

"For example?"

"You're an intelligent demon, Kobold, such a task will come easily to you," Reizend promised him. "When you're asked, you will simply say the first name that comes into your head. And you will remember that name, because it will be your alter-ego."

"You make it sound simple."

"It is. I've been doing this for a while, but I still remember my first excursion as a human. It was frightening, but I achieved everything I set out to achieve."

Kobold looked at Sadie. "But surely if I ... if I should approach her, then I will be corrupting her. She will become a sinner?"

"Some crimes are committed without malice, without knowledge that they are, indeed, crimes. Those sins, harmless to others, are overlooked by those sitting in judgement. Sadie has no knowledge of your true nature, and I know that she already is intrigued by you."

"I do not want to use her and then cast her aside."

"Something tells me, Kobold, that you will never do that," Reizend said, standing once more. "You should try to figure out the bigger picture, because there's more to you, to Satan, to Sadie and your future relationship, than you first think. You have a special destiny to fulfil. I have to go now. I have been on Earth for days. My powers are beginning to weaken. I have to return to Heaven."

"Will I see you again?" Kobold asked anxiously.

Reizend just smiled, and then disappeared in the crowd standing to the side of their table.

Kobold looked back at the stage, saw Sadie look at him. Their eyes met, she smiled as she sang, and closed her eyes as though embarrassed. Kobold couldn't help but smile – it just seemed to come naturally.

When Sadie opened her eyes and looked back at him, he was still smiling.

This couldn't work, he told himself. Reizend was wrong. This simply could not work. He was breaking all of the rules of Heaven and Hell, he was betraying Satan. Satan would know the moment he returned to Hell, and would condemn him as one of the Corrupted.

Satan would destroy him.

But even as he thought it, something was telling Kobold that Satan would not find it easy to destroy him. He couldn't put his finger on it, but he felt stronger than he had done in a long time. Or maybe it was that Satan was feeling weaker.

He didn't know.

All he did know was that Sadie was the most beautiful creature he'd ever seen.

And he wanted her.

13

Sadie couldn't believe how well the gig had gone. It was as though everyone in the club had been watching them, had actually listened to the entire set, and had enjoyed it. It was, she told herself as she left the stage to the sound of the audience cheering for more, the best gig they'd ever done. And she could tell by the looks on the faces of the rest of the band that they were of the same opinion. For some reason, they'd clicked out there like they had never done before. Oh, Sadie thought the band was good, but this was something else.

It was like magic.

As they walked to the dressing room, a few of the bar staff congratulated him. But it was Jeff who was waiting at the dressing room door for them, a bottle of champagne and five glasses on a tray in his hand.

"That was an awesome set, guys!" he proclaimed as they reached the door. "Man, you kids were something else out there tonight. Jesus!"

Nobody really said much, Sadie noted, probably because they were all too stunned. They stepped into the dressing room and took their seats, as Jeff popped the cork on the bottle, and poured out five glasses of champagne, handing them around to everyone and keeping one for himself.

"You guys really impressed out there, you know."

Finally, Mark spoke. "Yeah? But was there anybody out there worth impressing?"

"Hey, listen, you're building up a fan base. You keep doing gigs like that, people are going to travel to see you, because news does reach the outer parts, you know."

"We needed somebody to be in the audience, Jeff," Billy said grimly. "And we needed that person to be impressed. I mean, don't get me wrong, man, it's great that you're in here telling us how good we were. Jesus, nobody's ever said that to us with that much conviction, but at the end of the day, you can only offer us headlining nights here – and hey, there's nothing wrong with that. Shit, we'd really appreciate it. But we want a record deal, and much as you'd probably like to–"

"I can't give you one," Jeff concluded. "Well, you're right there, Billy."

"We appreciate the praise," Sadie said quickly, raising her glass, "and the champagne."

"Well, I just thought, you know, this might be the start of something big."

"Let's hope so."

There was a knock at the door, and Jeff went to answer it. He turned and looked at the band. "Martin Walsh is here to speak to you," he said, putting down his glass of champagne. "I'll leave you guys to it."

"Thanks, Jeff," Billy said, and the rest of the band followed suit.

And then all eyes turned to Martin Walsh as he entered the room and closed the door behind him. He was a smartly dressed man, his clothes slick and cool, no doubt expensive. He wore a white shirt with the top two buttons undone. His jacket was dark and open, and matched his trousers in colour and style. His shoes were handmade from leather – Sadie knew, because they were just like her father's used to be.

He was a handsome man, but the kind who clearly knew it, and who utilized it to his own advantage. His hair was blond, short and spiky, his eyes dark and brooding. He wore a gold chain around his neck, but it was understated rather than ostentatious.

He stepped up to the dressing table and lounged against it.

"People," he said, his voice laconic and laid back. "I heard something good out there tonight. Something that got to me. And I don't hear that very often." Nobody in the band spoke – it was odd taking this much praise from people, and praise that was sincere. In Jeff's case, he was sincere because he liked the band, and wanted to see them succeed. In Martin Walsh's case, it was sincere, but undoubtedly because he knew that he could make some money out of them.

In spite of those negative feelings towards him, Sadie found herself finding him strangely appealing, although not as appealing as the stranger she had seen in the audience. She pushed thoughts of that man aside – she'd probably never see him again, although she did recall saying that earlier in the day to Melissa. And he had smiled at her tonight.

"Now, I can't promise to make you stars," Martin was saying, "but I can offer you advice, get you in with the in-crowd. And in this business, that's what's important. That you should meet the right people, or if you don't meet them, you should at least have a connection that can meet them on your behalf, put in a good word. Do you hear me?"

"Well, what exactly is your proposal?" Mark enquired, his expression barely masking his distrust.

"I think you should lay down some more demo tracks," Martin said, removing their old demo CD from his pocket. "This has some good tracks, but it's definitely under-produced. Did you get the sound engineer to help you? I mean, far be it from me to knock a fellow professional, but you clearly didn't get a producer in, did you?"

"We did a lot of it ourselves," Billy explained, "with the help of the engineer."

"I can make your studio versions sound as hot as your live versions," Martin assured the band. "Because that's what you need. Your sound is dynamic, it all fits in, it has energy, it makes you want to listen. It sounds alive. You," he said, pointing at Sadie, "you get really intense when you're singing. You can see it on your face, such an exquisite expression, and you can hear it in your voice. Here, on this demo, you obviously can't see your face – but it's clear you're not giving it one hundred percent, probably because there isn't an audience in front of you. Now, you're a fantastic live band, absolutely fucking kicking, but you need to learn some lessons in the studio. And I want to teach you everything I know. Will you guys let me?"

The band all looked at each other.

They needed a break, and Martin Walsh was prepared to give it to them.

"We will," Billy answered for them – nobody protested.

"Listen, guys, I'm holding a party at my gaff tomorrow night," Martin said, sitting down in the seat next to Sadie. "And I'd like you to be there. There won't be any record bigwigs there, but there will be low level representatives. And they have the ears of the bigwigs. That's what it's all about. Networking. Get yourselves known, put yourselves about a bit, get to know a few faces. You'll probably need help from them in a few months."

"You really think we can make it?" Sadie asked him. Martin flashed her a smile that she found seductive, in spite of the fact that she knew she couldn't really trust him at all. But that didn't matter sometimes, did it?

Martin said, "I think with the right backing, with lucky breaks, you stand a chance. But it's not guaranteed. Nothing in this business is. God, the amount of bands I've seen that have really had the potential to succeed, but have only failed ... it's frightening, really. How somebody can destroy your hopes purely because they got out of bed the wrong side, or with the wrong person, or without the right person. You have to consider so many variables over which you have absolutely no control when you send in your demo tape, when you go for a meeting with some record boss. Did he get it last night? If he did, was it good? Is he high on cocaine? Has he got a cold? Does he need to go for a piss really quickly? Stupid little things that can affect a person's judgement, things that you can't do fuck all about. But with the right connections, you at least have a fighting chance, and with a demo that stands out as professional rather than merely entertaining to those who've heard you live, the chances of success are increased."

Sadie smiled. This man really did have a confident manner when it came to speaking. He sounded sincere, he sounded honest, he sounded so trustworthy.

She wondered whether he was selfish in bed, and immediately admonished herself.

She was certain that she'd blushed.

"And another thing," Martin said. "When a band walks into the room for a meeting that will probably secure them a contract, before even listening to the music, the guy who eventually signs them looks at them carefully. The lead singer – male or female – must be attractive, because they get the most exposure. If not attractive, well, then quirky rather than ugly or plain. They have to be confident and outgoing. The guitarists must also be attractive, though definitely not as much, because they'll detract from the attention the lead singer gets. And the drummer ..." He looked at Davey.

"Sorry, mate, but there isn't much stipulation on what the drummer looks like – so long as he doesn't look like some greasy child molester – because he's hidden behind the kit and people rarely notice him." Davey shrugged indifferently.

"I didn't join this band to get laid," he said nonchalantly.

"The thing I'm trying to say is that the band must look like a band, they have to look like they know each other really well, that they enjoy working with one another, because that way, they'll have staying power," Martin said. "Oh, there are exceptions – the Sex Pistols, for a start, they were manufactured, and they hated each other, but that's a different kettle of fish altogether. But you see, you guys, you all look like a band. Sure, I can sense some tension here between one or two of you, but you're not gonna be a fucking Christian band – you're gonna be an indie band, or a pop band, whatever you want to label yourself. At the end of the day, it doesn't matter about labels, because the press will call you what they want. But the tension doesn't matter, so long as at the end of the day, you get down, do the business, and don't let any disagreements get in the way of your professionalism. Because that's what this is, guys, a profession. You wouldn't expect a surgeon to arse about in the operating theatre, and you can't really arse about all the time when you're a professional musician. The Gallagher brothers can get away with it, because they're well-known, and because they're maybe ninety-five percent professional. You won't get away with it."

There was another knock at the door, and a woman entered. She was wearing the shortest skirt and the lowest cut top Sadie had ever seen, but she clearly had the assets for both. Sadie noticed that all three band members turned to look at her, and some of them lingered for longer than was gentlemanly. Martin got to his feet.

"Holly, come in," he said. The woman stepped up to him, gave him a peck on the cheek. Although pretty, there was something about the expression on her face that told Sadie something wasn't quite right. Her eyes were glazed over, her mouth droopy. She wasn't on anything – and that was the problem. She was coming down, and she wanted to go back up again.

"How long are you gonna be?" Holly asked.

"Not long," Martin said, a little impatiently. "These are Darcy's Box

– the band I was telling you about."

Holly smiled as best she could. "Hello," she said, somewhat wearily. "Martin, I need to go home."

Martin smiled, slightly embarrassed. "I'll be out soon, darling. You wait in the car," he told her, handing over a set of keys. "See you soon."

"You'll sort it out for me?"

"Of course," Martin promised as Holly left the room. "Sorry about that. She's a bit strung-out. Tired. She's an actress, you know."

"What's she been in?" Mark asked sceptically.

"*The Bill, Casualty* – that kinda shit. She hasn't hit the big time. She plays the victims."

Sadie wondered if there was something real in that opinion of Martin's. Holly, it appeared, was a victim – drugs and, doubtless, sex were her downfall. All at the hands of Martin Walsh.

Martin Walsh, she concluded was *evil.*

Evil? Wasn't that too strong a word? Adolf Hitler, he was evil – but Martin Walsh?

Why, she wondered, had that word entered her head? Her thoughts returned to the stranger who had watched the entire gig – in between talking to some pretty blonde. She found herself feeling slightly jealous, as though the man – she didn't even know his name, for Christ's sake! – was cheating on her. She had her sights set on him, and there he was, talking to another girl. And that girl, well, she'd been attractive, hadn't she? Virginal, angelic, a classical beauty.

Sadie shook her head. She needed to rest!

"So, you'll all come to the party tomorrow night?" Martin was asking. He handed a card to Sadie. "My address and contact number." He gave them to the rest of the band and walked over to the door. "I'll look forward to seeing you all."

And with that, he was gone.

Sadie stayed at the club a short while longer, a little upset that nobody other than Martin Walsh had made themselves known to the band. From that, she concluded that either they hadn't been that impressive to the record executives or else, and more likely, there hadn't been any present.

But it wasn't too late when she decided to return home. Jodie was alone, after all, in a strange place – they still couldn't think of their modest flat as home, and they still couldn't think of it being anything other than modest, in spite of the fact that it was still probably larger than most people's homes.

She took a taxi, leaving her Volvo in the club's locked car park because she'd drank that night, and didn't want to take the risk. Back at the flat, she found the hall light was on, Jodie's door was slightly ajar, and her little sister was asleep in her bed. She went in and gave her a kiss on the cheek. Her sister looked so young when she was sleeping, which was the complete opposite of how she looked when she was awake. When she was awake, she could easily pass for eighteen. Here, in her bed, with her long hair across the pillow, and her Forever Friends nightshirt, she didn't even look as old as her sixteen years.

She went to her own bedroom and closed the curtains, before stripping off, catching her reflection in the mirror. She still had a good body, in spite of the fact that she'd probably piled on a few more pounds than she should have, but no man had seen it in months. God, how she missed sex. It wasn't the same, being alone, with no one to kiss you, to take you to the very brink of satisfaction, before pushing you over the edge.

It just wasn't the same, she thought regretfully, switching off the light and slipping between the cool sheets.

If only she could have the comfort of a man, just for a few minutes, without people looking down on her like she was some kind of slut. It was okay for men to use women and toss them aside, but women who did the same were considered man-eaters, ball-breakers, whores …

Sadie closed her eyes and thought about Martin Walsh, a very handsome man with every confidence in his looks, who probably used them to bed any number of women every single week of the year, which was probably why his girlfriend, Holly, looked so hideous, in spite of her beauty. What would it be like, she wondered, to feel his soft caress, to feel him kissing her thighs, gently parting them, slipping his tongue …

She stopped herself.

The stranger, the guy whose name she didn't know, came to the front of her mind.

And she wondered what it would be like to nuzzle up to his chest, to feel his strong grip as he pushed her onto the bed, as he lifted up her dress, pushed her panties aside and forced himself into her, plundering her.

She slipped into a deep sleep with that thought in mind, and her dream consisted of the stranger making love to her. No, she corrected herself as he rammed his cock deep into her, her hands feeling his buttocks contracting with each push, he wasn't making love to her. He was fucking her. He was fucking her like she'd never been fucked before in her life. Then he pulled out and straddled her chest, the hairs on his muscular thighs brushing her nipples. His cock was inches from her face, standing proud, longer and thicker than any she'd ever seen before.

She reached up to grab him, but then the stranger's face changed.

The whole situation changed.

She was in a desert, staring out from a cave at the rocky plains beyond.

Her father and mother were lying on a blanket. Her father was kissing her mother, whose sarong had fallen open to reveal her shapely legs, something she'd always been proud of, in spite of her age. They were kissing passionately, and her father was pulling open her mother's top. Sadie wanted to look away, particularly when her father got up to his knees and began to unbuckle his belt, but she found she couldn't. She closed her eyes, but even when she did that, she still saw her father's erection, and felt disgusted by it. She could recall hearing her parents making love, even though in their mansion they were a couple of rooms away, but this was different.

She didn't want to see this, but had no choice but to watch.

Then the stranger appeared, walking up to her parents as her father pushed her mother's thighs apart, as he fell between them, as she hooked her legs around his back ...

The stranger had a rock in his hand.

He raised the rock.

And he brought it down upon her father's head with such force than Sadie actually saw his brains exploding from a huge hole in his skull.

Her mother began to scream, but she too had the rock slammed into her forehead.

Sadie awoke with a start, the sweat pouring from her naked body, the sheets stuck to her skin.

It was light.

She stood up, walked over to the window, and in spite of her nakedness, reached through the curtains, probably flashing her breasts to anyone who might've been in the car park to the rear of the block of flats, and opened the vent.

The curtains billowed out as the cool air blew in, and she returned to the bed, lying down on the damp bottom sheet.

The wettest portion, she noted, was right around her buttocks.

Something had turned her on, but surely not that dream. What the hell, she asked herself, was that all about?

She lay on the bed, fully intending to get more sleep, but the noise of traffic from the open window and the memory of the disturbing nightmare both conspired to prevent that. Soon, she was getting cold as the breeze blew across her naked body. She slipped between the sheets once more and rolled over onto her side, desperately trying to think of something else.

She thought of Martin, of the party she and the band would be going to tonight.

And eventually, she began to feel slightly better.

Then somebody began to shake her, and she realized that she'd fallen asleep again. She looked up to see Jodie standing over her. Her sister was already dressed and was making her way over to the window to close it.

"Man, it's cold in here! How long's this been open?"

"I dunno," Sadie said sleepily. "What time is it?"

"Ten-thirty," Jodie replied, going for the door. "And Melissa's here to see you. Wants to know how the gig went last night. And so do I, as a matter of fact." Sadie closed her eyes and rolled over. "Come on, Say, get up."

"Leave me alone," Sadie snapped, but she knew that she was fighting a losing battle. If she should fall asleep again, Melissa would be left waiting even longer, with only Jodie for company, and there was a good chance that she'd feel even more tired when she eventually woke up.

Jodie left the room, closing the door behind her.

"Goddamn it," she muttered, and pulled herself out of bed. A quick shower later, and she was ready to receive her visitor.

As she strolled into the front room, she saw Melissa sitting on the sofa watching Saturday morning kids' shows. Jodie was reading a book. Both of them looked up as she entered.

"Well, it's about time!" Melissa said. Jodie went back to reading her book.

"Hey, I had a rough night, okay, I'm hungover," Sadie told her, sitting down on the sofa next to her. "Jo, where's my breakfast?"

"I dunno," Jodie said, not looking up from the novel. "Where'd you leave it?"

"Oh, ha ha, what a goddamn comedian."

"My, who got out of bed the wrong side?"

Melissa smiled. "Come on, girl, tell me. How'd it go? Sorry I couldn't get along, but work commitments and all that."

Sadie realized she was going to have to lighten up. And the nightmare was now becoming more and more of a distant memory, the more hideous facts dispersing in her mind. She smiled and said, "Well, it was the best gig we've ever done. It was incredible." Jodie lowered her book and looked at her sister with something akin to admiration. "Jesus, we just, you know, gelled, like we've never done before. The audience were just totally wowed out!"

"So it went well?" Jodie asked.

"Better than that!"

"What about the record bosses?" her sister asked.

Sadie shrugged and sighed. "Well, if they were there, they weren't too impressed, because they didn't make themselves known. I mean, I've been trying to tell myself that nobody turned up, that we're just not that big a thing at the moment, but I've got to say, after last night's performance, we're getting there!"

"I wish I could've seen it," Jodie said.

"So do I!"

"But it was all in vain?" Melissa asked.

Sadie shook her head. "Not quite. We met up with Martin Walsh – he's a local record producer, got a few contacts, that kind of thing. He said he liked what he heard, that he wanted to work with us, get us a new demo laid down. He invited us to a party tonight."

"You're going?"

"The whole band is going," Sadie said. "Do you wanna come?"

"I thought you'd never ask!" Melissa said. "It's been yonks since I've been to a good party – and a record producer's party! God, there'll be all kinds of mad shit happening!"

"What about me?" Jodie asked.

Sadie frowned and looked at her. "What about you?"

"When do I get to have some fun? I mean, okay, so I can't see you play at some night-club, and I have to sit here all alone watching crappy movies that I've already seen a million times before. I deserve a night out."

"You're just a kid," Sadie said disparagingly. "You can't come to a party like this."

"Oh, come on, Say," Melissa said. "Jo needs to let her hair down. It's only a party."

"A minute ago, you said that all kinds of mad shit will be happening," Sadie reminded her.

"Yeah, but that's just me talking out of my backside!"

Sadie looked at her sister. Jodie, like her, had been through a lot, and she was probably right – she did deserve a night out. She needed to get her mind off things that could potentially depress her, and there were plenty of things, even in this flat that they had never shared with their parents, that could remind her that they were no longer here with them.

Melissa said, "Say, we'll both be there to look after her."

"I don't know," Sadie said, but she knew she was cracking. She didn't want to see her sister hurt again, even over something as trivial as a party. "Jo, fix me some breakfast, and I'll think about it."

Jodie was out of the room and already in the kitchen even as Sadie finished the request.

Sadie turned to Melissa and gave her a half smile. "Thanks."

"Hey, it was nothing."

"I've got to let her go now, haven't I?"

"Well, you're only young once," Melissa said, "and as I recall, you were a party girl yourself at Jo's age."

"Yeah, I was, wasn't I?" Sadie admitted, turning to the TV. Her silence didn't go unnoticed.

"What's wrong, Say?"

"Huh?"

"I don't know, something's on your mind, isn't it? You're not yourself."

"I saw that guy again last night."

"What guy?"

"That guy we saw in the Ragamuffin," Sadie said. "You know, the absolute hunk."

"Oh, *that* guy? I'd forgotten all about him. Can't even remember what he looked like."

"Well, I can," Sadie said. "Believe me, he was gorgeous. And he was at the gig, in the audience, watching us. Watching me. He smiled at me."

"So why don't you sound that pleased?" Melissa asked her curiously. "Is it because although he's an absolute hunk, he's showing all the signs of being a stalker?"

"No, it's not that," Sadie answered. She didn't want to tell Melissa about the nightmare. That's all it was, after all. A bad dream. No point in making herself sound neurotic. She said, "I'm just tired. It was one hell of a night!"

"And tonight," Melissa said with a wicked grin, "is gonna be just as good!"

Sadie looked to the doorway, where she could hear Jodie singing in the kitchen. Her little sister was as pretty as hell, she had to admit, but she couldn't sing. She really, really couldn't sing.

She listened to her sister singing, and wondered whether it was a good idea, letting her go to this party.

But she'd be there, Melissa would be there, and between them, they could keep their eyes on her, make sure she didn't come to any harm or mischief. Looking the way she did when she was all made up, Jodie certainly needed to have her big sister there to look after her.

And Sadie had a feeling that she'd be looking after Jodie long after she was out of her teens.

14

Sadie had tried as hard as she could to get Jodie to dress down – at least that's what she told herself – but the sixteen-year-old was determined to be one of the girls, and to be one of the girls, she had to dress like a young woman.

She wasn't a carbon copy of Sadie – her features differed slightly, because she took them mainly from their father, whereas Sadie took hers from her mother – but there were similarities. The fact that the two girls wore their hair differently – Jodie long, Sadie short – meant that it was difficult to confuse the two. However, it was easy to confuse their ages. Jodie, when dressed up as she was tonight, could easily look as though she were in her twenties. It was only when she opened her mouth, and her lack of experience of life showed in the words she used and the way she spoke, that people realized Sadie was the elder of the two.

All the same, as she climbed into the rear of the car, Sadie couldn't help but look at her sister and feel proud. Okay, she was a teenager, she had problems, she could be awkward – boy, could she be awkward! – but she was an extrovert, she was pretty, and she rarely embarrassed Sadie on the few occasions that she'd taken her out with her.

But because Jodie looked older than she was, the men she had met thought they were in with a chance. Jodie never let on about her age, but Sadie could never stand by and watch her sister getting mauled by drunken slobs. She didn't want her sister to end up losing her virginity at such a tender age to some worthless bastard. Jodie didn't understand that by dressing the way she did, she was attracting the attentions of men rather than boys her own age. Boys her own age could apply pressure, but they could easily be side-stepped, because much as they wanted it, they didn't expect sex from their girlfriends. Men, on the other hand …

The two girls drove to Melissa's house and picked her up. As ever, Melissa was dressed to kill, her dress short, showing off her long legs, and low-cut, displaying her ample bosom. Was there any other kind of dress in her wardrobe, Sadie wondered with a hint of jealousy. Okay, so Melissa probably had a perfect body, by most men's standards, and she was attractive – even Sadie could see that – but that brought its own problem. The men were just after one thing, and that thing didn't usually last more than one night. No more than a few minutes, in fact! Which was a shame, because in spite of the way Melissa dressed, she was the kind of girl most men could take home to meet their mothers. She was bubbly, but not in an overpowering way, and she was capable of dressing down, of hiding her assets, of presenting herself as a respectable young lady instead of a party girl.

But Melissa loved to party.

"I wonder whether there are gonna be any decent blokes there," Melissa said, as Sadie pulled the Volvo out onto the main road.

"Is that all you ever think about?" Sadie asked, glancing quickly at her friend.

"Well, I'm surprised it's not all you think about!" Melissa said. "Considering how long this dry spell of yours had been!"

Sadie felt herself flush. "For Christ's sake!" she said, looking up at the mirror to see her little sister beaming at her.

"You looking forward to this party, Jo?" Melissa asked.

"I'm looking forward to having a good time," Jodie answered. "I just hope I didn't get dressed up for nothing."

"And here's me hoping you did," Sadie muttered.

"Leave it out, Sadie," Melissa said. "She's a kid – she's entitled to have a good time."

Sadie looked at her sister again, and wished she could turn the car around and take them all back home. *'How does a pizza and a good DVD sound?'* But that wouldn't go down well.

This was a big mistake.

But pretty soon, they were pulling up outside the house where Martin Walsh lived, Sadie squeezing the Volvo into a space on the street. A small driveway that led up to a double garage was already packed with various prestigious vehicles – Porsches, BMWs, Mercedes, a few of the hot hatches from lesser makes. A few hundred thousand pounds worth of metal, demonstrating the type of guest that had been invited to the party.

As she climbed out of the Volvo, Sadie looked up the street and saw Billy's battered Fiesta – the boys had undoubtedly come together. Billy had a girlfriend, but neither of the others did. Davey was probably hoping to get lucky tonight – he was that kind of guy – and Mark would more than likely be looking for someone as intellectual as himself, someone with whom he could have a deep, meaningful discussion about politics. He wouldn't find that kind of girl here, Sadie thought, as they made their way up to the house.

The house was nowhere near as big as the Bartholomew's Harrow pad, but it was impressive nonetheless. Victorian, like most of the buildings in the immediate area, it had been upgraded – clearly it wasn't a listed building – with double glazing and a new roof. The garden, small though it was, was neatly trimmed and tended, doubtless looked after by a gardener, rather than Martin. He didn't look like the kind of guy who was into growing flowers. All the same, the house had a charm that had been totally bastardized by the party that was currently underway. Most of the windows on the ground floor had been thrown open, and the music filtered out, the deep bass riffs and drums vibrating Sadie's innards. A few revellers could be seen dancing, some holding bottles of drink, others just talking – a small number had already spilled out onto the front lawn, a couple blatantly smoking a joint. That activity, Sadie thought, would be better off taking place in the rear garden – if there was one. There were no lights on upstairs, so it was safe to assume that the first floor was out of bounds – either that, or the party hadn't spread yet.

It *was* early, after all.

There wouldn't have been any point in knocking on the front door, because nobody would've been able to have heard, so it was fortunate that the door was open. The three of them stepped inside, and found themselves immediately in a madhouse, a wild cacophony of sound and bustling bodies. Two large men dressed in bomber jackets and looking like neo-Nazis stepped up to them – doormen, bouncers, party security, call them what you will, they were here to maintain order.

"You ladies were invited?" one of them asked.

Sadie smiled. "I'm Sadie Bartholomew," she said.

The security guard just raised an eyebrow – clearly, there was no guest list. The doormen were probably just vetting guests and keeping out undesirables. It helped that this was a more affluent part of town, and the only people who would gate crash would be the ones driving BMWs – those, Sadie thought, were usually the worst kind.

The bounder nodded his head and let them through, oblivious to the fact that she was 'Sadie Bartholomew', a potential pop star.

They made their way along the wide hallway to the first door, which led them into the front room. It was a large room, and had been cleared of practically all of its furniture. It now held only people and a DJ with his sound system. Along the widest wall, videos matching the songs being played were being projected onto a screen. It all looked very impressive. But there was time to take it all in later. Now, they had to explore their surroundings.

As they fought through the crowd of dancers and money-talking yuppies, they found themselves at the doorway to the dining room, which contained a long, broad table upon which had been laid a full buffet.

Melissa smiled. "He doesn't do things by halves, this Martin Walsh."

"Did I hear somebody mention my name?"

Sadie spun around to see the music producer and host of the party standing against a backdrop of flashing lights and flickering dancers. Dressed in similar clothes to those he'd been wearing the last time they'd met, he was certainly an attractive figure to be greeted by, and not for the first time, Sadie wondered whether it would really be so bad to make love to him in return for a recording deal.

Melissa, she saw, shared her opinion.

"Great to see you here, Sadie," Martin said. "I think the rest of the band are kicking about. I saw them arrive, but haven't seen them since." Sadie couldn't think of anything to say, so she just smiled. "Well, aren't you going to introduce me to these two gorgeous babes?"

"Oh, sorry," Sadie said, letting out a laugh. "Uh, this is Melissa, my best friend. She got me my job."

"Your job? You mean you do something besides singing?"

"And this, this is Jodie," she said, adding for good measure, "my *little* sister."

"Jodie, Melissa, pleased to meet you both," Martin said. "Now, listen, you ladies have a good time here, okay? That's what this gig is for. For my friends and associates to enjoy themselves, to let their hair down. There's everything you could ever want from a party here – loud music, plenty of booze, whatever drugs you could ever desire, and bags and bags of sex." Sadie shot a look in her sister's direction – maybe this really, really was a bad idea, she thought. Martin added, "Of course, you're not obliged to take part in anything you don't like!" He leaned closer to Sadie. "Oh, you'd better keep an eye on your sister," he said quietly. "I'll let the doormen know as well. We don't want her to get up to any mischief."

Sadie smiled and nodded her head. "Thanks."

The music changed, merging from one track to another, and the DJ shouted something inaudible over the throbbing bass. Some woman started to sing, "Don't want no short dick man," and Jodie began to laugh. Martin patted Sadie on the shoulder, and then disappeared.

Sadie looked at Melissa, who said, "I dunno about you, but I'm gonna go and mingle!" And with that, she disappeared into the throng of dancers. Sadie turned to her sister.

"Well, just me and you, kiddo."

"Yeah," Jodie said, looking across the room, "and I reckon you're cramping my style." She made a move to leave, but Sadie stopped her.

"Hold it."

"Say, we're supposed to be enjoying ourselves, remember?" Jodie said, as though Sadie were simple.

"Just be careful, okay?"

"I will," Jodie promised. "I'm not about to jump into bed with any of the guys here. I'm not ready for that."

"Probably not," Sadie agreed, "but these guys here are. So watch yourself. I don't wanna stand by your side all night, Jo, so I'm putting a lot of trust in you to be careful. Don't disappear into any of the rooms with any of the boys here. Just stay downstairs, where there are lots of people."

"And if I need the bathroom?"

"Come get me, okay?"

Jodie folded her arms. "Can I go?"

Sadie sighed, and said, "Yeah, go on. Quit bugging me and leave me alone." And Jodie did.

Sadie watched both her friend and her sister get swallowed up by the dancing mob, and then turned to enter the dining room. She didn't feel like partying – not yet. In fact, she hadn't felt like partying in a long time, which probably explained why she didn't have a boyfriend. But she felt even less like partying tonight, because knowing that she had to take care of her sister reminded her of the fact that her parents were no longer here to look after the pair of them.

And that, in turn, made her think of the terrible accident that had claimed both their lives.

Not for the first time, she wondered what it had been like for her parents. She wondered what had been going through their minds when the car had spun out of control, tried to picture her father, powerfully built man that he was, vainly struggling with the steering wheel, fighting both a heart attack and the car as it fishtailed across the road. She tried to block out the mental image of the car slamming to a sudden halt as it hit the tree ...

Her mother had apparently received massive head injuries. So great, in fact, that Sadie had been advised not to view the body. She hadn't identified the corpse – that was merely a formality which had been handled by her uncle. Her father's body had received less substantial injuries. It had been the coronary that had killed him. That, Sadie thought, and probably the shock of having seen his wife die before him. If he'd lived that long, she corrected herself. The heart attack had probably knocked him out, and perhaps he'd never regained consciousness. Whatever, the crash hadn't killed him, because the injuries he'd sustained were light.

Sadie cursed in her mind. Her parents had suffered pain, terrible pain. Did they deserve it? Did even her father deserve that? A voice in her head told her that he did – after all, he was a criminal and he'd left his two daughters practically destitute. She admonished herself for that thought. Not for thinking that her father deserved, if he had to die, to die painfully, because she actually truly believed that. No, she admonished herself because she and Jodie weren't destitute. They were still wealthier than most, even if Sadie was working at McDonald's by day. They had cash in the bank

– a small amount, but certainly more savings than most – and Sadie's Volvo, which they could probably sell for a few thousand. They had a roof over their heads, and their home was fully furnished. They weren't, by any definition of the word, destitute.

But they were parentless. Orphans, although they didn't really need the guardianship of their parents any more. And Sadie missed her mother, and even her father, if she were being honest. But she missed her mother more. Her mother had always given her support, and was by no means weak-willed. She was a strong woman, who stood up both for herself and her children, and who supported her husband. A good wife, a good mother and a fantastic friend.

Sadie sat down in the dining room, watching the guests picking at the buffet with their paper plates and their bottles of beer or glasses of wine, and considered the horrific thought that her mother had probably been in complete agony immediately after the accident.

But no, a voice in her head was telling her, she hadn't been in agony. She'd died straightaway, without feeling any pain, and now she was in a better place, because she was a good person.

"Hello."

Sadie looked up, slightly stunned, to see the stranger who'd been at the Ragamuffin, and who'd watched the band play at the Billabong, looking down at her. He was smiling, and his face was so warm and open, that she couldn't help but smile back. The nightmare in which he'd featured was pushed firmly to the back of her mind.

"Hi," Sadie said.

The stranger sat down next to her.

He was smartly dressed, wearing a suit, but by no means did he look square or out of place. Slightly overdressed for a party, perhaps, but certainly trendy. His dark eyes, Sadie noted, were looking at her face, as though he'd never seen such features before.

Sadie smiled more broadly.

"I, uh, caught your band playing at the club last night," he said. His accent, she noticed, was American Midwest – a kindred spirit, she thought. What a coincidence! "You were great."

"Thanks," Sadie said coyly. She still wasn't used to the praise – she had never experienced adoration, and really, she didn't want to. The fame was second place to the money, if she was being honest.

"Oh, I'm Jordan, by the way. Jordan Weaver." He held out a hand, and Sadie shook it. It was quite cool to the touch. "You know, it's customary for the other person to introduce themselves as well," he said with a laugh.

"God, I'm sorry! I'm Sadie – Sadie Bartholomew." She felt her face flush.

"I know," Jordan said with a smirk. "I just wanted to see you squirm." He took a sip from the glass of whiskey he was holding. "Can I fix you a drink?"

"Uh, yeah thanks. Smirnoff and Coke, if there is one."

"Sure." Jordan walked over to a table in the corner of the room upon which were dozens of liquor bottles. She watched him as he poured her a glass and brought it back to her.

"Thanks."

"So, you know Martin Walsh as well, do you?" he asked her as he sat down.

"Only met him yesterday," Sadie answered.

"What do you think of him?"

Sadie frowned. "What are you? Some kind of police officer?" It was a joke and Jordan smiled.

"No, it's not that," he said. "I've only just met him myself."

"And what do you think of him?"

Jordan grinned. "Wouldn't be polite to say," he told her, taking another sip of whiskey. "You know, you don't look like the kinda girl who'd come to a place like this."

"Should I take that as a compliment?"

"No, I mean, you're here, sitting in this dining room, instead of out there, enjoying yourself. A bit of a wallflower, are you?"

"I never used to be," Sadie confessed. "But I've been through a lot lately."

"Really? Break up with a boyfriend?" Sadie smiled at that. "Or don't you wanna talk about it?"

Sadie didn't want to blow her chances with this guy. She had him in her grasp now, and she wasn't about to let him go. "No. No, it's worse than that. My parents ..." She tried to get the words out, felt the tears well up in her eyes and forced them back. "My parents were killed recently." Jordan's face seemed to drain of colour.

"God, I'm sorry," he said. "If I'd have known—"

"You couldn't have," Sadie assured him, secure in the knowledge that her emotions were back under control. She really, really didn't want to blow this opportunity. This guy was like the man of her dreams! "So, tell me a bit about yourself. You're from the States, clearly. What are you doing over here? Business or pleasure?"

"Well, it had been a business trip," Jordan answered. "But I've got this feeling it's going to turn into pleasure." A bit cheeky, Sadie thought, but probably true. She giggled slightly. "So, who writes the songs in your band?" He'd changed the subject, Sadie realized – he wasn't talking about himself any more. But she couldn't not answer the question.

"We all have a hand in doing it," she told him. "Billy, the guitarist, is the guy who comes up with the music. Mark, the bass player, and me, we come up with the lyrics. Mark does more than me though. I'm not good with words."

"Me neither," Jordan said. "Whenever I'm talking to a beautiful girl, I always get my turds in a whist." It took a few seconds for the joke to register, but when it did, Sadie couldn't help but laugh, almost spitting a mouthful of vodka across the buffet.

"Thanks a lot!"

"So, you here alone?"

Sadie shook her head as she sipped from her drink. "Uh-uh. My sister and my best friend are somewhere in this house – that's as much as I can say."

"They're having a better time of it than you?"

"Well, Melissa always was the party girl," Sadie explained. "And Jo, my little sister Jodie, she's probably due a good time. I'd like to see her enjoy herself again. I mean, I didn't want her to come here, but ..."

"You think she may get led astray?" Jordan asked with an arched eyebrow that made him look wicked.

"Well, I've only had a quick look around, but it's like the original

Sodom and Gomorra, isn't it?"

Jordan gave a crooked smile and nodded his head. "Well, I suppose it is."

"There are probably more sinners in this house than there are in the whole of Hell!"

"Oh, I wouldn't say that," Jordan said knowingly.

"So," Sadie said suddenly – she wanted to catch him unawares. "What is it you do for a living?"

"Me?"

"Yes."

"Oh, I'm in law," Jordan answered. "Sort of."

"Business law?"

"No – criminal law."

"Criminal?" Sadie frowned. "There can't be many law firms that send out lawyers overseas."

"I don't defend," Jordan told her. "I prosecute."

"That seems even less likely," Sadie said, unable to hide her scepticism. "I mean, prosecution lawyers work for the government, right? The DA? I mean, it's a long while since I've been to the US, and over here, everyone wears funny wigs, but ... well, what *are* you doing in the UK?"

"Can't tell you," Jordan said, smiling tightly. "Sorry ... it's the nature of my work."

"You work for the CIA or something?"

Jordan grinned broadly. "Something like that, yeah. Listen, I'm sorry, Sadie, but it's just, well, my work ... it's complicated. I could tell you, but—"

"You'd have to kill me," Sadie said in a bored voice. "I've heard that goddamned line two or three times in the last couple of days."

"Actually," Jordan went on, apparently not offended, "I was going to say that you wouldn't understand – or believe it."

"Now you've got me intrigued. What are you? Something to do with the government?"

"Sadie, can we sort of bypass this subject?"

Sadie nodded her head. If Jordan wasn't a bullshitter – and she had no reason to suspect that he was – then he clearly had an exciting career. But on the other hand, would some CIA spook really let his guard slip like that? Surely he'd already have a cover story? So what could that mean, if Jordan was telling the truth? Perhaps, she thought, he was a criminal, on the run. Like her father, like Alex Bartek. Maybe he was one of her father's associates. Either possibility seemed too fantastic to be true, but there was definitely something mysterious about Jordan, something that she couldn't quite put her finger on.

At that moment, Mark came over to where the two of them were sitting, bringing some intellectual-looking girl over with him. Sadie was stereotyping, but she could see that the girl was intellectual, because she was wearing glasses, had long, unstyled hair, and wore a superior expression and a long dress that certainly wasn't stylish.

"Hey, Sadie," Mark said. "We just came in here for the food." He looked Jordan up and down and then turned to the girl. "This is Karen. Karen, this is Sadie, and, uh—"

"Jordan," Jordan introduced himself. "Sadie and me just met."

"Another American," Mark said. His more relaxed persona told Sadie that he'd been drinking. "Hey, listen, do you mind if we join you guys?"

"We've been discussing near-death experiences," Karen explained as they sat down in a small circle. "Perhaps you'd like to throw your opinions into the hat?"

"What a morbid subject," Sadie muttered. Mark immediately looked distressed.

"Sadie, I didn't think—"

"Don't worry about it, Mark," Sadie assured him. "I wasn't talking about that so much as the fact that this is a party."

Jordan shifted in his seat. "No, if you don't mind, Sadie, I'd like to hear what these guys have got to say on the subject." He was looking at her as though seeking her permission. Sadie was astonished, but managed to nod her head.

"Uh, yeah, go ahead."

"Well, I'm a non-believer," Mark said first. "We all know that it's purely chemical imbalances in the brain being triggered off by a lack of oxygen. It's well-documented." Karen was smiling impatiently, and shaking her head.

"I take it you two haven't come to any sort of agreement over this?" Sadie said.

"Well, Karen is more spiritual than me," Mark said.

"Mark, you're just being ignorant."

"When we die, it's our body's way of making that passing as comfortable as possible, easing the distress," Mark said. "A defence mechanism, if you like."

"But why? Answer me that. I mean, biological defence mechanisms are in place to help us heal, to prevent or resolve a bad situation. But if I get shot in the head right now, clinically, I die immediately, right? I mean, my brain stem is gone, blown across that wall over there. So what part of my body decides that it has to prepare me for death? What part of my body is still functioning to decide that my mental state is so important, even though, if I'm not already dead, I'll be dying in the next few seconds. I mean, there's no need for defence under those situations – it serves no purpose. And in any case, some people have what is known as distressing Near Death Experiences, where they see images of Hell."

"It's a valid point, Mark," Sadie assured him. "I think she's got you there."

"Okay, okay, so scratch the defence mechanism," Mark conceded. "When the brain shuts down, when our thought processes are brought to a standstill, parts of us still function long after we're clinically dead. Now, as our brain is starved of oxygen, parts of it shut down, and with it, we lose some of our body's senses. Our minds are in a chemical turmoil, and they throw up images in any random order, because all of those neurones related to our memories and daydreams are being fired off. And with that, we lose our vision, hence the tunnel of light, and we also lose our sense of touch, hence the lack of pain, and the complete sensation of contentment and peace."

"Do you actually know what you're talking about, Mark?" Sadie asked him. Karen let out a little laugh. "I mean, do you really believe what you're saying?"

"I believe that when we die, when our physical bodies die, our mental capacity also dies," Mark said. "I mean, it's illogical to believe in an afterlife. If that were the case, and this afterlife is so wonderful, then what would be the point in living in the first place?"

Jordan responded quietly, though everyone listened to him. "You lead a mortal life so that your actions in life can determine your personality, and if your personality is a righteous one, then you will go to Heaven. If you are an irredeemable sinner, then you go to Hell."

"So, you believe in this NDE crap?" Mark asked him.

Jordan smiled. "There are no such things are near-death experiences."

Mark looked at Karen triumphantly. "Well, at least the boys agree."

"I don't think we do, Mark," Jordan went on. "You see, NDEs don't actually exist. I mean, in reality, you can have a near-death experience if you fall from a building and hurt yourself. You nearly died, ergo you experience a state which could be described as 'near-death'. But in the spiritual sense, as well as the biological sense, you are dead or you are alive. And if you're dead, then you will experience a taste of the afterlife, be it Heaven or Hell. You see, when your body shuts down, you're immediately sent to the afterlife, and it's only through the advent of modern medicine that more and more people are being brought back to report their experiences. They're not experiencing a state between life and death – they're experiencing the first stages of death, the introduction to the afterlife."

Sadie raised any eyebrow. "You're some kind of religious guy, aren't you?" She considered that maybe this was his role in the UK – something legal to do with the Church.

Jordan shook his head. "I'm not religious. I don't pray to God. I deal only with facts."

Mark got to his feet with a smirk. "Listen, I don't know about religion, but you're spooking the Holy Fuck out of me. I'm gonna go and take a leak."

Karen also stood. "Yeah, I think I'll leave you two alone." She looked at Jordan. "That's a little too deep – even for me."

After they'd left, Sadie turned to Jordan. "You know, it's okay to have beliefs."

"Even if I have beliefs that you don't believe in?"

"Hey, I'm an atheist, okay, but the way I see it, I can't lose," Sadie said with a smile. "I mean, God forgives everyone, doesn't He? So if I die, and there is an afterlife, then I put up my hands, beg for forgiveness, and I'm received into Heaven."

"Unless you've sinned," Jordan reminded her.

"Well, I don't sin that often," Sadie assured him. "And my sins are little white ones – that's all. Would that guarantee a place for me in Hell for all eternity?"

Jordan smiled. "Well, I doubt it."

Sadie looked into his eyes and instantly found herself falling in love. She didn't know why, but Jordan – a man who she barely knew, and who seemed mysterious and a little bizarre – seemed to give off this aura that she just could not ignore.

Then, behind Jordan, she saw a face that she recognized.

A girl's face, the one Jordan had been talking to at the gig last night.

Instantly, her heart dropped, and this clearly didn't go unnoticed by Jordan. "What's wrong?" he asked her, his expression and tone of voice concerned.

"Your girlfriend's here."

"My what?" Jordan asked, turning around. He looked at the girl, then turned back to Sadie, a confused look on his face, as though wondering how she knew the girl. "That's not my girlfriend," he said seriously as the girl came over. "She's in the same line of work as me. That's all. Except I guess you could say she works for the other side."

"She's a defence attorney?"

The girl stopped by the chairs and smiled at Sadie, who found that in spite of how she was feeling, she just couldn't summon up any hatred, or even dislike, for her. In fact, she even found herself smiling back.

"Hi, Jordan," the girl said pleasantly.

Jordan looked up at the girl and shot her an annoyed look. "I'm in the middle of something here."

The girl turned to Sadie. "Hi, I'm Mira. Jordan and I are sort of rivals at work." She was English, well-spoken, clearly well-educated.

Sadie nodded. At least that confirmed Jordan's story. Still, it didn't make it any easier, because this girl, Mira, was very beautiful, and although she dressed quite modestly, she clearly had some sex appeal, as demonstrated by the fact that a couple of men in the dining room had cast lecherous looks in her direction.

Sadie had a feeling that Mira wanted to talk to Jordan, even if the feeling wasn't mutual. She got to her feet. "I'll leave you guys alone," she said.

Mira's expression was one of gratitude, tinged with guilt. "I don't mean to chase you away, but this is work," she assured Sadie.

Sadie nodded her head. "It was great talking to you, Jordan. Maybe we could do it again sometime." Jordan got to his feet, but Sadie turned and walked away.

Her chance was blown, and she'd done most of the work herself. Mira, it was apparent, was not Jordan's love interest. The two of them handled themselves like work colleagues – nothing more. And yet ... the mysterious aura that Jordan emitted seemed to tell Sadie that there was more to this than met the eye, and she wasn't sure that she wanted to get mixed up in it.

Even if Jordan had been the most handsome person she'd ever met.

As she stepped into the front room, she turned and looked back to see Mira sitting down in her seat.

And the pangs of jealousy returned.

15

Kobold looked at Reizend and couldn't help but sneer. The angel shook her head slowly, as though admonishing him, but he couldn't help it. He'd been getting on great with Sadie. He'd felt almost human again. In fact, he'd almost forgotten what he really was. And Reizend had come along and destroyed that. He'd sensed Sadie's mistrust, sensed her anguish, and it was all because of the angel.

"You shouldn't sneer," she told him. "It makes you look inhuman."

Kobold's expression changed to one of warmth. He was learning fast, and was amazed at how natural it was to act in a way that was relevant to the Twentieth Century. He also knew that the conversation he was having with Reizend would not be heard by any of the partygoers. In fact, as the two celestial beings talked, their human bodies would be conducting a different conversation, one that was perfectly innocuous, inoffensive, and which would belie their true personas.

"What do you want?" he asked.

Reizend sipped from the Coke she was holding. "We need to talk, Kobold."

"About what?" Kobold asked, looking to the door through which Sadie had disappeared. "It was you who gave me the encouragement to speak to her—"

"Not about Sadie," Reizend said. "It's about Hell."

Kobold frowned and looked at the angel. "What about Hell?"

"Demons are dying in Hell, Kobold," Reizend went on. "Did you know that?"

"Hell is a large place, Reizend," Kobold said with a hint of sarcasm.

"This is serious, Kobold," the angel assured him. "Satan is feeling threatened, and he's responding in the only way he knows. He's destroying those demons he suspects of being the heir to the throne." Kobold shrugged his shoulders indifferently. "The heir – the heir is not yet powerful enough to prevent himself from being destroyed by Satan."

"Satan has ruled Hell in a fair and honest way, Reizend," Kobold said. "I don't see what the problem is."

"Until the heir reaches maturity, he should not be challenged by the devil."

"Says who?"

"Says God," Reizend snapped quickly. "It is one of the laws of Heaven and Hell, Kobold, and Satan is directly disregarding that rule."

"Does it matter that much?"

"Yes, it matters. Innocent demons are being destroyed, because Satan doesn't want to lose his seat of power. He's becoming like the Corrupted."

"Satan abhors the Corrupted," Kobold said. He should've been offended. This angel knew nothing of Hell and knew nothing of Satan. How could she sit in judgement over the greatest being in the universe after God? What right did she have?

"Satan is using the Corrupted, Kobold," Reizend told him. "He's offering them an amnesty in return for helping him find the heir. But the way they're doing it ... it's like a massacre. Mass genocide. Thousands of demons have already been destroyed, and Satan's personal guards are being replaced by Corrupted demons. Have you not noticed this?"

"Reizend, Satan is the most powerful being in Hell, and I don't sit around watching his every move. That wouldn't be possible – and it would also be disrespectful."

"Kobold, you have to understand that the heir must survive," Reizend said desperately. "The heir is the rightful successor, and his rule in Hell will be a just one. Satan has become corrupted by the power. He destroys demons without the proper authority, and he condones the deaths of innocent people – millions of innocent people – to claim the soul of just one sinner. He's abusing his power, Kobold, and he's not very good at his job."

Kobold shook his head in disgust. "We're on different sides of the fence, Reizend. You come from Heaven, I come from Hell. We both work for the same purpose, but we serve different masters."

"You serve God, just as I do," Reizend reminded him, "and just as Satan should do. We are all servants of God, every last one of us. And if we break His rules, then we have to have a very good reason for doing so, in order to justify our actions to God. Satan is breaking the rules. He doesn't trust many demons, you included. The only demons he can trust are the Corrupted, and he can trust them, because he knows that the heir cannot be one of the Corrupted."

"You're being serious, aren't you?"

"Of course I'm being serious," Reizend snapped. "When you go back to Hell, you have to watch your back. Satan can destroy you with the power he holds in his little finger. You could fight him, but it will be one-sided, and you will be destroyed. Do you know what it's like to be destroyed, Kobold, to be totally obliterated? There is no afterlife for angels and demons. If we are destroyed, then we cease to exist."

Kobold considered that thought very carefully. It certainly was a frightening prospect, even more so than being sent to Hell when your mortal body dies, though most would say that they'd prefer not to exist rather than spend eternity in Hell being tortured. He took a swig from the whiskey and experienced human emotions once more.

"But Satan trusts me."

"You really believe that?"

"I believe ... I believe that Satan wouldn't destroy me," Kobold said. "He told me that he was gathering up his most powerful demons for the fight."

Reizend smiled. "He was sizing you up, Kobold. He was trying to ascertain what kind of a risk you posed to him. You were lucky he didn't destroy you on the spot."

"I have to admit, Reizend, I was curious. How can I be one of his most powerful demons? I've been in this form for a couple of hundred years or so. It's just like the blinking of an eye." At that, Reizend smiled again. "What? You have to tell me what, Reizend."

"Do you feel weakened?"

"No. Why should I?"

"When demons and angels, celestial beings, appear in human form, our powers gradually diminish," Reizend explained. "Eventually, we lose the ability to return to Heaven or Hell. When that happens ..." She didn't conclude – she didn't have to. Kobold was fully aware of what happened to the Ensnared, those demons and angels who were trapped on Earth. They could never be brought back, but they could never be destroyed by a human. If their human form was destroyed, then they could never summon up another, and so they wandered the planet in their demonic or angelic form, visible to all. That could never be allowed to happen, because it would expose a celestial creature to the sciences of mankind, which were becoming advanced. The secret of the afterlife could never be revealed until the final moment of death.

So the Ensnared were hunted down by expert demons known as the Jäger, who had the power to destroy virtually any celestial being on Earth. The Jäger destroyed both demons and angels, and so far, only a few demons had become exposed to humanity. None had been exposed in the last three hundred years, which was many generations in human terms, but the mere blinking of an eye to an immortal creature.

Kobold considered his own wellbeing. As the hours dragged by in human form, most demons experienced some loss of powers, usually manifesting itself in a sensation of hunger, of feeling empty – emotions a celestial being should not experience. But he'd been in human form for three hours, and felt as powerful as he had done when he'd first left Hell. It had been the same yesterday. And usually, upon returning to Hell, a demon felt weak and needed time to recover – sometimes a week – before he could return to Earth in human form, the safest and only approved way. But he'd been to Earth twice in the last couple of days, and last night, he'd stayed for more than seven hours.

And he still felt powerful.

He looked at Reizend. "What does this mean?"

Reizend stood up. "I can't tell you that, Kobold. You're intelligent. Figure it out for yourself."

Kobold reached up, lightly grasped her hand and urged her to sit down again. "Reizend, I'm afraid."

"Afraid? A demon, afraid?"

"I'm confused, I don't know what's happening to me. Sadie – she just makes me feel emotions that I haven't felt for hundreds of years, and I don't know why. I just want to be human again, Reizend."

"You're way past that point, Kobold," the angel assured him. "You left humanity behind for good the moment you murdered your wife and her lover." Kobold felt his face blacken over. He didn't want to be reminded of his sins, but they were there with him every day, for all of eternity.

"I think I have paid for my sins, Reizend. I have repented. That is why I am now a demon."

The angel nodded. "That's right. But you are no longer human. You yearn to be human, but that can never be." Kobold ran a hand through his hair, a human action that made him even more distraught at the prospect of never being a man again. Reizend seemed to pick up on this. "I sometimes get upset," she said. "I didn't want to die, you know. I can still remember it ... we're not allowed to forget, are we? The pain, the discomfort, it's an eternal memory."

Kobold looked up at the angel and realized that they'd both been through the same thing. They'd both been human, and they'd both had it snatched away from them, never to return. "How old were you when you died?"

"When I was killed?" Reizend corrected him softly. "I was eighteen." She smiled as she looked down at herself. "I'm in my twenties now, aren't I?" It was a weak attempt at a joke. She sat down. "I was killed in 1943." At that, Kobold frowned. The war years, when countless souls had been snatched away from Earth at the behest of a handful of men.

It had been out of the hands of both God and the devil.

"What happened?"

"I was a Jew," Reizend explained. "A German Jew, which wasn't a very good thing to be in the Forties." She looked down at her drink and took a deep sigh. "I can remember the day they came for us – my family. My mother and father, my brothers, two of them. My youngest brother was eight, my older brother was twenty. He was studying to become a doctor. We weren't a fabulously wealthy family, but we had money. Not the kind of wealth the Nazis proclaimed." The last sentence was spat out bitterly. "They told us we were being relocated, because German was a country for

Aryan people, not for nationless bastards like us. We weren't the only Jews in our street, but the Germans came out to watch us leave, to watch us being led away by these soldiers. These *fucking* animals – they spat on us, called us names, threw stones ... it was unbelievable. The day before, they'd been talking to us. Now they couldn't wait to see the back of us. Ordinary people, men, women children – and they hated us overnight. I often wondered if they'd have been happy to see us leave their neighbourhood had they known what was really in store for us. Relocation?" Reizend shook her head. "That wasn't what the Nazis had in mind." The swearing and the bitterness betrayed her true emotions. She was speaking like a human, and that was permitted. There was no sin in swearing, nothing wrong with bitterness, because they were human emotions, and humanity was not inherently evil. "Do you want to know what happened to us? What evil was perpetuated in the name of mankind?"

Kobold said, "If it's not too painful to tell me."

Reizend shook her head. "It will always be painful, Kobold, to recall the crimes that were committed against me and my family, let alone those committed against the whole of the human race. But you have to know, *you have to understand*." She stopped, composed herself, as Sadie had done earlier that evening. "They enjoyed it, that was the thing. They actually revelled in torturing us." Kobold felt uneasy. He committed torture every day of the week, countless times every day, in fact. But this wasn't the kind Reizend was talking about.

She was shaking, Kobold noticed, a distinctly human reaction that was completely at odds with her celestial being. She took a nervous sip from her drink, then continued. "When we arrived at Belsen, we stood in this long queue of people, all of us holding suitcases with our belongings. Just a fraction of our belongings, all we could grab in the short time they gave us to pack. They came along, took everything from us, told us we'd get them back later, when we were settled in the camp. It was all lies, and I supposed that deep down, we all knew it. By that time, some of the rumours had got out about the resettlement programme. I remember ... I remember looking beyond the train station, through the steam from the train, where this thick, black smoke was being pumped up into the sky. And I remember thinking—*being*—scared. I remember being scared. Terrified. Because I knew that it wasn't a good sign." Kobold reached over and stroked her hand gently – he didn't consider the fact that he was behaving like a human. He was offering her sympathy, something that demons didn't do. They weren't put on the planet to sympathize. They were put on the planet to punish.

Reizend smiled weakly, and in that moment, she looked more human than she had ever looked before. If Kobold hadn't known that she were an angel, he would never have guessed. She looked vulnerable, sorrowful, and powerless. She went on with her story. "At the head of the queue were these two SS officers. I remember their black uniforms, with the white embroidery. *SS*. I remember seeing those initials, white lightning flashes, and thinking how terrifying they looked. They sent my younger brother into a different line – that's what they were doing, splitting us up into two lines. My mother cried – I think she knew." Reizend bit her lip. "I watched my little brother, his sweet, little face pleading with us. Pleading, but he never said anything. He just kept looking at us until he disappeared into the crowd of people. My mother was sobbing, but my father couldn't do anything. He just stood there, broken, because his son had been taken away, and he couldn't get him back." Reizend looked at Kobold. "I should think that you've seen lots of evil in your time, haven't you?"

"True evil comes along only once or twice every decade," Kobold told her. "But those men you're talking about, those SS officers, their sins against mankind were great, and they have all, each and every one of them, been punished for their crimes. And they will continue to be punished." Kobold thought about those men – although he'd never come across one, he did know that their excuse in life, that they were just following orders, would grant them no favours in death.

"We were sent into the showers – *real* showers, not the kind my brother had been sent to." Reizend caught a sob and held it in. Her eyes glistened as she looked to the ceiling. "When the water came out, we were all so relieved, those of us who'd heard the rumours. The other line had contained the weaker ones – the old, the young, the sick, though there were a few mothers who'd been sent to that line with their babies, because they wouldn't leave them. And a few fathers too, though the Nazis didn't want them to go that way. They wanted us all to work, you see. They shaved our heads, because they wanted to use our hair to make socks for submariners.

And then we were divided into men and women, and sent to the huts, where we had to work for the Germans." Reizend paused for a moment. "I was raped," she said blandly. "Countless times. Soiled and desecrated by these *fucking* pigs. They did it purely for their own pleasure, not because the Führer had commanded it. And for that, I condemned them, each and every time I lay beneath them." She shuddered. "I didn't protest, because I knew it wouldn't do any good. The first time it happened, I fought, and I was beaten. They broke one of my arms. It never did mend properly, but they didn't send me to the gas chambers, because I was useful to them. Useful, because they could rape me time and time again, and I would just lay there and let it happen. Then, after three months, I was dragged from the hut one night, along with a new girl. I think she was fourteen or fifteen, though she looked older. One of the men raped me, as they held the other girl down. Then they threw me into the corner, and told me that they had a new plaything, and that my usefulness had come to an end. I knew what that meant. I was going to be sent to the gas chamber. I looked at this girl, and her eyes were pleading with me as they stripped her. She fought, but they were men – what could she do? I remember her face well, because it reminded me of my brother's face the last time I saw him. And I let him down – I couldn't let her down. So I looked around the room, saw a pistol on one of the tables. It was in its holster. One of the SS officers had removed it so that he could rape the girl more comfortably." Reizend paused again and closed her eyes. "I took the gun. They didn't see me because they were all watching their comrade raping the girl. Watching and jeering and praising him on his technique. I could hear the girl crying, and I knew what I had to do. I aimed the gun, and I shot her in the head."

Kobold was stunned. "You killed the girl?"

Reizend nodded her head sorrowfully. "I dropped to my knees and I cried for God to forgive me. But if I had shot one of those men, they would've killed me, and they would've continued raping that girl until they'd got bored with her. I knew it was the only way I could save her from that torture. I prayed to God to forgive me, and as I was doing so, one of the soldiers took out his pistol and shot me in the face. I didn't die straightaway. I remember seeing them standing over me. Then another officer pointed his gun at me ... and then I died."

Kobold took a deep breath. It was some moments before he spoke.

"Thank you," he said sombrely.

"For what?"

"For telling me about yourself," he explained. "It must've been painful."

Reizend smiled weakly and nodded her head. "It was. I took another life, but it was a selfless act, and God showed mercy. I often wondered what became of my family, and I was shown their fate. My father was killed by the Nazis, but my mother and elder brother both survived the war. My brother is still alive now. I often go and visit him, though he doesn't know who I really am." She looked around the room, and then added, "I'm still trying to find my younger brother. He's in Heaven somewhere."

"There are lots of people in Heaven," Kobold said. "It will be a near impossible task."

"But I have to find him."

"One day, you might."

"I have to find him and apologize," Reizend said. "I need his forgiveness."

"You got God's forgiveness, Reizend, and because He forgave you, then so did everyone else in Heaven. Surely you must be aware of that." To Kobold, it seemed so obvious. And Reizend was obviously a very righteous person, or she would never have been allowed into Heaven in the first place, let alone been made an angel after such a short period of time.

"So many people loved me," she told Kobold, as though reading his mind. "In Heaven, everybody gives you support and love. For the first few years, you don't even think about those you leave behind. Some souls completely forget their previous lives – I mean, we're not encouraged to remember, are we? How many times have you seen people you've recognized in Hell?"

"In Hell, nobody has a face," Kobold explained. "Nobody, apart from those souls you've been assigned. We cannot allow recognition to corrupt our tasks." Reizend closed her eyes and nodded her head.

"I understand," she said. "But in Heaven, it's different, isn't it? We've been blessed with eternal happiness. Why should we be deprived of the ones we love?"

"We have eternity to find them," Kobold reminded her. "And your quest will be significantly easier than mine." He looked to the doorway through which Sadie had walked. "I had no one in life who I loved enough to want to see again."

"But you have somebody in death?"

Kobold smiled wryly. "We are not permitted to love, are we? Not humans. Not anymore."

"Some people have the power to change that," Reizend said, speaking cryptically again.

"I don't want to end up as one of the Ensnared," Kobold said. "And yet ... I think that I have fallen in love."

"With Sadie Bartholomew?"

"Does that sound ridiculous?"

Reizend smiled. "Not at all," she assured him. "There is nothing wrong with any of us desiring to be human once again."

"But do you think I will hurt Sadie?" Kobold asked – he didn't mean physically, and he didn't mean deliberately.

Reizend understood his question. She smiled once more and sipped from her Coke. "Enjoy your time on Earth, Kobold. You can't stay here forever, and you have more important work to do." And with that, she stood up.

This time, Kobold let her go, but her final comment lingered in his mind. What had she meant? He swirled the whiskey around in the glass and downed it in one gulp, as his human senses returned and all around him people walked, talked, danced and sang.

Sadie was important to him, because she'd opened his demonic mind to the thought of being human again, which he knew, in his heart, was impossible. He was dead, he was one of Hell's demons, and though he had the power to make himself appear human, he would never be human again. To maintain a physical body was difficult, and drained resources – though he appeared to be doing well at the moment – and to age that body as each day passed required even more of the precious power that demons could ill afford to squander.

He was in Hell, he told himself.

But as he walked to the front door and stepped out into a cold night that barely affected him mentally, but had distinctive physical effects upon his human form, he saw something that displeased him.

He could feel a surge of energy, the demonic form of adrenaline, pumping around the human body, enveloping his mind, as he watched Sadie climbing into a Porsche – the Porsche belonged to Martin Walsh.

And Kobold was perfectly aware of what kind of man he was.

16

Sadie didn't know why she accepted Martin's offer of a ride home, especially as Jodie was still alone at the party with only Melissa to look after her, but at the time, it had seemed like a good idea – an exciting prospect that numbed the pain of seeing Jordan with the angelic Mira. Although she'd only known Jordan for just a couple of hours, she was already jealous of watching him interact with another woman, as though Mira were a challenge to her own attractiveness. And Martin had come along at the right time – or the wrong time, depending on your point of view.

As Sadie glanced over at him, sitting behind the wheel of his powerful car, she wondered whether this really was brightest thing she'd ever done in her life. She wasn't concerned for Jodie's safety – whatever Melissa might be, she certainly wasn't irresponsible in that sense of the word. She'd assured Sadie that she'd look after her little sister, and Sadie had every confidence that she would. What concerned Sadie right now was her own wellbeing. The stories about Martin Walsh had come to the front of her mind again, and she wondered whether she was actually safe here in his car.

But then, what harm would it be? She hadn't been with a man in years, and she missed it immensely. More significantly, Martin wasn't exactly unattractive. She certainly fancied him, and the fact that she'd already thought about what it would be like to make love to him helped ease her mind. But then, was she doing this for the right reasons? Did she really want to have sex so desperately that she was prepared to have a one-night stand with a man she hardly knew? Or was the real reason because she'd been rebuffed by Jordan, and she was simply trying to get her own back?

If that was the case, then she had to put a stop to any ideas Martin might have.

And quickly.

That thought was in her mind as the Porsche pulled into the car park at the rear of the flats. Martin parked it in a space in the corner, and switched off the engine. A Sheryl Crow CD was in the deck, and he reached down and flicked a button. Immediately, a different CD began to play – this time, it was sloppy R'n'B crap that Sadie absolutely hated.

But it told her precisely what Martin had in mind.

He turned to her and smiled – she could see his face in the faint illumination from the dashboard.

"Well, here you go," he said.

"Thanks," she said quietly. She really should've just climbed out of the car, but something was compelling her to stay. She felt his hand brush her knee, and jolted ever so slightly at the shock of his touch. But all the same, a tingle ran up and down her spine. The first time in years ...

Martin leaned across and pressed the palm of his hand lightly on her cheek, directing his face to his.

"What about Holly?" she asked him.

"Holly won't mind," he assured her.

There was no get-out clause there, she thought.

Then his lips touched her, and she responded as only the desperate did – by opening her mouth and pressing her lips against his, her tongue probing the inside of his mouth, tasting the liquor he'd been drinking earlier.

She felt a hand cup one of her breasts, stroking the soft material of her dress, and her nipple grew erect.

This felt good ...

No, she corrected herself, this was all wrong.

But she couldn't stop it.

She wondered what Jordan was doing now, wondered if he was still talking to Mira, if he was kissing her right now, if his hands were touching Mira's nipples, if they were pushing up her dress, gently caressing the inside of her thigh ...

This was all wrong, the voice screamed out in her head, and she was unnerved, because it sounded so vivid, so real.

"Martin, I don't think we should be doing this," she said, breaking away.

"Come on, darling," he said softly, his lips gently kissing her cheek. "Don't you want to?"

"I'd rather not," Sadie said, "not in a car."

"But that's part of the fun," he told her with a smirk. "The risk, the excitement. Come on, it'll be great."

Sadie felt his hand rise higher up her thigh, and she felt an odd stirring between her legs, a buzzing sensation that was starting to drive her wild. It felt so good – and it wasn't as if she was about to make love to a monster.

She threw her arms around Martin's neck and pulled him towards her.

His hands worked quickly as they lifted her up and pulled her across the car and over him, her legs spread over his, her feet jammed in on either side of the driver's seat. She could feel him pressing upwards between her legs, through the material of his trousers and her panties. He was throbbing beneath her, desperate to get inside, and as she kissed him passionately, she really, really wanted him.

He tugged her panties aside, and then slipped a finger between her moist lips, gently stroking her with his thumb. But she wanted more than that. She put her own hand down there, and urged him to brush her more firmly. He obliged, and soon he had a couple of fingers inside, and was working more vigorously on her clitoris. She could feel that she was damp, and that was only to be expected. She was so aroused, so turned on, that she knew now she couldn't stop.

But still that nagging doubt at the back of her mind persisted.

This is all so wrong. You don't love him – that much was true, she conceded – and you don't really want to have sex with him. You're just aroused, and you're going to really, really, *really* regret this in the morning.

She had to admit that the voice spoke the truth

And yet, it wasn't her own voice that she heard.

It was Jordan's.

She pulled away from Martin and he looked up. His free hand had been desperately tugging at his trousers, as he vainly tried to prise his penis out. He was ready for it, she was ready for it, so what was she doing? She was putting a stop to it, she told herself, and rightly so. But how could she do it without sounding like some kind of tease, without ruining the band's chances of success?

"Wait," she said.

"What?"

"Not without a condom," she told him.

Martin smiled at her, and she felt her heart sink. He really wasn't making this easy. He reached in his jacket pocket and produced a sealed rubber, tearing it open with his teeth and handing it to her. "Here," he said, "you put it on."

Now she knew she was making a big mistake.

She didn't want this, not at all, and if she did it, it would only seem like a chore, like the bored housewife laying beneath her grunting husband for five minutes, doing her duty for her marriage. She wasn't going to enjoy it, not one little bit. Already, she could feel herself drying up.

She pulled herself away from Martin, resting her buttocks on his knees, and looked down at him, jutting out from his unbuckled trousers. It wasn't big – that much she could see – kind of thin, probably marginally longer than average. But it certainly wasn't impressive, not for such a large man. It throbbed angrily, and Martin threw his head back.

If they were going to do it, she wasn't going to risk anything, nothing at all.

She reached down and grabbed him with her left hand, pulling back his foreskin and placing the rolled up condom on the tip of his penis. As she did so, he jerked violently, and let out a pained grunt.

Thinking that she'd somehow hurt him, Sadie drew back both hands, the condom still in her fingers.

"What's up?" she asked.

Then she felt something hot and wet hit the top of her thigh, and she jumped. Two more drops hit her on the same leg, then another jet sprayed her hand.

"Jesus," Martin gasped.

And it suddenly dawned on Sadie what had happened. Another drop spurted across the inside of her thigh, and she jumped back, banging her head on the windscreen. That one, she told herself, was a little too close for comfort. She had to get out of here before Martin exploded.

"God!" he grunted, and she looked down to see his hand gripping his shaft, tugging it back and forth as he milked out the last drops. Clearly, her touch had caused him to suffer a premature ejaculation, and Sadie had pulled her hand away in mid-orgasm, which couldn't have been comfortable for him. But as he finished himself off, he was spraying it in all directions, and she didn't want to be caught in the crossfire, not anymore than she already had been.

She flopped down on the passenger seat, and pulled her dress down, feeling it sticking to the wet spots on her legs. God, she'd have to wash this dress, she thought to herself.

That thought was still in her mind as Martin stopped masturbating.

"God," he said again, breathlessly. "Sadie, I'm sorry. I don't know what the fuck happened there. It's never happened before. Christ, it's never, ever happened before!" There was a desperation and shock in his voice that was so sincere that Sadie had to believe him. For some reason, her touch had ignited his fuse, and he couldn't hold it back any longer.

It was just a shame, she thought, that he couldn't have waited until the condom was actually on.

She wiped her hand on the Porsche's seat, but it was made of leather, and so simply smeared the cum across her skin. All the same, he'd have to clean the car's interior, she thought smugly. She grabbed the door handle, but Martin reached over and held her wrist lightly with his hand – she didn't want to think about where his hand had just been.

"Listen, I'm sorry," he said.

"You don't have to worry," Sadie assured him. "What happened tonight, what was gonna happen, it would've been a mistake. I'm not about to tell anybody."

"It's never happened before," he said again.

"I believe you," she said. "But I have to go. My sister will be home soon, and I want to make sure that I get changed before then." At that, Martin winced, and she could almost hear his heart dropping inside him. "The party was great," she added, and opened the door. "And I hope that this won't prejudice your opinion of the band." It was a banal comment, and one that really didn't need to be said, but it just came out. She turned to look at Martin, but he didn't seem interested. He was more concerned with tidying himself up.

"Bye," she said.

Martin smiled sheepishly and fired up the Porsche's engine. "Yeah," he said, "bye."

Sadie closed the door, and with that, he drove off out of the car park.

Sadie stood in the cool air for a few moments, feeling the breeze against her skin, cooling her in the places where she was damp. A shiver ran down her spine, and she turned and looked around the car park. The sensation she was getting was one of being watched, but all she could see were cars. Two of them. A dark BMW and a Renault that she knew belonged to the neighbours. She couldn't see anybody sitting inside either of them.

All the same, she didn't want to stay in the car park a second longer, and fished in her pocket for the keys as she walked across the tarmac to the rear of the building. The rear entrance wasn't supposed to be used just for coming and going, so the landlord had proclaimed, but Sadie wanted to get inside as quickly as possible.

She wanted to strip off, throw the dirty clothes in the wash – by themselves, naturally – and take a shower. She didn't like showers, but didn't fancy the idea of sitting in a steaming bath with Martin's sperm for company. She just wanted to get it off her body, because she felt so dirty and used.

She wasn't always like this, she thought as she entered the building and made her way up the stairs to the second floor. She was quite adventurous when it came to sex, and enjoyed watching her partners climax. It gave her a thrill to see it shoot towards her. The further it travelled, and the more powerfully it struck her, the better, because she viewed that as a compliment to her sexual prowess. But she didn't like the idea of a facial on a first date, much less in the cramped confines of a Porsche 911.

And there was something about Martin that she didn't like.

She couldn't quite put her finger on it, but ...

She shuddered again as she entered the flat. Soon, she told herself, she'd be out of these dirty clothes, and tonight's exploits would quickly become nothing more than a distant – albeit seedy – memory.

* * * * *

Kobold watched from the front seat of the BMW, looking up at the window on the second floor as a light was switched on. Sadie was inside now, probably washing herself, washing away Martin's dirt. She had been about to commit an act that wouldn't have condemned her to Hell, but which would certainly have played on her conscience. And Kobold had stepped in to prevent that.

Now, she would not regret tonight's events in the morning, because nothing had happened. Nothing more than Martin Walsh shooting his seed unceremoniously across the interior of his expensive car and across Sadie's legs, keeping it away from the places where it could do the most damage to her decency.

He'd saved Sadie, but not to prevent her from becoming contaminated. He'd saved her because she meant so much to him, and because he knew that she didn't really want to go through with what Martin had in mind for her. He knew that – it wasn't something he was just telling himself. He knew that Sadie had gotten drunk, had gotten jealous, and that by accepting a lift from Martin, fully knowing what he had in mind when they reached their destination, she was avenging what she saw as Jordan Weaver snubbing her.

And so Kobold had saved her.

Because he loved her, and because the side of him that still felt human emotions didn't want to have to deal with that kind of emotional upset. He didn't want to feel cheated.

And besides, Martin wasn't really the ideal candidate to end a two-year dry spell.

And with that, Kobold closed Jordan Weaver's eyes and left the body.

Martin angrily tossed the car keys across the room to the dining table and stomped over to the drinks cabinet, where he fixed himself a very large Smirnoff Black and downed the contents in one gulp, savouring the painful burning sensation he felt. He wasn't in his own house, where the party was still in full swing, because he didn't really want to make his grand entrance with damp spunk stains all over his trousers.

He glanced down and shook his head.

"Fucking bitch," he mumbled. Then he poured himself another drink. No, it wasn't fair to blame Sadie. It wasn't her fault that she was so hot, that she made him want to cum every time he thought about her. But why, he wondered, as he took a swig from the vodka, did he find her so hot? It wasn't as if she dressed alluringly, and she certainly wasn't stunningly attractive. But nevertheless, she held him spellbound.

He just wanted to fuck her, wanted to impress her with his sexual knowledge and ability. Other girls had told him that he was good, and of course, he believed it. Why should they lie? Even Holly, who couldn't remain faithful even for a day, praised him constantly, though at the same time denigrating him for the size of his cock compared to other lovers, past and present.

But he'd blown the opportunity to fuck Sadie. She was hardly likely to agree to see him again – maybe with the rest of the band, but not alone. He'd made himself look like an inexperienced and desperate lover, and there was little possibility of him recovering his reputation to such an extent where Sadie would fall into his arms like a charmed maiden.

"Fucking hell," he muttered under his breath, and downed the vodka, quickly fixing himself another. Here he was, at Holly's flat, drinking her booze and waiting for her to return. She'd notice the spunk stains on his clothes, but she wouldn't say anything about them. She wouldn't say anything about them because she'd probably have spunk stains on her own clothes. That was the kind of relationship they had – open, and easy going. No jealousy, with plenty of opportunities to fuck one another and anyone else.

Why, he'd often asked himself, did he stay with Holly when it was clear that the both of them needed sex from others? Well, it was obvious – Holly was good in bed, so adventurous and daring, that he couldn't ever envisage himself without her. She knew every trick in the book, and she used her skills to full effect, always satisfying him. Which begged the question, why did Holly stay with him, when she could probably get far superior sex elsewhere?

That much was also obvious, Martin told himself ruefully as he downed the third large vodka. Money. Money and drugs, both of which he could supply. And Holly was both a shopping junkie and a cocaine addict. In his quieter moments, Martin sincerely wished that there could be more to their relationship than sex, money and drugs, but that was never going to happen. Not as far as Holly was concerned.

So he just laid back and enjoyed the sex.

He put down the glass and leant on the cabinet, feeling his eyes watering and his stomach burning. The neat vodka had certainly got to work, and he knew that he'd be suffering in the morning. But right now, oblivion seemed like a good place to be.

A voice said, "That can be arranged."

Martin frowned. Christ, that was so vivid, almost real. He'd drunk more than he'd thought.

"It's not the drink," the voice said again, and Martin was aware of a burning heat coming from behind him. By now, his heart was throbbing in his chest, valiantly pumping adrenaline around his body in anticipation of a fight of some sort. And Martin, reluctantly – because he didn't want to see the owner of that voice – turned around to face the source of the heat.

What he saw went way beyond his wildest fears.

The creature standing before him had the hairy legs of a goat, and the body of a man, coloured a brilliant crimson. The face was young, handsome, but at the same time, completely inhuman. The teeth that smiled at him were a dazzling white, and his head was topped with dark hair, slicked back with water, grease or probably sweat. Two short, stubby horns protruding from the creature's head added to the demonic effect.

"Well, hello, Martin," it said to him.

Martin blinked a few times, trying to clear the water from his eyes. Had he drank too much? Was he hallucinating? Or had Holly put some kind of substance in her vodka to enhance its effect? Whatever, this apparition before him most definitely could not be real.

"What the fuck are you?" he eventually asked.

"You know, I get bored answering that question," the creature said. "Let's just cut to the chase. What do I look like? That's obvious, isn't it?

And I'm here, Martin, for a very good reason."

"Listen, this is bollocks, man," Martin snapped, pouring himself another vodka. "Fucking bullshit. And on top of everything else, you've got an American accent!"

"You think I'm not real, don't you?" the creature asked with a smile. "You think that I'm just a figment of your drink-addled imagination, right?"

"The devil ain't real," Martin said, shaking his head. "And right now, I'm probably lying flat on my back on that floor there, pissed out of my skull, and having one of the worst nightmares ever. Whatever, this ain't really fucking happening."

The creature reached out with a hand, and threw a bolt of fire across the room. It slammed into the expensive hi-fi system, which exploded into flames. Martin could feel the heat, which was almost as intense as the heat that was coming from the creature.

"Is that real enough for you?"

"Hey, arsehole, explosions happen in dreams too, you know," Martin said. He took a swig from the vodka. He was actually starting to enjoy this nightmare. It was vivid and exciting, and had this ethereal feel to it that he knew would never fade. Christ, he'd be savouring the memory of this dream for weeks to come. If only Sadie would appear, then it would be complete.

"Well, remember it when you *wake up*," the creature said. "Because it will still be there then."

"Mate, this isn't happening, you know," Martin said, draining the vodka.

"Well, you better fix yourself another, and keep on telling yourself that," the creature told him. He took a couple of steps towards Martin, who glanced at the flaming stereo system. It sure looked real, it felt real, and it even smelled real.

What if ... no, this couldn't be real. This really could not be happening.

"What the fuck is this?" Martin asked slowly. He held up the glass of vodka, as though inspecting it for traces of some hallucinogenic drug, but he was only fooling himself. "Look, man, this just isn't fucking happening!"

"My name, in case you're interested, is Kobold," the creature said, the smile on its face broadening. "And I come to you directly from Hell, Martin, to give you a warning." It stepped across the room towards Martin, until its face was just inches away. Martin could smell the stench of sulphur, thick in his nostrils, potent enough to make him want to vomit.

Now this whole thing seemed far too real to be just a dream or hallucination.

"What warning?" he asked quietly.

"Stay away from Sadie Bartholomew," the creature said. "You have no right to force yourself upon her."

Martin's jaw dropped, and suddenly he felt so exposed and embarrassed at the spunk stains that were on his clothes. "I ... I don't know what you mean."

"You keep on fucking tramps like Holly, Martin, because that's all you're cut out for," Kobold told him. "If you should try to fuck anything that is out of your price range ..." The demon smiled and took a couple of steps back. "Well, I can always arrange for another accident, can't I?" Its eyes dropped to Martin's trousers.

Now Martin understood, but it just didn't make any sense, because this was reality, not some biblical movie. Demons, they only existed in fiction. But then, he had never suffered from premature ejaculation before, and it had come across him far too quickly for him to control, or to enjoy.

"And if you keep on insisting ..." The demon shook its head sombrely. "Well, I'll just send you straight to Hell, Martin. You see, God frowns upon that kind of activity, but the devil ... the devil, he just smiles. Not because he approves, but because he knows that it will mean another soul will be sent to Hell to keep the fires burning. We need people like you, Martin. And I'd be only too happy to take your life." Kobold let out a laugh. "And I'll take it even before you know it."

Martin threw the glass across the room, but it smashed harmlessly into the wall behind the demon.

No, not behind the demon, because the demon was no longer there.

The demon ...

Had it ever been there in the first place?

"Fuck," he exclaimed.

Then he staggered over to the drinks cabinet, found another glass and poured himself another vodka. In the corner of the room, the flames that had engulfed the stereo had burnt out, but the melted, mangled black hunk of plastic testified to the fact that some accident had happened there.

How was he going to explain it to Holly?

Fuck it.

It must've been his conscience speaking to him, though with a loud and visible personality. That was it. Nothing demonic, nothing supernatural.

Just then, there were sounds of the flat's front door being unlocked, and Martin stumbled over to the sofa and flopped down, spilling some his drink in the process.

Holly stepped into the room, wearing a little black dress, heels, and plenty of make-up. Immediately, her lip curled up and her nose twitched. "What's that smell?" Then her eyes fell upon the stereo. "What happened here?"

"Don't ask me," Martin slurred.

"Well, was there a fire or something?" Holly demanded, stepping over to the wreckage of the stereo.

"I said I don't fucking know," Martin snapped. "It was Satan, all right? He came in here, and set fire to the fucking hi-fi. That's as much as I can tell you." He gulped down another mouthful of vodka. By now, it didn't burn. It didn't have any taste or sensation.

Martin looked Holly up and down, saw the way the dress was pulled taut across her buttocks. "Come here," he said, tossing the glass onto the floor, where it spilled the vodka out onto the carpet.

Holly turned and smiled. "What? You feeling in the mood?"

"Ain't you?"

"I've already been satisfied," she told him, walking across the room towards the sofa. "And by the looks of your trousers, so have you."

"Oh that? That was an accident. It didn't satisfy me."

Holly straddled him and unbuckled his trousers, pulling out his cock. Already, it started to grow thicker and longer and harder. "Well," she said, "I'll have to see whether I can do any better." She began to wank him, her strokes long and firm, each one yanking his foreskin back as far as it would go. She dropped down onto her floor and pulled his cock towards her face, sniffing it and licking it. "It doesn't smell like you've been fucked," she said. "What was it? A wank? Did you get a wank off that singer?"

Martin threw back his head. "I don't want to talk about it."

"Well, enjoy this," Holly said, and she enclosed her lips around his shaft and bobbed her head up and down, her right hand still wanking him.

This was what he wanted, he told himself. This was what he needed. A good fuck from a woman who really knew how to satisfy a man.

She worked on him for five minutes, and he was enjoying every second. Then she stood up and pulled up her dress, showing him a neat landing strip of pubic hair. He reached up, slipped his hand between her legs, felt her lips soft, moist and slippery. He could smell the spunk on her, and without thinking, he pulled her towards him, and nestled his nose in her short hair, thrusting his tongue upwards between her lips, tasting the seed from another man.

Holly gripped his head tightly, and reached down to try to wank him, but Martin was already there, gripping himself and wanking vigorously as he lapped away at her pussy.

It was as he was about to climax that the vision of the demon entered his mind again, and with it, a horrible thought.

The spunk. Whose had it been? Was it clean? Or was he taking into his mouth a virulent strain of the HIV virus?

That thought was in his mind as his orgasm washed over him.

17

Sadie was working the morning shift at McDonald's on Monday when she spied Jordan coming in through the entrance. Immediately, she felt embarrassed. This wasn't the most prestigious of jobs, and in all likelihood, she'd end up serving him which, bearing in mind her present experience in the fast food industry – all of a couple of days – probably wouldn't be as impressive as she would've liked.

He smiled as he came up to the counter, and Sadie beat another girl to him, edging her out of the way with an elbow. Melissa, watching from the other end of the counter, smiled and signalled for the girl to come to her. With that, Sadie was now alone – as alone as she could be – at the counter with Jordan.

"Hey," she said.

"Hey," Jordan nodded a greeting. He was as handsome as ever, dashing in his suit, mobile phone in his right hand. "Listen, about the other night ..." That was all he said. It was probably as close as she was going to get to an apology. That was the way the other men in her life usually apologized. "I'm sorry. Mira turning up like that – kinda threw a stick in our spokes, didn't it?" He smiled.

And Sadie couldn't help but smile back. "Hey, don't worry about it," she said, her hands professionally gripping the electric till. It was the only part of the job she'd been able to master, because it came so naturally.

"No, but it messed up your evening, didn't it? And mine too."

"Well, I won't deny that I wasn't happy to be pushed aside for somebody wanting to talk shop," Sadie said, "but I had a good time while it lasted."

"Did you get home all right?" Jordan asked her.

At that Sadie almost flinched, as the memory of her lucky escape returned. "I ... I got a lift. From Martin."

"Dangerous guy, Martin," Jordan told her. "Hey, listen, I don't wanna get you into trouble. Fix me a Coke – let's at least make an effort to make this look like a genuine transaction." Sadie nodded and keyed the item into the till.

"That'll be—"

Jordan stopped her by holding up a fifty pound note. "Here," he said. "It should take you a few moments to get the change. Long enough for me to ask you out to dinner tonight."

Sadie grinned as she took the note. "Well, I'd be more than happy."

"I'll pick you up – seven-thirty?"

Sadie nodded and fished out Jordan's change. "Here you go," she said. She didn't bother counting it into his hand, and he didn't bother checking to see that he'd been given the right amount. More to the point, he didn't even bother waiting for his Coke.

"I'll see you then," he said, and with that, he turned and left the restaurant. It was only then that Sadie realized she hadn't given him her address, and Melissa chose that moment to approach.

"How'd it go?"

"Huh?" Sadie was a little bewildered – should she chase after Jordan, tell him where she lived? But a little voice told her that everything would be okay, and she found herself believing it. "Huh, sorry?"

"Did he apologize for messing up your date?"

"It wasn't a date, Melissa," Sadie said, turning to face her friend. "It was a brief encounter."

"Whatever, did he apologize?"

"He apologized," Sadie answered. "Though he didn't have to." Another customer came into restaurant, and Melissa nudged Sadie from the counter and round the back into the kitchen.

"One of the perks of having the assistant manager as your friend," she explained, as all around them, people worked frantically. It was a quiet part of the day, but there were few staff on duty. "You know, he is good looking. Better than Martin. Only you never did tell me what happened between the two of you."

Sadie smiled, and the smile turned into a grin. A few years ago, she would've been only too happy to tell Melissa precisely what had happened. Anything to embarrass an asshole like Martin Walsh. But she'd promised him she wouldn't tell – and besides, she really didn't want anyone to know that she'd been prepared to sleep with the guy.

"Nothing."

"Oh, come on! He wanted it, you wanted it—"

"He wanted it, yeah, and I wanted it," Sadie admitted, "but not from Martin."

"You mean you don't fancy him?"

"He's a good-looking guy, yeah, but he's not my type – too oily. I couldn't trust him. And I'm not looking for a casual fling here, Melissa, in spite of what you think. I want something that's gonna last – something good."

"So Jordan – is he something good?"

"He could be," Sadie said. "I'd really like that."

"I bet you bloody would!"

"He's asked me out to dinner tonight," Sadie said. "And I said yes." Then she remembered about Jodie. "But what about—"

"Forget about Jo, for God's sake, Sadie! Have a good time for once in your life. Jesus, Jo was fine at that party the other night," Melissa assured her. "Okay, so she got a little drunk," she said, raising an eyebrow and looking sheepish, "but I got her home safe and sound, didn't I? And she's still a target for vampires, isn't she?"

Sadie laughed. "Well, I hope so!"

"Just leave her to get on with her life, Sadie," Melissa said. "She's sixteen, for God's sake. She's a young woman, she knows right from wrong, and she's not a fool."

"Yeah, but I keep on remembering what I was like when I was sixteen," Sadie said. "You know, I wasn't a virgin—"

"Sadie, that was common knowledge."

Sadie raised her eyebrows. "You bitch!"

"Come on, we were all like it, weren't we? But Jo, she's different."

"Should I take that as an insult?"

"Well, take it whatever way you like," Melissa said, "but whatever you do, get back to work. The boss is watching us." And with that, she gave a wave to the manager, who'd just come out of the cramped office. "I'll see you at lunchtime, if I don't see you before. And stop slacking, Bartholomew!"

For Sadie, the rest of the day certainly didn't fly by, in spite of the fact that she was pretty busy between eleven and three. She was to go off duty at five, and those last two hours seemed to drag by, each second on the clock that hung by the side of the counter seeming to last a whole minute. Finally, she looked at the clock, and it said five to five – a glance to the rear of the kitchen and she caught Melissa's eye. Melissa came over and the two of them went into the locker room.

"Don't panic. You've got two and a half hours before he turns up."

"Yeah, but getting the stink of this place out of my hair takes ages!"

"Huh, you should try having hair as long as mine!"

"I hope he turns up," Sadie said, remembering that she hadn't given him her address. She contemplated telling a few of the evening shift what her address was in case he turned up here looking for a hint, but again the voice in her head told her that everything was going to be okay. Her guardian angel sure had an authoritarian voice today!

"Of course he will! God, Sadie, I wish I was you!"

"You wish you were me? I don't believe that for a minute," Sadie said, taking off her cap. "You get all the guys drooling all over you – they love you!"

"They don't love me, Sadie, they love my boobs or my legs or my blond hair. The guys I get aren't interested in me. They don't care that I like to read Shakespeare, or that I have this yearning to be an actress, or that I like writing stories."

"Well, Jordan doesn't know much about me," Sadie said sheepishly.

"No, but he will. I'm not insulting you, Sadie, because you've got a great body and you're beautiful ... speaking as a woman, of course." The two of them laughed. "But I've got all these bits that are exactly the right size to attract your average bloke. And we all know how the man's mind works. Childbearing hips, so there'll be no problem in childbirth; good sized breasts so that the baby will be able to feed easily; classical beauty, so the child will be pretty. That's how a man's mind works. It's conditioned to be attracted to all those kinds of things."

"I think you're being very negative."

"Do you know when the last time was that man actually asked me questions that taxed my mind? Or when a man actually asked me what I enjoyed doing? I don't think I can recall, because I don't think I've actually ever been asked those questions. Oh, I've been told, 'You should be a model, love', and all those bullshit lines, but that's hardly the same, is it? It's not even a compliment. It's more like an insult, because they're only doing it to boost their own egos. It's like, 'Hey, look at me, look who I'm shagging!'" Melissa threw open her locker door. "I want to be liked, Sadie, for who I am, not for my tits or my legs or my arse!"

"Wow," Sadie said quietly, as she opened her locker door and pulled out her jacket. "Melissa the feminist."

"Hey, it's not like that, and you know it!"

"You know, I never had you tagged for one of the hairy armpit brigade!"

Melissa took out a box of tampons and tossed a couple at Sadie. "Plug it up, Bartholomew!"

Sadie laughed as she tugged on her jacket. "You know, I'll be glad to get out of these flares," she said. Then she thought about the band, and about the possibilities that were being opened to her and the guys. "Maybe one day I'll get out of them for good."

"What, and get a job at KFC?"

"What do you reckon?" Sadie asked, smiling at her friend's flippancy.

"You mean, do I think you've got what it takes to become a star?" At that, Melissa appeared to consider her next comment carefully. "The band are great, Sadie. I don't go in for all that live music rubbish, but I listen to you guys – and you sound good. I mean, your demo's a bit raw, but the tunes are kicking." She bobbed her head up and down.

"I sense a *but* there."

"*But* – you need a lot of luck, Sadie, and there isn't much of that going around right now, you know."

"Tell me about it," Sadie said soberly. "And that's the problem, ain't it? I need a whole truckload of it, don't I? Well, I suppose I'm getting a truckload of it, but it's all bad luck, not good."

Melissa smiled sympathetically. "You're gonna be all right."

And Sadie had this optimistic feeling deep within her – a feeling that told her everything was going to turn out fine.

She was nervous that Jordan wasn't going to turn up right up until the moment the buzzer went. Jodie, who was closest, answered, and let Jordan into the building. A minute or so later, there was a knock at the door, and Jodie rushed to do the honours, much to Sadie's chagrin, though she knew that it was probably best if she didn't appear too eager. Jordan was one hell of a catch, and she didn't want him to know how desperate she was to reel him in.

As ever, he was gorgeous, dressed in a casual suit with a polo neck top, looking like the archetypal spy that she imagined him to be. Jodie, she noticed, couldn't take her eyes of him. Jordan, thankfully, only had eyes for her.

She'd tried her hardest to get her short hair neat, and she thought that she'd done a pretty good job. She didn't know where they were going for the meal, but she'd presumed it to be somewhere at least mid-priced, and so had dressed accordingly. She wore a knee-length skirt, matching jacket and stiletto heels. She'd thought, as she'd looked in the mirror just minutes earlier, that she looked like Jackie Kennedy – her style was so Sixties, and all she needed to top it off was a shocking pink lipstick and a hat.

Jordan, she could tell, was impressed.

"You look fabulous," he proclaimed.

"Am I dressed appropriately?"

"If anything, you're overdressed," he told her, immediately qualifying it with, "but that's not a bad thing – believe me, that's not a bad thing." He stepped up to her and kissed her lightly on the forehead, and she caught a sniff of his aftershave. It was so intoxicating, her knees almost crumpled beneath her. "I intend to make it up to you," he promised.

"You don't have to," she said. "It's not like we were on a date the other night."

Jordan smiled. "No, but I was impolite, and I won't be letting you down tonight."

"Glad to hear it," Sadie said, grabbing her matching handbag. The whole outfit had cost a fortune a year ago, when the family had money, and had only been worn once. Thankfully, it hadn't yet gone out of fashion. "So, where are we going?"

"Somewhere special," Jordan answered.

"Not McDonald's?" Jodie asked.

In the event, the restaurant certainly was special. Small, but not cramped and certainly exclusive. It was situated in one of the better parts of the city and clearly frequented by those with plenty of disposable income, and very high standards of cuisine. Sadie had never particularly enjoyed meals or dinner engagements, because they were either a phony environment for courting couples, or a phony environment for friends to get to know one another. A dinner party always had one boaster amongst its guests, and the men who'd previously taken her out to dinner usually spent the entire evening 'thrilling' her with their knowledge of French cuisine and fine wines, neither of which interested in her in the slightest. They spoke of money, of business, of fast cars. They never spoke of the little things, of the things that mattered.

Jordan was different

As they stirred their coffees towards the end of the evening, Jordan said, "So, have you heard any news about the band?"

"You mean, has Martin Walsh reared his ugly head again?" Sadie asked, trying to dispel the thought of Martin and his other ugly head from her mind. "Well, Billy – the guitarist in the band – he called me about an hour after I got in from work. Apparently, tomorrow, we've got a studio session booked."

"And Martin's producing?" Jordan asked, sipping his coffee. The liquid must've been boiling, Sadie thought, hiding her frown, and yet Jordan seemed unaffected.

"He does have experience," Sadie said, raising her own cup to her lips. She decided against taking a sip – it was far too hot. Instead, she blew on it, and put the cup back down on the saucer. "And people have said that our last demo was as little rough."

"So, you're gonna re-record a few tracks?"

"A couple." The band had discussed re-recording the demo only fleetingly, and at the most, three of the six tracks were worth a second attempt. But they had fresh material that they wanted to lay down on tape. "Martin sounds keen to get us started."

"I don't wanna come down heavy, Sadie, but you really should watch that guy," Jordan warned her. "He can be dangerous." His dark eyes were looking right at hers now, and she had this bizarre sensation of him reading her mind, as though he knew that she'd almost slept with the man in question. She shifted uncomfortably in her seat. It was the first time she'd felt uneasy in Jordan's presence, and the sensation reminded her of the horrifying nightmare in which he'd had a starring role.

"I'm sorry," Jordan apologized, as though he felt it too. "I'm sticking my nose in where it doesn't belong, aren't I?"

"I appreciate the advice, Jordan," she told him, "but this really is important. I mean, we all know that Martin's a little strange – Jeff told us. He's the guy who owns the Billabong." Jordan nodded as though he were already aware of that fact. "We're gonna be careful. But we have to do this, and Martin seems like our best shot."

"I understand that," Jordan said. "Okay, no more talk of Martin Walsh."

"How about talking about Jordan Weaver for a change?" Sadie asked with a smile that was forced, but genuine. "I still know virtually nothing about you. About your family. Come on, tell me everything."

"Everything?" Jordan asked, raising an eyebrow. "There are some things about me you don't want to know, and if you did, you wouldn't believe anyway."

Sadie frowned – Jordan certainly was a man of mystery, but she wasn't going to let him get away with it too easily. She knew next to nothing about him or his past. For all she knew, he could be an ex-convict, perhaps a killer on the run from the police ...

She pushed that thought aside.

He was too good to be a bad guy.

Jordan took another sip from his cup. "Well, my father was a farmer."

"He owned his own ranch?"

Jordan smiled. "Yeah, he owned his own ranch. He was ... he was quite wealthy."

"You speak of him in the past?"

"He's dead," Jordan said nonchalantly.

"Well, that's something we have in common," Sadie remarked grimly. She couldn't take her eyes off Jordan's lips as he took another sip of coffee. They were red, as though they'd been burned by the steaming drink, but Jordan didn't appear to be suffering any pain.

"Yeah, I guess it is – though my father died a long time ago."

"You were young?"

At that, Jordan seemed a little confused. He nodded his head. "Yeah, I was young – well, younger than I am now. I can barely remember him."

"You miss him?"

"Not anymore," Jordan answered. "I guess memories fade."

"That's sad."

"I didn't mean to upset you."

"You didn't. It's nice to know you're human." Jordan smiled again, and it turned into a grin. "What?" Jordan shook his head. "Jordan?"

"It's nothing, really, it's nothing."

Sadie decided to leave it there. There were so many things she didn't know about Jordan, she just didn't want to come down hard on him, not when she didn't know him very well. Some things were personal, and she couldn't expect him to tell her on their first proper date.

"So that's where the money comes from?"

"My money?"

"Well, you seem to be wealthy."

"We come from the same stock, certainly," Jordan said. "But my money doesn't come from my father. I ... I wasn't in the inheritance."

"You weren't?" Here was another mysterious fact. Had Jordan fallen out with his father before his death?

"My money comes from my job," he went on. "I have unlimited funds at my disposal."

"Unlimited? What kind of job do you do exactly?"

"I can't say, Sadie," Jordan told her. "At least, not now. I know I'm gonna sound like some kind of Walter Mitty, but my job is pretty unbelievable, and I just can't tell anyone about it. In fact, there is no one –

other than the people I work for and the people I work with – who know the nature of my work. It'd probably turn you against me if you knew what I did for a living."

"You work for the Inland Revenue?"

Jordan smiled, but continued. "In all honesty, it could be dangerous for you if I told you."

"You're some kind of spy?" Sadie said sceptically.

"No, I'm not a spy," Jordan replied. "I'm in law – chasing down the bad guys and all that. But that's as much as I can say."

"A bounty hunter, like Boba Fett?"

Jordan smiled again. "Like Boba Fett? No, I'm not a bounty hunter. Listen, can we change the subject?"

"Okay, so what part of the US do you come from?"

Jordan seemed to think about that question for a few moments. Then he said, "St Louis, Missouri."

"Beautiful city."

"I've gotta be honest – I never noticed."

The two of them stared at each other for a few moments, before Sadie felt a smile creeping across her face. "You know, I've got a confession."

"Go on," Jordan said, taking another gulp of coffee. He sounded intrigued.

"The first time I saw you, you were in the Ragamuffin," Sadie went on. "I saw you, and I just couldn't take my eyes off you."

"Well, that's not how I remember it."

Sadie felt her face flush. "You remember it?"

"Of course I do," Jordan said, grinning. "The way I remember it, I was looking at you – you were looking at me. You looked away. As I remember it, I couldn't take my eyes off you."

"I looked again," Sadie said, "but you were gone."

"Yeah," Jordan said with a wince, "I had work to do. But I had to get to know you better. Why do you think I went along to the Billabong to watch your band?"

"You know, I take that as a compliment."

"That's exactly how it was meant. I thought you were incredible."

"Thought?" asked Sadie, raising an eyebrow.

Jordan grinned. "Now I know."

Sadie flushed again. "You're embarrassing me," she said. "You'd better collect the bill and take me home."

"You don't wanna go Dutch?"

For a moment, Sadie was nonplussed – then she realized Jordan was joking. "You're such a gentleman," she said, watching as he signalled for the waiter. He removed his wallet and took out a Platinum American Express card. "You know, you really are wealthy, aren't you?"

"Fabulously," he said. "Hey, you're not only after me for my money, are you?"

"With looks like yours, Jordan, I'd be after you if you were working down the sewers," Sadie told him, all dreamy-eyed. "Where have you been all my life?" The line was cheesy, and she regretted saying it the moment it left her lips, but she couldn't help herself. The three glasses of wine had loosened her personality, and now she knew what she wanted more than anything.

This wouldn't be like it was with Martin. She wouldn't freeze up moments before, because she knew that there genuine reasons for being with Jordan. She liked Jordan, adored him, and she really did want to make love to him. But she didn't want to appear loose.

She rested her chin on her hand and said, "Do you want to come back to mine for coffee?"

Now it was Jordan's turn to raise an eyebrow, which gave him a cheeky appearance. "Are you propositioning me, Miss Bartholomew?"

"Well, I know I shouldn't, but there's something about you that I find irresistible."

Jordan looked away, his expression coy – but he looked like the cat that had got the cream. "I think you'd be doing me a great honour, Sadie, but I don't wanna rush things." Sadie felt momentarily stunned. Was she being turned down? Had she moved too quickly? "That came out wrong," Jordan said quickly. "I meant, I don't wanna rush you ... but I am open to offers."

"You're not rushing me, Jordan. I've been looking at you all night, and there's only one thing that would make this evening complete."

"And that is?"

The waiter returned with the receipt and Jordan's credit card.

The two of them left the restaurant and climbed into Jordan's BMW. Oasis were playing on the CD deck, but Sadie, who was always interested in music, particularly well-crafted tunes, wasn't really listening. She was thinking about their next move. Back to the flat, back to her room, where she would undress Jordan and reveal what she knew had to be the perfect body.

But what if it wasn't? What if he had a flabby belly, held in tight by some William Shatner-esque corset? What if the exterior didn't match up to the interior? She shrugged away those thoughts. She'd slept with a few men, and only one or two of them had possessed finely-honed bodies. The rest had all been average, or less – and it had never put her off before. It wasn't as though she'd ever made love to a sweaty, flabby old man, with stinking whiskers and false teeth.

She didn't really look at the bodies that much. She looked at the faces, at the expressions they made when they were in moments of high ecstasy. That turned her on more than anything. So it didn't really matter what Jordan's body was like, and she shouldn't have been thinking that way.

But what if beneath that expensive, quality-tailored suit, he was horribly disfigured?

Girl, she told herself, you've been out of the market for too long!

Then the next dreadful thought of those unused to casual sex and one-night stands entered her mind. What about her own body? What if it didn't measure up to Jordan's expectations?

Sure, she looked great fully clothed, but she was certainly sagging in a few places. She ate a little bit too much, so she was slightly podgy. Her breasts, though reasonably well-sized, pointed more downwards than upwards. And to top it all, she hadn't managed to outrun the dreaded orange peel on her thighs.

But then, there were few women out there who had the perfect body. That, Sadie assured herself, was fact. It wasn't just her own mind trying to boost her confidence. Women sagged and bloated in places they shouldn't, just as men did. The perfect woman that men drooled over didn't really exist. Everything bad was airbrushed out. The memory of a tale told to her by Billy. He'd told her that an art college friend of his had accepted a job with a porno magazine, and subsequently spent his days not assisting with photo shoots and lusting after leggy, busty girls lying spread-eagled on the bed, but airbrushing away the cellulite and piles in the finished prints. The very thought had been enough to make Sadie spit out her drink, but Billy had sworn that it was true, and she supposed that she had no reason to doubt him, even if he had told her many tales that were so tall, their heads were in the stars.

So Sadie considered herself to be an average woman, in a world which was full of average women. Most men didn't expect anything more. And she suspected Jordan didn't expect anything more. If he had, he would've chosen Melissa over her.

Sadie looked at Jordan, took in his wonderful profile, and felt nothing but passion for him. Having sex with Martin in the front seat of his Porsche did nothing for her – the thought of making love to Jordan here in his BMW aroused her more than she'd ever been aroused before. She reached across the car, and rested a hand on his thigh, feeling the powerful thigh muscles. She could feel them contracting as he used the clutch, and she imagined what it would be like to have all of his muscles contracting beneath her touch as he writhed between her legs.

Jordan turned to her and smiled. "You okay?"

"I'm fine," Sadie said, following it up with, "Well, I'm more than fine."

The rest of the journey passed in silence, with Liam Gallagher singing in the background. Finally, the BMW pulled into the car park and slid up alongside Sadie's Volvo. With that, the engine was silenced, and so was Liam. All that remained were the gentle clicks and ticks as the engine cooled and mechanical parts settled.

Sadie's eyes immediately went up to the windows of the flat, where she could see that no lights were on, which mean that Jodie wasn't up. She could still be awake, but had to be in her own bedroom. Either that, or she was in the front room with all the lights out waiting for Sadie to return. Whatever, Sadie just hoped that her little sister would leave her alone.

She looked at Jordan.

"About that coffee?"

"The offer's still on?"

"Of course," Sadie said, opening the car door and stepping out into the brisk air. Jordan followed, and the two of them made their way to the front entrance of the building. Sadie keyed in the combination, and the door buzzed. She pulled it open and they stepped into the warmth. Jordan followed her closely as they climbed the stairs, and she grabbed his hand as they neared the second floor. In the corridor outside the room, she stopped, and pulled him towards her. He had to bend his neck to reach, but he knew precisely what was on her mind. She kissed him passionately, her hand stroking the back of his neck as her tongue fought a pleasurable battle with his. His hands were lightly touching her, one caressing her shoulder, the fingers of the other dancing daintily across her buttocks, sending tingles of pleasure up her spine to her neck.

"How about we skip the coffee?" Sadie asked him.

Jordan just grinned broadly.

Within a minute, they were inside the flat, inside Sadie's bedroom, and she was peeling off his jacket, running her hands up and down his torso. She began to unbutton his shirt, as he kissed her lightly on the head, and soon his chest was exposed, along with its copious hair. She lightly scratched through the hair with her fingernails, and felt the tight muscles of his chest, before she pushed the shirt from his shoulders. He was everything she'd ever imagined him to be; in good shape, though not to the extreme of being vulgar, like a bodybuilder.

She felt the taut muscles of his arms as she wrestled the shirt from his wrists, and she couldn't help but run her hands along them, feeling the firmness of his biceps. She looked up into his eyes and he smiled at her, and they kissed again. As they did, Jordan removed her jacket, and his fingers found the buttons of her blouse, undoing them in a way that was almost professional, considering that he couldn't see them. For the first time that night, she felt nervous, with her breasts almost exposed, remaining half hidden beneath the frilly material of her Wonderbra. She was about to reveal all this to a man she hardly knew, a man she lusted after like no other man before in her life. She should've been far more embarrassed than she was, but she figured that was part of the excitement.

Speaking of which, she could feel Jordan pressing into her as they embraced. He was cupping her breasts in his hands, as though weighing them – not that they were large enough to require such actions, but the sight of him doing so aroused her even more. She wanted him to throw her down onto the bed and make love to her, but he wasn't about to do that just yet.

She reached up to the front of her bra and undid the fastener. Her breasts dropped slightly as her erect nipples were exposed. Jordan's fingers immediately pounced on them, and he brushed them softly as he kissed the side of her neck, just beneath her ear. Sadie reached down and rubbed his erection through his trousers, feeling its size. She was no expert, but it was impressive all the same. Jordan's hands slipped around to her back and found the button to her skirt. It came open easily beneath his touch, and the skirt quickly began to fall from her waist. Jordan peeled it over her hips and it fell to the floor with a soft hiss. Sadie shrugged off her bra and realized with a thrilling shock that she was now standing before Jordan wearing only her very brief panties. And Jordan's cock was pressing against them, straining against the front of his trousers.

So Sadie did the decent thing and undid them, peeling open the zip and letting them fall to the floor. Jordan stepped out of them, and Sadie chose that moment to look down. He stood before her now wearing a pair of tight trunks beneath which his penis jutted. Sadie didn't hesitate. She dropped to her knees and pulled his trunks down, freeing his engorged cock. As Jordan stepped out of the trunks, the massive organ bounced up and down just inches from her face, and Sadie found herself unable to resist seizing it, feeling its heat as she rolled back his foreskin.

It was probably nine inches in length, and thicker than any she'd ever seen before. The head was an angry purple colour, pulsating beneath her grip, and she responded by slowly jerking him off. She felt Jordan's hands lightly gripping her head, and she knew precisely what he wanted.

She had to open her mouth wide, but she managed to get his cock inside, her tongue lapping the underside of his glans. She considered herself to be quite adept at blowjobs – on the whole, she could make a man cum within a couple of minutes, just by using her tongue. Occasionally, it would take longer, but there was nothing wrong with that. She would just use her hand to jerk her lover at the same time. As she did now, slowly and rhythmically pulling his foreskin back and forth, while at the same time using her tongue on him. Jordan responded by running his hands through her hair.

She continued sucking him for a couple of minutes, before Jordan pulled her head away. He didn't want to come – and Sadie didn't want him to come either. Not yet. She wanted to feel him forcing his way inside her, his huge cock splitting her apart. As she stood up, she could taste the pre-cum, and thought that this wasn't going to last very long.

She was wrong.

Jordan lifted her onto the bed and tugged off her panties in one swift movement, exposing the thin line of pubic hair. He pulled apart her thighs and probed her with his fingers, which slipped easily inside her moist pussy. He was preparing her for the onslaught that would come when he finally mounted her – Sadie knew that it was going to hurt, but it would be pain mingled with pleasure, and she wanted him inside her as quickly as possible.

But Jordan wasn't about to rush things.

He got his knees and thrust his mouth against her pussy, his tongue working on her as hers had moments earlier worked on him. She could only take so much, because she wanted her orgasm to come when he was inside her. She pulled him up and soon he was laying on top of her, supporting his weight with his elbows. They kissed passionately, and Sadie could feel his cock throbbing against her belly like a dog straining at the leash. She could wait no longer.

Her hands reached down, and she guided him to her wet entrance.

He entered her, slipping inside slowly, until his cock filled her up and he could push no further. It hadn't hurt as much as she was expecting it to, and Sadie urged Jordan on by gripping his buttocks. They tensed beneath her, and then he began to slide in and out, slowly and gently at first, because he had to know that his cock was larger than normal, and liable to be uncomfortable for most women.

Sadie heard herself moan, and thought about Jodie lying in her own bed just a few feet away. She didn't like the idea of her sister listening to her having sex, but Jordan's technique was too wonderful for her to consider restrained modesty. Soon, she was moaning loudly with each thrust, and urging Jordan on by whispering in his ear.

"Fuck me," she muttered under her breath. Jordan obliged by speeding up his actions.

"Like that?" he asked breathlessly.

"Yes," Sadie groaned. "Oh yes, fuck me hard, Jordan – fuck me harder!" Jordan acquiesced to her command, and began pounding her violently. Sadie was vaguely aware of the bed springs squeaking beneath her, and she also considered the fact that Jordan wasn't using a condom. Prior to that moment, the risks involved hadn't entered her mind. Now, she found that she couldn't think of anything else.

She reached up and held Jordan's face between her hands, pushing him away. "Wait," she said breathlessly, and he stopped. They bounced a couple more times as the mattress rocked with the momentum of their lovemaking, and she smiled at Jordan. "I don't want to ruin the moment," she said, "God, I really don't wanna ruin the moment, but you're not wearing a condom."

Jordan raised an eyebrow, then said, "Hey, I'm sorry – I got carried away. I didn't think." He began to pull out, but Sadie stopped him.

"Wait," she said. She could feel his powerful cock twitching inside her. "I don't want you to think, you know, that I'm some kinda tease."

Jordan smiled and pulled out, which made Sadie's stomach contract. "That's okay," he said. "I understand. There are other ways we can enjoy ourselves."

"You don't have a condom on you?"

"Do you?" Jordan asked her. She shook her head. "I guess neither of us are the type of people who expect casual sex to come knocking at our doors on a daily basis."

"You can say that again!"

Jordan got to his knees, and Sadie caught sight of his cock again. It was huge, throbbing and bobbing before her like a python. It glistened as the dampness from her pussy caught the light.

Jordan grinned at her, then dipped his head between her legs again. He didn't say another word, but his tongue did a lot of talking. Sadie glanced down at him. She wanted to come. She needed to come. She watched as Jordan's eyes traced their way up her body, from her pubic hair, up her belly, to the shallow valley between her breasts. Finally, they locked onto her eyes, and as they did, Sadie felt the onset of an orgasm, and felt her face grimace. She called out his name softly, and then threw her head back into the pillow as the muscles in her thighs contracted.

The orgasm was intense, like nothing she'd ever experienced before, and lasted longer than any she could remember. Every muscle in her body contracted, and her legs shuddered violently.

"Oh shit," she groaned as the orgasm reached its climax and quickly subsided. "Fuck!"

She pushed Jordan's head away and snapped her legs together. Her entire body was quivering, as though she'd exerted herself, and she felt so out of breath, in spite of the fact that she'd just laid there as Jordan had done all of the work.

Jordan came up to meet her, and she smelled herself on his face. But in spite of the fact that she'd just climaxed, that turned her on. So much so that she reached down and gripped his cock. It had softened slightly, but still felt huge. She couldn't get her fingers around it. She began to slowly masturbate him.

"Was it good?" Jordan asked her. He looked so meek, so vulnerable, like a child seeking a parent's approval.

Sadie said, "My God, of course it was! I won't ask you where you learnt that technique. It'd only make me jealous."

"Well, it's nice to know I satisfied you."

"You, Jordan Weaver, are like a dream come true," Sadie said. "I only wish I could live up to you."

"Believe me, you're worth a hundred of me."

"You're just softening me up, aren't you?"

"Now, why would I do that?" Jordan asked.

Sadie smiled and tugged on his cock. "Sit next to me," she said. Jordan did, and Sadie immediately went down on him, sucking him into her mouth. She could smell and taste her juices on him – she'd tasted them before, on other men, and in a way it aroused her, though she'd never admit it, not to anyone. But this was Jordan's turn to enjoy himself.

She worked quickly, licking the underside of the tip of his penis, gripping the base with her left hand while her right quickly jerked him. She remembered that she hadn't told him to warn her when he was about to come, but considered the possibility that Jordan was too much of a gentleman to come in her mouth without first telling her.

Jordan began to groan, muttering under his breath, "Fuck, that feels good, don't stop – don't stop."

Sadie had no intention of stopping, even if it meant taking a mouthful of his cum, although that wasn't something she really wanted to do. She'd only ever swallowed one guy's cum, and he'd been someone she'd known for a couple of years. Much as she lusted after Jordan, she'd only known him for a few days. Hell, she'd only ever been on one date with him, and this was it. She wasn't ready to get that intimate, not with the risks involved in today's society.

But Jordan was, as she'd suspected, too much of a gentleman.

He pulled her head away and gapsed, "I'm coming."

Sadie closed her mouth and contined to jerk him off, his cock just a few inches from her face. It jerked violently in her hand, and the first stream of cum shot out, hitting her cheek. It felt hot, as though it had been stored in a furnace. More squirts erupted from his cock, and thick, lumpy wads of cum hit her face, spreading across her forehead, in her hair, up her nose and across her lips. Still Jordan's cock twitched, and more and more spurted out, coating her chin and her cheek, and dripping down onto the bed.

Finally, the squirts became less fruitful, and Jordan dropped down onto the bed, fully satiated, gasping noisily like only a man totally pleasured could.

Sadie felt the cum cooling on her face, and arched a damp eyebrow as Jordan looked down at her.

"Sorry," he said.

"I take it it's been a long time for you?" Sadie asked, grabbing the quilt and wiping the cum from her lips.

Jordan said, "You wouldn't believe how long it's been."

And Sadie laughed.

18

Sadie awoke to feel the wind blowing across her body. The quilt was wrapped around only a portion of her flesh, the rest exposed, covered in a thin layer of perspiration, which was evaporating in the draught from the open window. She'd slept fitfully, waking numerous times with memories of bad dreams. Jordan featured in most of them, and in all of them, somebody close to her had died. It was like her mind was warning her against associating with Jordan, as though her subconscious knew something she didn't.

But Sadie didn't believe in sixth senses. Her mind was disturbed, certainly, but she had been through a lot recently. The death of her parents, the loss of her home, the bizarre attempted sexual assault by Martin. She reminded herself, that wasn't actually a sexual assault. She'd been a willing, if slightly reluctant, participant. And it had all culminated in this meeting with a man who was handsome, kind and warm. A man who was too good to be true.

Perhaps, she wondered, that was why she felt so spooked by him, why her dreams were so vividly horrific.

She rolled over and threw an arm over Jordan's bare chest, her fingers tracing a path through the hair.

Then she frowned.

He was cold.

Well, it *was* cold in the room, but not that cold.

She propped herself up on an elbow and looked down at his face. His eyes were shut, his complexion somewhat pallid. She looked at his chest. It wasn't rising or falling.

Jordan wasn't breathing.

She felt her own heart rate increase, and pressed a hand to Jordan's neck. It felt icy cold to touch.

She'd been sleeping next to a corpse.

"Fuck," she said quietly. The word wouldn't come out any louder. "Fuck ... Jordan." She shook him, but her common sense was telling her that Jordan was dead. "Jordan!" she said more loudly.

And Jordan's eyes opened, rolling in his head momentarily before scanning the room and falling upon Sadie. At that instant, the heat also returned to Jordan's body, the change so drastic that it almost felt as though her hand had been burnt. She instinctively withdrew it.

"Sadie?"

"Jesus," Sadie said, her voice trembling. "Jesus, I thought ..."

Jordan sat up and put a hand on her shoulder. "You thought what?"

"Nothing," Sadie said, wiping away tears that had formed in the corners of her eyes. She could hardly tell him what she had thought. It would make her sound neurotic.

But then, he *had* been cold, hadn't he? Freezing. And he hadn't been breathing.

No, that was just ridiculous.

It was cold in the room, and as for the breathing, well, he was obviously breathing lightly. That was it. Nothing more to it than that. It was just the dreams – the nightmares – that had her spooked. That was all.

"Hey, what's wrong?" Jordan asked her. "You're shaking."

"A bad dream," she told him. It wasn't exactly a lie.

"You know, dreams are just that," Jordan said. "Not real. Nothing to worry about." His hand was running through her hair, straightening it, sending shivers of pleasure down her spine. She recalled the lovemaking that had taken place the night before, and closed her eyes. It had been passionate, exquisite, and she wanted more.

But she had to get up.

"You know, I'm gonna miss you," Jordan said suddenly.

"Miss me?"

"Well, you're going to the studio, ain't you?"

"The demo," Sadie said with a nod. "It has to be done, much as I'd like to stay here and have wild, passionate sex with you."

"Well, nice to know that I pleased you."

Sadie leant over and kissed Jordan firmly on the lips. It quickly transformed into a kiss of passion, but she broke away before it became too involved. "You're the best, Jordan."

"You're not bad yourself Sadie."

Sadie slipped out of bed, aware that she was naked and fully exposed to a man she felt she loved but barely knew. She felt a burning between her legs, a soreness that only came from being with a well-endowed man, and the thought entered her head that she'd taken one hell of a risk. Not with pregnancy, because she was on the pill – a precautionary measure, but merely a back-up to the other methods she usually adopted – but with AIDS, or indeed one of the less serious but nevertheless nasty STDs. She didn't know Jordan or his true background, she had no idea whether or not he'd been promiscuous, dabbled in drugs or loose gay sex, whether he was clean or dirty. She'd seen nothing crawling around him last night, and there had been no open sores on his penis, but that didn't matter. Some STDs remained hidden until they were revealed in ways that were not always attributed to sex.

She shrugged off that feeling and turned to look at Jordan.

His eyes were lingering on her body, and she felt awfully exposed and vulnerable. He, on the other hand, was partially hidden beneath the quilt. Eventually, his eyes moved from her lower body to her breasts, and then her face.

"Sorry," he said.

"Things always look different in daylight," she said.

"Better – not that I thought it could get any better."

"Have you got a gun under that quilt or are you just pleased to see me?" Sadie asked him. She couldn't actually see whether or not he was aroused, but she hoped that he was.

He pulled back the quilt in a smooth way that reminded her of a Chippendale and made her smile. She saw him standing to attention. Just as quickly, he pulled the quilt over himself again, his face reddening, clearly embarrassed by the fact that she'd smiled.

"I guess we're on an even keel now," Sadie said, pulling on her dressing gown.

"Maybe I shouldn't have done that," he said. "I feel like some kind of flasher."

"Hey, it's a way of breaking the ice," Sadie assured him. "Get naked, and all the borders get taken down. We're just a pair of nudists with nothing to hide."

"Yeah, but it's different for guys," Jordan reminded her. "If I'm horny, it shows. If you're horny, you can hide it."

"Yeah, but look what women have to put up with. Periods, pregnancy, childbirth, menopause, not to mention sexism. I'd trade all of that for an impromptu hard-on every now and again."

"Spoken with the ignorance of womanhood!"

"I never had you pegged as some kind of misogynist," Sadie remarked with a grin. She went to the door. "I've gotta take a shower. You have a lie-in."

"You're saying I need my beauty sleep?"

"After last night, Jordan, I need the sleep, so I'm sure you do too!"

And with that, Sadie left the bedroom.

An hour later, after kissing Jordan goodbye, she was parking her Volvo around the back of the recording studio. Martin's Porsche, no doubt the recent recipient of an interior valet, was parked close to the rear entrance. She saw the band's van, the only way to transport their equipment, parked alongside, the battered green Transit lowering the tone of the car park.

Sadie, dressed casually in jeans and an old tee-shirt, walked up to the rear entrance and pushed the intercom buzzer. A bored-sounding receptionist asked her what she wanted.

"I'm here with Martin Walsh and the band," Sadie told her.

The receptionist buzzed the door, and Sadie stepped into a dingy corridor and made her way along it to a door at the end. Through that, she found herself in the reception area, with a view that looked out onto the street. The bored receptionist sat at a desk, fingers tapping away at a keyboard, her eyes fixed on the VDU in front of her.

The decor of the reception was somewhat more sumptuous than the corridor that had preceded it. Silver, gold and platinum discs adorned the walls, which were painted a light shade of red, along with large framed prints of personalities who had laid down tracks in the studio. Sadie recognized a couple of them, but Martin was present in virtually all of them. As the studio's resident producer, that was only to be expected, although she doubted that he'd worked with every artist who had passed through the doors.

Three two-seater sofas, a brilliant orange in colour, were placed alongside the walls, and a wide coffee table in the centre of the room housed numerous music, film and art magazines. From invisible speakers, an RnB tune was being piped, inoffensive, soothing even, but instantly forgettable.

Sadie stepped up to the receptionist's desk and waited for her to look up. "Can I help you?" she asked when she eventually tore her eyes from the VDU.

"I'm with the band," Sadie said in a tone that implied she'd already told the girl once. "They're expecting me."

"Which band?"

"Darcy's Box," Sadie said. "We're working with Martin Walsh."

"I'll let him know you're here," the receptionist said, picking up the phone. Within a minute, she was being escorted into the studio by the girl. Martin, it appeared, had sent a rocket up her ass.

"Sorry I'm late," Sadie said.

Martin shook her apology away with a limp hand. "We're just getting started," he said. "And not to be insulting, but at the moment, you're the least important member of the band."

Sadie raised an eyebrow. "Well, I'll get the coffees, shall I?"

"We have people to do that," Martin said seriously, watching as Davey rigged up his drum kit. He nodded to the receptionist, who disappeared. "Well, now you're all here, have you decided on a playlist?"

Billy answered for them, handing over a sheet of paper. "Two new tracks, three from the old demo."

Martin read the titles. "Not bad, but how about dropping '*Welcome To Your Life*'?" All eyes turned to Mark, whose expression told everyone he wasn't impressed by the suggestion. "Believe me, it's been surpassed by '*Serious Hell*' as the song everyone remembers you by."

"That song's my baby, man," Mark snapped. "We play it."

Martin shrugged indifferently. "Fine, but how about doing '*Two*

Tears For You' as well?"

Mark wasn't taken in. "You wanted a five-track demo," he said. "And you're asking us to lay down six tracks. I'm not stupid."

"Let's just try it. It can't hurt. We'll have a debate afterwards and see which track is the weakest."

"Hey, you're not our manager."

"No, I'm your producer," Martin said, making his way to the studio door. "And believe me, Mark, I have a lot more experience in this business than you do." And with that, he left and made his way to the control room.

"Yeah?" Mark muttered quietly. "Then how come you haven't had any fucking hits, arsehole?"

Billy said, "Hey, cool it, dude. Let's just get on with it. Time is money, as they say."

Mark scowled. "Fuck this shit, man."

"Hey, this means a lot to us, Mark," Sadie said from her spot at the microphone. "Don't fuck it up for us."

"People," Davey said from the rear of the studio. "I think we need to lighten up." And with that, he started drumming, tapping his sticks on the rim of his snare. It took a few seconds to register, but Sadie finally realized what it was. And it wasn't the first time the band had played it.

"Fucking '*Antmusic*'," Billy said incredulously. "Oh man, I don't fucking believe it!" And with that, he chipped in with his guitar, as did Mark. Which left Sadie as the odd person out – unless she started singing.

Which she did.

Martin, she could see, was pulling his hair out, but there was nothing he could do. The band were revolting, and he just had to wait the full three and a half minutes of the 1980s tune before he could cut them off.

"Very funny, guys," his voice boomed from the speaker. "Now, let's just get on with it, for fuck's sake. Time is money here. You're playing with the big boys. And Suede want the studio in five hours."

"What, this studio?" Davey asked, looking around. It's a bit small for a band like them, ain't it?"

"No," Martin said. "They want the whole fucking building. Now, get your arses moving, and play me something we can lay down on tape!"

Sadie smiled.

She couldn't help it.

In spite of the bickering, the band got on with the business when it was required of them. Even Mark wasn't so much of a pain in the ass when they were working.

And that's what they did for the next four hours, laying down the tracks, overdubbing, re-recording, until they had six perfect tunes.

"Seven," Martin told them in the control room afterwards. "Against my better judgement, we recorded '*Antmusic*'."

"Cool," Davey said. It was his favourite tune, probably because the drums were the key instrument.

"Now, we listen to them, decide on five, and keep the other two on ice," Martin said. "Either that, or ditch them completely. But if this comes off, you can always use them as B-sides. I mean, this isn't some tin pot little studio, guys. These tracks are CD quality. If you crack the big time, you don't even have to re-record the tracks. Just use these ones. Of course, the chances are that the big labels will have you back in the studio to perfect them, probably without any intervention from me, but hey, that's show business."

"It begs the question, why are you doing this?" Sadie asked laconically. Mark nodded his head enthusiastically. He still hadn't lost his initial suspicion of Martin Walsh. The producer flopped down in a comfortable leather chair, alongside the sound engineer.

"Do you hear these guys?" he asked the bearded technician. "I mean, it's incredible, ain't it? I offer to help them, and they practically throw it back in my face!" He let out a laugh. "Listen, boys and girls, it's like this. If you guys hit the big time – and I've got this sneaking suspicion that, with my help of course, you will do – if that happens, then it also gets my name in the papers, now doesn't it? We all profit. Put it this way, I'm not just in this to make you guys famous. I'm in it for myself." He pointed to the engineer, then to the deck. "Play them the tracks, Eddie."

The sound engineer obliged.

And after listening to herself singing, and the rest of the band playing, Sadie realized that they were good. Very good. She'd only ever heard the third-rate demo, only ever seen poor quality video footage and even poorer quality mono sound of their gigs. But this was something else.

Martin put his hands behind his head and smirked.

"Sounds great, now doesn't it?" He looked at Mark, who cracked open a can of Carling.

"It makes us sound ..."

"It makes you sound tight," Martin told him. "It makes you sound more like a real band. The overdubs we did, they're in the right place, they're not too flash. Face it, you guys needed to be produced, and by somebody who knows what he's doing."

"Well, you're modest, Martin," Billy remarked, grabbing a Carling from the fridge in the corner of the room. "I'll say that for you."

"I've turned you guys from a pub band into a class act," Martin said immodestly. "Radio One material, that is. That could be sold in HMV, and nobody would know that you guys didn't have hundreds of thousands of pounds worth of production shit going on in the background."

"I hate to admit it," Mark said, "but it is good."

"So," Martin said, cocking an eyebrow. "Which tracks do we drop?"

And with that, the argument began.

And Sadie could only roll her eyes and leave it up to the boys.

Twenty minutes later, and two tracks had been dropped, both of them the tracks Martin hadn't particularly liked, which was no surprise. Martin shook all of their hands and told them were on the road to stardom.

Sadie wanted to believe him, but couldn't shake off the conman image she had built for him.

Then Martin said, "I wanna invite you guys to another party. Tonight. Bring a guest each, if you like. Christ, bring two. But I wanna show you off. There are gonna be a couple of bigwigs there, and I might be able to flash them a copy of the demo – the new and improved demo."

The boys immediately agreed, but Sadie wasn't so sure.

As they were leaving the studio, Martin stopped her.

"Can I have a word – in private?"

Fortunately, the only person to see or hear that brief exchange was the receptionist, and she acted as though she didn't care. She probably didn't for real.

Martin led her into an office – one with a glass wall through which Sadie could reassuringly see the receptionist.

"About the other night," Martin said. Sadie sighed. She didn't want to be reminded. "I was high, I really didn't know what I was doing. I'm sorry, Sadie. Really, really sorry."

"Me too."

"It was unprofessional of me," he went on. "I took advantage, maybe, I dunno, perhaps you felt compelled to go along with it. But in the cold light of day, I realize that I made a mistake. I mean, even if you had been completely willing, it should never have happened." He rubbed his face with his hands. "Can we forget about it? Put it all behind us?"

"I'm all for that," Sadie said blandly. She hadn't wanted to be reminded, and she just wanted to get out of this office. After the high of the recording session, this was a definite low. She just wanted to tell him to shut the fuck up, but she couldn't.

"I have to go," she said, making for the door.

"You will come to the party, won't you?"

"I don't know."

"Bring your sister and your friend, Melissa. I'll stay out of your way, I promise. Until I introduce you to the VIPs."

"I don't know, Martin."

"This will be important, Sadie," Martin said. "I promise you that. I'm not saying it'd be the end of the road, because it probably wouldn't, but it would get things moving more quickly. Please?"

Sadie came to the conclusion that Darcy's Box were probably a bigger lifeline to Martin than he was to the band. This was probably his last big chance of success, after his recent flops.

She nodded her head. "I'll be there. But I won't be stopping late."

"I appreciate it, Sadie, I really do," Martin said, the relief evident in his voice and on his face. "And let's keep everything business-like in future." He held out a hand, and after a short pause, Sadie shook it. "Thank you."

Sadie smiled tightly.

And as she left the studio, she wondered why she'd let Martin talk her into doing something she didn't want to do – again.

It was as though some hidden force was driving him, as though he held some kind of power over those around him. But then, Sadie thought as she fired up the Volvo's engine to the sound of Robbie Williams singing from the stereo, he was just good at his job. His job was to produce great work that could sell itself, but in some cases, a harder sell was required.

And Martin Walsh could sell sand to the fucking Arabs.

Next thing on her list of problems, however, was how to explain this to Jordan.

Because it was apparent Jordan didn't like Martin.

19

As she drove to the party, Sadie reflected on the fact that Jordan hadn't actually argued with her over her plans for that evening. He wasn't happy, that much was obvious, but he'd explained to her that this was her life, and that she had a right to choose what she wanted to do with it. But he'd followed it up with another warning that she shouldn't trust Martin Walsh. And when he'd said that, a shiver had run down her spine, because it was as though he knew precisely what had gone on between the two of them.

That eerie thought remained with her as she pulled into a parking space in the street close to Martin's house. She turned and looked at Jodie, who once again looked a lot older than the age on her birth certificate, and she once more felt a twinge of guilt. Jodie should've been at home studying, or listening to a CD of the latest boy band. She shouldn't have been coming to an adult party, where all manner of illicit substances were being taken, where sex was portrayed even more overtly than in an 18-certificate film.

"I'm sorry," she heard herself saying.

Jodie just frowned as she adjusted the front of her low-cut dress. "For what?"

"For dragging you here with me," Sadie said. It was like the mother who sat her child in front of the TV all day long – great for keeping the peace, but lousy on the guilt trip. She didn't want to leave Jodie at home all alone, because would've depressed her. And she didn't want to stay at home with Jodie, because that would've restricted her own social life. So she brought Jodie out with her, to places where sixteen-year-old girls should not have been taken, just to make things easy for herself.

She was being selfish.

Jodie, on the other hand, didn't see it like that. She thought it was great.

And she said that to Sadie. "Hey, I wanna be here, Say."

"Yeah, I kinda thought you would," Sadie said, opening the door. "Remember what I said – watch what you're doing, and be careful who you talk to."

"I'm not a kid," Jodie snapped indignantly.

"Oh, but you are, and the major problem is, you don't look it." Sadie smiled. "All I'm saying is, Jo, just don't do anything stupid. I don't wanna be watching you all the time we're here. I want you to have a good time, and you can't do that with me looking over your shoulder all the while. So just be careful and don't be stupid."

Jodie's face broke into a smile. "I know that's what you mean, and I'm sorry for having a go."

"Hey, you're a kid and that's what kids do – they overreact! I know, because I was a kid just a few years ago. I can still remember, okay? I'm not old and decrepit, like ..." She was going to say, *'Like mom and dad'*, but then the memory hit her, as hard a punch to the head.

Jodie caught the pregnant pause.

"Come on," she said, grabbing Sadie's hand and squeezing it. "Let's go enjoy ourselves. I want to have a famous sister with lots of money, and you're the only sister I've got." Sadie smiled back at her little sister, and realized that sometimes she could be more adult than she gave her credit for.

"You've grown up so much, haven't you?" she remarked. "I don't seem to have realized that." That much was true – and so was the fact that teenagers nowadays were so much more mature and advanced than they had been when Sadie had been the same age.

It made her feel so old.

"You'll always be my sister, Sadie," Jodie said, and the two girls embraced.

They walked up to the house, Sadie noting that the party was as rowdy as the previous one they'd been to. Melissa, unfortunately, couldn't come. A prior engagement, she'd told Sadie over the phone, which essentially meant that she had a date. She'd tell Sadie all about it the next time they met, that was for sure. So the two sisters entered the house by themselves, to be greeted by three drugged-up dancers, one of them a girl, her blouse open to reveal her pendulous breasts, which she proudly held and threw up and down, giggling loudly.

Jodie was shaking her head, and Sadie could only smile. Some people, she reflected, had started their celebrations early. At that moment, Martin sauntered up to them, pushing one of the boys aside.

"Sorry about that," he said, a frown on his face.

"We're a little late," Sadie said. "Sorry."

"Don't worry. There are a few people I'd like you to meet. The boys are already here. Do you mind?"

"No," Sadie said, turning to Jodie.

Jodie shrugged. "This sounds like boring business. I'll go and enjoy myself."

"Be careful," Sadie warned her, and then watched as her sister disappeared into the front room.

Martin put an arm on her shoulder. "Don't worry about her. There might be some nutters here, but they're all harmless. Besides, she looks as though she's got her head screwed on all right."

"Oh yeah," Sadie sighed, "she's very mature for her age."

But she couldn't hide the disconcerting feeling. It was as though someone was telling her to watch out for her kid sister, because something was going to happen. The feeling sent a shudder, which started right at the base of her spine and travelled slowly up to the nape of her neck, which didn't go unnoticed by Martin.

"You okay?" There was concern in his voice.

"Fine," Sadie replied. "Somebody just walked over my grave, is all."

"Well, let's get you known by the big boys," Martin said, leading her to the rear of the house, doubtless to a quiet corner. As she left the hallway, Sadie looked at the doorway leading into the front room. She could see the flashing strobe light effect, the dancers caught in stop-motion poses, but she couldn't pick out Jodie.

And the uneasy feeling didn't go away.

Jodie felt as though she'd been let off the leash, and that was great. She didn't like to think about the fact that her parents were dead, but when they'd been alive, her life had been so restricted. She couldn't go out partying, because her father wouldn't let her. He was never keen on her having boyfriends, although she could count them on the fingers of one hand, and that made any love life very difficult. She wasn't a wild child by any stretch of the imagination. She was just a teenager, she wanted to have fun, wanted to party with her friends, wanted to get off with boys, didn't want to take things too seriously.

In the past, the future didn't seem to matter. Her father was wealthy, she didn't really have to think about work, particularly as she would most probably meet some upper-middle-class boy with a position on the board of his daddy's company, and therefore what was the point in working hard at school?

Now, she thought as she sipped on the vodka and orange some guy had fixed for her, the future didn't seem so laid out for her. There was no money to support her, and her social status had taken a nose-dive as a result, hence the real reason she didn't want to return to school. Her 'friends' didn't really want to know her anymore, because mummy wasn't taking her to school in the Jaguar. She wasn't living in a mansion in an affluent part of town – she was living in an apartment. No, she corrected herself, apartment was Americano, and she was living in the UK. And in the UK, apartment implied wealth. No, she wasn't living in an apartment; she was living in a goddamned flat. A grody fucking flat, for Christ's sake!

She took another sip from the vodka.

She couldn't blame Sadie, because it wasn't her fault at all. It was their father's fault, because he was the one who'd broken the law. And she couldn't forgive him for that, for ruining her life. He'd done it to her when he was alive, and now he was still doing it from the grave.

Bastard.

He'd always been a bastard, she thought bitterly as she took another swig of the vodka.

What the hell was she doing? She was supposed to be enjoying herself, and here she was, badmouthing the dead and crying into her drink. She put the glass down on a table and made a move for the dance floor.

A man stepped in front of her.

"Hi," he said with a smile. It wasn't the greatest chat-up line, but when she looked at him, she knew that didn't really matter.

He was tall, black, wearing a tight teeshirt that showed off his finely honed body to perfection. His features were chiselled, handsome, and his dark hair neatly styled. His eyes were dark, and immediately drew her own to them. When he flashed her his smile, she was immediately won over.

"Hi," she said back, her eyes blinking coyly.

"I'm Theo," he said, thrusting out a hand, which Jodie felt compelled to shake.

"Jodie."

"You're American?"

"I've lived in the UK for longer," she assured him.

"Really? Listen, can I get you a drink?"

"I've just finished one."

"This is a party," Theo reminded her. "Come on. Let's go somewhere a little less noisy. I want you to tell me all about yourself." Jodie smiled. She wasn't too sure what Theo was suggesting, but she was certain she didn't want to pay a visit to one of the house's bedrooms with him. She considered herself to be mature, but not *that* mature, and she wanted to have fun, but not *that* much fun.

"We could try the dining room," she said.

Theo nodded. "Stay here. I'll go and get you a drink. What do you want?"

"Vodka and orange." She watched as he walked across the impromptu dance floor, nodding to a few people, patting others on the back. Whoever he was, he was well known by everyone, and that meant it was probably a good idea for Jodie to get to know him too. She smiled as she considered her life at that moment. Okay, so a few weeks ago, she'd had friends, lots of friends, because she'd been one of the in-crowd. And she'd been able to grab her fun in quite a few places. But it was nothing like this.

Her old friends were studying hard for their GCSEs, and in between all of that, they were partying. But they were just kids. They did childish things. They got drunk, got off with as many boys as they could, and they returned home. Mummy and daddy didn't really care, because the wild behaviour of their daughters wouldn't bring down the family business or get daddy fired from his city job.

But the parties were just kids' parties – that was all. Everyone was a kid, the boys acting immature as usual, while trying desperately to be men, and the girls holding their glasses of champagne and their cigarettes as though they'd been doing it all their lives.

This was different, Jodie thought to herself. There wasn't another kid in sight. Everyone, it seemed, was at least in their late teens, or even their twenties. Some were older. The younger ones were dancing, drinking, rolling around; the older ones stood in quiet corners, talking business, unconcerned with their rowdier fellow guests.

It made her feel so adult, so much superior to her friends.

This was a showbiz party!

Theo returned with her drink, and the two of them stepped into the large dining room. Once again, there was a buffet on the table, along with other, as yet unopened, bottles of liquor and beer. They found a seat in a corner of the room, and sat down, Jodie thankful for the lull in the noise from the other room.

Theo broke the silence. "So how'd you manage to get an invite here?"

Jodie shrugged. "I came with my sister."

"Your sister?"

"Yeah, we're very close." She wasn't about to reveal the difference in age between them. She took a sip from the vodka. "What about you?"

"I'm a friend of Martin's," Theo explained. "We go back a long way."

"You're in the music business?"

Theo laughed. "No, darling, not the music business. I guess you could say I'm in the entertainment business, because I move through all the elements of showbiz. Music, TV, films ... even sport, if you can call sport showbiz. I suppose it is, though, isn't it?"

"So you know plenty of famous people?"

"Lots," Theo said, raising his eyebrows. "Course, I'd never divulge names. That wouldn't be wise, not in my line of work."

"Which is?"

"I provide recreational facilities for the rich and famous."

"Which means?"

"Listen, enough talk about me, darling," Theo said. "So, your sister

– she knows Martin, does she?"

"She's the singer in a band," Jodie explained, undaunted by Theo's reluctance to answer her question. "Martin's just produced a demo for them."

"Your sister's the singer with Darcy's Box?"

"You've heard of them?" Jodie was surprised.

"Like I said, I mix with these people," Theo answered. "I see things, hear things ..." He took a sip from his drink. "Maybe one day I'll be providing services for your sister's band."

"Well, it depends. You still haven't said what kind of services you provide."

Theo smiled and looked around the dining room, where a dozen other partygoers were sitting, having a time-out from the makeshift dance hall in the next room. "You see, these people – okay, they're probably having fun, but they could be having a whole lot more fun."

Jodie was beginning to catch on. "I see," she said, more maturely than she would've expected. "You sell drugs?" She asked the question cautiously.

"I sell recreational products," Theo said. The euphemism didn't make it sound any more impressive.

"Drugs?"

"People want to have a good time. I'm not hurting anyone."

"But people die of drug overdoses."

"You're a very intelligent girl," Theo said, "but you're misguided. Only fools die of overdoses. I don't sell to fools. I supply quality products to discerning customers. I couldn't afford to sell any old crap. It has to be good stuff."

Jodie frowned. She'd chosen the wrong person to speak to here. Okay, so she was occasionally wild, but sex and drugs were something she let other people do. There were safer ways of enjoying yourself, and she would never entertain the thought of doing drugs.

"You're prejudging, without having all the facts, Jodie," Theo went on. "I'm a supplier, not a pusher. I only supply to those who want it. And take a look in that room there," he added. "All those dancers, they look like they're having a great time, don't they?"

Jodie raised an eyebrow. The people dancing in the other room certainly seemed to be enjoying themselves, but she doubted whether Theo could take all the credit. For sure, some had their experiences enhanced by the use of narcotics, but not all.

"You don't believe me, do you?"

"Hey, if people want to do drugs, that's their business," Jodie said, shrugging indifferently. She took a sip from her vodka. The drink certainly was going to her head. Already, she felt dizzy, slightly confused. "I'm not about to stand in judgement."

"But you're not interested in doing drugs yourself? For recreational purposes? I'm not talking about getting hooked on smack or crack. I'm talking ecstasy, coke, weed. The softer stuff."

"Well, coke isn't exactly soft, is it?" Jodie said.

"Well, it can fuck you up, sure, if taken excessively. But the people here, the people I supply, they do a few lines maybe once or twice a week at most. They don't start clucking if they don't get a fix, because they do it for fun. Like drinking – alcohol's a drug too, you know."

"And tobacco," Jodie agreed. "But neither are illegal, are they?"

"So I guess this conversation's turned you against me?"

Jodie smiled. So, Theo was a dealer, and she didn't agree with that, but he seemed unconcerned, he wasn't getting aggressive defending himself. He was just answering her questions and arguments concisely. He came across as intelligent and friendly, in spite of what he did for a living. And Jodie supposed that there were worse jobs and worse vices. She took another sip from her vodka – it tasted just the same, but it sure was strong.

"Let's just say," she said, her mind vividly aware of her words becoming slightly slurred, "that I'm not convinced by your argument, but I'm not gonna castigate you for your chosen career."

"Jesus, for a minute there I thought you said you weren't gonna *castrate* me!"

"That neither."

"Well, tell you what, let's get off the subject. Tell me a bit more about yourself. Where do you work? Or do you lead a life of leisure?"

Jodie didn't really know how to respond. She could hardly say she was at school, because she certainly didn't look old enough to be a teacher.

So she decided to lie. "I'm at college." It was only one step away from the truth.

"What are you studying?"

A friend had once told her how to respond to such a question. Simply think up a boring subject that no-one's interested in, then you don't get asked any awkward questions. But Jodie didn't want to lie completely, so she said, "English, mainly – I'm hoping to break into journalism."

"Yeah?" Theo said, raising an eyebrow. "You're gonna do an exposé on me?"

"No, you're safe," she assured him. She took another sip from the vodka, draining it from the glass, and shook her fuzzy head. Her vision was beginning to blur, her whole body seemed to vibrate, and none of her thoughts seemed to make any sense. She looked at the clear glass, and for the first time, saw colours as the light reflected on the cut crystal. She closed her eyes – she didn't feel very well.

She stood up. "I have to go."

"Was it something I said?" Theo asked. He was wearing a smirk, and his voice came out of his mouth slowly, as though he were speaking to somebody who was hard of hearing. Jodie could hear the pounding beat from the music system in the next room, and it seemed to shake her innards, making her feel nauseous.

"I don't feel too good," she told him. "I have to go to the bathroom." And with that, she staggered through the door leading into the front room, pushing her way past the writhing mass of dancers, the strange lights that dazzled her eyes and painted bizarre images right onto her retinas, the loud music that made the whole house throb. She stumbled as she entered the hallway, and someone held her up. Somebody else asked if she was all right, but she couldn't recall responding.

She made her way to the foot of the stairs, passing a couple sitting on the bottom step, kissing. They were half-naked, their eyes bulbous and staring at Jodie. She tripped as she tried to climb the stairs, and people shouted at her. But she wasn't concerned. She needed the bathroom, she had to puke. Maybe if she puked up the vodka, it'd stop wrecking her body, stop making her feel like this.

As she reached the top, she stopped and almost toppled over

backwards. A hand stopped her, but she fought with it. The whole staircase seemed to be rising and falling beneath her feet, and all she could hear now were laughs and taunts, the faces of her school friends surrounding her, teasing her, and she just wanted to get away.

Then she was floating ...

Floating down ...

Then there was a loud crash, and the lights dancing before her eyes ceased.

21

Sadie heard the commotion through the closed door of the office where she and the rest of the band were sitting with Martin and two of his music contacts. The music was still pounding, shaking the framed prints on the walls of the room, but there were fresh sounds, not usually associated with parties, or quasi-raves. For a second, she found herself listening to that instead of the conversation that was going on within the office.

She turned to the group and saw that Billy was frowning. He too had heard the sounds. "What's that all about?" he asked.

"What?" Martin said impatiently, evidently disturbed at having been interrupted when he was in full flow.

"Some kinda fight going on," Sadie said, getting to her feet.

"Who cares?" Martin said, waving a hand dismissively. "The security guys'll take care of it." At that moment, the door to the office flew open, and one of the security guys in question burst in, a look of panic on his face. There was vomit down his trousers and blood on his hands.

Martin immediately got to his feet, though his expression seemed to say that he was of the opinion that this was nothing more than a drunken brawl. "What's wrong, Steve?"

"We've got a problem."

"What kind of problem?" Martin demanded to know. Sadie glanced at the two record executives. They were looking at one another nervously.

"Some kid," Steve went on. "She fell down the stairs, puked her guts up. I think she's took something." Sadie immediately got to her feet. She instantly thought of Jodie.

"Let's take a look," Martin said. He turned to the executives. "Won't be a second."

Sadie and the band followed Martin and the security guard to the hallway, where a crowd of people were standing in a semicircle. Martin pushed his way through, and Sadie followed.

She recognized Jodie's dress straightaway, and felt her knees go weak. Billy held onto her, but Sadie had to look at her sister. She shoved Martin out of the way and dropped down beside Jodie's unconscious body. The vomit that had spattered the doorman was also down Jodie's dress, spilling onto her legs. Blood was pouring from a wound at the back of her head, soaking into the carpet, and her lip was split, already swollen, the blood covering the lower half of her face.

"Jesus," Sadie muttered. It was all she could say.

"We have to call an ambulance," Billy said. "Has nobody already fucking rang for one?"

Martin snapped, "No way. We'll end up with the law down here."

"Don't be a fucking nipple!" Mark said. "She's in a bad way. She needs medical attention." He was fumbling for his mobile phone.

"We'll take her to the hospital," Martin volunteered.

"Fuck you," Sadie snapped, looking up at the producer. "You fucking asshole. My sister needs an ambulance." At that moment, the music from the other room ceased, and Sadie was aware of the fact that nobody else was talking. From upstairs, came the sound of some people having sex, the woman screaming in pleasure.

If it hadn't been for the gravity of the situation, it might've been comical. Under the circumstances, it turned Sadie's stomach. She cradled her sister's head. "It's gonna be okay, Jo, we'll get you sorted out."

Then she heard Mark's voice. "Yeah, ambulance, please." He was talking on his mobile. Martin reached across to stop him, but Davey stepped in the way.

"I wouldn't do that," the drummer advised.

"Fuck you! This is my fucking house! I say what goes on here!"

"Not when someone's fucked up like that, you don't," Davey said. "Now, don't be so fucking arrogant, and let Mark call for an ambulance." The two security guards moved a little closer to the man who paid their wages, but Davey was far from intimidated.

Despite the situation, Sadie felt a warm gratitude as she looked up at her three friends. Mark switched off his phone.

"Ten minutes, maximum."

Martin rolled his eyes and threw out his arms. "We could've had her at the fucking hospital in that time."

"Don't you get it?" Mark snapped. "If she has took something, she could fucking arrest at any time. Do you know how to resuscitate her? Have you got a fucking defibrillator in your car?"

"If the law turn up—"

"If the law turn up, what? You're worried about your reputation? Christ, Martin, this really is fucking serious, man! If you're that fucking concerned, we'll tell them she must've took something before she got here."

Sadie looked up at Mark, then her gaze shot across to Martin. "But she didn't, did she? She got whatever she's taken from this party." She was amazed at how calm she was. "Who gave her it? You know, don't you?"

"I haven't got a fucking clue," Martin answered laconically.

"Don't take me for a fucking fool, Martin. Now, there must only be one dealer here, because this party isn't big enough for any more. And you have to know who that dealer is. Now I want to know who sold my sister that fucking shit!" She looked around the hallway, but nobody could meet her eyes. They all knew who the dealer was – maybe the dealer was standing amongst them. But he – or she – would not reveal themselves, and nobody was going to speak up.

What difference did it make anyway? What good would it do to find the person responsible? Jodie had made a mistake, she'd experimented with drugs, and now she was paying the price.

Sadie looked down at her sister and gently stroked her hair. And she said, ever so softly, "You stupid little bitch."

The sirens could be heard in the distance, and Sadie realized that some minutes must've passed. Some of the bystanders and partygoers were gone, probably frightened off by the prospect of police presence. Others remained, if only to witness the possible death of a teenage girl.

And Sadie was caught up in the middle, furious with her sister for being so stupid, and yet deeply concerned for her safety. She couldn't lose another member of her family. Jodie was so important to her, more so now than ever before, because she needed a friend who had been through everything she had, a friend who understood, a friend she could vent her anger and frustration out upon, a friend she could love and sympathize with.

She felt a hand on her should and looked up to see Billy standing right behind her, sincere concern on his face. At that moment, there was a knock at the door and the paramedics entered, one of them immediately dropping to his knees alongside Jodie's body.

"What's her name?"

"Jodie," Billy answered – Sadie couldn't speak. "This is her sister."

"What happened?"

"She fell down the stairs," Steve, the security guard, responded. "I reckon she's taken something."

The paramedic inspected Jodie's injury, then asked his partner for a neck brace. He looked across to Sadie, saw the anxiety evident on her face. "A precaution," he explained. "After the fall." He looked up at Steve. "What kind of thing are we looking at? Ecstasy, or worse?"

"No idea," Steve said, shrugging his shoulders. Sadie wanted to punch him, because the bastard certainly had an idea of who it was who'd given her the drugs. "But I've seen this kind of thing before – probably an E." The paramedic nodded as his partner returned with both a stretcher and a neck brace. The two of them worked quickly but methodically, and soon Jodie was being strapped onto a stretcher.

Sadie finally found her voice. "Is she gonna be okay?"

"We'll do everything we can," the paramedic assured her. "You're her sister?"

"That's right."

"Take a ride with us." There wouldn't have been any stopping Sadie even if the paramedic hadn't offered. She wasn't leaving her sister, not when she was this vulnerable. They were both vulnerable, in fact. Jodie to the drug and her injuries, and Sadie to her sanity – she was in danger of losing it. More importantly, she felt as though she were in danger of losing her sister.

The journey to the hospital was brief, the sirens wailing only occasionally, but the blue lights flashing constantly, their reflections visible through the smoked glass as they bounced off the walls of buildings. Throughout the journey, Sadie couldn't remove her eyes from her sister, and kept her own hand clamped firmly on Jodie's. Jodie didn't move, didn't stir once, and were it not for the fact that she could see her chest rising and falling, Sadie would've sworn she were already dead. The paramedic's face wasn't overly concerned, but he was carefully monitoring Jodie's vital signs.

As the ambulance pulled up outside the casualty entrance, the rear doors were opened by nurses, and Sadie was gently nudged out of the way as the stretcher was removed from the vehicle. A nurse, young, probably fresh out of nursing college, held onto Sadie's arm and smiled warmly.

"Do you want to come with me?"

Sadie looked anxiously at Jodie as the stretcher was wheeled through a set of double doors that had opened automatically. "My sister," she said, "I should stay with her."

"Let's get her stable," the nurse said. "We need to get a few details from you. As soon as we've done that, I'll take you straight through to see her."

"I shouldn't leave her," Sadie insisted. She didn't want to add that she thought there was a chance that Jodie might die and she didn't want her sister to die alone.

"She's in the best place now," the nurse assured her, leading her through a side door. Once inside, she faced a barrage of questions, starting with Jodie's name and address, her age, then switching to the cause of her injuries and finally to the type of drug she'd taken.

"The paramedic heard that it was probably ecstasy," the nurse said. Alongside her was the staff nurse, a tall, thin man with a friendly face. The nurse turned to Sadie. "Do you know what she took?"

"No, I don't," Sadie answered. "And to be perfectly honest, I can't believe that she'd take anything. She wasn't – *isn't* – that kind of kid. She's not stupid."

"A lot of teenagers experiment, Miss Bartholomew," the staff nurse assured her. "And the vast majority of them come through it unscathed. It was unfortunate that Jodie had the accident. That may well have complicated matters."

There was a knock at the door of the office, and a middle-aged woman entered, a stethoscope around her neck and a clipboard in her hand. "I'm Doctor McCutcheon," she said.

"This is Sadie Bartholomew," the nurse said. "Jodie's sister."

"Ah, the older and wiser sister?" the doctor said. She gestured for Sadie to sit, and the two of them chose comfortable, if a little worn, chairs in one corner of the room. "I've just come from seeing your sister."

"How is she?"

"She's stable, for the moment. We'll be sending her up for a CT scan in the next fifteen minutes or so, so we should know the full extent of her head injuries shortly."

"How serious does it look?"

The doctor sighed. "Well, I've examined her briefly, and it would appear as though may be dealing with some slight swelling on her brain. I'm also not ruling out a bleed. If that's the case, we'll have to get her straight into theatre. Which leads us to the next problem." The doctor consulted her clipboard, but it seemed theatrical. "The drugs."

"I've already said to the nurse, I don't know what she took. I left her for a few minutes, that's all, and as far as I knew, Jodie wasn't stupid enough to try drugs."

"Nevertheless, there is a suspicion that she's taken something. Now the most likely substance is ecstasy, but that's a very volatile drug, and there are so many different types. It's a dangerous drug to take, because most of the time, the stuff they put in it really isn't designed for recreational purposes."

"Spare me the lecture," Sadie snapped. "I don't do drugs, and I never thought Jodie would either."

The doctor nodded. "Is there any chance that somebody could've slipped her a drug without her knowledge?"

"Why?"

The doctor paused, looked at her colleagues, then continued. "For sexual purposes. Did you see your sister with a man during the party?"

"You mean like the date-rape drug?"

"It's not uncommon," the doctor said. "Miss Bartholomew, I'm simply weighing up all the possibilities. In cases like this, we cannot afford to disregard any scenario."

"My God," Sadie muttered. What had she done to her sister? This was all her fault. If she hadn't taken Jodie to the party, none of this would've happened. If she'd stayed with Jodie, or took Jodie to the office with her, then she'd still be okay.

Her selfishness had placed Jodie in a situation that was way beyond her control.

"We'll run tests," Doctor McCutcheon said, "but we have to consider the possibility that any operation Jodie undergoes might result in serious complications."

"Because of the drugs?"

"If she has taken drugs, it will be more difficult to keep her stable throughout the operation ... if she has an operation, that is. I'm probably worrying you unduly—"

"No, you're worrying me, but I don't think it's unduly. I want to know what her chances are if she has to have an operation."

"It's a straightforward enough procedure, but it's not without its risks. And the possibility of there being drugs in Jodie's system only compounds that."

"But the odds?"

"Impossible to say."

"You must have an idea," Sadie snapped.

"I won't be doing the operation, so—"

"But you're a doctor. The odds?"

"Maybe seventy-thirty in favour," the doctor replied, standing up. "But really, it is something that cannot be accurately predicted. I don't want to increase your concern, I don't want to sound alarmist, but I also don't want to build up your hopes. Jodie is stable, but serious."

An hour later, and Sadie received the news that an operation was necessary. The doctor also had the lab results back. "We found traces of a number of drugs in your sister's system," she said. "As well as MDMA, which is the traditional ingredient of ecstasy, we also found slight traces of Ketamine."

"Is that bad?"

"Well, the MDMA isn't good, but thousands of kids are taking it, with few ill effects," the doctor explained. "With careful use, it shouldn't really be that dangerous – although I'm not advocating its use, you understand, but like smoking and drinking, it's a drug that people enjoy, in spite of the fact that there are inherent risks associated with its consumption.

But the Ketamine, well, that's different altogether. Ketamine is an anaesthetic, and depending upon the volume taken and individual user, it can have different effects, varying from inducing sleep to inducing coma."

"And that's what Jo took?"

"She took a bad E," the doctor said. "Just one, judging by the amounts we found. Whether by choice or whether somebody slipped one in her drink, we have no way of knowing, and for the moment, that really isn't important. The police will probably want to speak to both you and Jodie, but let's forget about that for now. We have to consider your sister's health."

"And the verdict?"

"She's stable as far as the reaction to the drug goes, but as you know, we have to send her up for surgery to relieve the pressure on her brain," the doctor said. She looked at an older man who had entered the room with her.

Dressed in a suit and looking stately, he took a couple of steps forward. "There has been a slight bleed on the inside of her skull," he said in a deep, well-spoken accent. "This is putting undue pressure on her brain, which we have to relieve." He wasn't telling Sadie anything she didn't already know. "The procedure will take a couple of hours, although ..." He paused, held up his hands in an effortless surrender gesture. "... it has been known to take longer. The CT scan can only reveal the state of the brain at that precise moment in time. We can predict from the knowledge it gives whether the bleed will get worse, and if so, how quickly, but like forecasting the weather, medicine is not an exact science. You or I could stand here right this minute and suffer a massive brain haemorrhage without any forewarning. We will do our best for Jodie – of that, have no fear – but the unexpected does occasionally happen. And though we are very well-placed to deal with the unexpected, nature sometimes does win the battles it begins. If you'll excuse me, I have to prepare for surgery." And with that, he was gone.

Sadie looked across to Doctor McCutcheon. "Can I see her?"

"Of course."

Jodie was located off the main ward in a side room which was full of hi-tech machinery that bleeped and whirred to confirm she was still alive. Graphs of her vital signs were being constantly plotted out on rolls of paper that dropped almost to the floor. An EKG monitor beeped rhythmically and reassuringly in one corner of the room, and a nurse in blue was jotting down the information on a form fixed to a clipboard. She looked up and smiled as Sadie entered the room.

"We're just about to prep her for theatre," she said, "but you can have a minute or so with her before we begin."

Sadie nodded. "Alone?" she asked.

The nurses left the room, but they also left the door open so they could return at once if their services were required in a hurry. That, Sadie thought as she walked over to the bed, wasn't reassuring.

She looked down at Jodie, at the blood-soaked bandage that had been wrapped around her head, and the way the blood had dried down the side of her face. She looked a mess, and the nurses hadn't cleaned her up – probably had more important things on their minds, she told herself, but that didn't excuse it.

Jodie was alive, and although she tried not to keep telling herself, this could be the last time she would ever see her. She didn't want to remember her dressed in a hospital gown, with a bloodstained face and a blood-soaked bandage around her head.

But the image, she thought with a horrified expression, would forever remain with her.

She reached down and grabbed Jodie's hand. A cannula had been inserted into the back of her wrist, the entry point bruised and bloody, as though they'd had trouble inserting it. Jodie's hand felt cold, like she was already dead.

She lowered her head until it was level with her sister's, and then she kissed her bloody cheek, her remaining hand gently caressing the bandaged head. Jodie didn't move, but she was still breathing.

What had the doctor said? Something about the drug inducing a coma? Sadie had heard somewhere that under certain circumstances, comas were a good thing. But then, she also seemed to recall that bizarrely those comas had been induced by the doctors. This, she reminded herself, was totally different.

"I'm sorry I let you down," she said quietly. "I didn't mean to leave you. God, if I could turn back the clock." Jodie didn't respond, not even the flicker of an eyelid to let Sadie know that her words were being heard. But still she continued speaking. "Please, pull through this, Jo. I need you. I reckon I need you more than you need me. I don't know what I'll do if ... if anything happens to you." She felt the tears well up in her eyes, and then she heard footsteps behind her.

The nurse came up to her and put an arm around her shoulder. "Come on, let's go somewhere quiet and wait." Sadie nodded. That was all she could do now, just sit and wait, and watch the expression of the doctor when he returned. If he returned, she thought as she stepped back into the relatives' room with its homely appearance and clinical odour. If the news was particularly bad, he might just send one of his juniors to inform her. No, she thought, shaking her head. He seemed like the kind of man who was accustomed to death, and who could deliver news about tragedies without it affecting him a great deal.

The nurse asked if she wanted a coffee.

Sadie shook her head. She didn't feel like eating or drinking.

She just waited.

Alone, because the nurse had other jobs, other patients, to attend to.

She didn't know how long she'd been waiting when the door finally opened. She looked up expectantly.

And Jordan stepped into the room.

Instantly, she felt as though a weight had been lifted from her shoulders, and she rose to her feet to meet him, as he gathered her up in his arms and hugged her tightly. She didn't ask how he'd found out – she presumed one of the guys in the band had told him or he'd found out through the grapevine. He seemed to have connections with Martin Walsh. More to the point, she didn't care how he'd found out. All that mattered was that he was here with her now.

The tears came, and her body was wracked by heavy sobs. Jordan squeezed her gently, soothingly, and said nothing for a couple of minutes. His hands caressed her head, sending pleasant shivers down her spine, and for a brief moment, she felt as though everything was going to be all right. Then the odour of the room and the stark realization that this was all too serious brought her back round.

She pulled away from him, but allowed him to continue holding her.

"How is she?"

"She's having an operation," Sadie replied, clutching a hand to her mouth in a vain effort to fight off a sob. "God."

"It's gonna be all right," Jordan assured her.

"Thanks for the confidence, Jordan, but we don't know that, do we?"

"What happened?"

"She fell down the stairs," Sadie replied. "Hit her head pretty hard. Apparently, there's a brain ..." She stopped, sobbed, wiped her damp eyes. "There's a brain haemorrhage, and they've got to relieve the pressure. It's a dangerous procedure, but the consultant tells me they do this kind of thing every day."

"It's second nature to them," Jordan said. But he was frowning. "She fell down the stairs? Is that all that happened?" It was as though he already knew the full facts, but wanted her to tell him.

Sadie didn't question him. Instead, she said, "She took some drugs – so the doctors tell me. I can't believe it myself. I mean, Jodie just isn't that kind of girl."

"What else are they saying?" Jordan asked, leading Sadie over to the chairs, where they both sat down.

Once again, Sadie felt compelled to answer. "They suggested that maybe somebody slipped Jodie something in her drink."

"Spiked it?"

"It was a suggestion," Sadie said. "I think the doctors are more of the opinion that Jodie was just experimenting. They only said about spiking her drink for my benefit. But I know Jodie, for God's sake. I know she wouldn't take drugs. She's a sensible kid. Moody, sure, bratty, occasionally, but on the whole, sensible. I mean, drugs? She's just not like that!"

"Have you spoken to the police?"

"Not yet. Though what good that's gonna do, I don't know."

"So you've no ideas as to who was pushing this shit to her?"

"None whatsoever. And Martin won't tell me. That bastard knows, but he's not talking. I mean, in a way I don't blame him – he can't really afford any kind of scandal. Do you know, that lousy bastard didn't even want to call for an ambulance?"

Jordan shook his head. He looked furious, as though he were holding his rage inside, stopping it from bursting out. She had this strange feeling that he wanted to find the dealer and strangle him. It sent another shiver down her spine, but not a shiver of pleasure. This one scared her, because it was something primal, some base emotion that she'd uncovered. And it all seemed to stem from Jordan, who was sitting just inches away from her with a non-threatening expression on his face.

He seemed to sense her unease, and he reached across to touch her hand. "Trust me on this one," he said, "she's gonna be fine. It may take a while, but you'll soon have her back home." He spoke with such conviction that Sadie was almost convinced. Unfortunately, he also sounded like some bible-belt preacher from back home, and she was half-expecting him to tell her that God was looking out for Jodie and that He wouldn't let anything bad happen to her, which ruined the effect.

Coming from anyone else, she would've responded by telling that person to shove their bullshit up their ass – but she couldn't say that to Jordan.

The door to the room opened again, and the consultant neurosurgeon entered. He looked down at Jordan and then sat down opposite Sadie.

"Miss Bartholomew," he said. She couldn't read his expression, and it was apparent that there had been no rush to get here from the operating theatre, because he was wearing a smart suit. "We've finished the operation on Jodie, and I'm pleased to say that we've stabilized her. There was a massive haemorrhage to the rear of her brain, but we think that we've minimized the bleed. There was a certain amount of swelling to the brain itself, but that was to be expected, and we cannot be certain of the true nature of any damage until Jodie comes out of the coma. We're hoping the damage will be minimal. Indeed, we're hoping that there will be no lasting effects."

"So she's gonna be okay?"

"Oh, I didn't say that. She's stable, that much I can guarantee you, so she is in no immediate danger. We've got her in the ICU, but that's nothing to be unduly concerned about."

"But what are her chances?" Sadie asked timidly. She felt as though she were in limbo – she didn't know whether to be happy, to look forward to the future, when Jodie would be coming home, or worried, because her sister might not have much more of a future remaining.

The consultant sighed heavily, as though he didn't like answering such questions. He finally said, "I would be cautiously optimistic, were I in your shoes." And with that, the doctor got to his feet.

"Can I see her?"

"Probably wisest to leave it for a couple of hours," he replied. "Go home, catch up on your sleep—"

"I'd rather stay."

The consultant nodded. "I'll tell one of the nurses." Then he left the room.

"You're gonna stay here?" Jordan asked her.

"I want to stay here, for when she wakes up," Sadie explained. She didn't add, *If she wakes up.*

Jordan crouched down before her and squeezed her hands. "Do you want me to go back to your apartment, pick up a change of clothes for you?"

"Yeah, I suppose that might be an idea," Sadie admitted, looking down at her bloodstained dress. Even without the stains, it was hardly the kind of thing she should be wearing in a hospital. "And some toothpaste and a toothbrush."

Jordan smiled and nodded. "Have you got enough cash to get yourself something to eat and drink?"

"Yeah, but I don't want any—"

He stopped her by putting a finger against her lips. "You need to eat, Sadie, or you'll pass out, and that won't do anybody any good, will it?" She reluctantly agreed to get herself something to eat, but not right now, and Jordan relented, getting to his feet. She gave him her keys and kissed him goodbye.

Then she was all alone again, waiting apprehensively for a visit from one of the nurses or the doctor. She wondered what her sister looked like now. Her head, probably shaven where they'd removed part of her skull. She hadn't thought to ask about scars, but at the time, it hadn't seemed important. It was more important that they save her life. Now, bizarrely, it did seem important.

She couldn't imagine Jodie walking around with some of her hair missing, never to grow back where they'd cut her head open, with a thick scar running across her scalp. It just didn't seem right somehow.

It didn't seem fair.

Jodie deserved more, a lot more than having her life hanging in the balance, than living out what remained of her life, be it hours or years, horribly mutilated.

Sadie shook way the thought as a nurse entered the room. She was drawing conclusions without being in possession of the full facts. The nurse, she thought fearfully, would have all the information she needed.

And thankfully, the nurse was smiling at her.

22

Jordan walked through the club doors without raising so much as a glance from the two doormen. One or two lads in the queue pointed fingers at the door and protested as he disappeared, but the doormen simply ignored those also. Once inside, he was greeted by the loud music pouring out from the dance hall through another set of double doors which were propped open so that he could see the writhing, dancing masses. And in amongst those heaving, sweating people was one man.

One man alone he was interested in.

He strolled confidently across the foyer towards the doors, ignoring the looks he received from a handful of girls standing nearby. Just as there was only one man he was interested in here, there was only one woman on the entire planet he was interested in, and she wasn't here. Though that interest, he had to say, could not be more different between the man and woman.

The woman, he loved.

The man, he'd come to kill.

His first port of call was the bar, and he ordered himself a whiskey, his eyes scanning the faces of the people standing alongside him. Within a couple of seconds, he'd discounted them all as being his potential target – not that he knew what the man looked like, not physically, but he *could* spot a sinner when he saw one.

It hadn't been easy finding out the identity of the man responsible for Jodie's condition, but if anybody could've done it, nobody could've done it better than Jordan. He'd asked only one man – Steve, the bouncer at Martin Walsh's party. At first, Steve had simply told him to go forth and multiply. But Jordan was proficient at his job, and without revealing his true identity, it had taken a mere four seconds to persuade Steve that it was in his best interest to allow the information to be extracted by the least painful method.

From the bouncer, he'd gleaned a name and a description. More importantly, he knew where this Theo Blackwood was moving onto next to peddle his wares. And that was exactly where he was now, surrounded by the young and the wild, most of them teenagers, all of them looking for sex and fun and drugs to enhance their thrills. A veritable den of iniquity, and here he was, ignoring the masses to pass judgement upon just one.

He took the whiskey and downed it in one gulp, the burning sensation barely registering with him. He felt powerful, having nourished himself in the bowels of Hell, and he could see behind the faces of those who surrounded him, ignorant to his true nature. His eyes, appearing lifeless and soulless, scanned the crowd, penetrating the flesh and bone, peering right into the minds.

Here was a girl who had on two occasions charged for sex; another who had bedded five men at the same time; a man who had forced himself upon a girl he barely knew; another who had taken part in the gang-rape of a fifteen-year-old; yet another who had, with friends Jordan could not detect, kicked a man to death round the back of this very nightclub. Sinners, dozens of them amongst the lesser sinners, the ones who would scrape into Heaven when their time came — sinners who should be taken at the earliest opportunity. But that wasn't the way, Jordan thought. No, with a simple sinner, the kind who had violated another human being in any sense by raping or killing, the preferred method of punishment was to allow them to live out their lives in full, let them forget the solitary crime of their youth, and then, when their time came, remind them of their sin as they were dashed to pieces on the rocky floor of Hell, ripped apart by the winged demons, tortured for all eternity.

That was the preferred method.

It was not, Jordan thought angrily, *his* preferred method.

And here, he thought with a smile, here was the man he sought.

His eyes penetrated this man's soul, and saw his crime, his most recent crime ...

Slipping a pill in Jodie's drink, with the intention of taking away her virginity.

Jordan moved quickly, pushing two large men aside. One of them made a grab for him, but Jordan simply glanced in his direction, and the man quite literally dropped to his knees, a look of terror on his face as his own crimes were visited upon himself in a horrifying vision he would never relate to anybody for the rest of his days. By that time, Jordan had disappeared into the crowd of dancers, his gaze fixed once more upon Theo Blackwood.

As he crossed the room, Blackwood moved towards a set of doors above which was inscribed the word 'Toilets'.

Perfect, Jordan thought.

Absolutely perfect.

He passed a bouncer, who paid him scant attention as he stepped through the door, whereupon he found himself in a dank corridor. There was a door on either side, one for females, the other for males. Jordan straightened his tie, and took the door on the right, stepping into a clean, white room, with tiled walls and a tiled floor.

Six cubicles were along one side of the wall, three of them locked. That didn't concern Jordan, the fact that there may be witnesses, for no mortal police force could entrap him. They could capture his body, but his demonic form would simply leave it catatonic, return to Hell, and generate another human body.

Of course, it would mean leaving Sadie behind, for she had fallen in love with Jordan, not Kobold.

Jordan shrugged that thought away. He wasn't here on human business. He should never have had any human business whatsoever. He was here on demonic business.

Looking around the rest of the room, he saw eight urinals against another wall, all but one of them vacant, with a row of sinks along the wall directly opposite. Theo was washing his hands, checking his reflection in the mirror. Jordan walked up to the sink next to him and turned on the taps. The peddler gave him a sideways look, curious as to why he'd chosen the sink directly alongside him, when there were nine others to choose from. Jordan caught his eye.

"What the fuck are you looking at?" Theo hissed.

Jordan finished washing his hands and turned off the taps. He shook the water from his hands and raised an eyebrow. "You don't know who you're talking to, do you?"

"Should I?"

"I heard you were the kind of man I could cut a deal with," Jordan said, shrugging his shoulders. "Seems like my information was bogus." He made to move away, but Theo, clearly intrigued at Jordan's US accent, quickly spoke.

"Cut a deal?"

Jordan walked over to the hand-drier and switched it on. He rubbed his hands together beneath the hot air until they were completely dry. Then he switched the drier off and turned to look at Theo again. The peddler had followed him across the room.

From the other side came the sound of a bolt being thrown, and a man stepped out of one of the cubicles and walked over to the sinks. Jordan watched as he washed his hands. When he'd finished he came over to the drier, but Jordan didn't stand aside.

"Use a paper towel," Theo snapped at him. The man did as he was told, then left the room. "So what kind of a deal?"

"Here," Jordan said, walking over to the cubicles. He chose the one on the end, the disabled toilet, which was larger to accommodate a wheelchair, and stepped inside. Theo followed, and locked the door behind him.

"Is this gonna be worth my while?" he asked.

Jordan smiled. "Oh yes," he said. "The first sample comes free. After that, well, we can work out the cost."

"But it will be beneficial to me?"

"Oh, it will be beneficial," Jordan assured him, pulling a syringe from his pocket. Theo eyed it curiously.

"What's that, man? Fucking H? I don't deal in H."

"Don't you?" Jordan asked, taking the cap off the end. The syringe was full, a millilitre of clear solution. It was clear, because it was 100% pure. In one swift movement, he stabbed the needle in Theo's neck and pushed down hard on the plunger. There was a slight resistance as the liquid was forced into Theo's jugular vein, but it was all over within half a second, and the syringe was empty by the time the peddler pushed Jordan's hand away.

"What the fuck are you doing, man?" he asked, his eyes watering as he held his neck. "That fucking hurt! Jesus fucking Christ! You some kind of madman?"

"Right now," Jordan said calmly, "you have one millilitre of pure heroin pumping around your circulatory system. Within a few seconds, you will begin to feel the first effects." The realization of his fate was evident on Theo's face. "Perhaps as Jodie Bartholomew did earlier this evening ... only she had no warning, did she?" Jordan smiled. "At least I'm giving you that, allowing you to repent before you face the final justice."

"What the fuck are you, man?" Theo asked, but already the colour was draining from his face, and the beads of sweat that had broken out on his skin were vibrating as he trembled.

"We will meet again, Theo," Jordan assured him. "But I estimate that you have less than ten seconds of life left." Theo fumbled with the lock on the toilet door. "That's it, work harder, pump that blood around your body, because you're in pain, aren't you? And the quicker you can get that heroin to act, the quicker your life will be over." Theo dropped to his knees. "But don't think, Theo, that your pain will end then. Because your pain, my friend, will only just be beginning."

Theo clutched his chest, gasped loudly, and fell onto his face. He jerked violently once or twice, and then was still.

"That," Jordan said quietly, "was so easy."

He couldn't believe how easy it had been, in fact. Theo, without any persuasion, had believed Jordan right from the start. His curiosity, Jordan thought wryly, certainly had got the better of him. He kicked the body gently to see if it moved, but it felt dead beneath his foot.

Crouching down, Jordan felt for a pulse.

Nothing.

Right now, he thought, Theo would be falling.

Falling to the stony ground miles below, in a confused state, probably not comprehending what had happened, recalling the heroin overdose, and attributing the sights, sounds and smells around him as some hallucination.

How wrong he would be.

And with that, Jordan laughed loudly.

Five minutes later, he was sitting in his BMW. He had to drive it to the lockup Jordan Weaver had rented out for the next three months. It would take maybe twenty minutes to get there. Theo would already be in Hell by then, dragged into one of the myriad caverns by Kobold's small army of imps, awaiting the arrival of the demon who would administer his punishment. From now on, Jordan was unconcerned with time. He had all the time in the world.

For now, he had to stash the BMW and the human form in which he currently existed somewhere safe, away from prying eyes. Then he could get on with his work.

23

Theo was still breathless ten minutes after hitting the ground. It didn't help that both his legs had been shattered by the jagged rocks upon which he'd fallen, and that his right arm was twisted behind his bruised and battered back. If this was some heroin-enhanced hallucination, it certainly was vivid. The smell of sulphur was so authentic, the screams of tortured souls echoing around inside his head so graphic, like nothing he'd ever experienced before, that it just seemed so real, as though it were actually happening.

But this couldn't be happening. This just wasn't possible. In spite of the pain, Theo's mind tried to reconcile the events he could remember and knew for certain were genuine with the situation he now found himself in. It just didn't seem to make sense. But his limited knowledge of theology allowed him to gradually realize that he was dead, that this was the afterlife, and that the creature that was walking towards him was here to punish him.

He looked up at the creature's red face, and knew instantly that this was a demon standing before him. A demon with the face of the man who had, only minutes earlier, injected him with pure heroin in a toilet cubicle in a nightclub. The demon grinned as he looked down at Theo.

"I'm sorry I've been so long," he said, "but I had a few things to attend to before I came here." He reached down and pulled Theo to his feet. The drug pusher looked around and saw this scene duplicated thousands of times as fallen souls were dragged, some kicking and screaming, towards a mammoth set of gates which opened into a cityscape unlike any Theo had seen before.

"This can't be happening," a voice next to Theo shouted. Theo looked at the demon, who simply smiled.

"It is happening to each and every one of you," the demon said. "You pay here for the sins you've committed on Earth. There is no escape."

Theo closed his eyes and allowed himself to be pulled by the demon through the Gates of Hell, and into the stinking furnace beyond. As they neared a cavern set into a wall full of similar caverns, Theo spoke for the first time.

"I suppose if I said I was sorry, it wouldn't do any good?"

The demon smiled. "It's too late, Theo, way too late for apologies, Sinners are those who fail to repent the moment their lives end. It should be your dying thought. I believe your dying thought," the demon said, shoving Theo into the cavern, "was that you hoped the bitch that sent me to kill you dies of cancer. That was it, wasn't it?"

"You can't keep me here," Theo said determinedly. This was just like being in a prison that was located right in the middle of a large city, and there appeared to be plenty of places to hide. And he just knew that there had to be some escapees, an underground movement, out there.

"I know exactly what you're thinking, Theo," the demon told him, "which makes your plans for escape very difficult." He dragged Theo back over to the entrance and pointed down at the city of caves and huts below. "Take a look — what do you see?"

Theo could see the buildings, and people walking among them. He looked up at the demon.

"But take a good look — the people. Notice anything about them?"

Theo looked again there were two kinds of people. Those with fair or black skin in other words, human-like — and those with a red complexion. "Nothing significant," he said.

"The humans — the souls of the humans — take a look at them." Theo did, and it took a few seconds to register. Each and every one of them was accompanied by a red skinned creature. Indeed most if not all, of them were shackled to the creature. Their expressions were worn down, depressed, not at all vibrant like the demons and imps.

"A human soul does not leave the torture chamber alone," the demon said. "In fact, a human soul rarely leaves the torture chamber at all." He moved his hand and Theo involuntarily dropped to his knees, realizing at that moment that he too was shackled to the demon. When it had happened, he could not recollect. But what the demon said hit him hard. "Those souls, they are all on their way to their final resting place. If you did somehow manage to escape from this chamber ... well, you wouldn't get far before somebody picked you up. The winged demons, overhead there, see them? They pick up a few hundred every day. And I really wouldn't recommend leaving the city walls. There are things beyond those walls that are so terrible, even I am afraid." The demon laughed. "Now, enough of the small talk — that is such a human trait." The demon's expression changed, and he seemed more downcast. He shook his head lightly, as though shaking troubled thoughts from his mind, and then dropped down to his knees to look at Theo. "There are many ways to die, Theo, and from here on in, we can explore each and every one of them in explicit detail."

And then, the demon let out a bellowing laugh that seemed to shake the whole chamber.

Kobold didn't enjoy the torture any more.

As he stared impassively at the wrecked body of the drug dealer, he wondered whether he ever did, back in the beginning, when he'd been given the opportunity to administer rather than receive. Perhaps, he wondered, the enjoyment he might've felt at that time had been nothing more than a release of his pent-up anger and bitterness.

He hadn't really relished the thought of torturing another human being.

And that was the problem.

The other demons didn't view the victims as human beings; they were souls. Condemned souls. And the demons certainly didn't view themselves as human beings.

Kobold was finding it increasingly difficult to draw any distinctions. As far as he was concerned, those souls were humans — didn't they still have flesh and bone that was ripped apart by the torture, even if it was reconstituted at the end of every session? And didn't he have flesh and bone? Could he not be touched, could he not feel pain, more so when in human form?

It was something that Kobold just could not shake from his mind. That bond with humanity, it was becoming so strong recently. Usually, excessive time spent in human form, wandering Earth, left a demon feeling physically drained. So much so that extended periods of recovery in Hell were required to regain enough power to return to Earth, enough power even to carry out their duties in Hell.

But Kobold didn't feel the strain as much as he used to.

His power was increasing — that much was obvious.

And as he felt the familiar pull of the devil on his thoughts, realizing that he was being summoned to appear before Satan, he knew that he had sufficient power to resist perhaps only for a short while, but long enough to make a point. However, he also knew that Satan's power was far greater, and in the end, he could use it to destroy Kobold — could, and most certainly would. So he allowed himself to be taken, feeling the familiar tingling sensation of every atom in his body being disassembled and pulled through the rocky ground, deep down into a pit where only a few journeyed.

When the atoms were reassembled to make up his familiar shape, he realized that he was kneeling before the devil's throne, and he had to look up to see Satan glaring down at him. A pair of succubi, naked and beautiful in spite of their crimson colouring, were delicately handling his penis, which hung limply, disinterested, between his legs like a man's forearm.

Satan rested an elbow on the arm of the throne, and laid his chin on a clenched fist.

"When I issue a summons, Kobold, I expect it to be obeyed," he said, his voice deep, echoing throughout the huge chamber.

Kobold bowed his head. "I apologize, my lord, but I was otherwise engaged."

"So I have been led to believe," Satan said. Kobold looked up to see the succubi still fondling the devil — their efforts were being rewarded. The huge penis was beginning to bob upwards slightly. "And I am disturbed by what I have heard."

"My lord?"

"You have been spending excessive amounts of time on Earth," Satan said. His penis was now fully erect, but the devil was showing no signs of enjoyment. The succubi were each using both of their hands to pull back the foreskin, revealing an enormous, grotesquely purple head. "I would like to know why."

"I feel that I would be better placed to judge humans from this time were I more aware of their lifestyles," Kobold said. It was a lie, with a slight foundation of truth. He did want to know about what humans had to contend with in this lifetime, but only in so much as he wanted to be closer to humanity.

"You are talking utter rot, Kobold." the devil said, leaning back in his throne. The succubi were working quickly now, using all of their physical strength to masturbate him as frantically as they could. "You dare to come into my chamber and lie to me? You dare to insult me?"

Kobold began to feel nervous — the anxiety was creeping up on him slowly, a rumbling deep in his bowel that seemed to originate from the ground upon which he knelt. He remembered what Reizend had told him, about the demons that were being systematically destroyed by the Corrupted, empowered by Satan himself, and he genuinely feared for his own existence.

He looked up at the devil, trying not to look at the succubi as they worked on the devil, desperate to drink his semen. His heart was pounding in his chest, another sign of his growing humanity — demons didn't possess hearts, didn't possess much in the way of emotions. Like automatons, they did as they were instructed, with very little deviation from what was commanded. There wasn't any need for initiative, for they were here to do the devil's will.

And Satan was fully aware of what each and every one of his demons was getting up to. And he knew precisely what Kobold had been doing.

"You didn't have the authority to take that last life," he said. "What you actually did, Kobold, was commit a murder."

At that, Kobold jolted. A murder. He hadn't thought of it like that. As a human, he had plunged a syringe fill of pure heroin into the bloodstream of another human being, thereby killing him. And although the drugs and the syringe had been created by Kobold out of the atoms that surrounded him, there had been no supernatural powers used in the taking of that life.

Therefore, it had to be a murder – a human taking the life of another human.

It was some time before Kobold responded. "I may have reacted rashly, my lord—"

"You were thinking of the Bartholomew girl," Satan said. He was smiling, and Kobold believed that it had very little to do with the succubi masturbating him, nor was it a sign of friendship. "It is not your place to use your powers purely for the purposes of revenge. Neither, Kobold, should you be cementing any relationship with a human. Surely you know where that path leads."

Kobold shook his head.

"It is how some of the Corrupted became so inclined," Satan said. "Bonding with humans, believing themselves to be human. Is that what is happening to you, Kobold? Is that what you desire?"

Quickly, Kobold shook his head. He could feel a surge of power that was no doubt caused by the adrenaline that raced around his body ... he stopped. There was no adrenaline racing around his body. Flesh and bone he looked to be, but those atoms were only in place to present a form to the souls. He was nothing but an empty shell.

But the surge of power, and that was no misguided delusion.

He really felt it.

All the same, he knew that Satan could smite him simply by raising one finger.

Smite him, destroy him, send him to an oblivion from which there was no return. You couldn't kill a demon — you could only totally obliterate him.

"I am sorry, my Lord," he said. "I have made some poor decisions in the past."

"You have," the devil agreed. "Some of them unforgivable." He leaned forward in his throne, and still the succubi worked on his penis. "You will stay away from the Bartholomew girl."

Kobold nodded.

But even as he did so, he knew that he couldn't stay away from Sadie.

She was the closest thing to making him feel even part way human again, and he wasn't about to throw it away.

He would use his powers, he thought to himself as he left the devil's chamber, to mask his visits to Earth. If he could use them for nothing else, if he didn't have the power to destroy Satan, he certainly had the power to hide his true intentions. Sadie needed him, especially at a time like this, and he wasn't about to let her down.

That, he realized, was another human trait he was adopting.

And it felt so good.

Satan leaned back in his throne and threw back his head, trying to enjoy the sexual stimulation administered by the succubi. But this was a task, nothing more. They needed his semen; he certainly didn't need the pleasure. He wasn't decadent, he didn't destroy or abuse just for the sake of it – that had been Beelzebub's downfall. Perhaps he broke the rules occasionally, but didn't everyone? Even God? So what had he done to deserve this? To have his position of authority within Hell challenged, to have the threat of total annihilation hanging over him. He didn't deserve this.

And Kobold ... there was something odd about that demon. He had power that Satan had only rarely seen before, and only in demons with more than a thousand years of experience. Kobold didn't have that. Which made him a threat.

But could he be *the* threat, the pretender to the throne, to Satan's throne?

Satan pondered on that thought for a moment, as he felt the surge of an almighty orgasm wrack his body, sending a spray of semen showering over the succubi, who drank greedily on it. Before Satan's eyes, the succubi seemed to physically change, outstretching their arms and sprouting wings. letting out screams of agony as the transformation took place, turning them from minor demons into winged demons, with gnarled horns that signified their new importance.

Then they took to the air on their new wings, and flew upwards to the ceiling of the cavern thousands of feet overhead, leaving Satan bored and alone.

But wasn't that always the way? It was lonely at the top, that was the maxim most successful businessmen had, and Satan had to agree that it was true. Not that Satan required friends — that was a human trait and Satan hadn't been human in more than two-thousand years. In fact, he hadn't taken human form once in the last two millennia, hadn't needed to.

His court was a lonely, miserable one.

Satan got to his feet and descended from his mighty pedestal, standing on the rocky ground below. It was rare that he left the sanctity of his throne, and everything looked different from down here. The pedestal was high, although its actual size could be altered at will by Satan, and it certainly presented an imposing sight to all who entered his capacious chamber. He looked down at the ground beneath his cloven hooves, and saw the narrow cracks that zigzagged across the rocky surface, cracks that exuded foul-smelling steam from the bowels of the Earth. It was a sickening odour that permeated the whole of Hell — but was more pungent here in Satan's chamber. A stench that was naturally revolting to the souls sent here on the moment of death, but seemed perfectly familiar to Satan and his legions of demons.

And that was it, wasn't it? This was familiar to Satan, this was his life, more than any false life conjured up by the mystical powers of demons and devils. He could barely remember his life before Hell; it seemed like this was all he'd ever known, all he'd ever been. So he really couldn't understand the desires of the few demons he'd seen like Kobold, who tried so very hard, and all in vain, to become human once more. Tried hard enough so that their Hellish personas were almost swallowed up. Some had paid the ultimate sacrifice in surrendering their powers, destroying themselves in the process. Others, the *Ensnared,* so called because they could not return to Hell, were mercilessly hunted down and destroyed by the Jäger.

Satan looked up to his throne, and with a slight tensing of his body, was instantly transported back to the top of the pedestal. He sat down, flexed every muscle in his body, and considered his current situation. There were billions of demons in Hell, and he knew every one of them. He knew their names, their strengths, their weaknesses, the severity of any threat they posed to his rule. And yet, there were some, some whose ultimate powers remained a mystery even to him.

And there really was only one way to deal with them.

Destruction.

Resting his chin on his hand, he pondered the decision he'd taken, and wondered whether it had been the right one.

The Corrupted, those demons who had gone bad, who took human lives not for punishment, but for fun, played with humanity in ways that broke every celestial rule. The Corrupted were the demons who gave Hell its bad name, the ones who snatched babies in their sleep, who guided people into the paths of bullets, or speeding cars, or inflicted them with cancers. And the Corrupted were also targeted by the Jäger, though with less success, because their powers were not seriously diminished as were those of the Ensnared.

The Corrupted were to be avoided at all costs – avoided, if not destroyed.

And Satan, Lord of Hell, had offered a considerable number of the Corrupted demons amnesty, in return for helping him. Amnesty, enabling them to return to Hell, to become fully fledged demons once more, no longer running from the Jäger, no longer hiding far out in the mountains of Hell, torturing the few runaway souls they found to rejuvenate their powers before returning to Earth to create mayhem.

Satan was offering them another chance, setting a precedent, because the Corrupted were not given second chances. It was an irredeemable act for a demon to commit a sin, because demons could not be restored to the status of a sinned soul. A demon could only be destroyed.

Yet Satan was offering them forgiveness.

And in return, he was asking a lot.

Not of the Corrupted, for their demonic souls had already been condemned. No, he was asking a lot of himself, because what he'd asked them to do for him broke the laws of Hell. It was an abomination, and yet he'd still asked it of them. Why had he done it? To preserve his own status as Lord of Hell, as the devil. Wasn't that selfishness, wasn't it greed for personal gain?

Was not that a human trait?

Was that not what Kobold had succumbed to?

Satan growled and held out a hand.

Instantly, what seemed to be a small demon appeared, standing in his palm.

But this was no demon.

It was an imp, the lowest of the celestial beings in Hell.

"Mörder," Satan hissed. "I have a task for you."

The imp bowed its head. "My Lord."

He told the imp what he required of him, and then leaned back in his throne as the imp disappeared.

And in his head, Satan heard the screams of another hundred demons being destroyed.

And he knew that one day, he would have to pay for his sins, not as Beelzebub had, for Beelzebub had lost the challenge to his authority, and had been destroyed by the successor to his throne. Satan, on the other hand, was breaking God's laws in order to maintain his seat of authority, and when the punishment came, as it surely would, it would be agonizing and final.

The only way to ensure he wasn't destroyed by God was to fight Him. He certainly had the power to challenge God, but God would win, of that Satan was in no doubt, for God created Heaven, Hell and the Earth. Satan merely maintained control over Hell and the demons. Satan was an employee, not a deity.

There was another way, Satan told himself. God was forgiving.

He should stop the Corrupted and throw himself down before God and beg forgiveness.

Satan scowled.

He would never do that.

He was Satan, he was the devil, and he would ensure that he remained so whatever the cost – even the price of his very existence.

To have his authority usurped by a young pretender, to be sent into oblivion by a demon who would be the devil, that very thought Satan found insulting.

To be destroyed by God Himself ...

If oblivion was to be Satan's fate, then he could choose no more honourable or memorable way to meet it than that.

24

Kobold knew that what he was doing was wrong, but it didn't seem to matter anymore. He no longer thought of himself as Kobold the demon. He was Jordan Weaver – not the Jordan Weaver who had four hundred years ago murdered his wife and her lover, but the Jordan Weaver who had fallen in love with Sadie Bartholomew.

And here he stood, outside the door to Sadie's flat, the devil as far from his mind as he could possibly be, a young man preparing to take the young woman he loved to the hospital to see her seriously ill sister.

A human, with human feelings, human emotions, and human sentiments.

Sadie opened the door, and he saw immediately that she'd been crying. Straight away, he stepped into the flat and held her tightly, squeezing her into his chest as though he could squeeze away the poisonous emotional heartache she was experiencing like the pus in a spot. It was an instinctive reaction to seeing the woman he loved so upset – and a uniquely human reaction.

For five minutes. they remained embraced, the door to the flat still open, Sadie seemingly oblivious to the fact that anyone could look in on her distressed state — that didn't appear to matter to her, not after what she'd been through at the hospital. There were more important things in life. Jordan was oblivious to anything or anyone other than the woman he loved.

He just wished that he could make it all better for her.

But he only had the power to dish out death; prolonging life wasn't something he was capable of performing. That side of things belonged to those like Reizend, and he doubted whether even Reizend could restore life when all hope was lost. Only one possessed power of such magnitude, and to Him, the life of one teenager was insignificant.

And that was another thing that disturbed Jordan, that turned him away from his alter ego, Kobold, into the totally human Jordan. It was the way that God rarely intervened to save a life. Even the life of His own son, mortal Jesus. The way He allowed innocent children to die daily across the world, from cancers, at the hands of murderers, or in terrible accidents.

God wasn't as powerful as those who worshipped Him believed.

God was nothing.

Jordan — as Kobold — could recall the discussion that passed from the lips of demons in Hell during the Holocaust. Curious asides, bewilderment, and a feeling of helplessness. Demons were not evil — they punished the evil. And to have to sit by and watch the most evil man most of them had ever seen order the butchery of children, innocent men and women without intervention from those on high ... it was more than they could take. The demons took the lives of those who were to be punished. It wasn't in their place to decide who those people were to be. But God and the devil were making no moves to put a stop to it. It was as though it were all part of some greater plan.

But as more and more bodies were scraped out of the gas chambers and into the crematoria, so the unrest among the demons increased. A handful had decided to take the law into their own hands, and efforts were made to put a stop to the murder. Those efforts failed, and none of the demons in Hell knew how or why. But the rebellion was crushed, and the war was soon over, Hitler dying at the hands of one of his loyal followers, a man who'd subsequently escaped the clutches of the Allied forces, and lived out the remainder of his life in South America.

All the same, there were demons in Hell — and no doubt angels in Heaven – who wondered as to the purpose of the master plan behind the Holocaust, if indeed there was one. And Kobold was one of those demons who just couldn't see the reasoning behind such a massacre. It was as though everything that was rotten in Hell had spewed forth its influence upon one man and one nation, and Kobold, like many demons, was just as confused and angry as the millions of humans who had witnessed or heard of the atrocities.

Jordan, as he held Sadie tightly, considered that it was probably around that time that his love and his loyalty for the celestial life began to dwindle, until it was now non-existent. He would gladly trade in his immortality to be vulnerable once more, and be able to love and live another life unmolested by the devil and his hunters. He would trade in the opportunity of another afterlife just to live even a few years as totally human, as a complete man.

But that wasn't possible, and he knew that he would have to make do with snatched moments of illicit love with a woman who could never know him for what he truly was. It was a secret he could never tell her, not just because to do so would violate the laws of Heaven and Hell, but because he couldn't bear to tell her truth for fear of turning her against him. What woman, what *human* woman could love a creature from Hell?

She could never see him as he truly was, red-skinned and inhuman, a manifestation of evil that for most people existed only in the deepest caverns of their imagination.

And yet, he couldn't bear to keep such a secret from her. He looked down at her, beautiful and tender, innocent and trusting, and wondered how he could expect to be human if he was capable of withholding such a terrible secret from such a delicate creature as her. She deserved more than he could offer her, a part-time lover, a mostly absent partner, a friend who couldn't totally confide in her.

She deserved a human.

But his own selfishness wouldn't allow him to cast her aside, to give her a few days, a few weeks worth of heartache, so that she could eventually have a lifetime of happiness.

Jordan wanted her — Kobold wanted her ...

She looked up at him. "I love you," she said. And it moved him more than he'd ever been moved before, mostly because he felt the same emotions for her.

He ran his fingers through her short hair and smiled at her. "I love you too," he said. "And I'll be here for you."

"But what about your work?" she asked him.

His work? The work that was so secretive, he couldn't confess it to her for fear of revealing state secrets. He was like a *Walter Mitty* character, a dreamer, the kind of guy who usually pumped gas, or served up greasy fries and floppy buns with wafer-thin burgers. But she didn't suspect him of being a dreamer, of inventing a lifestyle. Sadie knew he had something to hide, and knew that whatever it was, it was something he was unable to tell her, probably ever. How right she was, Jordan thought wryly. If she knew, if she ever found out the terrifying truth ...

"Let's not think about my work," he said to her. He didn't think that he really had to think about his work, because Hell was far from his mind, and he felt powerful enough to remain on Earth indefinitely. He even felt confident that any Jäger who came after him could be easily defeated.

Overconfident?

He shook off that thought. "You wanna go to the hospital?"

"Please," Sadie said.

"Have you heard any other news?" he asked her, genuinely concerned.

"No. The last time I phoned, she was still critical but stable." Sadie stepped over to the coat rack and grabbed a suede jacket. "I'm so worried, Jordan. I just keep getting this image ... this image of Jodie, lying in a coffin".

"Hey, don't talk like that," Jordan admonished her. He grabbed her again, almost as though he were going to shake her like she was an unruly child. "You have to remain positive." He didn't say anything crass, didn't make any rash promises or predictions. Jodie might die, but he didn't want to say that to Sadie. What he did say sounded like the best option — honest, yet not too negative.

It was an hour before they finally arrived at the hospital and made their way into the ICU, where Jodie lay in one of four beds, closely monitored by a team of nurses. Almost immediately, the doctor came out to see them.

"There's been no change," she said, fingering a clipboard. "Would you like to speak in a side room?"

"Should we?" Sadie asked harshly. "I mean is there something wrong?"

"Nothing more than you already know," the doctor said.

"Only I was wondering why she was still in intensive care?"

"Your sister is still seriously ill, Miss Bartholomew," the doctor told her. "Coma patients need constant medical care, particularly in the early stages. She really is in the best place, and I'm sure that's all you want for her."

"Don't patronize me," Sadie hissed, uncharacteristically bitter – Jordan placed a hand on her shoulder, and attempted to calm her. He half-expected her to shrug it off, but she didn't. Unfortunately, she didn't calm down either. "Don't you people understand what it's like to have a relative seriously ill in hospital? You don't, do you? To you, it's just another patient, somebody without a face, without a name. She could die right here, and in a couple of days, there'll be somebody else in this bed, and you'll have forgotten all about her, what she looked like, what her name was. You're just interested in statistics."

"I'm interested in saving lives–"

"I don't doubt that," Sadie said. "But that's because it's your job, and you want to do a good job, don't you? You're just a mechanic, and like a mechanic, you fix problems, but you don't give a shit about that car or its owner if the problem is terminal. You move onto the next patient. And that's why you have no idea how to treat people like me — the families of your patients. We deserve respect."

"Miss Bartholomew," the doctor said — she sounded and looked embarrassed. There were a couple of other visitors in the room, and one or two of the nurses were also listening in. "Please, let's not have this discussion. It really isn't appropriate."

"Yeah? Well, fuck your appropriateness" Sadie snapped, and flopped down on Jodie's bed, tightly gripping her sister's hand. The doctor looked at Jordan, who could only shrug his shoulders. In a way, he agreed with what Sadie had said — but he also understood the doctor's problem. She was only doing her job, and she had neither the time nor an interest in arguing with her patients' relatives.

The doctor walked off without saying another word.

Jordan looked down at Sadie, and then his eyes turned to Jodie. And he stopped.

There on Jodie's face, like some fictional ectoplasm, was the imprint of a hand.

A small hand print, red in colour, spanning Jodie's mouth and nose.

It had been suffocating her.

Jordan shuddered, and his eyes scanned the room for signs of creature that had left the print. He saw nothing, but he certainly felt the presence of something evil. Another demon should not have had this effect on him. Demons did not give off auroras of evil, because they weren't evil. Not unless ...

The Corrupted, they were evil.

And Satan, wasn't he working with the Corrupted?

But this, this wasn't right, because only demons could become the Corrupted, and the presence he sensed was not great enough to have been left by a demon.

And the hand print on Jodie's face ...

An imp.

The gophers of Hell.

Jordan squinted his eyes and looked around the room. Even in human guise, he should've been able to see any celestial creature. But he saw nothing. The imp, or whatever it had been, was no longer here. No doubt it had darted back to Hell the moment Jordan turned up. Which meant that Satan would now know precisely where Kobold was, that he wasn't in Hell, that he had completely and utterly disregarded a direct order from the devil.

Jordan cursed inwardly.

And then he considered another thought.

If only the Corrupted were truly evil, why was he sensing an evil presence? The imp could not have given off such an aurora, even if carrying out an act that was ultimately evil, because the imp was merely carrying out instructions given to him by one of a higher standing — therefore, the imp wasn't evil. Not in the true sense of the word.

Jordan clenched his fists and realized that he was changing in ways that he didn't truly understand. His powers were increasing, yet at the same time metamorphosing, so that he saw things differently, more vividly. The human sensations, they were becoming far more clearer – taste, touch, smell, sight and sounds, they all had a crisper, more realistic edge to them.

He wondered ...

Was he changing into the most powerful creature in Hell or was he turning human?

Or was it both?

Sadie turned to look at him, tears in her eyes, and it upset him so much to see her like this. He'd known her only for a short while, but he already loved her more than anything. He knew that she would always be the most important thing to him, whatever happened. For four hundred years, he'd sought liberty, and now he was getting a taste of it, he didn't want to surrender it.

He sat down next to her, carefully, supporting the bulk of his weight on his legs, not willing to allow himself to rest completely on the hospital bed. He put an arm around her shoulder, and pulled her towards him, squeezing her tightly at the same time.

"You have to be strong for her," he said. What he really wanted was to get her out of the way, get her back home, and to return himself as Kobold the demon, and locate the imp who was obviously trying his hardest to snatch away Jodie's life. But he couldn't rush Sadie – that wouldn't be right. Besides, so long as he was here, Jodie was safe from the imp. It was only when he left that the imp would sense that it was safe to return – and that was the dangerous time, when he would find it difficult to get back to the hospital. At least he was assured in the knowledge that imps had little in the way of power, and consequently, it would not be an easy task for the imp to take a human life, even one in such a fragile condition as Jodie's.

All the same, he would have to rush back to the hospital as quickly as possible – more accurately, he would have to get Sadie home and out of the way as quickly as possible, for then he could adopt his demonic form, and return to the hospital in the blinking of an eye.

He couldn't allow anything to happen to Jodie. Not only was she innocent, he also couldn't bear to see Sadie so distraught. But it was going to take a lot of work to prevent any harm from coming to her.

He looked around the room once more, his eyes scanning every surface, every item of furniture, for signs of any celestial presence. He could see none. The imp must've simply have returned to directly to Hell, its atoms dispersing without touching any other surface in the room. Perhaps it had returned to rejuvenate its powers.

That didn't matter, Jordan thought, because he was certainly powerful enough to destroy an imp.

But in doing so, wouldn't he be breaking every rule in Hell?

What would the devil do to him then?

Would he be hounded by the Jäger? Would he become one of the Corrupted?

He felt Sadie kiss his cheek, and it brought him back to reality.

"You don't have to stay," she told him. "I know this can't be much fun for you."

"I'm here for you," Jordan said. "I'm here for Jodie too, but I'm here for you to lean on."

"Will you always be here for me?"

Jordan smiled, even though he didn't feel like doing so. "Of course," he told her, "Of course I'll always be here for you. You don't get rid of me that easily."

And he stayed with Sadie until early evening, until she decided that she had to go home. An assurance from the doctors and nurses that they would call her the moment there was any change didn't seem enough to comfort her, but she left all the same.

"I need sleep," she said. "Sleep and food."

"I'll make you a sandwich and put you straight to bed," Jordan told her. He had to get back to the hospital as quickly as possible. An imp could not take a life as quickly as a demon could, but they could take a life all the same.

Thankfully, Sadie agreed, and soon they were driving back to her flat in his BMW. Once there, he put her to bed, his eyes lingering longingly on her body. As he made her a ham sandwich he used his powers to make her drowsy, and by the time he returned to her bedroom, a tray in his hands, she was already well on her way to falling asleep

"I doubt I'll find the energy to eat it," she said.

"Well, I'll let you catch up on your sleep," he told her, tucking her in and kissing her gently on the lips. If only, he thought ... if only there was time to make love to her, to know that truly magnificent human emotion once again. The other night with her, it had been like losing his virginity all over again. It had been the most wonderful experience he could ever recall having.

But there just wasn't time. There were more pressing matters that required his attention.

Soon, he was out of her flat and on his way to the BMW. The worst part was, he had to drive the BMW to some secluded spot, where Jordan Weaver's body could hide while Kobold the demon travelled to the hospital. The lockup, he thought solemnly, was the safest place, and so he drove as quickly as he could, assured in the knowledge that should he be stopped by the police force, he had special powers at his disposal to curtail their conversation.

He reversed the BMW into the large lockup, and switched off the engine – not that carbon monoxide could kill him, but it could render the human body he had created effectively useless. He stepped out of the car and walked to the doors, closing them and throwing the bolt to lock them. Then he returned to the BMW, climbed in and switched off the car's headlights.

Within a second, he was standing in the intensive care unit, just a few feet from Jodie's bed.

And so was the imp.

25

The imp looked warily at Kobold, his hand resting on Jodie's face, effectively smothering her in her sleep. Already, she was showing signs of becoming distressed, her comatose body shifting slightly, barely imperceptibly beneath the evil creature's touch. The imp made no effort to remove his hand. All the same, Kobold could see the concern on his face.

"Leave her," Kobold commanded.

"Fuck off," the imp hissed.

"You dare to disobey an order from a higher rank?"

Now the imp smiled, like a naughty child who knows that he is getting the upper hand, who senses victory in a minor battle of wits. "I do the bidding of the devil himself," he said. "I obey none other than Satan."

Kobold took a couple of steps towards the bed, but the imp didn't shrink away.

"You think that Satan is watching over you now, imp?" he asked with a sly grin. "You think that he will extend the hand of protection when you require it of him?" Kobold widened his eyes and laughed. "You are nothing to him, imp. He will see you destroyed, and he will not lift a finger. You are mere cannon fodder, a pawn on a chess board. And to me, you are nothing more than an annoyance — a fly buzzing around my head." Now the imp's anxiety was more visible on his face. His hand moved away from Jodie's mouth. "And like a fly, I shall swat you."

And with that, Kobold launched a bolt of flame from the palm of his right hand. It shot out across the bed and caught the imp in the chest, blowing him back against the wall. Celestial though he may have been, solid objects were just as solid to the imp. Slightly winded, he dropped to the floor and looked up at the demon standing before him.

Kobold just laughed again.

"Who do you fear the most, imp?" he asked. "That is the question you should he asking yourself. Do you most fear the wrath of the devil, with whom you may well be able to bargain with for your life or do you most fear me?" The imp got back to his feet and clenched his lists, adopting a pugilist's pose. "Let me assure you, imp, with me, there is no bargaining."

"Satan commands," the imp said, though there was a frightened edge to his voice now, "and I obey."

"Then you shall be destroyed," Kobold said laconically.

"As you destroy me, Kobold, so Satan shall destroy you," the imp had the audacity to proclaim.

Kobold reached out and grabbed the imp by the throat. "Let me tell you something, imp. Satan does not have the power to destroy me. If he had, then he would already have done so. You have chosen the wrong team and you will pay dearly for that mistake." The imp struggled to free himself, but Kobold merely tightened his grip. He could sense the overwhelming build-up of power, and knew that he could destroy this celestial being as easily as he could destroy a mortal. The imp also seemed to sense that his survival was very much in doubt.

But still he would not deny his master.

"If you destroy me," he gasped hoarsely, "then you condemn your soul to the Corrupted."

"A very brave proclamation from one in such a delicate position," Kobold said, his grip loosening slightly. "Tell me, imp, what is your name?"

"Mörder," the imp said.

"Well, Mörder, you have seconds to argue your case," Kobold told him. "You see, I want that human behind me to survive. You are threatening that desire, and I cannot have that."

"If it isn't me, it will be another." the imp said. "Satan will not rest until he has taken her soul from her mortal body. That much is obvious. You can destroy me, but what will it achieve?"

"It buys me more time," Kobold said, slipping into his human persona for a moment flawed and vulnerable. Mörder appeared to notice this and seemed to think that he stood a chance of survival. He'd argued his case — that was enough. Kobold didn't want to listen to any more. "Have you anything else to add?"

"Once she's taken, you will be next," the imp said defiantly. "Already, the Jäger will be preparing to hunt you down."

"You underestimate me," Kobold said. "I have tenfold the power of the Jäger. And I will be victorious."

"I applaud you on your confidence," the imp said, "however misplaced and misjudged it might be."

"And I applaud you on your intrepidity, Mörder," Kobold told him. "But I am bored playing games. Your time, like my patience, is at an end." And with that, he plunged his free hand into the imp's chest and gripped tightly on the soul that was inside. It writhed and squirmed in his hand like some thick, stubby snake, desperate to break free. But Kobold held it tightly — the life-force of the imp, the precious entity that was keeping him in Hell.

And once that was gone ...

"Please," the imp said suddenly. "Don't do this." There was desperation in his voice, and Kobold recalled what he had been like when he'd first been transformed from tortured soul into celestial being, how powerful he'd felt — how powerful, but also how vulnerable, for the imp was the lowest rank of demonic entity in Hell, the lowest in Heaven and Hell, in fact.

At least when you were human, if you had faith, then you believed you went to a better place when your life was lost. To celestial beings, the end was so final, for there was no other place. How could there be any other place beyond Heaven and Hell, any deity more powerful and higher in rank than God Himself? And so there was no belief in the afterlife, in Heaven and Hell — there really was nothing more.

And so the imp was understandably terrified as he stared into eyes that were unforgiving.

"I'm pleading with you," he said.

For a moment, Kobold felt sympathy.

Then he remembered about Jodie, and what this creature had been doing to her.

And he wrenched the life-force from within Mörder's chest and held it up in front of the terrified imp's eyes.

"Please," the imp gasped. Without the life-force, the Hellish body

Mörder had been using would soon shrivel up and decompose. But while the life-force still beat in Kobold's hand, Mörder would survive – he would have to resurrect another form, but that would take only a matter of days, during which time he would be unable to leave Hell, be unable to torture souls, be unable to interact with anyone or anything.

But he would survive.

"Please," Mörder gasped again. "Please don't do this."

"You have argued your case, Mörder, and you have lost."

And with that, Kobold squeezed the throbbing life-force, grinding it into slime with his hand, and tossing it down on the floor of the hospital where it would remain forever, unseen by any human eyes.

Mörder shook his head, unable to comprehend what had just happened.

"You have destroyed me," were his last words.

And then the imp seemed to explode into a billion particles of dust, and Kobold realized that the hand that had been gripping Mörder's throat now grasped thin air.

With that realization in mind, he took a couple of steps back from the shredded life-force, and considered the severity of what he had just done. He had destroyed a fellow celestial, the worst crime that could be committed. He was now one of the Corrupted.

And yet, hadn't he been trying to prevent the imp from taking an innocent life, from doing the bidding of the devil who himself was not averse to using the Corrupted to his own ends? Didn't the two of them cancel one another out, or would he forever be condemned to a lifetime of trying to evade the deadly Jäger that Satan would surely send after him? Wouldn't that make it impossible to have any kind of life at all with Sadie?

He turned and looked at Jodie. He'd just saved her life, but Satan would doubtless send out other imps, perhaps even a demon, to claim her, as Mörder had predicted. He couldn't be with her all of the time and he couldn't lead a human life, not any more, not with legions of Jäger out for his blood. Jäger commissioned by Satan – who clearly wanted him dead – and sanctioned by Heaven.

What hope did he have?

And yet, as he stared at Jodie, he saw her stirring, moving her head gently from side to side, opening and closing her mouth like a fish. Secure in the knowledge that in his present form, he could not be seen by humans, not by the patients nor the nurses in the room. Kobold stepped over to the bed and looked down at the face of the girl whose life he'd just rescued. Her complexion was pale, now devoid if make-up, a handful of spots dotting her face, her hair lank, unkempt, unwashed, all evidence of her previous vanity now gone. She was a child, an innocent child, and in her face it showed.

Her eyes moved beneath her lids, and then flickered open, rolling backwards in her head as she blinked quickly. Then they opened fully, and her eyes darted around the room ...

Then they settled on Kobold.

As though she could see him.

She opened her mouth to speak, but no words would come.

Kobold considered leaving, disappearing into a fine vapour only to materialize in the body of Jordan Weaver a few miles away, but he was curious. She could see him, and yet ...

She wasn't afraid.

He smiled. "Get some rest," he told her.

She frowned, confused, and then her eyes stared right through him, and he knew the moment was gone. However she had once managed to see him, she could see him no longer.

In a way, he was relieved.

But he was also confused.

His appearance, the red skin, the horns, the hairy, crooked goat legs, they should've shocked her, should've terrified her, and yet it had been as though she hadn't seen those malformations. It was as though he'd appeared to her as a total human.

Kobold backed away from the bed. He had someplace else to be.

Within a second, he was sitting in Jordan Weaver's body, using all of the human senses that it provided him with. For a moment, he felt chilly, the air being particularly biting that night.

And he was suddenly aware of somebody sitting alongside him.

Demon though he was, he still jumped, startled by the presence of another, as he twisted his head to see who was sitting in the passenger seat.

"Did I give you a fright?"

It was the angel, Reizend.

Jordan felt the colour returning to his face. "Fuck yes!"

Reizend smiled. "Sorry."

Jordan felt his heart rate beginning to return to normal. "Jesus fucking Christ."

"You know, you shouldn't be taking the Lord's name in vain."

"I'm not religious," Jordan said wryly. "Besides, I work for the other team, remember?"

Reizend gave a crooked smile, as though she'd found his comments amusing, but couldn't allow herself to laugh.

"Anyway, to what do I owe this pleasure?"

"I saw what you did," the angel said quietly.

"What I did?"

"To the imp."

Jordan frowned. "You were watching? Where were you?"

"Nowhere," Reizend responded – it was a banal answer to a human, but to a demon, it made perfect sense. "You realize now you've overstepped the mark."

"It was something I had to do."

"It was an unselfish act," Reizend said, "and for that, you have nothing to fear from Heaven."

"But I have plenty to fear from Hell?"

"Something like that," Reizend told him. "You know Satan's not going to be happy about what you did."

"Tell me about it," Jordan said. Even now, he could feel an invisible pull on his soul, as though somebody were dragging him downwards. He was being summoned by the devil. He tensed his body, though that wouldn't do any good – it was his spiritual form that he had to tense up, his soul that had to fight the summons. "There's no going back now, though, is there?"

"Satan has two forces at his disposal," Reizend explained to him – but she wasn't telling him anything he didn't already know. "He has the Jäger, who are sanctioned by God Himself, and who have practically unlimited authority to achieve their aims. But more significantly, he has the Corrupted, who in some instances are more powerful than the Jäger, because they feed directly off human suffering."

"And that makes them stronger?"

"It's a concept you wouldn't understand, Kobold, because you're one of the righteous ones. Human misery is a potent source of energy, but it still isn't as potent as the source that is feeding your powers." She looked at him squarely, and raised an eyebrow. "Have you solved the riddle yet?"

"The riddle was easy to solve, Reizend," Jordan said. "The tough part was trying to figure out why I was chosen."

"Few are chosen, Kobold, and only God knows why," Reizend said, "But I can assure you of this – you have a fearsome battle ahead of you if you are to survive. Satan is using the Corrupted, and they will see this as a test of their own personal strengths. Long after Satan is gone, the Corrupted will still be baying for your blood, keen to bring about your destruction."

"So, you're saying that my chances of survival are slim to zero?"

Reizend didn't answer immediately; she looked away, through the windscreen of the BMW, neither of which improved Jordan's confidence, particularly as it didn't afford much of a view by way of distraction.

Another human trait, he realized.

"You have to destroy Satan," she told him. "But first, you must gather your strength. You're too weak at the moment, in spite of how powerful you may feel."

"There's only one place to improve my strength," Jordan said soberly. "Here on Earth, it's being constantly eroded."

Reizend nodded. "You have to return to Hell."

"Where I'm surrounded by billions of demons who will do whatever Satan commands of them?"

"Your powers can be rejuvenated outside the gates of Hell, Kobold," Reizend reminded him. "Far from the gates, in the caves of the mountain ranges surrounding the plains."

"You know Hell, do you?"

"I've seen Hell," Reizend told him. "We are all shown what Hell is, the first moment we arrive in Heaven. We're reminded of our weaknesses, and rewarded for our strengths."

"The caves of the Corrupted?" Jordan said with a scowl. "I don't know which is worse."

"The Corrupted aren't as many as the demons in Hell, Kobold," Reizend said. "I'm sure you can find a quiet corner to hide."

"Hiding isn't something that comes easy to a demon, Reizend."

"And you want to be human again?" she asked him with mock incredulity. "You still have a lot to learn about human nature."

"I'm constantly being reminded how fragile humans are, Reizend," he said. "For the moment, it is that which takes precedence over all else."

"You're talking about Jodie, aren't you?"

"An imp nearly claimed her soul," Jordan said. "If Satan should send a demon ..."

Reizend smiled. "I will guard her," she assured him.

"You'd do that for me?"

"Not for you" she said. "For Jodie. She will go to Heaven if her life is taken, but her time most certainly hasn't come yet."

"But if Satan sends a demon–"

"You think I'm not strong enough?"

"You're an angel."

"And over the years, I've fought demons," she told him. "As have many angels before me. Fights to the death."

"You've destroyed?"

"Only the Corrupted," she added quickly. "Other than that, and in spite of what you said earlier, demons and angels are on the same side. Only we generally dish out rewards and you dish out punishment."

Jordan smiled.

Then he remembered what he had to do. "I don't think I dare spend too much time in Hell."

"Your powers are being constantly drained, Kobold," Reizend said. "If you stay on Earth, you will surely die. It's something you have to do."

"But what about Sadie?"

"You must say goodbye."

"But I want to be with her."

"You want to be human," Reizend corrected him. "That's different."

"No, I want to be with Sadie," Jordan insisted. "I love her. And it's because I love her that I know I'm almost human. I'm more human than devil, Reizend."

"Then use the best of both to achieve your aims, Kobold," the angel told him, before disappearing.

Jordan didn't return to Hell that night. Instead, he remained awake and considered his options.

He had to leave Sadie, if only in the short term, because if he didn't feed his powers, he would never be strong enough to defeat Satan. Oh, he felt powerful enough to take on a dozen Jäger, and certainly more of the Corrupted, with their crude methods of combat, but Satan was different.

He didn't get to become the devil without having even more power than the previous incumbent.

And Jordan had to ensure that he was even more powerful.

And so he would have to say goodbye to Sadie.

And that was why he didn't rest that night – because with every minute that passed, he was taken ever nearer to the time that he would have to kiss her for the last time.

And he didn't want to face that.

Wasn't that ever so human of him?

26

When the telephone rang at three-thirty in the morning, it had given Sadie the fright of her life. She'd been in deep sleep, trying to regain some of the energy that had been zapped from her over the last few days, and she'd shook violently as she'd reached across the bed to pick up the receiver, her mind not fully awake, her heart beating heavily and noisily in her chest. She hadn't really had time to consider the possibility that it could be bad news, that telephone calls at this ungodly hour only delivered bad news. Not until the person on the other end had responded to her hoarse grunt of a greeting.

"Is that Sadie Bartholomew?"

"Yeah," Sadie said, her voice still shaky. She rubbed one of her eyes, which refused to come open thanks to a thick crust of sleep.

"It's Doctor McCutcheon."

At that, Sadie sat up immediately.

"Yes?"

"Jodie has regained consciousness," the doctor said.

It hadn't been what she was expecting, and her body still felt crushed by an overwhelming sense of loss, even though none was evident. She clutched a hand to her face and stifled a sob. "My God."

"Miss Bartholomew? Did you hear what I said?"

"Yes," Sadie said softly. "Yes. I'll be right there."

And she cradled the receiver and flopped back on the bed as her body and her mind tried to come to terms with the news.

Her sister had regained consciousness.

Her sister was alive!

For the next few minutes, she simply ran around the flat, trying to decide what to do next. She threw some bread into the toaster, switched it on, and then fixed herself a bowl of cereal. But midway through, she decided to take a shower, and rushed into the bathroom, switching on the faucet. The water was icy cold, and she reconsidered, switching the shower off and putting the plug in the bath. She switched the hot water tap on full, and poured in some bubble bath, then stopped what she was doing. She wanted to get there in a hurry, not spend an hour lounging in a hot, soothing bath.

She darted back into the front room, looked across to where the telephone was, and made her way over to it, feeling so light-headed, it was almost as though she were floating across the room, her feet barely touching the floor.

She scooped up the handset, flopping down on the sofa at the same time, and pushing the speed-dial button for Jordan's cellphone, the only method of contact she had with him. She didn't think it suspicious that he hadn't supplied her with a home number — unusual, maybe, but not suspicious. And he always answered her calls.

Tonight was to be no exception.

"Sadie?"

She didn't ask how he knew it was her – she knew his phone had caller ID. And she was also conscious of the fact that it was late, and that Jordan had every right to sound anxious.

Strangely, he didn't.

He also didn't sound tired.

But that was of no consequence to her right now. Right now, she wanted to tell him the good news "It's Jodie. She's regained consciousness. She's ... she's making a full recovery."

"Wow. What, the doctors told you that?"

"Well, not exactly, they just said she's awake, but hey, it's the first step towards full recovery, isn't it?"

"Are you going over to see her?"

"Well, that's just it," Sadie said coyly, tucking her legs beneath her body. "I wondered if you could come over and go with me. I mean, I know it's late, and I'd understand if—"

"Hey, I'd be honoured. In fact, I'm on my way over anyway. I was going to check in on you."

"Don't you ever sleep?"

"As little as possible, sleeping's for the dead," Jordan said — and she could tell he was smiling. "I'll be there in five."

"That quickly? I'm not ready."

"I'll help you get ready," Jordan told her.

And Sadie couldn't remove the smile from her face.

Five minutes later, almost to the second, Jordan arrived, and she let him in, before hopping into the shower. Within twenty minutes, they were on their way to the hospital, driving towards a sky that graduated from brilliant red on the far horizon, to a fiery orange, to a pale blue, becoming a deep navy dotted with stars overhead. It was a beautiful sight, and one that Sadie rarely saw. Getting up at the crack of dawn was not high on her list of priorities.

But she knew that she'd never forget this sunrise, or the joy it was already bringing her.

"You know," she said as Jordan drove. "I really thought I was going to lose her. And it was bad enough losing mom and dad, but to lose Jodie ..." She shook her head. "I don't think I could've taken that. I mean, I've never thought about suicide, you know, throwing myself off a high-rise, but I would've just blamed myself for it. For the rest of my life."

"It wasn't your fault," Jordan assured her. "It's the fault of some drug-pushing scum. I hope he fries in Hell. He deserves to." There was a sneer on his face that Sadie couldn't remember ever seeing before. In a way, it frightened her. Then he turned to look at her, and his expression softened. "I'm sorry. I guess you didn't wanna hear that, did you? I shouldn't be bringing you down like this."

"No, that's okay," Sadie assured him. "Hey, we all have opinions. It's just ... well, I never considered anything so drastic for criminals before. I was always one of those guys who protested for the abolition of the death penalty back home. I think it's pretty barbaric." Jordan nodded his head slowly, and he was wearing a pained expression, as though something about the death penalty was affecting him personally.

For a moment, she thought she'd touched a raw nerve.

She reached across and brushed her hand against his.

"Hey, how about we change the subject?"

Jordan nodded.

But he didn't reveal any secrets to her.

And they spent the rest of the brief journey in silence, and for the most part hand-in-hand.

Sadie practically ran to the ICU, and was met *en route* by one of the nurses, who assured her that there was no need for her to rush, that her sister's condition certainly wasn't worsening, and that Jodie was, at that precise moment, asleep, and that this probably wasn't the best time to be visiting.

But Sadie wasn't to be put off, and she sat down next to her sister and grabbed her hand, as Jordan followed behind.

Jodie looked as peaceful as she had done ever since she'd first been hospitalized, but that was misleading, because she was no longer in a coma. She was simply sleeping. That was all. She could be back at home, in her own bed, if it wasn't for the monitors, drips and wires that surrounded her.

Doctor McCutcheon came over, bags under her eyes, stethoscope around her neck. She said in a tired Scottish accent, "We've sedated her. It's the best thing for her, because she needs to rest. I don't think she's ready for any excitement."

"We're not going to throw a goddamned party!" Sadie snapped, feeling tears forming in her eyes. She felt Jordan rest a hand on her shoulder.

"How soon before she recovers completely?" he asked.

There was a pause, and Sadie looked up at the doctor. "She's very weak," she finally said. "We'll be keeping her in for at least another week, though we'll be moving her out of the intensive care unit tomorrow, uh, today," she corrected herself, looking at her watch. "But as for a full recovery ... we can't really say how much damage her body's received as a result of the drugs. It's looking like she might get away with no ill effects, but the blow to her head is something that we're very concerned about. As I said to you on the phone earlier, Miss Bartholomew, Jodie regained consciousness, but she wasn't very coherent. We couldn't make out much that she said, and we certainly couldn't ascertain the severity of any brain damage. We're hoping it'll be minimal, if there is any, but we can't say. The next few days will reveal more answers to us."

"She was talking?" Sadie said, looking at her sister's beautiful face. In spite of a pale complexion, sunken cheeks, the dark eyes, the bandage covering the bald spot where her head had been shaved prior to the operation, Jodie was as pretty as she'd always been. "What did she say?"

"Dream talk," the doctor replied. "Nothing important."

"To me it is," Sadie said quietly.

"She was talking about angels and demons," the doctor said. "If you'll excuse me now, I've already run way into my rest time. I've got a new shift coming up in about four hours. I'd like to get some sleep."

"Sure," Sadie said, and her attentions turned back to Jodie.

She was going to stay here until Jodie woke up again. She wanted to be here, if not for the first time her sister woke up, then certainly for the second time.

In the event, it was some hours before Jodie finally awoke, and by then, Sadie had drifted off to sleep herself, only to be roused by her sister squeezing her hand lightly. She looked up, slightly confused, and her eyes fell upon Jodie, upon her tired, but smiling, expression.

"Hey, sis."

"Hey," Jodie said hoarsely. She reached up to her throat. "Thirsty," she said.

"I'll see if I can get a drink sorted," Jordan said, and Sadie wondered whether he'd been awake all this time. He was sitting in the chair on the other side of the bed, and a magazine was spread out across his lap. He stood up and tossed it onto the seat behind him.

Sadie smiled as he walked off and then she looked back at her sister.

"You know, you had us all worried there."

"Why? What happened?"

"We'll talk about it later," Sadie said. "When you're a bit better."

"Sadie, I'm scared. What happened?"

Sadie reached up and stroked her sister's greasy hair. "You're fine now," she said. "But somebody spiked your drink at the party."

"I don't remember any party," Jodie said grimly. "I don't remember anything."

"You were high, and you fell down the stairs," Sadie went on. "Banged your head pretty hard. You had to have an operation, you were in a coma for a few days, but we think you're okay now."

"My head hurts," Jodie said, instinctively reaching up to the bandage. She grimaced. "It's kinda sore."

"It will be," Sadie said with a smile, "they cut out part of your skull."

"That's gross," Jodie said, smiling weakly. "Did they put it back?"

"Yeah, right after they realized you didn't have a brain."

"Nice to know you're not treating me with kid gloves."

"Just trying to make you feel at home," Sadie said. "How are you feeling?"

"Pretty rough," Jodie said, closing her eyes. "Tired, whacked out, sore and aching. I just wanna sleep for a hundred years."

"You nearly did," Sadie said grimly. "But I'm glad you're back."

"Did you and Jordan come in to see me when I was out of it?"

"Of course. Why?"

"Did you come to see me last night?"

"Yeah, we both did."

"Jordan was here when I woke up," Jodie said.

"I don't think so, honey."

Jodie closed her eyes. "He was. Only it wasn't him. He was ... he was sorta weird."

"What do you mean, weird?"

Jodie shook her head. "I dunno. Like he wasn't human. Like he was evil. But it was like ... like he was saving my life. He had this fight, right over there by the wall. This smaller guy, some kind of devil, was trying to kill me."

Sadie smiled slightly. A hallucination, nothing more. But her sister wasn't finished.

"He stood there, right at the bottom of the bed, and I should've been scared of him, but I wasn't. Then I fell asleep. When I came to, this angel was sitting right where you're sitting."

"An angel?" Sadie said, trying her hardest not to sound sceptical.

"I remember seeing her somewhere before, but I can't recall where," Jodie said, not noticing her sister's incredulity. "She said her name was Reizend. She said that although Kobold was a demon, we shouldn't fear him. He wasn't evil."

"Kobold?" Sadie asked.

"Miss Bartholomew?"

Sadie looked back to see Jordan and the doctor standing behind her.

"She's fine," Sadie said.

The doctor nodded, and Sadie knew that if she could, she would've said, "I'll be the judge of that." But doctor kept her mouth shut and sat down next to Jodie.

"How are you feeling now, Jodie?"

Jodie shrugged. "Rough – like I've just run a marathon and then been knocked down by a car, but otherwise I feel fine."

"You have been in the wars," the doctor told her. "We'll be moving you onto a ward later today, but I want you to get some rest, okay? You've got a long recuperation ahead of you."

"Does this mean I don't get to go back to school?"

"Not for a week or two."

"You know, I actually feel really, really bad," Jodie said, closing her eyes and pushing her head back into the pillow. "Maybe two weeks won't be long enough."

"She's back to normal," Sadie said, smirking.

The doctor smiled tightly. "Well, it may be some time before you're well enough to get right back into the swing of things, but you'll certainly be well enough to go back to studying in a few days. We'll know more after we've run a few tests."

"You're still concerned?"

"Jodie suffered a serious head injury, and there is always a risk that there could be complications, even after this length of time," the doctor said. She turned to Jodie. "I'm sure you're all right, but we just want to make doubly sure. And you're in the right place. Better here than back home."

"How long before I can leave?"

"We'll see how you're doing in a week or two," the doctor said, standing up. "But even then, you may have to stay in bed for a few more weeks."

"Sounds great."

Sadie smiled again – the wit was there, but it was delivered by a tired girl. As the doctor strolled off, Sadie squeezed her sister's hand. "We should go, let you get some sleep."

"You look as though you need it as much as I do," Jodie said. Her eyes switched to Jordan, and she smiled knowingly at him. "Look after her like you looked after me." Sadie looked up to Jordan, who was giving her sister a half-smile. She frowned suspiciously, then recalled what Jodie had said earlier, and how Jordan must've caught the end of the conversation.

Later, in the car, she asked him about what Jodie had said about him.

"Angels and demons?" he said with a smile. "A concoction of drugs and sleep deprivation."

"She'd been in a coma."

"It's not the same," Jordan said. "She was pretty mixed up. She's been through a lot."

"To hell and back," Sadie muttered.

"You'll never realize how close that description is," Jordan said mysteriously, as he wove his BMW through the late afternoon traffic. "I feel sorry for her."

"Like those near-death experiences, she's gonna be talking about that for the rest of her life," Sadie said, not picking up on Jordan's comment. Then she remembered the conversation Jordan had had with Mark a few days ago, the one about death. The conversation that had spooked the hell out of her. "Mind you, you'd say that was something else altogether, wouldn't you?"

"You mean because of what I said about NDEs?" Jordan asked. "Hey, I'll admit to that, yeah, and freely. I've got an open mind – in my line of work, you learn to believe anything, however unimaginably unfeasible it sounds."

"You're beginning to sound more like Mulder every day," Sadie remarked. "Just remind me what it is you do again."

"Law," Jordan replied. "Anyway, this thing with Jodie, it's not the same. I'm not saying she's mad, because she isn't, but she was dosed up with some pretty heavy shit back there, and the body produces its own powerful narcotics in times of stress."

"All the same, she seemed pretty sure," Sadie said, realizing the moment she said it how ludicrous it sounded.

"Yeah? Well, do I look like a demon to you?" Jordan asked her as they pulled up in the car park behind the flats. He turned to her and smiled.

"Well, you look like a little devil," Sadie replied, lightening the mood. "You wanna come in for a night-cap?"

"It's a bit early for that."

"My body clock is all screwed up," Sadie offered by way of explanation. "How about dinner?"

"How about I take you out for dinner?"

Sadie had to agree that was a good idea.

27

Detective Chief Superintendent Saddington was at home when the call came through on the mobile, and he quickly made his way to the Vauxhall Senator parked outside, a car that the Metropolitan Police paid for, but which he used mainly for things that were entirely unconnected with work. Tonight, however, was something different altogether.

He drove quickly, secure in the knowledge that with his exemplary driving record behind him, and the fact that he was on the way to a job, that he wouldn't be prosecuted, even if he had the misfortune to be pulled by some of his colleagues. Within ten minutes, he was parking in the street to the rear of the house in question. As he locked the car and armed the alarm, he noticed that curtains twitched in a couple of houses, and was reminded of the fact that this was a neighbourhood watch area.

He could only see the rear of the house he was heading for, but a net curtain twitched in one of the upstairs windows, and Saddington smiled to himself as he opened the tall gate and walked up the path to the back door, which was opened by a young detective whose name he was ashamed to admit escaped him. He nodded a greeting, and stepped into the house, where he saw Gerry Egan waiting at the foot of the stairs.

"What have we got, Gerry?" Saddington asked, as he followed the DI up the stairs.

"A suspicious car," Egan answered in his thick Belfast accent. "The Yanks spotted it. We didn't have any boys on duty. I was nearby, on my way home, so I came straight here – and called you the minute I confirmed what we have."

"Which is what, precisely?" Saddington wanted to know as they stepped into one of the front bedrooms.

"It's a Mondeo," Egan said.

Saddington raised an eyebrow. He could make out shadows in the room, but no faces. The room was in total blackness, and a pair of curtains at the front were drawn almost totally together, with just a four-inch wide gap between them through which both a video camera and an SLR camera pointed.

A bright red glow preceded the shadowy figure who stepped out from the far corner.

Saddington recognized the voice. Rothschild.

"A hire car, rented out from Heathrow Airport to an American whose name is unimportant, because it doesn't match any of the names we've got," he said. "One thing's for sure, these pukes ain't gonna be using their own names."

"What about descriptions?"

"We got the information from the hire firm's computer – our boys hacked in there earlier – so we haven't questioned any of their people," Rothschild said, "and it would be a thankless task, because those guys rent out a hundred cars or more a day. Besides, the pukes left Heathrow in a taxi. Which means they have to have a third man over here."

"A money man," Saddington muttered. "Well, apart from suspicion, what have you got? I mean, an American renting a car at Heathrow Airport isn't unusual. There's thousands of you bastards go through there every day."

"The car's parked in the lot behind the apartment block," Rothschild went on. "Which is a pretty strange place for an American tourist to hole up. And inside, two guys, we can't get a decent description. We had one of our girls do a walk-by, but she couldn't get close. The car lot isn't a through route. All we know is that there are two guys in the car. That's suspicion enough."

Saddington nodded. "You're right," he said, turning to Egan. "Get some units here. We'll pull them in."

"We can't do that," Rothschild protested.

"You mind telling me why not?"

"For starters, they haven't broken the law."

"They're behaving suspiciously," Saddington said. "Which is cause enough for us to give them a tug."

"We need to know where the money is," Rothschild said. "Listen, these guys ain't gonna go in there shooting. They're gonna ask questions."

"And how does that help you?" Saddington questioned. "You're in here, they're across the street."

In the gloomy light cascading from the gap in the curtains, Saddington could see Rothschild smiling sheepishly, and he closed his eyes, knowing precisely what was coming next. "We have a directional mike," the American said. "We point that sucker at the window to the front room of that apartment, and we can hear everything."

"Well, I was expecting you to say you'd bugged the flat, so I should be grateful," Saddington said, "but tell me, how much have you been hearing?"

"Pillow talk reveals a lot," Rothschild said, "though for that, we have to send a car round to the rear of the building."

"And how much has this pillow talk revealed so far, besides proclamations of love and a lot of squelching?"

Rothschild didn't answer. He dragged on his cigarette, the tip glowing fiercely. "We're just monitoring the situation. This new guy she's got hanging around – I've got my suspicions about him. He's American too."

Saddington stepped up to the window, pushing aside one of the FBI men and peering through the lens of the camera. "Can't see much."

"We're loaded with infrared film," the FBI man explained. "Take a look through the video camera," he suggested. "It's got night-vision capability." Saddington did just that, and saw a fuzzy image of the Mondeo, with two men visible sitting inside.

"Is Sadie Bartholomew there?" he asked, stepping up from the eyepiece.

"She came back from the hospital with her boyfriend about four-thirty." Rothschild answered. "They stayed about an hour and a half then went out again. The pukes turned up about seven-thirty, and the Bartholomew girl returned with her American chum about midnight." Saddington saw that it was about one-fifteen now.

"Why'd it take so long for you to call this in to us?" he asked the American.

Rothschild didn't answer at first. Then he said, "We had to be sure these were our guys. We ran all the checks, they came back suspicious, we gave you a call."

Saddington didn't believe the American for a minute. "Why haven't they made a move yet, then? They've had over an hour."

"Waiting for chummy to leave," Egan suggested. "He's a big, hard-looking bastard. If he weren't a Yank, I'd say he was a face. He's got that presence about him. Something fucking scary about him, so there is."

Rothschild nodded. "We have guys at the hospital," he said. "They say pretty much the same thing. It wouldn't surprise me if he didn't have some powerful connections from wherever the hell he comes from."

"What's his name?"

"Jordan Weaver. We've ran all the checks. Came up with Jack Shit. No records on that name, nothing identifiable from any prints or any photographs."

"You ran his prints? Where'd you get them?"

"From the outside of his car," Rothschild confessed. "Hey, this is big to us, Derek, you know."

"I'm beginning to realize that, yeah," Saddington said grimly. "You reckon those hitmen know him?"

"Maybe – could be why they're not making a move."

"But what does he want with Sadie?"

"Maybe the same thing they want."

Saddington considered that opinion for a few moments. He couldn't leave Sadie Bartholomew at the mercy of these animals, in spite of what Rothschild wanted. And yet if he moved in now, he'd blow an FBI operation, and probably find himself being hauled up in front of his superiors for wrecking the relationship between the Met and the FBI.

"If anything happens to her–"

"It won't," Rothschild assured him. "As soon as they leave the car, we'll send over some guys to the apartment block. We'll be listening in, and if things start to get loud, we'll move in."

"We'd end up with a hostage situation, and two heavily armed lunatics," Saddington said. "I can't risk that."

"You have to," Rothschild told him.

"You don't have any legal jurisdiction here," Saddington retorted.

"You'd blow our operation for this?"

"I don't want her death on my hands."

"You won't," Rothschild promised. "We can see the front room of the apartment from here."

"The curtains are shut," Egan said. "You can't see a fucking thing."

"We can hear everything," Rothschild assured. "Hey, our guys are trained in this kind of thing."

"Your *guys* certainly don't have any jurisdiction," Saddington said. "If anything happens, we'll move in."

"You don't have enough people here."

Saddington turned to Egan. "Call in CO-19," he said.

"Wait!" Rothschild said. "If you call in the armed units, you're gonna alert those pukes. They're not stupid."

Saddington considered his options. "What are you suggesting? Listen, you guys don't have any powers of arrest here, you know."

"Who's talking about arrest?"

"I can't go along with that," Saddington said.

"You don't have any choice," Rothschild said. "We want that information, this is the only way we're gonna get it, and we certainly ain't gonna sacrifice Sadie Bartholomew for it. We can't let this develop into a siege situation so we'll move in, take them out."

"Where did you get your guns from?" Saddington wanted to know.

"The people here came straight from the embassy," Rothschild said. "They have diplomatic immunity."

"This is insane," Egan muttered. "Christ. Sir, you can't let them do this."

Saddington turned to the Irishman. "You've changed your tune. I thought Sadie Bartholomew was way down your list of priorities."

"This is Britain," Egan said, looking at Rothschild, "and not the bloody USS Great Britain. These boys think they can come over here, do what the hell they like. If this thing goes belly up, Sir, we're gonna take the flak, not them."

Saddington nodded. "I think you're right." He looked at Rothschild. "Paul, if things get hot, if Sadie Bartholomew gets killed, or any innocent bystanders, you're going to hop on a plane and fly back to the States with your career intact, leaving us to pick up the pieces."

"So this is all you're worried about? Your career? We're talking about the big picture here."

"Aye," Egan said, "and you want us to be the sacrificial lambs."

Saddington saw Rothschild shaking his head, as he said condescendingly, "It's not like that at all."

"Sir?" one of the FBI men near the window said seriously.

All eyes turned to him.

"I have Target Two leaving the building."

"Target Two?" Saddington queried.

"Jordan Weaver," Rothschild told him.

28

Something was wrong.

Jordan could sense evil in the vicinity.

Not demonic evil, but human evil, which in some ways was worse, because human evil could never be controlled. He could sense it close by, and he knew that it threatened Sadie.

He couldn't allow that.

He stood up walked over to the window, peering out through the curtains, but he couldn't see anything that presented any kind of threat. Sadie stood up behind him and put her arms around his waist.

"What's up?"

"Just wondering about the weather."

"Why?" Sadie asked him. "You're not going home, are you?"

"I've got an early start in the morning," he lied.

"I was hoping you were going to stay the night," Sadie said.

He turned and faced her, and the sense of doom increased. "I have to go," he said. "It's very important. I don't wanna leave you–"

"Then don't."

"I have to," he said.

"When will you be back?"

"Tomorrow," he promised her. "Late morning."

"I have your word?"

"Have I lied to you yet?" he asked her, raising an eyebrow.

"Well, you haven't always told the truth," she said.

"Hey, that's not fair," he said, feigning hurt. "I've probably kept things from you, but I've never deliberately told you a falsehood."

She hugged him. "Why won't you tell me everything?"

For a moment, he was tempted to. But common-sense prevailed. "I wish I could," was all he said.

He didn't want to rush things, but he had to get out of the flat, had to find the danger, had to eliminate it. He had to make his excuses — but Sadie was still vulnerable, and he didn't want to just drop her.

"Are you gonna be okay?"

"I'm gonna have to be, aren't I?"

"I'll be thinking of you," he promised her.

They kissed, at first tenderly, then more passionately, and Jordan feared it would turn into something that he wouldn't want to stop, and so he reluctantly broke away. "I'm gonna miss you," he said.

"I thought you were coming back in the morning?"

"Does that make a difference?" Jordan asked with a smirk.

A thought entered his head, and he reached into his pocket, pulling out a small, silver crucifix, which he handed to Sadie, "Here," he said. "I want you to wear this always."

Sadie looked at him with uncertainty. "You're scaring me, Jordan," she said, fingering the necklace. "You're making it sound like I won't see you again." Jordan kissed her lightly on the forehead, and pointed to the crucifix.

"It will protect you when I'm not here," he said. "Keep evil at bay."

"You really believe all that?"

"I have very good reasons to believe it," he told her cryptically.

Sadie saw him to the door, and he kissed her again, before making his way quickly downstairs as the sensation of evil caused adrenaline to pump around his body, giving him a heightened sense of awareness. Human bodies, he reflected, were so fragile, so receptive to their environment. And coupled with his own heightened senses, it made for an almost overwhelming combination.

In the lobby he stopped and pulled his overcoat around his body in preparation for the cold outside.

But that wasn't it, he told himself. He didn't fear the cold — he didn't fear anything ...

But the human side of him was anxious, shivering with trepidation, as though preparing him for a battle.

He was being unreasonable.

There was nothing on the planet that could destroy. Nothing human, anyway.

But then, why did he feel fear?

He shrugged away the sensation.

Whatever human threat awaited him, he would deal with it summarily.

And that threat, he realized, was coming from the rear of the building — from the car park.

Outside, in the cold night air, the stars sparkling overhead, the moon glowing brightly, he looked around the car park, and saw the usual array of vehicles lined up in tidy rows. But there was an extra car parked there, one he didn't recognize.

And it was positively glowing with evil.

Jordan rolled his head around his neck for a few seconds, hearing some of the bones crack, and then made his way across the car park towards the car in question. Something was telling him that the men in this car — he could sense there were two — presented a threat to Sadie. As he neared the car, one of the windows slid down with a hum.

"Hey, how you doing?" Jordan asked as he stepped up to the door.

"You got a problem, buddy?" the man in the passenger seat asked — he was American.

"Me? Nah, just wondering what y'all are doing here."

"Fuck off," the passenger growled.

"Now, you see, I can't do that," Jordan said with a smile.

The passenger leaned back ever so slightly, and there was a brilliant flash of light, a deafening bang, and Jordan was looking at the sky. By the time he realized what had happened, he felt himself being sucked out of the human body, downwards, falling towards Hell.

Jordan Weaver was dead.

And Kobold was returning to a place that was now hostile towards him.

Saddington jumped as the gunshot sounded, and he rushed towards the curtains, pulling them aside to see the Mondeo's lights sweeping across the car park, leaving a body in their wake. All around him there was panic, as FBI agents grabbed guns and rushed out of the room, clambering noisily down the stairs. Rothschild was with them, and Saddington followed, with Egan close behind.

"Bloody hell!" the Irishman was cursing. "This is a total balls-up, sir!"

"Tell me about it," Saddington snapped breathlessly, as he rushed out of the open front door. The Mondeo was gone, and two FBI agents were jumping into a Golf, ready to give chase.

Rothschild threw out his arms in exasperation. "Well, this was totally fucking unexpected!"

"Is that why you didn't have men out here?" Egan demanded to know.

The American turned on him. "Hey, I know this is a total cluster fuck, but we weren't expecting those fucking assholes to waste somebody right outside."

"No," Saddington said grimly, "you expected that to happen in Sadie Bartholomew's flat, didn't you? And when it happened, you'd be ready and waiting to mop up the pieces." He looked across to the car park, where three agents were tending to the wounded man. One of them hopped to his feet and dashed back across the road as the VW screeched away from the kerb perhaps twenty seconds too late to catch up with the Mondeo.

"He's dead," he said as he approached Rothschild. "Took away half his fucking head."

Rothschild shook his head. "Man, this is a total fuck up!"

"You said it," Saddington agreed. "Did somebody call an ambulance?"

"That poor sucker doesn't need one," the FBI agent said.

"It's procedure," Saddington snapped, turning to Egan. "Get it sorted. And call this fucking mess in at the same time." He looked at Rothschild and scowled. "You satisfied?"

"Not particularly," the American said, as he casually lit a cigarette. "They're still out there, and we don't know any fucking more than we did before this whole goddamned thing started."

"Well, I hope you've got an explanation planned for your bosses, Paul, because we certainly ain't taking the shit for this."

"You won't have to," the American assured impatiently. "So long as we have your continued co-operation–"

"Paul, you'll be lucky if the Met doesn't throw you out of the country," Saddington said, looking up to the flat where Sadie Bartholomew lived. "Somebody had better tell her that her boyfriend's just had his brains blown out," he said. "Before she hears about it on the news."

Rothschild took a drag from his cigarette.

"I'll do it," he volunteered.

"I don't think so," Saddington said. "I'll do it."

Sadie almost collapsed when the Chief Superintendent gave her the news. It couldn't have been more than five minutes ago that Jordan had left the flat, and now he was dead. She just couldn't comprehend it. She'd gone from relieved exhilaration to complete shock within a few minutes, and it was certainly taking its toll on her.

The detective was looking at her sympathetically, but that was no consolation to her. After all, wasn't this the very same man who had taken away her house and her finances?

"I'm very sorry, Miss Bartholomew," he said.

Sadie could only nod as she sat down on the sofa. It was some moments before she spoke — it had been the first thing she'd said since the police officer had entered her flat. "Outside, you say?"

"In the car park," the detective said solemnly.

"I ... I didn't hear anything."

Saddington didn't respond.

"I still can't believe it," she said. "Are you sure? Are you certain it was Jordan?"

"Yes," Saddington replied.

"But how can you be sure?"

"Well, we'll need you to formally identify the body," Saddington said, "unless you have an address for a next-of-kin?"

Sadie shook her head. What did she know about Jordan? He was the mystery man, and she had no idea where his family — if he had a family – lived. Under those circumstances, she was the only one who could formally identify Jordan—it would be the third body she'd have to identify in her short existence.

"I don't, sorry."

"What about work? Where did he work?"

"I have no idea," Sadie answered. "He was very mysterious." Saddington nodded knowingly. "Who would do this to him?" She suspected that Jordan, who had implied that he carried out shady work for the US government had been the victim of some James Bond style killing.

What Saddington said stunned her even more. "We believe that the men responsible were after you."

"After me?"

"Mafia hitmen, over from the United States. Professional killers."

"And they were after me?"

"Your father owed a lot of money to some very powerful and unscrupulous people back in the US," Saddington told her. "The FBI believe that the hitmen were over here to interrogate you, to see whether you had information as to the whereabouts of your father's money."

"But I don't."

"I don't doubt that," Saddington said, and she believed his sincerity. "But these men are not so forgiving or believing."

"My God," Sadie said, running her hands through her hair. "Jesus fucking Christ! How much more is gonna go wrong with my life?"

"You have had it rough," the detective agreed. "And I'm very sorry."

Sadie looked up and saw the sadness in his eyes. "Thank you," she said.

"Is there anywhere you can stay tonight?"

"No," Sadie replied. "Not anymore."

"It's just ... well, the car park is an official crime scene," Saddington said cautiously.

"You mean Jordan's still out there?" Sadie asked softly. The detective nodded. "This is getting worse."

"It may be some time before he's moved."

With that thought in mind. Sadie resolved to sleep in Jodie's bedroom, which overlooked the front of the building. "I've nowhere else to go."

"We'll have armed officers posted outside the building," Saddington assured her, "but for your own peace of mind, I think you should consider a hotel for tonight."

Sadie shook her head. "I don't think so," she said.

"Is there anyone who could stay with you?"

Sadie nodded. "A friend," she said. Melissa. She would call Melissa. "Thank you for ... well, if you don't mind, I just want to be alone."

"I understand," Saddington said, going for the door. Sadie followed him. "Your friend?" he said as he opened the door. "His or her name?"

"Melissa." Sadie told him.

And with that, he left her alone.

Sadie was too stunned to take it all in. She walked into Jodie's room and fell face down on the bed, smelling her sister's deodorant and perfume on the sheets. If she could have slept in her own room, she would have been able to smell Jordan's aftershave, his distinctive odour, but she couldn't go into her room, not with his body just twenty or so feet away, probably still warm.

In a way, she wanted to go and see him, wanted to hug him while he was still warm, but she knew they probably wouldn't permit that, wouldn't allow her to contaminate the crime scene. And she wasn't sure that she could handle it. It would rip out her heart to see Jordan lying lifelessly on the tarmac of the car park.

She couldn't deal with that.

She couldn't deal with losing him.

She remembered the crucifix he had given her, no more than fifteen minutes ago, and she reached to her neck, grabbing the tiny cross with the figure of Christ embossed upon it. It would keep her safe, he had told her, keep evil at bay when he wasn't around.

In a way, he'd been right.

The evil had been kept from her, and instead, it had struck him down.

The tears came suddenly, and were quickly followed by the sobs. She continued to cry for half an hour, and then a sense of peace overcame her.

It was as though Jordan were watching over her. Jordan, or some fantastically righteous presence.

She fingered the crucifix again.

Perhaps Jordan had been right all along. Perhaps he was in Heaven, looking down at her.

She smiled slightly, ever so slightly.

And then she reached for the telephone to give Melissa a call.

29

Kobold awoke — which in itself was strange, because demons didn't sleep — to find himself lying on jagged rocks and smooth boulders, a dusty red surface with a pink sky that might resemble Mars to an ignorant human. But this was no distant planet. This was Hell, and it existed on another plane to the planets of the Solar System.

Kobold pulled himself to his knees and looked across the horizon, towards the city of Hell many miles in the distance. He could see the familiar sight of souls falling to the surface, tiny dots against the glowing sky, to be collected by demons who would drag them back to their lair. Kobold shrugged away the sense of confusion, and took in his current surroundings.

He could see that the uncomfortable surface upon which he now lay was situated on a small plateau, no more than fifteen feet wide, and maybe ten feet deep, and located some two hundred feet above the vast plain that stretched between the walls of Hell and the mountain ranges surrounding it. Behind him, set into this particular mountain, was a cavern, its gaping mouth black and uninviting.

But it presented him with cover from the eyes of the Jäger, who undoubtedly were already on their way from Hell, having seen him fall from the sky. They would've seen where he'd fallen, and the cavern was the first place they'd look. No, he thought, he had to get away from here.

But where?

He'd intended to return to Hell, upon the advice of Reizend, to rejuvenate his powers, but he hadn't expected a mere mortal to send him here. Kobold scowled. He would have that mortal's life — that much he promised himself. He hauled himself to his feet and looked skywards, taking in the sheer face of the mountain. This was where he had fallen, by sheer chance, and there was no way he was able to physically climb out of this location, which meant he would have to use the powers at his disposal.

Unfortunately, he could sense that his spiritual powers were weak—weaker than he'd thought when he was in Jordan Weaver's body. Now, naked and in Hell, he realized that the symptoms signifying the loss of his powers hadn't been that strong. He could only hope that they would regenerate more quickly than normal.

The Jäger could be here in seconds, if they knew precisely where he was. The chances were that they didn't, that they had received a summons from Satan, who had sensed Kobold's arrival back in Hell, and that they had then been dispatched to locate and destroy him — or take him back to Satan.

The way he was feeling right now, Kobold knew that he didn't have the energy for a prolonged fight — he also knew that once his powers were back to normal the Jäger would not be able to contain him. It would be a fight to the death — hopefully not his.

He glanced back up at the sheer face of the mountain, which stretched for more than a mile overhead, and considered his options. Here, he was an easy target, but on that sheer face he would present an even easier one. There was no escape, nowhere to run. He looked over the side of the plateau upon which he stood, and saw the almighty drop. A fall down there would shatter his demonic body — on Earth, it would do nothing to him. Here, in Hell, it would be the equivalent of a man falling the same distance on Earth. It wouldn't kill him, but it would render his body useless for days while he recovered.

The only consolation was the fact that the Jäger would suffer the same fate if they fell.

So he wandered over to the mouth of the cavern and peered inside, his eyes trying vainly to penetrate the inky blackness beyond. The cavern could hold many things – the Corrupted, any number of them, with powers that would easily outmatch those he possessed now, which would mean him becoming embroiled in a fight he didn't want, and could probably not win in his present condition. It could also contain some of the lost souls, some of the escapees from Hell, and it would ordinarily be his job to transfer them right back to the city — but he had more important things to worry about.

The cavern might well be deep, might afford him some cover that could delay the inevitable.

He took a couple of steps into the mouth, feeling his entire body being swallowed up by the darkness.

He felt nervous and demons didn't feel nervous.

His humanity was showing again.

He resisted the temptation to look behind him, wanting his eyes to become accustomed to the dark as quickly as possible, and that process would be destroyed if he looked back at the city, at its many fires burning against the pink horizon. It wasn't long before his eyes could make out lighter smudges against the black, and he could see the walls of a tunnel that twisted off to the right a couple of hundred yards ahead. Realizing that he could be walking straight into a dead end from which there was no escape, he nonetheless began to walk. He had to hide, had to go to ground, if he was to stand any chance of surviving for even a few more hours.

Around the bend, the tunnel began to widen out, and Kobold paused momentarily.

Was that light he could see ahead?

He frowned.

It certainly looked like light, or at least something that was causing the lighter grey smudges of the walls to flicker haphazardly. What *was* this place he wondered, as he took a few more steps. With each step that he took, however, each of them echoing quietly up and down the tunnel, he became more and more certain that it definitely was light up ahead.

And where there was light, especially unnatural light, and especially in a place as dark as Hell, there was usually life — or in Hell's case, death.

He continued walking, rounding another bend, and was suddenly greeted by the sight of flaming torches embedded into the walls, their flames causing eerie shadows to dance against the uneven rocky surface. He took a step back in surprise, and then looked further ahead, to an entrance cut into the rock. What, Kobold wondered, lay beyond that entrance?

Grabbing one of the torches, he proceeded up the tunnel, walking slowly, keeping his eyes fixed dead ahead, and with his ears paying particular attention to his rear. It took him no more than a few seconds to reach the entrance, and there he paused, allowing his eyes to take in what lay beyond.

He could see the walls on the other side of the room, which appeared to be circular in shape, and adorned with many torches. If it was circular, then it was at least two hundred feet in diameter. The floor of the room was well illuminated, and Kobold could see that the Star of David had been carved into it, each line more than four feet thick and cut down into the rock at least two feet. Kobold took a couple of steps forward, and looked upwards. He couldn't see the ceiling, just the sheer walls of the circular room that stretched upwards to a point that was beyond his line of sight.

Kobold braced himself— yet another human trait — then stepped into the room.

The walls were at least three hundred feet high, and the ceiling, far overhead, was domed. Whoever had carved out this room had worked for many, many years, and with much devotion — more than Kobold could ever have expected from one of the Corrupted. There was dedication here, Kobold thought to himself, as he walked around the Star of David on the floor, to the crackling sound of flames from the myriad torches. He saw the throne in the centre of the Star, and then he saw the hole in the ground, that undoubtedly led to other rooms, what humans would call living quarters.

There, he thought, he would find the owner of this cathedral.

"Not there," a voice behind him said.

Kobold spun around to find himself face-to-face with a demon the like of which he had never seen.

The demon was old, had the features of a ninety-year-old human, and the hair on his crimson head was white in colour. His eyes, rather than being black, were a deep blue, in direct contrast to the glowing red complexion of his face. The expression he wore was one of ambivalence and Kobold felt as though he had nothing to fear, even though his demonic senses hadn't alerted him to the presence of this bizarre member of the Corrupted.

"I am not one of the Corrupted," the demon snapped indignantly, as he walked across to the throne as though in pain. He sat down, and Kobold realized that this demon didn't possess the legs of an animal, but rather those of a human.

Now he was intrigued.

"Then what are you?" he was compelled to ask, as he walked up to the throne and stood before it.

"You ask me that?"

Kobold didn't respond.

"Well?"

"You look like a demon," Kobold said, and the demon shook his head. "Then what are you?" Kobold said repeating his earlier question.

"My name is David," the demon said.

"David — the King of the Jews?"

David shook his head and laughed. "You really are naive, aren't you, Kobold?"

Kobold was going to ask how this David knew his name, but nothing much surprised him now. Instead, he said, "Would you care to enlighten me?"

"Maybe, maybe not." It was said with something akin to petulance, like a child in a bad mood.

Kobold sighed. "Listen, I'm in trouble here, and I haven't got time to fuck around!"

David smiled and wagged a finger. "You are becoming more and more human every day, aren't you?" He let out a chuckle. "Oh, the Jäger, they are coming for you ... may take them the best part of today to find you."

"How do you know that?"

"I know," David assured him confidently.

Now Kobold was angry. "Your answers don't seem to provide me with much in the way of explanation, old man."

"Indeed I am old," David confessed. "Older than you could imagine."

"I don't know," Kobold said. "I can imagine quite a lot. I know, for instance, that Satan is more than two thousand years old. I myself have been in celestial form for four hundred years."

"Like the blinking of one of my eyelids," David said.

"So, how old?"

"As old as the universe."

Kobold shook his head. "I don't believe that for a minute. God created the universe."

"He did," David agreed. "And then He desired a companion."

"And He created you?"

David smiled, "Don't believe everything you read in the Bible, Kobold," he said. "The Bible was written by man, and man has been known to exaggerate, to tell stories, to jazz things up and play things down."

"God created you as His companion?" Kobold asked, wondering how, when his very existence was being threatened, he could be having this conversation.

"He created me as His equal."

"You're wasting my time you know, I could destroy you right there where you sit now."

David smirked. "No you couldn't," he said confidently, shaking his head. "Not in your present condition. You would be fortunate to win a battle with an imp, now wouldn't you?"

Kobold had to admit that David was probably right, but he couldn't believe what this insane-looking demon was telling him. "God doesn't have any equals," he said, not answering David's question.

"Not anymore," agreed the old man.

Kobold was beginning to become intrigued – in spite of everything, he wanted to know what story this old man had to tell, even if that meant risking his own destruction. "Is this going to change my life knowing what you're about to tell me?"

David smiled and shrugged. "It may — or it may not. In any case, it will neither delay nor advance the arrival of the Jäger, and since you have to regain your strength, and you have time to spare, you may as well listen to what I have to say."

"I'm all ears," Kobold said, sitting down in one of the niches that formed the Star of David.

"For many, many millennia, God and I lived alongside one another," David said, "and I grew to think of him not as a father, which to me — *to everyone* — he truly is, but more as a brother."

"Brothers?"

"Hardly in the conventional sense," David went on. "You could never hope to comprehend what it was like, before all of that up there and all of this down here was created."

Kobold shook his head. "What was it like?" he asked.

David tutted. "We talked ... you see, we had dreams, as many humans do, and all of ours involved us having more and more companions. But you see, God had used up the bulk of His powers creating me — hence the absence of any other companions. I had the powers, but not the skill to mould characters. And it was many millennia before God found the necessary power to create the rest of the universe."

"He created everything?"

"*Everything*," David said. "Oh, don't get me wrong. The universe is a self-functioning, self-sufficient environment, and gets by without any interference. Even the Earth – and those planets like it – can manage themselves."

"Other planets?"

"Life didn't begin as it says so in the Bible," David said with a smile. "The Earth was an experiment and it wasn't the first. Some of the earlier ones ... well, let's just say that it is fortunate that we spaced the planets as widely apart as possible."

"So, how did life begin?"

"It was almost as scientists describe it," David explained. "God didn't simply mould humans into shape. He is powerful, but not that powerful. We had to mix up the chemicals, and watch life form within them. At first, simple single cell organisms. On Earth, it began the same as it did on other planets. But whereas it didn't evolve successfully elsewhere, here we created life that appeared to evolve intelligence."

"We? You said God created everything."

David smiled. "He did – I merely assisted. Perhaps I am building up my part somewhat."

"Perhaps," Kobold said. "I'm curious to know why you ended up here."

"All good things, Kobold, all good things," David said. "God considered this planet to be a success, and He began to nurture the life here."

"With religion?"

"That wasn't planned," David said with a smile. "That was a side-effect, dreamt up by mankind itself."

"But the Bible says—"

"The Bible says that God intervened, that He spoke to selective members of mankind, that He gave advice and instructions," David said. "All true ... but it wasn't to bolster His own standing. It was simply to prevent mankind from destroying itself."

Kobold frowned. "Mankind was hardly capable of destroying itself three thousand years ago."

"And it wasn't capable of destroying itself ten thousand years ago," David said. "Which is when God first showed Himself. Time for us is different to the time humans experience. A thousand years is nothing to a being who lives for all eternity. But you see, God had this idea. He knew that mankind would increase their intelligence and their scientific understanding, and with it, their ability to create weaponry and ideas of mass destruction. He believed that by planting this seed of religion, of Himself as the greatest power imaginable, he would ensure that mankind feared his retribution."

"But they didn't," Kobold said.

David shook his head solemnly. "Even before God first appeared to them, when they were barbaric and uncivilized, they were worshipping any object that they thought would bring them good fortune. The sun, animals, even strange-shaped rocks. God had to make His wrath known to man."

"By plagues, floods and earthquakes?"

"God is capable of manipulating the weather, of manipulating the planet itself even," David said. "And in the days before civilization reached the scientific level that allowed it to understand the way the planet worked, the way the planets revolved around the Sun, and the way the Sun revolved around the centre of the galaxy, and the way the galaxy revolved around the centre of the universe, which is, ultimately, where God sits, His powers had an effect." David sighed. "But mankind does not believe what it cannot see, and God cannot appear before man anymore."

"Why not?"

"With the creation of Heaven and Hell, rules were created, rules that not even God Himself can disobey," David said. "You see, there isn't a soul in Heaven or Hell that is older than ten thousand years, because before that time, there was no Heaven or Hell."

"What was there in its place?" Kobold asked, intrigued.

"Nothing," David said. "And because there was nothing, there was no way to reward the righteous."

"So there are millions of people who've never experienced the afterlife?"

David nodded. "When mankind first became aware of God, He decided that he must have some method of reward and punishment. And this is what He came up with. Everlasting life. Everlasting happiness or perpetual torture, depending on your point of view. And where there is Heaven, there is God and where there is Hell ..." David broke off.

"There is a devil," Kobold finished his sentence. "Then you ... you are the first devil?"

David didn't answer. He said, "There is a bloodline that runs for more than ten thousand years to the present day. That bloodline is responsible for Jesus, and for all the highest angels in Heaven – the Seraphim. They are all descendants of that bloodline, as was Jesus himself, who was descended from God. Only Jesus revealed his true identity to humanity – and he was dealt with summarily by mankind, because his point of view did not accord with theirs."

"So, why didn't God help him?" Kobold asked.

David smiled. "I always wondered myself. He never gave me an answer – and He never gave Jesus an answer. But you see, Jesus achieved so much, didn't he? Perhaps it was all part of God's big plan."

"You know, that's how humans console themselves when something bad happens," Kobold said. "And the more intelligent ones know that it's just a lie. There is no big plan – you've as good as admitted that yourself."

David shook his head. "God has these incredible powers of prediction," he said. "He can look down, see an event happening, and know whether his intervention will make it better or worse. He is, after all, omniscient."

Kobold asked the one question he'd always wanted to ask. "Then why does He sit around and watch genocide? Why does He allow that?"

"As I said, He can predict the outcome of any particular action with startling accuracy," David said. "And in addition, the Earth is not the only planet He has to watch over. In fact, there are one or two with life forms as intricate and intelligent as those on Earth. Some are evolving far more quickly, in fact."

"But He allowed millions of innocent people to be killed," Kobold said, referring to the Holocaust.

David could only shrug. "To a human, a lifetime is no more than, what, eighty years? A century seems like eternity. A millennium, impossible to conceive, all of the changes that take place over a thousand years. But to us, to the immortal, to God Himself, what is a thousand years in a lifetime that has lasted billions of years and will last many, many billions more? What are four million lives to a being that has seen the passing of quadrillions of lives, and will see the passing of quadrillions upon quadrillions more?" David shook his head. "No, God has His own plan, his own scheme, and humans do not even play a part in that. I'm amazed that you haven't realized that, since you're a celestial immortal yourself."

Kobold could only give a half shrug. What David had said was perfectly true. There was no need for time in Heaven or Hell, because years could pass in the blinking of an angel's eye. The passing of four million lives in six years was apparently insignificant to one as powerful and immortal as God.

David said, "Perhaps you are more human than celestial, more mortal than immortal."

Kobold bowed his head. "Perhaps you're right," he said.

David snorted. "No matter — I was talking about bloodlines, wasn't I?" Kobold looked up again. "How the Seraphim are created out of the mortal DNA that Jesus Christ himself shares. The Seraphim come from humans who are so righteous that they exist only once or twice every century. Some of the bloodline becomes corrupted by human misery and horror, so that those rightful heirs never become more than angels."

"They fall to Hell?"

David shook his head. "Never. That could never be permitted. God Himself smites these potential Seraphim down while they are still human should they ever exhibit signs of corruption, before they commit acts of evil that would otherwise condemn them to Hell."

"So the demons?" Kobold asked. "I have always wondered. Where do they come from?"

David smiled knowingly and outstretched his arms. "As there is a bloodline that comes from God, so there must be a bloodline that comes from the devil."

Kobold frowned. "Then you ... you *are* the devil!"

"The original," David said, "instructed by God Himself to punish the wrongdoers."

"This is unbelievable," Kobold said, his mouth agog. "I just don't believe it."

"Believe it" David said. "My first heir, Lucifer ... it was intended that he become my chief assistant, that he appear before mankind as a warning, much in the same way as Jesus later did." He shook his head solemnly. "But Lucifer was already corrupted before his life was taken away by God. When he came to Hell ... well, he didn't see me as a father, he saw me as a rival. I fought him, I destroyed him ... my own son, for want of a better description."

"But I thought Beelzebub—"

"You thought Beelzebub destroyed Lucifer?" David asked with a smile. "Beelzebub came from my bloodline, from Lucifer's bloodline. Fifteen generations passed before Beelzebub fell to Hell. He was little more than a common murderer, with nothing to distinguish him from the rest of the fallen souls. And yet ... I recall he was always powerful. Powerful, unrepentant, truly evil. Maybe even worse than Lucifer."

"I thought the devil wasn't evil," Kobold said. "I thought that was the whole point. How can one so evil punish others for their sins?"

David shrugged his shoulders. "Power corrupts," he said. "And absolute power, the kind held within the hand of the devil, absolute power corrupts absolutely."

Kobold shook his head. "And Beelzebub — what happened to him? How did he become the devil?"

"Hell was in turmoil by this time," David said. "Full of corruption, demons destroying demons, taking the lives of innocent souls. The revolt was massive, and I couldn't stop it. Beelzebub arrived in Hell to be punished, as all other sinners are. He wouldn't be punished. He fought. He was powerful — extremely powerful." David added ruefully. "He was a mere soul, and yet he destroyed demons. Countless demons fell before him — my most loyal servants. Even I could not contain him. He threatened to destroy me. And I have been here ever since."

"Beelzebub was more powerful than you?"

David lowered his head and smiled. "I was God's first creation. I didn't have, to use a human expression, an evil bone in my body. The power did not go to my head, because I was not interested in power."

"You gave it up?"

"I feared destruction," David said. "As one of God's creations, I can be destroyed. I didn't want that."

"So you've remained here, in this temple, ever since that day?"

David gave a half smile. "Does that make me sound like a coward?"

Kobold didn't answer immediately. The demon inside him – and there was still a demon inside of him – believed that David had given way to cowardice. But it was the human inside of him that eventually said, "No. It makes you sound sensible."

"Thank you."

There was a pause. Then David said, "Beelzebub got his comeuppance — after a time."

"Satan?"

David nodded. "Satan, the most worthy holder of the post of devil. I had high hopes for Satan. I've even sat in counsel with him on a number of occasions." He sighed. "But like I said earlier —power corrupts."

"Is that what is in store for me?" Kobold asked quietly. "Corruption and evil?"

"You come from my bloodline," David said. "And I guess the evil, the corruption ... part of it must come from me."

"And from the woman — Lucifer's mother."

David nodded. "That possibility was brought to my attention," he said solemnly. "I chose the wrong woman. I will forever be cursed for that, for creating monsters like Lucifer and Beelzebub — and Satan."

"And me?"

David paused. "You, Kobold, you are different. You have no desire to be the devil. And yet, you are the strongest of all of my bloodline currently in Hell other than Satan. It's your destiny, Kobold, to fight Satan. And you must defeat him."

"I cannot do that," Kobold said.

"You will have the power," David assured him.

"But when?" Kobold asked with desperation in his voice.

David just smiled. "You will know when you are ready," he assured him.

"But I feel weak enough to be destroyed by the Jäger," Kobold said, and was reminded of the fact that the devil's hunters could not be far behind him now, especially after having been delayed by this demon claiming to be God's first devil.

David stood up, and Kobold could see now the power within his frame. For an old demon, he was muscular, and in spite of his gentile appearance, his white hair, his glowing, blue eyes, his wrinkled face, in spite of all of this, he certainly gave off an aura of power.

"I want to see the structure of Hell returned to its previous state," he said. "I want to see an end to the corruption at the highest levels. As the saying goes, the fish always stinks from the head down. I need a devil to take the place of Satan who will be just, who will punish the wrongdoers, and keep his demons away from those who have chosen a path of righteousness." David walked over to the far side of the room and looked up at the domed ceiling, far overhead. "Up there," he said, "where humans tread, I see demons offering temptation to those who otherwise would never have strayed from the highway to Heaven. They plant evil thoughts into minds, subverting souls who may well have been harbouring sinful ideas, but who would never have acted them out. That has to be stopped, Kobold. It was Satan himself who presented temptation to Jesus — and in those days, Satan was far from being full of corruption. To Satan, who had only been the devil for a handful of years, it was simply a case of following the examples set before him. That was what Beelzebub did. That was what Lucifer did. Sent forth demons to corrupt mankind. And when Satan saw Jesus — the son of God — he felt obliged to tempt him." David gave a deep sigh. "You know, I don't think God ever forgave Satan. Why He didn't destroy him then and there, I'll never know."

This was all very interesting, Kobold thought, even highly intriguing, but it wasn't helping him at all. Another time, another place, and he could listen to David all day. David took his time saying what he had to say, but he left nothing out. He was honest.

And he had uncanny powers. He raised an eyebrow. "I sense your concern, Kobold, and I can assure you that when the time comes, you will be ready."

"Can you tell me how long I've got?"

"Before your battle with Satan?" David asked. "A matter of days, which is why you must remain in Hell and rejuvenate your powers. As to your battle with the Jäger, well, that will come a lot sooner, but it shall be over very quickly."

"You seem sure."

David said sternly. "I am always sure."

And somehow, Kobold almost became convinced of his inevitable success.

Until he heard the shouts and echoes from down the rocky corridor.

30

All at once, Kobold felt a tremendous surge of power rush through his body – it was as though his muscles were simply inflating. More significant was the sense of his mental powers inflating, his whole head throbbing as they did so. Kobold outstretched his arms as though he were being crucified, and outstretched the fingers of each hand, holding the palms away from his body. It was a pose of sheer defiance and strength, and as the Jäger entered the cavern Kobold could see the uncertainty on their faces.

On the faces of all six of them.

Kobold smiled, whilst at the same time sensing that David was no longer with him, that he had shrunk away to the hole in the floor. And yet, he didn't feel alone.

He certainly didn't feel afraid.

The Jäger encircled him, each of them brandishing long spears with a tip that split into two arrowheads, each of them tipped with a venom that was particularly lethal to demons. Kobold turned slowly in a circle, his eyes meeting each of the Jäger in turn, a smile on his face as though he were looking forward to the forthcoming conflict. Two of the Jäger met his gaze defiantly, clearly confident with their own abilities – the other four seemed less assured, one of them even dipping his head subserviently.

Kobold's smile broadened, and he felt the power building up within him once more.

One of the Jäger, clearly the most senior of the troop, took a couple of steps forward.

His face was crimson, but striped black, like Maori tattoos, and his horns were long, curling inwards so that their tips pointed down at his own bald head. His mouth was open, snarling, showing his sharpened teeth, and he held his spear expertly.

"I have destroyed many demons," he said in a hissing voice, "and each of them begged for mercy. I showed them none, because the Corrupted deserve no mercy." He lifted the twin tips of the spear upwards, displaying the blood that had stained them. "What makes you think that you will be any more of a challenge than they were?"

Kobold continued smiling, sensing the Jäger standing behind him, secure in the knowledge that he would immediately know if they tried to make a move on him. "What is your name, Jäger?" he asked.

"I am Zerstörer," the Jäger answered. "Know my name — know the name of the demon who will take your life, who will send you into oblivion."

Kobold nodded. "In that case, Zerstörer, you had better know my name. My name is Kobold, and if you – all six of you – believe that you will destroy me, then you had better be prepared for the toughest challenge of your life."

"Talk is cheap, Corrupted," Zerstörer spat. "And the time for talking is at an end. You will die — whether you die fighting or die screaming for mercy is of no concern to me. But be sure of this – you *will* die."

Kobold's smile broadened.

He looked in the direction of the weakest Jäger, the one whose head had dipped earlier, and pointed a finger.

Instantly, the demon's body was consumed by fire, and the screams echoed through the domed room as smoke drifted upwards and the celestial flesh turned to a greasy, powdery residue sticking to shiny, white bones. The unfortunate Jäger, still clutching his spear, fell to the floor screaming as his soul was sucked out of his body and burnt.

Long after he was gone, the screams still echoed through the room. Kobold looked at Zerstörer and raised an eyebrow. "One down — five to go."

"He was inexperienced," Zerstörer said. "Which is probably why you chose to attack him. Your sins are multiplying by the second, Corrupted. By the powers vested in me by Satan, the devil himself, and under the authority of our Lord God, I will destroy you."

Kobold took a step back, closer to where the ashes of the fallen demon lay, so that there was no longer a Jäger behind him. "You keep saying that, Zerstörer, but you seem unwilling to carry out your oath. Could it be that you are afraid?"

"Never," the leader of the Jäger hissed, and at the same time, another of his troop lunged for Kobold, who clasped his hands together in a praying gesture, and sent a bolt of fire in the attacker's direction. The Jäger was thrown back, slamming into the wall of the cavern, while his spear flew through the air in Kobold's direction.

Kobold caught it neatly in one hand, twirled it around so that tips were facing away from him, and then threw it like a javelin.

It impaled the unfortunate Jäger to the wall of the cavern, its poisonous tips penetrating his chest and inflicting a mortal wound. As the life force ebbed from the Jäger's tortured body, he let out a bellow of agony and expired in a cloud of steam.

Kobold turned to the remaining Jäger and smiled.

Three of them were backing off.

Zerstörer, however, remained defiant.

Kobold knew why. With each attack, he was using up his powers, and soon he would be weak.

At least, that was Zerstörer's thinking.

Unfortunately for the experienced Jäger, he was not fighting an ordinary demon.

Kobold had plenty of power in reserve.

"Does anybody else wish to make an attempt on my life?" he asked.

One of the Jäger backed away, closer to the entrance of the cavern, ready to make his getaway. The other two took up position on either side of Zerstörer, and slightly behind him, clearly fearful for their own safety.

Kobold didn't want to waste any more time. He still felt strong.

He held out his hands and used his powers to rip the spears from the hands of those two Jäger. As they flew towards him, he caught them and plunged their tips deep within the rocky ground.

"You are no challenge." he said. "I take no pleasure in destroying demons weaker than myself. Leave here now, and spare me from any further guilt." The two demons, terrified expressions on their faces, looked at one another, and then at Zerstörer.

"Leave here," their leader commanded.

The Jäger didn't need any further instruction, and they darted through the entrance of the cavern, following the third, who was already well on his way to Hell, doubtless fearful of retribution from Satan, but evidently more fearful of what Kobold would do to him. Zerstörer, however, seemed unperturbed by his comrades' lack of courage, and adopted an aggressive stance, the spear held out before him.

"You will pay for that indiscretion," he promised.

Kobold simply smiled. "Whenever you feel you are ready, you may try to make me pay. But I warn you, unless you have fought Satan himself, you will never have faced a more dangerous adversary."

Zerstörer growled and lunged for Kobold, who rolled out of the way and outstretched a leg, tripping the Jäger over and causing him to topple into one of the crevices that formed the huge Star of David. The spear, however, remained firmly in his hand. He hauled himself to his feet and hopped out of the crevice, scowling at Kobold.

"Child!" Zerstörer snapped, as he took a couple of steps back and gripped the spear more tightly.

Kobold tried, using all of his powers, to wrench the spear away, but found that it wouldn't come.

Zerstörer smiled.

"Not as powerful as you would have yourself believe, are you?" he said.

Kobold said, "No matter. If you feel the need to fight me using a weapon, then by all means do so. You will not be having an unfair advantage – perhaps it even balances us out."

At that, Zerstörer tossed the spear aside. "I will fight you like a demon," he said. "I will destroy you without resorting to unfair advantages."

Kobold grinned. "I admire your bravado – but you will surely die for doing so." And with that, he gathered up all of his powers and flung out a thunderbolt across the cavern. It caught Zerstörer in the face, flinging him back against the wall. For a moment, the Jäger was stunned, but he quickly recovered, and flung out a hand, sending a ball of flame hurtling towards Kobold, who merely deflected it with a forearm.

Kobold realized that Zerstörer was certainly a tougher opponent than he'd expected, and came to the conclusion that he'd have to adjust his fighting style to defeat him. Demonstrations of supernatural powers were not sufficient, for the Jäger was armed just as lethally. Kobold needed something special. But in the meantime, he had to grind the Jäger down, reduce his overall strength without reducing his own too considerably.

He dived across the cavern and onto Zerstörer, the two of them tumbling backwards into a crevice. The Jäger lashed out, his fist catching Kobold on the jaw, but it was little more than a minor annoyance. Kobold, who was on top, lifted his own fist, and clenched it tightly. Sharp spikes grew from the knuckles, and he swung the fist down into Zerstörer's face again and again, pounding the flesh and bone. Zerstörer cried out in pain, and fought violently, eventually succeeding in throwing Kobold off of him.

Kobold rolled and jumped to his feet, looking down at Zerstörer's battered and cut face, the blood visible only as liquid on the demon's crimson skin. He smiled and watched as Zerstörer climbed to his feet, all the while keeping his eyes on Kobold. But Kobold could see the uncertainty on the Jäger's face now, a small hint of resentful respect. Clearly, he could see that this fight was not going to be as easy as his previous battles.

He could see that Kobold was no ordinary demon.

"You could always run back to Hell," Kobold offered him.

"Never," Zerstörer spat viciously, blood dripping from his face. "I have not lost a battle yet, and I do not intend to start now."

"You will lose this one," Kobold said, reaching up and, with supernatural powers, pulling a hunk of rock from the ceiling. It began to fall, its jagged tip aimed right for Zerstörer's head. But at the last moment, the Jäger seemed to sense that he was in danger, and he looked up, instantly diving out of the path. The boulder slammed into the ground where he had, a split-second earlier, been standing, and drove its tip deep into the rocky surface.

Kobold laughed. "You have been blessed," he said, "with powers of precognition. But they will not save you."

"I have more powers than you could ever imagine," Zerstörer assured him. "As you will find out."

"But you have yet to use them," Kobold mocked.

The Jäger snarled, and held out his arms, palms up, raising them slowly. The ground trembled beneath Kobold's feet, and he barely had time to leap into the air when a huge split tore open the Star of David, spitting chunks of rock into the air. Kobold landed to the side of the split, and looked down at it — it was deep, but not so deep as he could not see the bottom.

He looked at Zerstörer and smiled broadly. "Not bad," he said, "if you were a child. I was expecting something far more impressive." At that moment, there was a buzzing in his head, and he instinctively hopped to the side as a rock tore into the ground. As he leapt down into the hole Zerstörer had created, he realized that the Jäger had used the minor earthquake as a diversion then, as he fell down, he came to the conclusion that perhaps, like a chess player, Zerstörer was thinking half a dozen moves ahead. He clearly hadn't got to the position where he was – probably the most experienced Jäger in Hell – without having shrewd powers of reasoning.

All of which didn't help Kobold as he fell, feet first, down the deep hole Zerstörer had created.

His powers were low, but Kobold still mustered up the strength to allow him to slow his descent to a hover. Looking up, he could see that the cavern from which he'd fallen was easily five hundred feet above him, and it would take a lot of supernatural strength to materialize back in the cavern itself.

Which meant it was probably wiser for him to simply use his physical strength to scale the wall of the pit. Whatever he decided, however, he had to do it in the next few seconds, because with every second that passed as he hovered within the pit, his powers were being drained even more.

So he made a decision.

And he found himself standing in the cavern beside the pit in the blinking of an eye.

Zerstörer was still smiling — but he looked drained.

"That was a clever move," Kobold praised. "But you simply won the battle, Zerstörer. The outcome of the war itself has yet to be decided."

Zerstörer continued smiling, apparently basing his mood on the fact that Kobold was probably as weak as he was.

It was a misguided belief.

Kobold clasped his hands together, and sent a thunderbolt across the cavern, slamming it into Zerstörer's battered face. The Jäger, stunned by the attack and wounded by its ferocity, staggered backwards, falling down into a crevice. But he was not defeated yet.

The attack had left Kobold almost supernaturally drained, but the war of attrition between him and Zerstörer was almost at an end – and he had come out on top.

He almost felt sorry for Zerstörer as he stepped up to the crevice. Though this demon, this Jäger, had come here with the intention of destroying him, Kobold could not summon up the hatred required to destroy him in turn. He looked down into the crevice, saw Zerstörer gasping and clutching his chest and his face — the thunderbolt had ripped open the Jäger's cheek, tearing away some of the bone. He clutched his chest because his life-force was threatening to break away. And when that went ...

Zerstörer jumped as he saw Kobold, and his eyes widened in fear. But he did not beg.

"Will you not plead with me?" Kobold asked him.

Zerstörer shook his head. "Never."

"But you have lost."

"I fought a worthy opponent," Zerstörer said with begrudging praise. "And I meet my destruction with honour."

Kobold stepped down into the crevice and held out a hand. Zerstörer shied away from it to begin with, then realized that the hand meant him no harm. He realized what Kobold wanted.

He gripped Kobold's hand, and was pulled to his feet.

"Return to Satan," Kobold told him. "Tell him if he desires my destruction, then he must seek it out personally."

"You have to destroy me."

Kobold shook his head. "I could never destroy a demon whose only trespass against me is to carry out his legitimate business."

Zerstörer blinked. "I don't understand."

"You will soon understand," Kobold assured him. "Satan is the corrupt one. It is he who must be removed, whose destruction should be sought. This is not a fight I have with you, or any of the Jäger. This is a fight between Satan and me, a fight that will soon be fought."

"If I return to Hell, Satan will destroy me."

"Then you must stay here," David said. Kobold spun around to see the one-time devil standing behind him. Zerstörer frowned at the newcomer. "You will be our guest."

"Who are you?"

"I am the one who will nurse your wounds," David said. "And I will tell you all you need to know, while we await the birth of Satan's successor."

Zerstörer looked across at Kobold. Then he realized.

And he bowed down before Kobold.

31

Two weeks had passed since Jordan's death, and the true meaning of it still hadn't hit Sadie. She supposed that it hadn't helped having Jodie in hospital, still weak, still recovering from the overdose — more stress that she really didn't need, couldn't really cope with, at this moment in her life. Oh, her friends had been great – Melissa, the boys in the band, they'd all given her sympathy, all listened to her – even Mark – when she'd broken down before them. But they didn't really understand. They were all young, had never lost anybody they'd loved and few people in the world could've lost the person they loved in such an extraordinarily brutal and tragic way.

Just feet from where she'd lay, thinking about him, imagining him making love to her, when at that precise moment in time, his brains had been slowly leaking out onto the car park just twenty feet from her bedroom window. She knew that if she ever became aroused with another man, her mind would return to that night, to the fact that she had been touching herself, dreaming about Jordan ...

As she showered, she thought about the last two weeks, about how she'd tried to give herself plenty to do, in the hope that occupying her mind she might not have to think about Jordan, about his death. It hadn't worked, of course, and the fact that the band was garnering more interest from record labels – in particular, a local label, and one of the few truly independent labels in the country – only made things worse. It was simply more pressure, because she knew that she couldn't fail, couldn't let the boys down. She had to perform well at both of their recent showcase gigs, in spite of the fact that all she'd wanted to do was break down and cry.

And the patience of her friends was wearing thin – at least, she was under that impression.

After all, surely they were wondering why, after just a few days of knowing him, she'd become so attached to Jordan that losing him was far worse than losing her parents. She supposed that a psychologist would tell her that losing her parents was the worst of the two, but that Jordan's death, coming on top of the original tragedy, and in addition to Jodie's near-brush with death, made the murder seem worse than it really was.

But that was all bullshit.

Of that she was convinced. She knew how she felt. She'd seen the bloodstain on the car park floor, the chalk line that had marked the position in which he'd fallen. She knew that this was worse — far worse. All children flew the nest, and they prepared themselves for the deaths of their parents. Some came sooner than others, but they were expected — anticipated. But the death of a lover, a partner, somebody you intended to live with for the next forty, fifty, sixty years?

No, you didn't expect that person to die, not until you were old and grey.

Stepping out of the shower and towelling herself dry, Sadie did something she'd been doing every day since the murder. She tried to blot out Jordan's image, tried to forget him, so that she no longer suffered. But as before, it was still impossible. She could still see his face, still see him smiling at her, smiling that devilish grin that had doubtless captivated many women before her, but which had been hers exclusively for all too brief a period of time.

The telephone rang as she pulled on her clothes, and she slouched through to the front room of the flat, picking up the receiver and not even attempting to sound cheerful as she answered.

It was Melissa. "Are you ready?" she asked.

"Look, I'm not sure about this—"

"Are you crazy? Sadie, this is a big night for the band! Hobnobbing with the rich and famous."

"We've done all that," Sadie muttered. "I seem to recall that's how Jodie ended up in hospital."

"You have to do this for the boys, Sadie," Melissa said, without trying to put her down. "I mean, this is important, isn't it?"

"I know it's important," Sadie said grimly, flopping down into the sofa. "I just don't think I'm up to it. I'm tired, I'm run down, I look like shit ... I'm just not ready."

"You've been doing okay for the last week or so," Melissa said.

"I've been putting on a brave face," Sadie snapped. "And two weeks isn't long enough for me to—"

"Sadie, I'm sorry," Melissa said sincerely. There was a pause. "I just can't imagine what it must be like for you. I mean, you're coping so well."

"Outside, I am," Sadie admitted. "But inside — I just wanna collapse." She closed her eyes, tried to seal in the tears, and did a good job of it. Her nose began to sting, which in turn made her eyes want to water even more. She gulped down some air, and let out a sigh. "I've been trying to keep myself busy, just so as I don't have to think about things, but it doesn't really work. He's always there, always at the back of my mind, if he isn't standing right there at the front. I've not given myself the opportunity to really mourn, Melissa. I still haven't cried properly – listen to me, talking about it rationally, like it didn't happen to me. I'm just not dealing with it properly. All of this hurt, it's just crushing my chest — my whole body aches. I want to let it all out."

"Then why don't you?"

"Because I know that if I start, I don't think I'll ever stop."

"Hey, do you want me to come over? I can blow the party off."

"No, no, it's okay," Sadie said.

"You can't stay in by yourself," Melissa said.

"I probably won't – I've got myself all ready for the party."

"Well, then you should come."

"Melissa, I really don't know."

"You've had it tough over the last couple of months, and you can't just curl up into a ball and hope that it goes away. It won't go away, not ever. It'll always be with you — what happened to your mum and dad, what happened to Jodie, what happened to Jordan — life has been really cruel to you, Sadie, and you can't let yourself be beat like this."

"I'll come to the party," Sadie relented. "But I don't feel like enjoying myself. It's not just a case of feeling guilty, Melissa, I just don't feel in the mood for fun."

"Then come to the party and we'll talk about Jordan," Melissa said.

"We'll all get pissed, we'll sit around off our faces and talk about Jordan, and talk about old boyfriends, and have fun." There was mock frustration in Melissa's voice, and Sadie was grateful for the effort her friend was putting into the conversation, something that she herself found impossible to reciprocate.

Nevertheless, she still found herself sitting in a minicab forty minutes later as it pulled away from the front entrance of the flats, Melissa already inside, struggling to keep her body within a little black dress. She was dressed to kill, and she was hungry for love — at least, that was the first thing she'd told Sadie when she'd climbed into the cab. There wasn't a melancholy atmosphere in the car, just jovial, boisterous good humour – Melissa wasn't about to let Sadie get miserable.

They were going to have fun.

"So," Melissa said, as the cab was well on its way to the location of the party Martin Walsh had organized specifically for the band. "Do you reckon there'll be anybody there worth me taking a look at?"

"You mean, are they all gonna be old farts with more money than sex appeal?" Sadie asked.

"Something like that," Melissa said with a grin. "I mean, this outfit doesn't leave much to the imagination, does it? Boobs hanging out the top, and I'm really nervous about bending over in case you can see my knickers. I don't wanna have wasted the money on it for nothing." The two girls giggled as they looked at the driver, a handsome man in his thirties, whose eyes shifted nervously from peering in the rear-view mirror to the road ahead. Sadie was certain that had it been light, she would've seen him blushing.

Melissa could be cruel. Fun, but cruel.

The driver shifted uneasily in his seat, then fiddled with the stereo, turning up the volume slightly, so the girls could hear the Manic Street Preachers singing about Kevin Carter. Melissa began to tap her foot, and Sadie found herself smiling — probably for the first time in the last fortnight.

Maybe, she thought, she could get through this thing without breaking down.

As the cab pulled up outside the swanky apartment block where the party was happening, they hopped out onto the pavement and Melissa paid the driver. The two of them looked up at the attractive, modern building, and Melissa gave her a nudge.

"Nice place," she said.

"Yeah," Sadie said grimly, remembering that her family had once owned such an apartment. She shrugged the memory away, and resolved to think only positive thoughts tonight.

Even facing Martin Walsh wasn't going to be that difficult for her.

She'd seen him a couple of times during the last fortnight, and he'd treated her with kindness and respect and, even if he hadn't meant it, he'd at least made the effort to ensure that there was genuine sounding sincerity in his voice. At that moment in time, as they stood in the car park of the apartment building, surrounded by Porsches, BMWs, Mercedes, Ferraris, and other flash cars, she felt as though she could face anything the world had to throw at her.

Jodie was getting better, no longer in any immediate danger, and so it seemed unlikely that anything terrible was going to strike the Bartholomew family in the not-so-distant future. The Mafia hitmen who had killed Jordan hadn't put in an appearance since the murder, and Chief Superintendent Saddington had assured Sadie that both the hospital and her flat were under constant observation by armed police officers.

Things could not possibly get any worse.

And sad though it was, that was a boost to her confidence.

Melissa laughed, and pointed to the entrance of the apartment block, where a man stood, wearing stockings and suspender belt, a pair of matching panties and a bra clearly stuffed with old socks. His face was hidden behind a gimp mask, and he tottered in front of the door in a pair of ludicrously high heels.

"Jesus," Sadie groaned. "What the hell are we getting ourselves into?"

"Welcome to decadence," Melissa said, dragging her up the entrance.

They passed the man, with Sadie half expecting him to wave his penis in their faces, without incident, and made their way to the lifts. Piped music played as they rose to the top floor, to the penthouse level, where the party was being held. As the doors swished open, the sound of pounding music replaced the muzak in the lift, and Sadie felt her insides vibrate as they made their way along a richly decorated corridor, passing smartly dressed guests holding glasses and bottles chatting away in small groups.

"Well, it's more subdued here," Sadie said, as they reached an open set of double doors. A butler greeted them, and they stepped into the wide hallway of the luxury apartment, from which three doors spread – one on either side and one directly ahead. The side doorways were closed, but the one in front – another pair of double doors – was open.

The room beyond was dark, and strobe lights flashed to the pounding beat, catching the dancing throng in various poses.

"You know, I always hated raves," Sadie said.

"Well, you Americans are a bit backward, aren't you?"

"You know, I should be insulted," Sadie said.

At that moment, one of the side doors opened, and Martin stepped out with the boys from the band. Smiling broadly, he wandered over, and took Sadie's hand.

"Hey, thanks for coming," he said. "I wasn't sure whether or not you would."

"I made the effort," Sadie said, smiling tightly.

"It's appreciated," Martin told her. "I've a got a few people I want you to meet — including the head of Lazy Records. But I'll get you fixed up with a drink. I take it you don't wanna go through the dance hall?"

"Not really," Sadie said. She turned to see Melissa looking longingly at the dancers. "Hey, you don't have to stick with me."

"I'd feel so guilty."

Billy stepped up to Sadie and put an arm around her. "We'll look after her, Mel. You go and do what you do best."

"Which is?" Melissa asked, raising an eyebrow.

"Partying," Billy said with a grin.

And with that, Melissa was gone.

Martin led the band through the doorway and into a large dining room, taking them through one of two doors at the other end. As they walked, Billy said, "It's a wild party. I know you don't like wild parties, but I'm glad you came."

"It certainly is wild," Sadie remarked. "That guy downstairs, for a start."

"The gimp?" Mark asked with a lopsided grin. "Man, that's unreal."

Martin stopped them at a set of double doors at the end of a short corridor.

"I wonder what the neighbours think of that," Mark went on.

Martin raised his eyebrows. "That guy *is* one of the neighbours."

The whole band laughed, as Martin swung open the double doors, showing them the modern office beyond, and the glass-topped table around which sat two men and a women, all of them casually dressed.

"Darcy's Box, meet Brett Somers, head of Lazy Records."

So dazzled and impressed by the speed at which their career seemed to be moving, Sadie found herself not thinking at all about Jordan, for the first time since his murder.

This was the good life, away from the horror and misery of the outside world. She took the champagne from the woman who was dressed in jeans and a tee-shirt, and allowed the bubbles to tease her nose and throat as Martin led them to the table.

Here, she thought, the next few years would be decided.

This wasn't the first rung on the ladder.

This was almost at the top of the ladder.

The hard work was almost over.

They'd been discovered.

32

Samuel Mirkin turned to the other man in the car and raised an eyebrow.

"What do you reckon?" he asked, taking in the other man's blank, emotionless expression.

"I reckon we wait," Luke told him.

"We might not get the opportunity out in the streets," Samuel said. "Those bitches have got the fucking local law watching them. We already saw that car following them."

"You gotta ask yourself, Samuel, why the fuck is that?" Luke said calmly, taking a drag from his Marlboro. "If you hadn't have gone fucking loco a couple of weeks back, blowing away that asshole right on their fucking doorstep, they wouldn't be watching those bitches now."

"That's fucking bullshit, man," Samuel snapped. "A crock of total shit, and you fucking know it. They were already watching those two bitches – someone had to have known we were coming."

The two men remained silent for the next few minutes, and that gave Samuel Mirkin time to reflect on the events of the last fortnight. Reflect on, and admit to – though only to himself – the mistakes he'd made. The biggest had been the one Luke had thrown in his face – shooting Sadie Bartholomew's boyfriend. That had only served to increase the intensity of the police surveillance.

But at the time, Samuel had believed there wasn't any other option.

It was well-known that Sadie Bartholomew's old man had connections. Christ, the bastard was well in with the Mafia back in the States — well, before he'd screwed them out of a fortune, that was. For all Samuel knew, that asshole could've been some kind of bodyguard, could've been packing, could've pulled a piece on Samuel and Luke, and blown them both away before they'd had time to react.

You didn't survive long in the hitman business by being slow to react to any given situation.

You could never be too careful.

Unfortunately, as Luke had later argued, with some degree of truth, there were two kinds of reaction involved with being careful. One was to overreact, and the other was to under-react — and by under-react, Luke had meant they should've just got the hell out of there, leaving behind the smoke from burning rubber instead of a weapon discharge.

But there was something about that bastard, about the way he had walked calmly up to the car, about the way he'd confronted them – something special, maybe even frightening. So, maybe Samuel *had* overreacted, but he was certain he'd averted a disaster for the two hitmen. And Luke had trusted his reactions in the past.

"We can't go home empty-handed," Samuel said, breaking the silence.

Luke sucked on his Marlboro, then filled the interior of the Range Rover with smoke. "Well, what the fuck do you suggest? That we gatecrash that fucking party, interrogate that stupid bitch, and then shoot her dead? You reckon we could hold back a hundred or so partygoers? You reckon none of them are gonna have the time or the opportunity to call in the police?" Luke shook his head in disgust, took another long drag from his cigarette – winding the window down at the same time – before tossing it out into the road.

He wound the window back up.

"So what's your plan?"

"When she comes out, we follow," Luke said. "We find the right moment, and we strike."

"But what about the police?"

"There were two cops in that car," Luke said. "Now, how many cops have you wasted in the past?" The question was asked with a smile. Samuel raised an eyebrow. "Exactly. I don't see it being a problem. The chances are that they've backed off their surveillance after these last two weeks – one car, two cops max. Maybe a unit back at the apartment block, waiting for her to come back, making sure we don't slip inside while she's out. That's all. We can take out two fucking skanky cops. We just have to make sure we waste the motherfuckers before they get a call through to backup."

"No problem," Samuel said with a smirk. "Those bastards are gonna be so concerned with self-preservation that picking up a goddamned radio is gonna be the last fucking thing on their minds."

"But we don't overreact, okay?" Luke asked — it was more of a command than a question.

Samuel nodded.

They'd already made a total clusterfuck of this operation, and he for one didn't want the goddamned Mafia hunting him down the way he and Luke had been hunting down Michael Bartholomew and his prick of a partner.

But that wasn't going to happen, he thought with a smile as he settled in for the evening.

Because tonight, somebody was going to die.

The evening had gone reasonably well, Sadie had to admit. Okay, so she hadn't totally forgotten about Jordan but at least she was able to think about other things. About the future.

The guy from Lazy Records had been very encouraging, but said that he couldn't commit to a contract — not just yet. It was clear that they didn't have the money to take on any new talent. After all, they were only a local indie label. But they were an indie label who had managed, with a couple of their bands, to make valuable inroads into the national charts. A top five and a top twenty hit weren't to be sniffed at.

He put it into simple words. "You guys have got this incredible sound, but I just can't afford to take you on. We're working with a limited budget, and we can't take on any new bands right now. It's a total pisser, because there are two other bands we'd like to sign up, but our finances are already committed to other projects. But I can promise you this — give it three months, till we can free up some additional funds, and you guys are top of the list."

"You know, high praise is all well and good," Billy told him, "but no disrespect here, we're hearing that kinda shit from all corners. And high praise doesn't get us in the charts."

Brett Somers took a sip from his champagne. "Billy, I'm not pulling your chain. High praise from someone without power is worthless shit. But high praise from someone who can help you is significant. I can't help you now, but I don't forget. I'm in this business to make money — and I think you guys can make me money. All of you. I'm not gonna lie — if I didn't like one of you, I'd tell you here and now to come back in three months with a new band member, and we'd talk then. But you guys gel together perfectly — the chemistry is great."

Sadie looked at Mark, who looked back.

He gave her a half smile she responded in the same way. When it came to important situations like this, they could get along fine.

"Now, if you guys are still together in three months, by all means come back and see me. Hopefully, you'll have new material, and we can lay down maybe twelve or fifteen or so tracks, get us an album and a few B-sides out of it. And I promise you. I will sign you up. I mean, we're not talking hundred thousand pound contracts here — I won't get drawn into amounts, but it won't be much over four figures. Call it the first rung on the ladder. I mean, great, I'd love you guys to stay with me for the rest of your careers, but I'm realistic, and as I said, I'm here to make money. I'm here to keep myself living in the lap of luxury — Porsches, fancy apartments. And I can see that at the very least, you guys will make a mark on the charts and if that catches the eye of one of the major labels, and they want to put in a bid for your contract ..." Brett smiled broadly. "Well, we all profit, don't we?"

"Can we have all this in writing?" Mark asked with a raised eyebrow. It was a joke, but Brett took it seriously.

"I would love to give you all this writing, but let's call this a gentleman's agreement," he said. "It's in both of our interests. I mean, it might be that in three months, Lazy Records are up shit creek. Maybe one of our top bands will leave us in the lurch, or maybe we'll put out something that's total bollocks and lose a shit load of money. Conversely, you guys might get an offer from one of the majors, and they probably won't wanna pay me a hundred grand to take over your contract, not without you even touching the charts. The way they'd look at it, they'd have to pay me, pay you, and pay for your publicity. They won't take the risk. So let's just keep this all on a sensible level. You guys remember me and I'll remember you."

"So we'll see you in three months?" Billy asked.

"Three months and you guys will be recording an album for Lazy Records," Brett told them.

And with that, the meeting was over. It was time for the band members to enjoy the party.

All Sadie wanted to do was go home, but the rest of the band wouldn't let her.

"Look, Sadie, soon we're gonna be on Top of the fucking Pops," Davey said to her. "You've gotta know how to party, haven't you? And this is the kinda crowd you've gotta mix with."

Sadie looked around at the people around her. For the most part, they were dancing, drinking or kissing — and the ones that weren't doing any of the first three were in the bathroom or one of the other rooms doing drugs or having sex.

"This is depraved," she remarked, as Martin came wandering over.

"So, I hear the meeting went well," he said. He'd been asked to leave by Brett early on, and hadn't been happy to do so. Before he'd left the office, he'd told Brett that the band worked well with him as a producer, a fact that Brett didn't seem to pay much attention to.

Mark said, "Yeah, if you call waiting three fucking months for your big break 'well'."

"Hey the way I see it," Martin said as Holly tugged at his arm, "it's like knowing you're up for winning the lottery on a certain day. You guys are gonna crack it. I just know it. All you gotta do is just sit back and wait."

"I can't help thinking that he was bullshitting," Mark said.

"Did he come across as a bullshitter?" Martin asked him seriously, as they all sat down in the dining room.

"No," Billy answered quickly. "I think if he wasn't interested, he'd never have agreed to see us in the first place. But my main concern is that there are three months to go before he can even look at us again. And in that time—"

"In that time," Sadie said, "some of us could be dead."

"I was going to say that a couple of other bands could turn up and push us further down the queue," Billy said quickly.

Sadie looked up to see Melissa approaching the table.

"How'd it go?" she asked.

Sadie shrugged. "Better than I thought, but not as well as I'd have liked."

"That sounds rough," Melissa said, sitting down.

"How you doing?"

"Met up with a couple of guys," Melissa said, adding hastily, "and another girl, before you start talking about threesomes." Some of the band laughed. Martin looked up at Holly and the two of them smiled, something which Sadie didn't really understand. "But if you want to get off—"

"No, you stay," Sadie said.

Melissa smiled. "I know it sounds selfish, but I was hoping you'd say that."

"Which is why I said it," Sadie told her. "I'm just that kinda girl."

"You're leaving?" Billy asked.

"I'm not in the party mood," Sadie said. "I came here because the band needed me to. I'm not ready for all of this kinda thing."

"You can't go by yourself," Mark said. "One of us will come with you."

"I'll be fine," Sadie said, but she knew that nobody believed that. She also knew that nobody would come out and say why. "Really, I'll be fine. The police are still following me around."

"We'll take you home," Martin offered, hugging Holly to him. "We're about to leave as it is."

"Bit early for you, ain't it?" Davey asked. "Or are you on a promise."

"I hope so," Martin said. He looked at Sadie. "You ready to go now?"

Sadie nodded. The memory of what Martin had done to her in the past was still firmly fixed in her mind, but he'd shown her a lot of concern over the last few days, and besides, he was with Holly. What harm would it do? She stood up. "Will we all fit in your Porsche?"

"We came in my Mondeo," Holly said.

"Slumming it, Martin?" Mark asked, laughing raucously.

"Well, you've just insulted my girlfriend's car," Martin responded, "So I suppose with that, we'd better be on our way."

They all said their goodbyes, and were soon sitting in Holly's red

Mondeo. Holly was driving, and as they made their way across town, she suggested to Sadie that she should come back to theirs for a coffee. The night was, she said, still young.

Sadie agreed. After all, she had nothing to rush home for, and a quiet coffee was better than a loud party.

She'd never been back to Holly's apartment before, and as they entered, she looked around at the modern furniture, the blacks and whites, the hi-tech electronic stuff. On the wall over the fireplace, close to the ceiling, a long black tube was situated — a cinema screen, Martin told her, which automatically dropped whenever he turned on the projector, which was to the rear of the room, suspended from the ceiling. It, in turn, was connected to the DVD player.

It was also possible, he told her, to watch TV via the projector.

"Though seeing Grant Mitchell's face four feet tall isn't exactly my cup of tea," he added, as he wandered off to the kitchen.

"Sit down," Holly said, and the two of them sat down on the black leather sofa. Holly made a big show of leaning back and crossing her legs, and Sadie was given the impression that Martin's girlfriend was proud of her body. But she was putting on a display to the wrong person — the wrong sex.

"So, how long have you known Martin?" Sadie asked.

Holly smiled and threw back her head. "Too bloody long!"

"I heard that!" Martin shouted from the kitchen.

Holly laughed. "Well, we get on well enough," she said. "We both have things to offer each other."

"Really? Like what?"

Sadie realized as soon as she'd asked it that the question wasn't appropriate.

"Sex and drugs," Holly answered candidly. "I give Martin sex and he gives me drugs."

Sadie didn't really have a response to that — it was clear that Holly was a druggie, though at that moment, she looked quite respectable, in spite of a skirt that almost showed off her underwear. Well, she wasn't a dirty smackhead – she came from a wealthy family. That much Sadie did know.

"Have you ever tried drugs?" Holly asked bluntly.

Sadie shook her head. "It doesn't appeal to me," she said, thinking about what had recently happened to Jodie.

Holly seemed to realize her blunder, and her face drained slightly. "Oh, Christ, sorry — I forgot. I didn't mean—"

"That's okay," Sadie assured her as Martin came into the room with a tray of coffees. He handed them out, offered Sadie milk and sugar, both of which she refused.

"Holly and me met a couple of years ago", Martin said as his girlfriend switched on the television — the volume was low. Out of the corner of her eye, Sadie could see some movie was playing. A group of men and women were sitting in a room not unlike Holly's front room — they were talking. "Some wild, crazy party – she was right in the middle of the action, standing there waving her top over her head."

Holly smiled. "I was the original wild child," she said.

"It was when she dropped her skirt that I just thought ... well, I knew that I had to have her."

Sadie began to feel slightly uncomfortable. The conversation was turning into something somewhat perverse — she didn't really want to be given any more details than they'd already provided her with.

"We slept together that night," Holly said. "It was pretty intense. I also tried H for the first time that night as well. Been hooked ever since."

"Martin got you hooked?" Sadie asked with a frown.

"I was already into Charlie," Holly said. "Charlie, dope, ecstasy — I was already a dope child before Martin came onto the scene."

"And I thought I'd tried it all before I met Holly," Martin said, putting a hand on his girlfriend's thigh. The gentle caressing, Sadie deciding, was a little bit too personal for him to be doing in front of her. "But Holly's just wild. She can't get enough."

"I go all ways," Holly said.

"I'm a one-guy girl myself," Sadie felt compelled to say.

"That's commendable," Holly said. "But haven't you tried it both ways?" Sadie noticed that on the TV screen, some of the actors had stripped off. And this wasn't some Hollywood blockbuster. They didn't show erections at the movie theatres. When she looked back to Holly and Martin, she saw with horror that his penis was out, and that Holly was gently stroking it.

"I think I'd better go," she said, getting to her feet.

"Wait," Holly said getting up. She pulled Sadie to her, kissed her softly on the lips, and then gently stroked her buttocks. Sadie just froze.

Until, that was, Holly slipped her hand between Sadie's legs, her fingers rubbing her through the material of her dress. Sadie pulled back.

"I think you've got me wrong," she said, blinking rapidly. "I'm not ready for this kinda thing no, scratch that — I'm not into that kinda shit!"

"Come on," Holly said seductively, and Sadie could see why she was so attractive to men. "You're a beautiful woman. Aren't you in the least bit curious."

"Not at all," Sadie said. "Look, have you two assholes forgotten what has just happened to me?"

Martin was smiling, and stroking his penis as he looked the two of them up and down. "Come on, Sadie, don't be so frigid."

"Fuck you!" Sadie snapped, going for the door. Holly reached it at the same time, and Sadie found herself staring into a pair of firm breasts. Holly pushed herself against her, rubbing her erect nipples against Sadie's face.

"For Christ's sake!" Sadie snapped in disgust, pushing Holly away. "You fucking weirdo! You pair of fucking sick freaks!" And with that, she wrenched open the door and rushed out into the hallway. As she stomped down the corridor, she could hear Holly laughing loudly, before the door was slammed shut.

"Fucking assholes!" Sadie snapped.

And then she looked at her surroundings.

She'd climbed down a couple of flights of stairs, and now she stood in the lobby, which was dimly lit. Though she was assured that the security of the building was good, and that the people who lived here were all wealthy, that certainly didn't make her feel any safer. Martin and Holly were both wealthy, but they were as crazy as hell, and they lived here, in this supposedly safe residence.

No, she didn't fancy stepping out into the street, not with a couple of hitmen after her, even if there were police officers out there somewhere, watching her every move.

And she didn't fancy staying here.

But she had to go home.

She pulled out her cellphone and pushed a speed-dial button for a taxi service she used regularly. The dispatcher assured her that a cab would be on its way immediately — ten minutes maximum. All she could do now was sit in the lobby and wait for the cab to pull up outside.

It gave her plenty of time to reflect on the way the evening had gone. From the relative high of meeting the record boss, to the utter dregs of finding herself trapped in a room with a pair of deviants. It was amazing how quickly fortune changed.

One minute she was kissing Jordan, and the next ...

She cursed under her breath.

"Where the fuck is that cab?"

33

Samuel watched as Luke lit another Marlboro, and he gave a little sigh, casting his eyes up to the window where a light had gone on just a minute or so after their target had entered the building.

"What the fuck is she doing in there?" he snapped.

Luke, somewhat calmer, merely shrugged.

"We should fucking do it there, man, off the streets."

"We make a move on that fucking apartment, and those cops are gonna call for back-up," Luke explained quietly. "We'd have to take the cops out first."

"I don't see the problem, man."

"That doesn't surprise me," Luke said. He dragged lazily on his Marlboro.

"Well, what you're suggesting ain't no fucking saner, man," Samuel said. "You're talking about doing it in the street. Jesus, we'd have no cover."

Luke turned and looked at him, one eyebrow raised. He took another drag from his cigarette, then wound down the window and tossed the butt outside. "We're talking about doing a snatch. We get in between the cops and that bitch's car. At a set of lights, we waste the cops then we pull her car over. I thought you was cool with this shit?"

"Just a few things wrong with that, man. What if there are no red lights? And what's to stop her from getting away while we waste the cops?"

"She left home in a cab," Luke said calmly. "She'll leave here in a cab too."

"How can you be certain?"

Luke gave Samuel a withering look, and then turned back to the apartment block, where a car was pulling up in front of the lobby.

"How'd you know that?"

"Those two assholes she came here with — it was obvious they lived here. They got into that building by keying in a combination on the buzzer. The chances are, they're in there getting loaded and smoking dope – they're not gonna be driving her home. Although I gotta admit," he said as Sadie Bartholomew came out of the building and got in the taxi, "she's leaving a lot earlier than I thought she would."

With that, he fired up the engine and prepared to follow the taxi.

Gerry Egan looked up in the vanity mirror as the Vauxhall Senator followed the Peugeot down a deserted main road. He didn't get to where he was in the police force without being observant, without knowing instinctively when something was amiss. The detective sergeant driving the car shot him a look of curiosity.

"Guv?"

"That car behind," Egan said. "Can you see whether or not it's a Range Rover?"

The DS looked up into his mirror. "It's a tall motor, some kind of off-roader. Can't tell what kind. Why?"

"Because when we pulled up outside that first block of flats, the one with the fucking pervert outside, a Range Rover parked up the street behind us," Egan said, flicking a cigarette out of a packet and using the lighter. "I didn't see nobody getting out."

"You think it's them?"

"I think somebody else was watching that party," Egan said. "As far as I know, there were no other surveillance operations planned — of course, I can't be certain, because nobody tells anybody else a fucking thing at Scotland Yard, but the way I see it, there's only one other bunch of guys with a reason to watch that party." He paused momentarily before revealing some more startling information. "And back there, at that second block of flats — it was there again."

"Shit," the DS hissed. "I don't like the sound of this."

Egan automatically felt the weight of his pistol in the shoulder holster — the weapon, a SIG Sauer P228 — was loaded, and he had a couple of spare magazines. But it was no match for a submachine-gun — these guys were professionals, and there was a very good chance that they'd be packing something more substantial than a 9mm semiautomatic.

Egan reached for his mobile phone and pushed the number for Saddington.

The Chief Superintendent answered on the second ring.

"It's Egan."

"What you got, Irish?"

"We're following Bartholomew," Egan said. "She's been on a party crawl. I reckon the vice squad could've filled up every prison in England with the filth that was going on."

"Well, that's all very enlightening, but—"

Egan cut off his superior. "We've got a tail. It's been with us since the start. A Range Rover. Don't know the registration number."

"You sure?" Saddington sounded concerned now.

"Aye. We're following a taxi now. Bartholomew's inside. Alone." He read off the index number of the taxi. "The tail is behind us. We've got about five miles to go before we get back to home base. Five miles, and half a dozen sets of traffic lights."

"You reckon they're going to make a move?"

"Aye," Egan answered, surprised himself at how nonchalant he sounded. "I give 'em a few more minutes before they get past us, in between the taxi and our car. They'll go for it when we hit a red light."

"If you hit a red light." Saddington said.

It wasn't a very reassuring statement — everyone hit a red light at least once during their journey. Egan didn't say that to Saddington. "We're heading down Hereford Road," he said. "I'd appreciate it if you could get back-up out to us ASAP. Oh and guv, if I don't see you again, it's been a pleasure working for you."

"Gerry, don't be so melodramatic—"

"Fucking hell," the DS muttered under his breath, and Egan turned his head to see the Range Rover overtaking. "What do I fucking do, guv?"

"Let 'em past" Egan said.

"What's going on?" Saddington asked him, panicked now.

"This is it, guv, this is it," Egan said. "Can't talk." And he switched off the phone. "You know, it's times like this that I think maybe the police union should've argued more strongly in favour of bullet proof cars," he said laconically.

"This ain't no fucking joke, guv!" the DS snapped as the Range Rover pulled in front of them.

"Take it easy,'" Egan said calmly. "There's a set of lights coming up. They're green. If we hit a red set, you stop the car, you open your door, you draw your weapon, and you run to the rear of the car. Right?"

"Right," the DS said breathlessly.

"It gives us the best protection," Egan went on. "But we've got to assume these guys know how to take the police down. Their first objective will be to hit the petrol tank, try to make it explode. Which means we've got perhaps five or six seconds to look for alternative cover." The procession of three cars passed through the green light. Egan breathed out, "The closer we get to home, the nearer we are to back-up. But there's a long way to go. You think you can deal with this?" He wasn't offering the DS a chance to pull out — there was no opportunity for him to retire from the forthcoming fight. If they did that, then Sadie Bartholomew was already dead.

The DS nodded. "I didn't join the police to get blown away," he said. "But I did join to protect people like that girl in front."

"Very commendable," Egan said, his tone slightly sarcastic. "I'm sure your ma and da would be very proud of you. But this ain't the movies. When this goes down, as it surely will, there's gonna be a lot of shooting. There's two of them and two of us, but we've got to assume that they've got submachine-guns — fully automatic. If they're packing anything heavier ..." He didn't finish his sentence, partly because it didn't need finishing, but mainly because they were now approaching another set of lights.

These ones were on red.

The taxi was braking.

34

Samuel couldn't help but smile as he saw the red light ahead, even though this plan wasn't his, and in spite of the fact that his stomach was tightening with the anxiety that often accompanied such operations. Here he was, about to spill blood again. And those cops in the car behind them, they weren't your average traditional British Bobby – these guys were armed. Armed, and probably already on full alert. After all, what Luke had just done was highly suspicious overtaking in the middle of town, screeching in front of the unmarked police car.

It was so blatant.

"Get ready," Luke told him as they approached the lights. He was already braking, Samuel feeling himself being forced against the restraints of the seat-belt. Already, the Uzi was in his hands, a round in the chamber, the weapon switched to three-round bursts. He would be out of the Range Rover and spraying lead at the unmarked police car behind them within a second. The cops wouldn't stand a chance.

Tyres squealed as Luke floored the brake pedal, and momentum threw Samuel backwards into the seat when the car finally screeched to a standstill.

He reached for the door handle.

Then stopped.

Something was there, behind him. He could feel it.

"Come on!" Luke shouted.

Then he too stopped.

Both men turned their heads.

Sitting in the rear of the Range Rover was a man, naked from the waist up, and wearing a pair of furry pants. Samuel frowned, then dropped his jaw. The man smiled and leaned forwards, and Samuel could see his dark hair, slicked back. He could see the protrusions on his skull that looked a lot like horns.

"Who the fuck ...?" Luke began.

He clearly realized who the man was at the same moment as Samuel did, because they both said in unison, "You're fucking dead!"

The man Samuel had shot twice in the head two weeks earlier smiled more broadly. "Good evening, gentlemen," the man said, apparently clearly alive. "Hey, I'm not disturbing you, am I? I mean, I didn't fuck up your plans?"

Samuel was vaguely aware of someone in the distance shouting, "Police! You in the car — come out with your hands up!"

But that seemed to be in a whole different world, in a place that didn't really matter at all.

"Actually, I know what your plans are," the man said. "That's why I'm here."

"I fucking shot you, man," Samuel said in disbelief "I blew your fucking brains out!"

The man gave a crooked smile and laughed. With one finger, he tapped one of the horns on his head. "Didn't nobody ever tell you? You can't kill a demon."

Samuel shuddered. He could hear the police officers shouting at him and Luke again, but wasn't really paying that much attention. "Who are you?"

"They call me Kobold," the man said. "I suppose it is only courteous of me to allow you to know the name of the person who kills you."

Luke raised the gun he was holding and pointed it at the man's head.

The man — Kobold simply continued smiling. "You know, that's gonna hurt you a whole lot more than it's gonna hurt me. I promise you that, Luke."

"How the fuck do you know my name?" Luke snapped vehemently.

Now Samuel could hear sirens – the police were sending in reinforcements, and here they were, talking to some guy who was dead, who resembled some kind of devil, who was threatening them.

"Luke, this isn't fucking happening, man," he said quietly. This had to be a dream – a nightmare. But how could him and Luke both be having the same hallucination? "Fuck this, man, we've gotta get out of here!"

"Shoot me, Luke," Kobold said with sneer. "Go on — I dare you."

"Luke, he isn't there," Samuel said — he knew that the demon was tricking them. He had to be tricking them. You couldn't kill a demon – the demon had said that himself. And it was obvious, really. How could you kill a demon? Demons didn't exist. For once in his life, Samuel actually felt as though he were right. "Luke, don't fucking do it, man!"

"In the car— this is the police! Come out with your hands up! Now!"

Tyres screeched, and Samuel looked out of the windows of the Range Rover to see half a dozen sets of flashing blue lights.

"You're surrounded!"

"Fucking shit, man, we're fucked!"

"Luke," Kobold challenged quietly. "Go on — shoot me. Prove me wrong. If you dare. If you've got the balls."

"Luke, no!" Samuel screamed.

Gerry instinctively flinched as the gunshot rang out, ducking behind the rear of the car as the rear window of the Range Rover was shattered. The DS gasped out in shock, and Gerry noticed that the sergeant's gun hand was quivering uncontrollably. A lot of fucking use he was going to be. So it was fortunate that two ARVs had just arrived, their officers armed with MP5 semiautomatic submachine-guns.

There were more gunshots, a lot of shouting, and the men and women from CO-19 opened fire without any instruction from him – not that they required it. This was a situation to which they had no other option. Two armed gunmen were shooting in a residential street. They had to be taken out before a stray bullet took out an innocent civilian.

The sounds from the MP5s were totally different to the muffled shots from inside the Range Rover. Loud cracks in double-tap bursts from four different weapons, each shot making Gerry jump. More than thirty rounds went into the Range Rover, and then a noise unlike anything Gerry had ever heard before erupted from within the off-roader. Flashes filled the interior of the vehicle, and windows that weren't shattered were punched outwards as one of the hitmen opened fire with a sub-machine-gun. Gerry ducked as lead flew in all directions, the hitman totally unconcerned with where his bullets were going, and simply spraying rounds everywhere.

The armed police officers responded quickly, their MP5s cracking with a more restrained accent, as they spat their rounds out just as effectively as the sub-machine-gun the hitman was firing.

More effectively, Gerry thought, for the shooting from inside the car had stopped.

But had the hitman simply ran out of ammunition? Highly likely he had, but with the amount of rounds that were fired into the car, it was also highly unlikely that he wouldn't have been hit. Him and his partner.

Gerry's mobile phone chose that lull in the fire-fight to ring, and he snatched it out of his pocket with his left hand, punching the green button with his thumb as he raised it to his ear.

"Aye?"

"Egan?" It was Saddington. "You're okay?"

"You're calling at a bad time," Gerry said wryly. The armed officers were shouting at the occupants of the Range Rover to get out. No one was shouting back.

"What's happening?"

Gerry stood up.

Then the Range Rover exploded in a furious ball of flames. Everyone instinctively hit the ground, expecting shards of metal and glass shrapnel to fly out.

None came.

Curious, Gerry got to his feet again, and watched in amazement as the Range Rover burned.

Burned on the inside, the flames licking out of the shattered windows and across the roof.

"Fuck me," the Irishman muttered under his breath. "Fucking Mary Mother of Christ."

Another car screeched noisily as it halted in a cloud of blue smoke, and Saddington emerged, running across towards Gerry, mobile phone in his hand. Gerry automatically switched his off and returned it to his pocket as the Chief Superintendent approached.

"What the hell happened?" Saddington demanded. Behind him was the FBI arsehole, Rothschild.

Gerry sighed heavily, the adrenaline pumping through his body almost preventing him from talking. "I have absolutely no fucking idea," he finally said, throwing out his arms.

"We wanted them alive!" Rothschild stormed. "Man! We're never gonna fucking find out what we wanted to know now!"

"Aye, well fuck you too," Gerry snapped, taking out a cigarette and lighting it. He watched the Range Rover burn as one of the armed officers called for the Fire Brigade — an ambulance too, though the crispy critters inside wouldn't be needing one of those.

"Gerry, just tell me what happened," Saddington said quietly.

So Gerry told him.

And the two police officers watched the Range Rover burn together, neither of them comprehending why it had caught fire, and why it was only burning on the inside.

Eventually, Gerry said, "She got away."

"Did she see any of this?" Saddington asked him.

Gerry shook his head and sighed. "You know what, I don't know. I was too busy watching those guys in that Range Rover. Aye, mebbe she did," he added, considering the fire-fight from start to finish. He and the DS had shouted at the occupants of the Range Rover to come out. Nobody did. There were shouts from inside the car, then the armed response vehicles turned up. By that time, Gerry could remember that the lights had turned to green.

That was when the hitmen opened fire.

"Well, the important thing is, she got away," Saddington said. "I'll go round and see her when we've finished here."

But Gerry wasn't interested.

He was still watching the car burn, and wondering exactly whatthose hitmen had been carrying that had been so flammable.

It was just so weird.

He could never have known that within the next half an hour, the night was about to get a whole lot weirder.

35

Kobold materialized inside the mortuary and quickly looked around.

The whole building stank of death, a horrid, rank funk that only demons could smell. Humans thought that they could smell death, the decaying flesh of their loved ones, of bodies they discovered rotting away in homes, in hospitals, where dead pieces of humans were disposed of like litter. But that wasn't death – that was simply the odour of putrefaction. That wasn't the smell of death.

Kobold took a deep breath sucked in a heavy lungful, and almost choked.

The smell of death was something different. Here, were vessels that once carried souls, but which were now lifeless, empty shells that no amount of mourning or weeping could ever bring back. The soul was gone, powerless to breathe life into the body that had carried it through an all too brief existence, unable ever to return even if it could, for Heaven or Hell had claimed them, and from there, there was no coming back.

Except for the angels and the demons.

Kobold felt his eyes water from the stench of the dead, as he looked at the freezers, where the corpses were stacked, on metal trays, one on top of the other, in rows and rows, some perhaps enemies in life, but brethren in death, their bloated flesh hollow and empty.

Kobold stepped over to the freezers, his eyes scanning the doors as though he could see through them. And in a way, he could. Well, not see, but sense. Here was a man who was righteous, whose soul was right now in Heaven, and here, another man, a common thief whose sins had condemned him to serve purgatory before being allowed into Heaven, because he was not inherently evil. A woman there, who was being tortured by the demons in Hell for being cruel to her children – she had taken her life, right after battering her three-year-old son's head with her bare fists.

He knew what all of them had done, how each of them had died, and where their souls were currently residing. And as he scanned the freezer doors, he came across an area that was blank, that gave off no odour, and from which he could not perceive any life history. This was the one he was looking for. Reaching out with a muscular red hand, he yanked open the freezer door and stared at the five trays inside, each of them holding a body zipped inside a black bag. It was the one second up from the ground that Kobold was interested in, and he pulled out the tray, hearing it squeal as it slid along its metal slides.

The body wasn't as bloated as some of the others in the freezer, but Kobold's limited human senses could still detect an odour of putrefaction. He reached down and unzipped the body bag, staring into the bloated, pallid face of Jordan Weaver, one eye closed, the other open a slit, the mouth slightly ajar. A hole slightly less than an inch in diameter was above the left eyebrow, the flesh around it puckered and bloody. The hair was matted with blood, and a deep scar ran around the hair line, where the scalp had been sliced for the autopsy procedure. Kobold felt with a hand, tilted Jordan's head to one side, and inspected the exit wound. It was of considerable size, probably large enough for a woman to insert her fist. Scalp, bone and muscle tissue extruded outwards, and what brain matter he could see was torn and bloody. Whoever had carried out the autopsy had replaced the brain, and made a good job of it too, for Kobold could see the hole in the brain aligned almost perfectly with the hole in the skull.

Kobold inspected the rest of the body, could see signs of advanced decay, though the freezer had delayed it somewhat. The y-incision dissected the chest and belly, and had been roughly sewn up. Not many people wanted to see a dead relative naked, so that part was usually concealed under clothes or a burial gown – that much Kobold did know.

He considered his next move, and knew that it was going to use up a lot of resources, but he had no choice. He loved Sadie, he wanted nothing more than to be human again, and there was only one way that was going to happen. He'd ensured that no more Jäger would come after him, which just left Satan a few loyal servants. Satan would never leave Hell, and his servants were no match for Kobold. The Corrupted, however, gave him more cause for concern, but even Satan wouldn't be that blasphemous as to disobey a direct commandment from God Himself.

Surely not.

He looked down at Jordan Weaver again, and then laid hands on the body, watching them glow brilliantly, as before his eyes, the scars began to heal, the torn skin knitting together, the colour returning to the pale flesh as blood was created out of molecules, and arteries and veins received fresh supplies. Kobold felt the heart start to pump, but the body wasn't ready yet and the blood oozed out of the wound in Jordan's head as it began to decrease in size, bone growing to replace that which was lost and which had been swept up by police investigators from the car park behind Sadie's apartment. Jordan's eyes flickered, and both sealed up, making him look asleep, as his chest began to rise and fall.

Kobold corrected himself – there was nobody inside this body to be called a life. Although blood pumped through its arteries, although lungs breathed in oxygen, although the brain was capable of coherent thoughts, eyes were capable of seeing, ears capable of hearing, this body was little more than a mindless vegetable — its capacity to be human counted for little, because the body was soulless.

Kobold needed to enter the body, to twist the molecules of his demonic form so that they existed on a separate plane, leaving only his soul behind. And it would be the soul that entered the body, assuming a position that no other soul had ever assumed, for Jordan Weaver was not a man in the true sense of the word. Jordan Weaver had no parents, hadn't even been born, in fact. Kobold had created him in his own image, using the centuries-old memory of himself as a living being, throwing together molecules and atoms, using all of the materials at his disposal, crafting like an expert sculptor, so that the body he would occupy would be capable of passing for a human being.

Now, he stood before his creation, feeling slightly weakened by the exertion of spinning together more molecules to rejuvenate this once dead body. Fortunately, it hadn't decayed too much, but although the initial injury, the one that had caused the death of this body, was a relatively minor fault to repair, and confined to a single area, there was additional damage caused by the autopsy. And it was ironic that it was this damage that had caused him the most problems, that had taken the most energy to put right.

But now it was time to occupy the body. He had work to do, and quickly. He knew that soon he would have to face Satan in combat, for there could only be one demon occupying the throne of the devil. And he, Kobold, had been chosen for the role.

It was not a challenge that he was looking forward to.

For now, Jordan's body was his, and holding out his arms to ease the disruption of the molecules, he quickly forced himself into the human form, and opened his eyes. He was looking up at the stark white lights that illuminated the morgue. The body itself felt different, but he figured that was because for the last two weeks, he had been in demon form. It felt weak – considerably weaker than it had done before, but he presumed this was because he was a lot stronger as demon now, and the power differential between the two forms was considerable.

After taking a few seconds to orientate himself, Kobold — now Jordan – sat up, feeling a cool breeze from the air-conditioning system blowing over his body. The hairs on his legs, on his chest, on his arms, all stood on end. The hair on his head, greasy and still matted with blood, shifted in the breeze. He would have to get it washed before he left the building. He would have to wash all of the body, in fact, for the smell of death, of two-week-old blood, was still evident. Jordan's nose could smell it, and he had no doubt that the people he passed on the street would he capable of smelling it. More importantly, he realized, he needed clothes, ones that fitted him.

He stood up, feeling the cool, tiled floor beneath his feet, as he looked around the large room. Here, he figured, was where they carried out the autopsies. The floor cambered from each of the four walls, leading down to a sluice grate, where the fluids from the autopsies were flushed away. Three tables were placed over this grate, enabling the medical examiner to carry out one post-mortem while the previous one was cleaned up and the next one was prepared.

He wouldn't find his belongings here, not his clothes, nor his keys, nor his mobile phone.

They would be in a separate office, probably locked away.

He walked over to the double doors and looked out into a corridor. There was a door directly opposite, and through the glass in the top half, he could see a light on. Stepping across to the door, he peered inside, saw a morgue attendant sitting at a desk, the TV on in front of him, a magazine to one side, a lunchbox open next to it. In his hands, the attendant held a novel, his eyes rapidly scanning the text on the page, clearly not interested in either the magazine or the late-night show on the television. He dipped into the lunchbox and took out a sandwich, not even inspecting it before taking a bite.

Jordan felt his own stomach rumble. It had been two weeks since his last meal, he thought with a wry smile. He looked beyond the attendant and saw a row of lockers – either they belonged to members of staff, or more likely they held the belongings of the people in the freezers. The chances were, somewhere in there were his clothes, his cellphone, the keys to his BMW. He had to get into the room, which meant that somehow, he had to draw the attendant out of the office.

He chose to bang on the morgue doors, slapping them loudly with the open palms of both hands, and then swinging them open, before retreating to an alcove ten feet up the corridor. It was some time before the attendant came out of the office, walking warily across the corridor and halting before the swinging, creaking morgue doors.

"Who's there?" he asked nervously, his voice shaky. Jordan was certain he could hear the man's heart beating, hear the blood pumping through his arteries. But it was just a trick of his imagination. "Doctor Travis, is that you?" The attendant shuddered visibly, then pushed open the morgue doors and with a sense of dread, he stepped inside.

Jordan moved quickly, and was inside the office before the morgue doors had stopped swinging behind the attendant. He ran his eyes along the doors to the lockers, and found one with his name scrawled on the label in red felt-tip pen. Wrenching the locker open, he dug out his clothes and pulled them on, noting that the suit jacket and the shirt was bloodstained. But he couldn't worry about that now. He had the means to acquire more clothes, but he had to get out of the morgue – he had to find his BMW.

As he buttoned up his trousers, the attendant returned to the office, his face already pale.

He'd discovered the open freezer door, and the empty tray.

Then he discovered the person who should've been on that tray dressing himself in his office.

It was almost too much for him, Jordan noted.

"Jesus Christ!" the attendant shouted, staggering backwards. Jordan just smiled and continued dressing. "Uh, sorry about this," he said. "A case of misdiagnosis. I should never have been declared dead."

"But I saw you," the attendant gasped. "Your head!"

"Just a scratch," Jordan said, rubbing his blood matted hair. "Got nicked by the bullet, is all."

"No way! Half of your bloody brain was missing!"

"The answer is clear for you to see," Jordan said, reaching in his jacket pocket and pulling out his mobile phone. He switched it on. "Do I look dead to you? Does my head look like it's been blown apart and excavated?"

The attendant couldn't deny that Jordan looked remarkably healthy.

"You can't leave," he stupidly said.

"Why not?"

"Because ..." the attendant said. He stammered and stuttered, then said. "Because the doctor will want to see you."

"No disrespect to your doctor, but if he couldn't tell that I was still alive, well, it doesn't inspire confidence, does it?"

"He cut you open," the attendant said. "I saw it with my own eyes. I even saw them take out your brain and weigh it."

"And a very good job he made of it," Jordan praised. "Believe me, I didn't feel a thing." He pulled on his jacket. "Is there anywhere here I can take a wash — I'm pretty dirty. You buggers didn't even clean me up."

The attendant shook his head. "You're a bloody ghost!"

"Believe me, I'm as human as I look," Jordan said. "And I also stink. I need to take a bath, but for the time being, a wash will do. Is there a sink here I can use? Some soap, shampoo?"

Amazingly, the attendant found all of these things for him, and watched as Jordan washed away the dirt and the blood, staring in disbelief at his torso, where a y-incision should've been. He also couldn't believe that there was no wound visible on Jordan's head.

He said, as Jordan towel-dried his hair. "I saw that bullet hole with my own eyes. It was a horrific wound."

"It was a scratch," Jordan said, "and all the time I've been in that freezer, it's been healing."

In spite of his help, the attendant still didn't believe what he was seeing, and Jordan knew that it was just a matter of time before he cracked. The most likely moment would be when he ventured out of the morgue, and the attendant was left all alone, with only his thoughts for company. His thoughts, and one less corpse in the freezer. And he would have to explain it away somehow.

As Jordan thanked the attendant and stepped out into the street in his bloody suit – the attendant didn't have any fresh clothes for him, other than those belonging to the other corpses, and Jordan neither liked the idea of stealing nor of wearing a dead man's jacket — he knew that he had to leave the area as quickly as possible. Of course the police wouldn't believe the attendant's story. Corpses didn't just get up and walk away but they would know that Jordan Weaver's body was missing, and they would want to know where it had gone.

It didn't leave him much time at all.

He made his way across town on foot, to where the BMW was parked in its lockup. A journey to a nearby menswear shop, and Jordan broke in without setting off the alarm. Soon, he was sitting in the BMW in fresh clothes, the bloody suit in the car's boot.

And he drove quickly, heading for Sadie's apartment.

36

Saddington was *en route* to Scotland Yard when the call came through. Egan took it, and his jaw dropped visibly as he handed the mobile phone over.

"Yes?" Saddington snapped, expecting a call from one of his superiors asking about the gun battle in the middle of a residential area – either that, or someone from the FBI, demanding to know why the British bobbies had fucked up a federal operation.

Instead, it was a CID inspector, who introduced himself, then added, "I'm at the St Augustine's morgue."

Saddington frowned, then looked at Egan, whose expression was still one of subdued shock. "Go on."

"You'd better get over here," the inspector said. "I understand it was one of your bodies so to speak."

"What the hell are you talking about?"

"Jordan Weaver," the inspector went on, "his body's gone walkabout. Literally, by all accounts." He gave a little chuckle.

Twenty minutes later, and Saddington's Vauxhall Senator was parked up in the morgue car park, alongside two ominous black vans used for collecting corpses. The Chief Superintendent rushed inside, Gerry Egan following closely behind.

Saddington was one of a majority of people who hated hospitals – the smell made him anxious, even nauseous, and the morgue was possibly the worst area of any hospital, and yet it was the area to which he had made the most visits in his career. He recognized Mr Travis, the pathologist, who dissected dozens of corpses every week, many of them for the police. He was sitting behind his desk in the large communal office, with a young man sitting alongside him. Two men in suits, along with two uniformed officers, stood behind the medical people.

Everyone looked as Saddington entered.

"Chief Superintendent Saddington. I understand there's a slight problem here."

"You can say that again," the young man said in a strange, high-pitched voice. Mr Travis stood up and shook Saddington's hand.

"I informed the inspector, here, that you would be interested in this," he said.

"It concerns Jordan Weaver?"

The local CID inspector stepped up to Saddington. "Tell me what's so important about Jordan Weaver?"

"He was shot dead by two hitmen in Harlow a couple of weeks ago," Saddington explained.

"That explains it," the inspector said.

"Explains what?" Saddington asked. "All I've had is some cryptic call saying that one of my bodies has gone walkabout. So does someone here mind filling me in on events?"

"Jordan Weaver's body is missing," Travis said.

"And there's a good chance that these hitmen took him away," the inspector declared. "To dispose of evidence relating to their crime."

"Hardly," Egan said laconically. "They're still counting the bullets in their bodies."

The inspector looked slightly bewildered. "Huh?"

"The two men who shot Jordan Weaver opened fire on armed police officers about half an hour ago,"

Saddington said. "They're both on their way here – in body bags. If the bullets didn't kill them, then the fire did." He looked at Travis, who merely shrugged indifferently. He'd seen it all, and mostly, nothing shocked him. There were those child murders a few years back, but he'd been unlucky to get that case — and the nightmares weren't as frequent now as they had been maybe a dozen years ago.

"Well, someone certainly had a reason to walk out of here with Weaver's stiff," the inspector said – Saddington had already forgotten his name, and he wasn't particularly interested in asking him again.

"I presume we have an informant?" He looked expectantly at the young man, no doubt the nightshift attendant. Chances were he wouldn't he asking to do this shift again in a hurry, in spite of any overtime pay.

"This is Ronnie Henman." Travis said. "He has an unusual perspective on this matter."

"Really," Saddington said, pulling up a chair and sitting down. "I'm intrigued."

"Nobody came in and got him." Ronnie said, nervously toying with a handkerchief. "He just walked out. Even asked me to provide him with washing tackle."

Saddington arched an eyebrow. He'd heard these kinds of tall stories before, and he recalled the events in Brazil a few weeks back, where the captain there was insistent that some kind of devil had killed Anthony Bartek, Michael Bartholomew's partner in crime.

"Hmm," he said, frowning seriously. "You understand how this all must sound?"

"Of course I do," Ronnie snapped. "Christ, I've been telling myself that I imagined it, that the hours got to me, that I'm just, I dunno, *cabin crazy* or something. But I checked the bathroom. There's blood in the sink. Jordan Weaver's blood. He washed it out of his hair."

"Are you sure someone else didn't wash it out for him?" Egan asked sceptically.

"I know this sounds mad." Ronnie said impatiently. "But I'm not a nutter. I'm telling you it like it happened."

"From the start," Saddington said. "Tell us how it happened right from the start."

"I heard a noise," Ronnie said. "From the morgue." He was pointing. "So I went out into the corridors. The morgue doors were swinging, as though somebody had just walked through them. So I entered the morgue."

"You must've been nervous," Saddington said. "Must've taken a lot of guts, you being here all by yourself, and all those corpses in the next room. Christ, it'd give me nightmares."

"You tend to get used to it," Ronnie said. "Well, until something like this happens."

"What did you find in the morgue?"

"One of the freezer doors was open," Ronnie went on. "A tray had been pulled out, but there was no corpse on it – just the body bag. I went over and had a look, and I knew that a corpse should've been in that drawer – a fatal gunshot wound – but it was gone. It wasn't anywhere in the morgue. So I came back into this office, intending to call the police, and report a body snatching. I mean, I wasn't about to go running around looking for it. If someone's crazy enough to take a body, who knows what else they're crazy enough to do."

"So, what happened next?" Saddington asked.

"When I came in here, a guy was over by the lockers there," Ronnie said. "He was getting dressed. For a moment, I thought he was some kind of tramp, thieving from the dead, and I was pretty outraged — scared, because you don't expect to see anyone else in this building this late at night — but angry. Then, I saw the blood on this man's head — and down his body. Across his chest, in a sort of y-incision." He traced a path across his own chest. "An autopsy scar. Except, there wasn't any scar there —just the blood. And I realized at that moment ..." Ronnie shuddered. "It was the man from the missing drawer. I recognized his face. Weaver, the gunshot wound. The headshot."

"He was standing in front of you?" Saddington asked.

"It sounds crazy, but yeah, he was standing there."

"Then what happened?"

"I said something like, '*you should be dead*', or something," Ronnie went on. "And he just laughed and said he'd been alive all along. I mean, it sounds ridiculous, but ... he was standing there. Right there by the lockers. You can take some fingerprints if you like!" Saddington looked at the open locker door and gave a half smile.

"We'll do that, Ronnie," he said. "But that really wouldn't prove anything. Anybody could've swiped Weaver's corpse across that locker. Dead man's hands leave prints behind too."

"I knew you wouldn't believe me!" murmured Ronnie, resting his head in his hands.

"You have to see it from our point of view, Ronnie. Mr Travis here carried out the post-mortem and I saw the wound myself. Jordan Weaver was dead, totally dead. We didn't even recover all of his brain.

There is no way that he could even have breathed, let alone stood in front of you." Saddington smiled tightly.

He didn't want to upset this witness – their only witness – but the story he was telling was just so unbelievable, it had no credence whatsoever.

"That's the way we see it."

"I don't know why I bothered," Ronnie said, standing up. "If you don't mind, Mr Travis, I'd like to take tonight off."

Travis nodded, "Certainly. And Ronnie, we'll talk about changing the shifts around."

"I can't afford to lose the nightshift." Ronnie protested.

"We'll talk about it."

"Ronnie, we may need to speak with you again," Saddington said.

"What's the point?" Ronnie asked glumly as he walked to the door. "You don't believe what I'm telling you, and I'm not going to tell you any different in a couple of days. I saw Jordan Weaver with my own eyes. He was alive, or doing a very good impression of a man who's alive. That's what I saw. I didn't imagine it, I didn't dream it — the body's gone, I saw nobody else. That's as much as I know."

Saddington looked at Travis after the young attendant had left.

"What do you think?"

"About Ronnie?"

"About his story."

"His story is absurd," Travis said. "That much is apparent. Even if by some miracle Jordan Weaver was alive when he was brought in here, and even in the extremely unlikely event my colleagues and I missed any signs of life, the autopsy procedure would've killed him. Well, no, let's add something there — the autopsy procedure would've caused some reaction from him. If you were sleeping, and I sliced you open, you'd wake up."

"A coma?"

"There'd be some response," assured Travis. "But as I said, the autopsy procedure would've killed him. We remove organs, and yes, we replace them, but we don't waste time sewing them back up in the right places. Mostly, we place them in a bag and stick them back inside the chest cavity. We're not here to keep people alive, because they're already dead."

Saddington shook his head and snorted. "This is insane. Somebody took that body — why?"

"As the inspector said, there would've been evidence inside that body," Travis said. "But that would only have mattered prior to our autopsy, which we carried out over a week ago. And besides, if the man's killers are now dead, well, dead men don't walk, and they certainly don't steal the bodies of other dead men from morgues."

"This is a puzzling case," Saddington said, looking at Egan. "It reminds me of Brazil."

Egan pulled a surprised expression, then said, "Well, it's bizarre, guv. I'll give you that."

"I'm afraid you're not going to be able to work in here for the next few days," the inspector said. "We're going to have to seal this entire building off until we've made a thorough search for clues."

Saddington ignored the inspector. "What about security cameras?" he asked.

Travis shrugged. "I believe there's a camera on the entrance, but I don't know if it's switched on. We don't keep cameras in the theatre. This isn't America, and we don't have problems with our staff molesting the bodies."

Saddington smiled distastefully. "Right. Well, in a way, I guess you could say that's a shame. But maybe we'll be able to pull something from the camera situated on the entrance. Who do we speak to?"

Half an hour later, they were speaking to the hospital's head of security, in his untidy office. He was fumbling around with a TV and some kind of digital recorder, trying to get a picture. Saddington wanted to take over, because he was certain the man was doing something wrong. Eventually, they got a picture.

"We need to wind it onto approximately eleven-thirty," Saddington told him. "That's what time Ronnie Henman says this all happened." The head of security raised a sceptical eyebrow.

"Working in that place is bound to fuck with your mind," he said. "That boy must've been taking something. Did you test him for drugs?"

"Ronnie hadn't committed any crime, Mr Matthews," Saddington told him patiently. "And we're not in the habit of routinely testing witnesses for signs of drug abuse."

"Maybe you should," Matthews hissed as he wound the footage on. "Little bastard. Sits in that office all night watching crap on TV, wanking over porno mags, snorting Christ knows what! He should've called me straight away, you know. It's my job to contact the local police when something like this happens. He overstepped the mark when he called you people direct."

"If we could just concentrate on this," Saddington said, his patience now wearing thin. He'd seen these men before. Ex-coppers, now heads of security, bitter at losing their old jobs. Usually, they'd screwed up in some way, some way that had been kept quiet for the good of the force, which meant that they were unleashed on an unwary potential employer with plenty of excess baggage about they wanted to keep quiet. Matthews, he knew, had been a Dl on some local force, before he was caught getting free oral service from a prostitute in the front seat of his unmarked Astra.

Now he was head of security for a hospital.

It was a strange world, Saddington thought ruefully.

Finally, the footage reached eleven-twenty, and from here, Matthews took it slowly, as the jerky time-lapse images played out before the eyes of the two police officers and one ex-copper. Saddington could see the entrance to the morgue on the right-hand side of the screen, and the car park to the left.

"What's the time lapse on this thing?" he asked.

"A second per frame," Matthews said. "The playback machine runs it so each frame is on screen for a second – makes it real time for viewing."

Saddington nodded, and watched as the seconds in the top left of the screen ticked past. Finally, at 11:43:38, the doors to the morgue opened, and a man stepped out into the car park.

"Pause it there," Saddington instructed, and leaned forward to inspect the man on the screen, He immediately frowned. "He's wearing Weaver's clothes."

"Nothing peculiar in that," Egan said. "The locker had been broken into."

Saddington viewed the man's face, taking in the hairstyle, and features – they were blurred, terribly poor quality images, but all the same ...

He looked at Egan. "It looks like Weaver — that much is apparent."

"But it can't be him," Egan said.

"Of course it's not," Saddington said. "A brother, maybe, come to take the body away. Hide his true identity?" He looked up at Egan. "What do you reckon?" The footage now continued to play, and they watched the Jordan Weaver lookalike walk away into the night.

"Good theory," Egan said. "The only one that makes sense. But where's the body?"

Saddington turned to Matthews. "Is there another way out of that morgue?"

"There's a door that leads through the hospital," Matthews said. "Though it'd look highly suspicious if they walked through there, one of them being dead, like. And there's the fire escape at the rear. But that's alarmed."

"No camera there, I suppose?"

Matthews shook his head. "We don't usually have problems with burglars at the morgue. For obvious reasons."

"Someone must've taken the stiff out the fire exit," Saddington said.

"Then why's your man there coming out the front, as bold as brass?" Egan wanted to know. "And why's he wearing Weaver's clothes? It doesn't make sense."

"You're right," Saddington said, standing up and frowning. "But then, nothing about this case seems to make much sense, does it?"

"You're talking about Brazil?"

Matthews pricked up his ears, a fact that didn't go unnoticed by Saddington. He replied cautiously, "This case is full of goblins and devils and all kinds of X-File shit, so I guess I shouldn't be surprised." He thanked Matthews for the memory stick holding the footage, and the two officers left the hospital.

"Where to now?"

"Back to the Yard," Saddington replied. "We need our tech-boys to take a look at this, see if they can enhance it any more. We have a suspect — all we need is a firm ID."

"Aye, and the luck of the devil himself," Egan remarked sarcastically.

Saddington had to admit that Egan was probably right.

37

Sadie had been home more than an hour, the memory of Holly and Martin's attempted assault still fresh in her mind. She could recall the journey home in the taxi, in between tears, but not much of what the driver had said to her. She remembered paying him, and the look of panic on his face. He seemed perplexed that she was in such a calm condition, and drove off shaking his head, as though he'd said something outlandish to her during the journey and she'd totally ignored it.

Whatever it had been, Sadie didn't care, as she made her way up to her flat. There were men out there trying to kill her — they'd already killed Jordan — and she didn't want to stay on the streets a moment longer. She wanted to be indoors, wanted to go to bed, where the quilt would make her feel safe, as though she were encased in a bullet-proof jacket rather than flimsy material and duck down. It was something that went back to her childhood – feeling safe at night whenever she was under the bed sheets.

She'd showered and grabbed herself a bite to eat before going to bed, slipping beneath the cool covers and listening to the sounds from the street outside. She was still in Jodie's bed – her own room brought back too many painful memories. And besides, Jodie's bed was a constant reminder of her own sister, still recuperating in hospital. It was as though Jodie were with her constantly when she slept, at a time when she felt as though she had no one.

She heard cars passing, people talking as they strolled beneath the window, some shouting. Loud music could be heard, throbbing from some party in one of the side streets. It wasn't loud enough to disturb Sadie, though she presumed that neighbours closer to the source might well have cause to call the police. Not that it would've worried her too much had it been loud enough to disturb her. She wasn't sleeping well at the moment – hadn't been for a while, which was understandable. She knew that it would be three or four hours before she drifted off.

She'd always suffered from insomnia, though in the past, she'd pulled on a set of headphones and listened to a CD – that had always helped to send her to sleep. Now, all alone in the apartment, she couldn't do that. She wouldn't be able to hear those noises that terrified those who lived alone – the non-existent axe murderers, the rapists, the burglars, the demons. She wouldn't be able to hear death coming before it took her.

She switched on the bedside lamp, picking up a Patricia Cornwell novel she'd been trying to read. So far, she'd only got a dozen pages into the book, which was a sad indictment on her current state of mind, she told herself as she found her place in the book and recapped by reading the last few paragraphs.

She'd managed to read maybe three pages when the door buzzer sounded, startling her out of her skin.

She stood up and looked out of the window, which offered a partially obscured view of the building's entrance. A BMW was parked just outside, its parking lights on, but she couldn't see who was pushing her buzzer. It certainly wasn't the police, because they didn't travel in BMWs. She put down the book and walked to the hallway, pushing the intercom.

"Yeah?" she said, trying to sound confident.

"Sadie?"

The voice came right from the grave, and caused Sadie's legs to turn to jelly. She shuddered uncontrollably, and released the intercom button, sliding to her knees on the floor. This couldn't be. Somebody was playing a trick on her – they had to be.

The memories of the man she loved came flooding back to her.

And that was Jordan's voice — there was no mistaking that.

"Sadie? Please answer me."

Sadie reached up and pushed the button. "Jordan?" she asked — she was in tears now, just moments away from an uncontrollable sob.

"Sadie, you have to let me in," Jordan said.

"Jordan, I don't understand."

"You don't have to," he told her reassuringly. "I'll tell you everything. But you have to let me in."

There was a knock at the door, and Sadie jumped back, slipping onto her backside and swearing.

"Sadie?"

It was Jordan at her door.

Now she knew that it had to be a trick. She'd been speaking to him on the intercom, and within a second, he was standing at her door. Even if she had have buzzed him in, there was no way he could've got here that quickly.

She got to her feet and walked up to the door. "Jordan?"

"Sadie," Jordan said quietly. "Come on, let me in. We have a lot to talk about."

"Jordan ... Jordan, you're dead," Sadie said. "That can't be you. I'm calling the police." And she grabbed the cordless handset from the table in the hallway. "If you don't leave ..." Her threat hung in the air — there was no response from Jordan, or whoever he was. After a pause, Sadie said, "Jordan?" She stepped up to the door and peeked through the peephole.

It was more startling than hearing his voice.

He had one hand on the door frame, and his head hung low— but she recognized his hair. She'd kissed it, nuzzled into it, could remember it tickling her in places she would never have told her mother. And when he raised his head, almost as though he sensed her looking at him, she found herself staring into the face of a dead man.

"Jordan," she said softly. "My God, it is you."

"Please hang up the telephone and try again," a robotic voice said, jolting Sadie back into reality. She switched off the phone and put it back on the table, peering once more out into the corridor, and seeing a wide-angled view of the man she loved. Within a second, the door was open, and he was pulling her into his arms, squeezing her tightly as though he never wanted to let go, which was fortunate, because all Sadie wanted to do was collapse.

"But how?" she finally managed to gasp.

"It's a long story," Jordan said, and he led her into the front room, where they sat down on the sofa. "I've missed you."

"You wouldn't believe how much I've missed you," Sadie said, wiping her eyes. "God, this is so unbelievable. I thought my life had hit rock bottom, I thought it couldn't get any worse, and I also thought it was never gonna get any better — and then, in the blinking of an eye, it just turns completely around." She hugged him. "God, you're alive. I don't know how, but you are, and that's all that matters. Please, tell me this isn't a dream. Tell me you're real. A real, living, breathing human, and not some crazy dream. God, it'd be a nightmare, not a dream!"

"I'm not a dream," Jordan promised her.

"So how? I don't understand," Sadie said, shaking her head. "This doesn't make any sense. They came and told me what happened."

"That I'd been shot?"

"That you were killed," Sadie said. "Hitmen, after me."

"The hitmen, you don't have to worry about any more," Jordan assured her. "That's all been taken care of."

"But if they killed you—"

"They didn't." Jordan said with a smile. "It was ... we played a trick. We, uh, pulled a fast one."

"We?"

"I can't tell you who 'we' are," Jordan said. "At least, not yet."

"Why not? Jordan, I have to know! I have a right to know."

"You do have a right," Jordan agreed. "But we've just found each other again, and I don't wanna ruin that."

"Is it really that bad?"

"It's ... let's just say that I'm not the kind of person you want to introduce to your family and friends," was all Jordan would say.

Sadie really wanted to pursue it, but so much of Jordan's past and present was shrouded in mystery, and she was just so happy to see him again, that it didn't really seem that important. Not right now. Not this minute. Not when she'd just discovered that the man she loved, the man she'd thought was dead, was actually alive and well, and embracing her, and showering her in his comforting aroma.

"You're not going to leave me again?" she asked him.

"I'm never going to leave you," he promised her. And this time, she really did believe that it was true. He ran a hand through her hair and kissed her softly on the forehead. He looked into her eyes, and she suddenly felt as though the last few days had finally caught up with her. She felt so exhausted. And Jordan could see this, because he said, "Come on —let's get you to bed. You look as though you could do with a good sleep."

"I've found you again, Jordan, just when I thought you were dead," Sadie protested. "There's so much I want to say to you."

"And I'll still be here in the morning," he assured her. "But right now, your health is more important."

Sadie couldn't argue with that. Right now, she felt so tired, she could sleep standing up, and that really wasn't doing her any good at all. This was like a dream come true, and she felt that she could finally sleep, and not have any worries, any deep concerns to trouble her.

As Jordan led her to the bedroom, she so wanted to feel his touch, to have him caress her, to make love to him, but she was so tired, so very tired. Before she knew what was happening, she was lying down between the sheets, and Jordan was kissing her on the forehead.

"Where are you going?" she asked meekly.

"Nowhere," he told her, and he lay down on top of the quilt alongside her. "I'll be right here."

Satisfied that he was here with her, that he was back for good, she closed her eyes, and drifted into a warm, comfortable sleep.

Kobold looked down at this beautiful creature resting with her head on his stomach, this human he had fallen in love with, who made him want to be human once more, and he smiled. She filled him with such happiness unlike anything he had ever experienced, and he was prepared to give up what was rightfully his, to abdicate from the throne of Hell, just to be able to spend the next forty or so years with her.

But the future wasn't that assured. First, he had to dispose of Satan. He felt powerful enough, but he knew that the forthcoming battle would be perilous. Satan was not a mere demon — he had powers that had been finely tuned over the last two millennia, whereas Kobold was a juvenile in comparison, a future devil still experiencing puberty.

He wanted to see Sadie one last time, before the battle, because there were no guarantees that it wouldn't be him who was destroyed. Satan would not gladly surrender his throne. He would fight, and he would draw on the experience he had garnered over the centuries, using skills that Kobold simply didn't possess. The fight would be difficult, but Kobold had to defeat Satan if he was to stand any chance of ever becoming human once again, something which, in itself, contravened God's own law.

He ran a hand through Sadie's hair, and it was soft to touch. He was experiencing the warmth of being human and it was a sensation he did not wish to readily surrender.

He frowned.

Satan would be destroyed, and order would be restored once more in Hell. He would see God, and he would beg Him to allow this one transgression. How could He refuse Kobold that?

First things first, Kobold thought with a sneer.

He had some unfinished business to attend to.

Sadie's honour had been offended— and he couldn't allow that.

Jordan Weaver slipped into a deep sleep.

Almost instantly, his body was cold to touch, as though it were a corpse.

Jordan Weaver was merely a soulless, lifeless cocoon.

Sadie wasn't aware that she was sleeping in the arms of a dead man.

38

Martin Walsh looked at Holly as she came up to kiss him, spit and semen dribbling from her smiling mouth, her eyes half-closed in a drug-induced, semiconscious state. For a brief instant, he was disgusted with her, with what she had become. More than that, he was momentarily disgusted with himself for allowing this to happen to her. She prostituted herself to the highest bidder, in return for heroin, cocaine or some other worthless commodity nobody should have to sell themselves for. He'd reduced her to this — he'd pumped her full of heroin and cocaine, then pumped her full of semen. He'd ruined her future — like a hard-core porn star, she could never recapture the innocence of her youth. Though it might eventually become her past, it would forever remain a part of her. And like the porn star unable to shake off the reputation, she would never be able to shake off the stigma of addiction.

If the hard drugs didn't kill her, the chances were, she'd do it herself.

It was sad really.

"What's wrong?" she asked him lazily, as she flopped down on the bed next to him. "You look as though you've got the weight of the world on your shoulders." She laughed loudly, and for a moment, Martin thought she was going to collapse into hysterics. Fortunately, she caught herself.

"Nothing," he said, unable to shake off the hostility.

"Didn't you like it?" she asked him.

"Of course," he answered — well, he wasn't lying. Holly was very proficient when it came to sex. She did things to him that drove him wild, and she never expected anything sexually in return. And wasn't that typical of a prostitute? Hating sex and hating men, but at the same time, using one to garner favours from the other?

Now, Sadie Bartholomew, she was something else. She was aloof, playing hard to get, probably because she didn't like him, a tiny voice said in the back of his mind. But that was part of the attraction. Here, he had a woman who pleasured him, but who clearly didn't enjoy doing it. In fact, Holly didn't even bother pretending any more. She did the job, did it well, and then held out her hand for her next fix. Ten years ago, Martin might've found that exhilarating, supplying her with two or three fixes a night, just so he could have three goes at her, but now ...

Well, he was older, and it wasn't exciting having sex with Holly anymore, because she clearly didn't want it herself. And the drugs were costing him a fortune. He knew that he could get sex elsewhere, and a damn sight cheaper. Christ, he could find an eighteen-year-old who would be turned on enough by his Porsche, his fancy bachelor pad, and his job not to require the added incentive of a fresh supply of drugs every day. He didn't love Holly, and she didn't love him — they made no secret of that fact. They never had. There wasn't much more than a physical side to their relationship. Maybe at the start, there had been, but now it was simply sex and drugs.

And Martin had had enough.

He wanted Sadie.

And as Holly fished around for a fresh supply of coke, he pondered how he could turn Sadie back onto him. It was apparent that she'd been disgusted by Holly's advances earlier that evening, which at the time, Martin had thought was a shame, because he was so aroused just imagining Holly sitting on Sadie's face while he alternated between fucking the pair of them. But that wasn't to be.

And now Martin knew that wasn't what he wanted.

It was time for him to settle down, to put this decadence behind him.

It was time for him to try and make Sadie understand how much she meant to him.

His erection reminded him how he felt about her, but he knew that it probably wasn't a very tactful starting point for the conversation.

Holly, a gram of coke in her hand, wandered off to the bathroom, and Martin thought about Sadie.

He felt a throbbing between his legs, and then a sharp pain.

Grimacing, he looked down to see his foreskin was red, with spots of blood in a couple of places. He pulled it back and exposed his head which was almost raw in places. Well, he and Holly had been having pretty wild sex a few minutes earlier, before she'd finished him off with her mouth. He'd managed to keep it going for more than an hour, with Holly manipulating him manually in the quieter moments. It was only natural that his penis should be a little sore. Christ, she was probably in just as much pain.

"Pain is an indicator that something is wrong," a voice that Martin recognized spoke up.

Chilled, Martin turned his head to see the evil creature that had paid him a visit a few weeks earlier standing by the side of the bed, his arms folded. Instinctively, he shielded his penis.

"A little late for that," the creature said dismissively. Martin blinked at the inhuman form, but this wasn't a figment of his imagination. He'd drunk only a little, and hadn't taken any drugs that night. He was wide awake, he could even hear Holly sneezing in the bathroom.

"Who the fuck are you?"

"Oh you know me, don't you, Martin?" The creature's face bobbed closer. "Perhaps if I had half my head missing, you'd recognize me." Martin frowned.

Then it dawned on him who this creature looked like. That guy Sadie had been dating. He'd seen him once, and only briefly, but Martin never forgot a face.

"Jesus fucking Christ!" he mumbled loudly.

"You know, people are always calling me that," the creature said with a bemused smile, "and I keep telling them they're thinking of the wrong side."

"This isn't real."

"Just like last time, Martin, this is about as real as it gets," the creature said, placing its hands on its hips.

"What do you want?" Martin managed to gasp.

"You know, Martin, there's a big difference between a girl like Sadie and one like Holly," the creature said, looking to the bathroom door. "Do you know what that difference is?" Martin shook his head. He had an idea, but he didn't want to be conversing with this highly vivid figment of his imagination. "Their virtue, Martin, that's the difference. Sadie has had a handful of lovers. Holly — well, we all know about Holly, don't we? She knows everybody — and I mean that, Martin, in the biblical sense." The creature frowned. "Do you know how many lovers she's taken, Martin?" Martin shook his head. Working it out quickly, he thought she'd probably averaged maybe two or three a week at least for the last six months. Maybe more. He didn't want to think about it, really.

The creature raised an eyebrow, as though able to read Martin's thoughts. "It's scary stuff, isn't it? And those lovers? How many lovers have they had? Let's say an average of maybe ten. And those lovers? How many lovers have they had? You know, Martin, effectively, each time you sleep with Holly, you're also sleeping with another couple of hundred people. All those germs, that bacteria, passed from person to person, until finally, they reach you. But it's not merely symbolical bacteria you have to worry about in this day and age, is it? There's something far more serious."

Martin shuddered. "What do you mean?" he asked, though he had a pretty good idea. He'd thought about it often enough, and on each occasion, the possibility had terrified him.

"Acquired Immune Deficiency Syndrome, Martin," the creature said. "Otherwise known as AIDS."

"That's a moderate risk," Martin said quietly.

The creature looked at the bathroom door again. "She has it, you know," it said.

"Fuck you!"

"Before she came here tonight, she had sex with somebody," the creature went on. "At that party — where you and Holly tried to tempt Sadie over to your depraved sexual lifestyle. A man — bisexual — he was unfortunate enough to have contracted HIV from a partner whose morality was somewhat lacking. He thought he knew the man well. He was a careful man himself. But condoms burst, don't they?" Martin was shaking his head. "That man doesn't know yet. And when he finds out ... well, it will destroy him. He is but an unfortunate casualty, totally innocent, a man of high morals who will go to Heaven. All the same, he still infected Holly and you."

"You're lying!" Martin snapped. This wasn't happening, this wasn't fucking real!

The creature shook its head. "I'm not," it assured Martin sincerely. "Go for a test in the morning, wait a couple of weeks for the result. It will tell you precisely what I'm telling you now. You're dying, Martin, and you have maybe a couple of years left. At most. And when you do eventually die ..." The creature grinned. "I will be waiting for you in Hell. If I were you, I'd consider your suffering with AIDS as a blessing, because what you suffer here on Earth as a result of your depravity will be nothing compared to the suffering you will undergo in Hell. I'll be seeing you soon, Martin – and if not me, then somebody like me."

And with that, the creature disappeared.

Martin gasped breathlessly, and looked down at his penis, which had shrivelled up into a hairy walnut between his legs. There was blood on the tip, a few streaks across his foreskin — the perfect path into his body for the lethal AIDS virus Holly was carrying.

"Jesus," he muttered as she returned to the bedroom suitably refreshed.

She stopped in her tracks and looked at him, her eyes dropping down to his groin and then rising to take in the expression on his face.

He knew what that expression must've looked like.

"What?" she asked him.

"You fucking bitch." he muttered.

"What? Martin, lighten up, for fuck's sake!"

"Do you know what you've done?" Martin shouted, getting to his feet. He knew that he was acting irrationally, that what the figment of his imagination had told him only seconds earlier could not possibly have been true, because it hadn't existed. It was just his own fears being voiced in a vivid way — an extremely vivid way, he had to admit, but nevertheless, it wasn't real.

"Martin, have a toot," Holly said to him with a smile, "before you lose it."

Martin rushed across the room and grabbed Holly by the throat, pushing her against the wall. She banged her head and blinked, her eyes watering.

"What the fuck are you doing?" she screamed, her voice betraying her hurt. She raised a hand to her head and rubbed it. "You're crazy!"

"Who did you fuck earlier tonight?"

"Huh?"

"Who the fuck did you fuck earlier tonight?" Martin shouted, shaking her head back into the wall again.

"Get the fuck off me, you stupid bastard!" Holly said, trying to push his hand away. He wasn't holding her tightly, but it was still tight enough to prevent her from shaking loose.

"I know you fucked somebody earlier," he snarled. "Now, who the fuck was it?"

"Fuck you!" Holly said, but there was fear on her face, and the defiance in her voice certainly wasn't sincere. "Christ, what's wrong? It's not like I've never done it before."

"That person gave you AIDS, you stupid fucking bitch! And you've given it to me!"

"What?" Holly said. She smiled nervously, then frowned. "Did you know him or something? Do you know something about him?"

"I know he's bisexual," Martin told her. "And I know that he's got AIDS."

"You can't possibly know that," Holly said, shaking her head.

"You've given me AIDS, you fucking whore!"

Holly shook her head.

Martin punched her in the face. He didn't know where it came from, because he couldn't remember the last time he'd ever struck anybody — it must've been years ago, when he was at school — and he felt something give beneath his fist. As he pulled back his hand, he saw blood pouring from Holly's lip, which was split up to her nose.

She didn't make a noise as she slithered to the floor, leaving a trail of blood on the wall behind her from where she'd also banged her head.

But Martin wasn't done yet.

This stupid bitch had given him a death sentence. She couldn't be allowed to get away with it. She deserved to be punished.

And so he kicked her hard in the stomach, then again in the head. When he realized that it was hurting his bare feet, he stepped back and looked around for something else to beat her with. Holly lay at his feet, coughing up blood, resigned to her fate, a pathetic human being. But Martin didn't feel pity for her – he felt only disgust, as he walked over to the far wall, where a 20" TV rested on a small cabinet. He grabbed the TV, wrenching the plug from the socket, and walked back over to where Holly lay.

She looked up at him, her eyes full of sorrow and sheer disbelief.

But she didn't move. She lay where she was as he raised the television over his head.

"You bitch!" Martin bellowed, and threw the television down on top of her.

A loud bang shocked him back to his senses, and he staggered back and sat down on the bed, staring in horror at the sight before him.

One of Holly's legs twitched, and an arm jerked beneath the TV, flopping loose and banging into the wall. He could see blood seeping from beneath the broken hunk of plastic and glass, and suddenly the full impact of what he had just done hit him with a force that seemed mightier than the impact between the heavy TV and Holly's skull. He forgot all about AIDS, and thought only of Holly, at her sad expression as she'd looked up at him with disbelieving resignation.

Somebody behind him laughed, and Martin knew exactly who it was.

"Are you happy now?" he asked, hanging his head in his hands.

The creature sat down beside him. "Ecstatic," it said. "That saved me a job. She had to die."

"What are you saying?" Martin asked, looking up.

"For her sins."

"Her sins? You mean drugs and sex?" Martin shook his head and scoffed. "Those aren't sins, for fuck's sake!"

"I suppose you think that the drugs made her a victim? And I suppose you think that because of the drugs, she had to sell herself to the highest bidder?"

Martin looked down at the bloody mess on his bedroom floor, and threw his head back into his hands. "She *was* a victim."

"No, she wasn't," the creature said. "I can show you victims, if you like. Just follow me to the nearest cemetery. Those are victims."

"You're perverse," Martin snapped. "She was a fucking human

being, and you're saying she deserved to die."

"She did," the creature said. "But not because of the sex and the drugs. Drugs harm only the person who takes them, and sex ... well, sex is fun, isn't it? But when you have to harm people to fund those addictions ..." The creature paused. "She was a nasty piece of work, Martin, but then, I suppose that made you a very appropriate couple, didn't it?"

"Fuck you."

"The defeated man resorts to empty insults, Martin," the creature said. "And I know you're defeated, Martin, because I'm looking at the thing that's going to see you serve the rest of your life in prison. An unprovoked attack, a mindless and savage murder, with your fingerprints all over the murder weapon—"

"It wasn't unprovoked!" Martin snapped. "That fucking bitch gave me AIDS!"

The creature smiled. "Uh, yeah, sorry about that," it said. "Bit of a mix-up at the lab, you could say. You know that bisexual I was talking about earlier? Well, it turns out that although the guy he slept with had AIDS, the condom didn't break. He's perfectly healthy and so is – *was* – Holly. Consequently, so are you."

Martin's jaw dropped and he blinked wildly. "You mean, I haven't got AIDS?"

"No," the creature said. "Mind you, thirty years in prison, a pretty boy like you, who knows what could happen?" The creature stood up, walked over to Holly's body and bent down. "Don't you fancy taking a look? You know, death always fascinates me – injuries too. It demonstrates how fragile the human body is, seeing the various ways it can easily be destroyed."

"You lied to me!" Martin hissed in utter disbelief.

"Two things, Martin. Firstly, I'm a demon. I come from Hell, and it's part of our job to lie to assholes like you. And secondly, and perhaps more significantly, you believed I was a figment of your imagination, and yet you took me seriously enough to cave in your girlfriend's skull with a twenty-inch Sony Nicam stereo TV. If you're that crazy, well, you deserve to be locked away." The creature pulled away the TV to reveal the bloody mess that was spread across the carpet where Holly's head should've been. The skull was shattered, with bloody squares of her scalp, complete with clumps of hair, mashed in with her crushed brain. The creature nodded its head approvingly. "Would've killed her instantly. Right now, she's falling to Hell."

"You've destroyed me," Martin said softly, as he began to realize the full implications of his actions.

"No, Martin, you've destroyed yourself," the creature said. "Of course, you could always try that old defence, couldn't you? These voices told you to do it, the devil told you to do it. That might work. I doubt it very much, but you can always try it, can't you? The police are on the way — a neighbour called them, because he heard all the shouting and the loud crash, so I've got to go. Before I leave, would you like to know how you die?"

"Does it really matter?" Martin asked with a dejected sigh. "My life's already over."

"You get run down by a car," the creature said. "Driven by Holly's brother."

"But Holly's brother's only eight," Martin said.

The creature smiled. "That's not the whole story. You spend thirty years in prison, and on your first day out ... well that's what happens. You've got that to look forward to, Martin. And knowing the way you go, well, that's torture, isn't it?"

"You only exist in my imagination." Martin said, and snapped his eyes shut. In the very least, the devil creature should disappear. At best, he was hoping for this whole sorry affair to be a nightmare.

When he opened his eyes, the creature was gone.

Holly was still there, dead on the floor.

Martin hung his head in his hands and sobbed as the sirens grew louder.

39

Satan thoughtfully stroked his chin and pondered his future.

The Jäger he'd sent out after Kobold had been unsuccessful, and only two had returned alive, reporting to him that the demon they'd pursued was far more powerful than any of them had suspected. And Zerstörer, the most powerful Jäger in Satan's army, hadn't returned. The most disturbing thing was Satan had this feeling that Zerstörer hadn't been destroyed, that Kobold had somehow turned him against Satan, and over to his own side. More disconcertingly, the surviving Jäger had reported that they'd fought Kobold in the chambers of a demon called David. Satan was one of the few beings in Hell who knew about the existence of David. More importantly, he was possibly the only person in Hell who knew precisely who David was, who understood the full significance of his existence.

Well, up until recently, that was, because it was a definite fact that Kobold was the young pretender to Satan's throne, and it was also undoubtedly likely that David had supplied Kobold with all of the information he needed to gain an unfair advantage over Satan in the battle that would surely be fought between the two of them.

Right now, Satan was concerned for his future. In the coming battle, there could only be one victor, and consequently one survivor. The loser's soul would be tipped out and dashed on the stony ground, crushed underfoot, as he was sent into oblivion. Satan was not overjoyed at the prospect of being the loser, and that in itself was a bizarre notion. The fear, the lack of confidence, both sensations he hadn't felt in a long, long time. Human sensations that he had wrongly thought would never penetrate his crimson hide and yet, here he was, fearing the loss of a battle with one who should never be as powerful as him.

Satan had plans — of course, he had plans. You could not be the devil and not successfully plot the downfall of others. And that, he told himself wryly, was half of the problem, wasn't it? He had plotted the downfall of those who didn't deserve to be destroyed, and as a consequence, had succeeded only in plotting his own downfall. He could see it happening, unless he reacted drastically to the potential threat. Which was why he'd despatched the Jäger, led by Zerstörer, who had probably been the fiercest and most powerful demon in Hell. And yet Kobold had survived that conflict, which was a frightening indicator of the actual strength of his powers.

So there wasn't a demon in Hell who could destroy Kobold, but that was probably because the demons of Hell obeyed the laws laid down by God — even if Satan himself disobeyed them, and twisted them to his own ends. But Satan didn't just have the demons of Hell at his disposal. He'd been dealing with the Corrupted for some time now, and the Corrupted obeyed no one. In fact, Satan was aware of the fact that outside of Hell, the most powerful of the Corrupted – those who had been in the wilderness for centuries – were easily a match for him. It was only when one entered Hell that Satan had the upper hand. And that meant that they would be more than a match for Kobold.

Of course, that all depended upon how mature Kobold was.

A demon materialized before him, muscular arms outstretched, the horns on his head long and wiry, having grown out of control. A thin strip of short hair ran down the centre of the demon's head, and he looked up at Satan with the wild eyes of a madman.

"You will forgive me if I do not kneel before you," the demon said. "But the Corrupted bow before no one." He lowered his arms and placed them on his hips. "I understand that you wish to speak with me."

Satan nodded his head, for the moment ignoring this demon's impertinence. He was fully aware of the fact that he could destroy this demon, probably without even breaking into a sweat, because in Hell, he was the strongest, but he was also conscious of the fact that the Corrupted were a socialist population, and their union was powerful. When one was destroyed, others came to his rescue.

Their population was minuscule when compared with the full

population of demons of all guises in Hell, but should they converge on Satan's chamber, they could easily overpower and destroy him, particularly with him being tired out after a vicious battle.

"I have a task for you, Ubel," Satan said.

Ubel nodded and smiled. "You speak of the one known as Kobold?"

Satan frowned. The story of the wayward demon must've travelled beyond the walls of Hell. And if it had travelled beyond, then more importantly, it had travelled within, which was something Satan did not want to worry about, having the loyalty of his demons put in question because they were awaiting his downfall.

"You have heard of him?"

"Heaven, Hell, and everywhere in between has heard of him, Satan," Ubel said. "And judging by your reaction, the stories are true."

"What of these stories?"

"That your time as the devil is almost at an end," Ubel said with a smirk. "That you are shortly to be overthrown by one who is younger, more powerful, and less corrupt." He said that final word with a lopsided grin. "I can see the effect such tales are having on you."

"There is a battle about to take place," Satan admitted with a sneer, "But it is Kobold who will be destroyed."

"Then why do you desire my services?" Ubel asked bluntly. "Surely if this Kobold is no match for you, I am superfluous."

"I do not need to be bothered by this insignificant annoyance," Satan said. "I have more important things to concern myself with. Which is where you come in, Ubel. You can unburden me of some of this load by ensuring that Kobold is dealt with."

"But Kobold is the successor to the throne—"

"Only if I am destroyed," Satan snapped.

"Why yes," Ubel said, continuing, "however as I was saying, he has been appointed as your successor, which means that he must be powerful."

"Undoubtedly," Satan said. "But he will be no match for you, Ubel."

"The way I see it, Satan," Ubel said, strolling around in slow circles, "is that there are two possible outcomes. Firstly, I destroy Kobold, which rids you of an annoying problem you do not wish to sully your hands with. Secondly, he destroys me, but in the process sustains injuries from the obviously monstrous battle, from which he finds it difficult to recover, thereby rendering him an easy target for you."

"How perceptive of you, Ubel."

"Just tell me, Satan, what do I get out of it?"

"A change is about to take place in Hell, Ubel," Satan said, "and you can be a part of it. All I ask for in return is your loyalty. And doing this for me will demonstrate that loyalty."

"Telling me that a change will shortly occur in Hell is no incentive, Satan," Ubel said, folding his arms. Satan avoided glaring at this impertinent demon — he knew that Ubel was the best chance he had of defeating Kobold. Ubel's cunning and strength were legendary, and it was certainly better to have him as an ally than as an adversary. "That much," Ubel went on, "is apparent. I need to know what my reward will be. This vague promise of yours, talking about a change, is not enough".

"The changes that are to take place are far greater than those imagined by the demons who oppose me," Satan growled. "My powers are supreme, and I oppose the current selection process. I propose to change all of that."

"You propose to fight God Himself?" Ubel asked with a raised eyebrow. He wasn't impressed — it appeared as though he were simply regarding Satan as a fool.

"There are few who are truly righteous, Ubel," Satan went on. "And yet there are countless hundreds of thousands who pour through the gates of heaven every single day. Almost all of them have sinned in some way, and they need to be purged of those sins."

Ubel nodded his head in agreement. "That would mean regressing to the way things were before."

"Under Beelzebub," Satan said, "before God and David both stepped in to put a stop to it."

"I agree that it is a worthy cause," Ubel said, "though whether you succeed is another matter."

"With powerful demons by my side, Ubel, I can succeed," Satan said. "I can restore you to Hell, allow you to regenerate your powers. You will become a force to be reckoned with."

"And does that hold no fear for you?" Ubel asked with a smile.

"Would you not see me as a challenge?"

Satan laughed. "There can only be one devil," he said, "and I am he."

"And Kobold?"

"Kobold is the designated heir to the throne," Satan said dismissively. "As I am sure you are aware, a devil has to put an end to insurrections. Indeed, Beelzebub and Lucifer both crushed opposition and challengers to their respective thrones before they were finally defeated. You are no heir to the throne, Ubel, and Kobold is not even a worthy challenger. He will be crushed."

Ubel's eyes turned oily black. "But not by you?"

"I cannot afford to become wounded."

"And I can?"

"If you lose, as you rightly say, Kobold will almost certainly be mortally wounded," Satan said. "Your place in the history books shall be assured."

"A place in a history book, Satan, is not particularly attractive, especially when it comes at price of my destruction," Ubel said. "But no fear, I shall destroy Kobold, and I shall enjoy doing so. And I will expect to receive full support from you when I am victorious. Full support for myself and for my legions."

Satan shuffled nervously, but tried not to let it show. He had a feeling that Ubel would demand something like this. He wanted his loyal demons, thousands of the Corrupted, to join him in Hell, a veritable army that could oppose Satan at any time. And if that happened, chaos, not a devil, would reign in Hell.

Satan lied. "Of course," he said. And like the devil he was, he lied convincingly.

Ubel frowned with uncertainty, then nodded his head. "Consider it done, Satan. But know this — if you betray me, I will see your throbbing soul ripped out and smashed on the ground of this very chamber. I will see it torn to pieces before your dying eyes, and shared amongst the hungry mouths of the hounds of Hell."

Satan smiled. "I do not betray the faithful, Ubel. Of that, you have my word."

And with that, Ubel disappeared, leaving Satan to ponder the wisdom of his decision.

40

Kobold awoke, the body of Jordan Weaver already warm, because his soul had remained within — it was, he had decided, the safest place for him. In Hell, he would be continually harassed by rogue elements of the Jäger, undeterred by Zerstörer's failure, and he had considered the fact that battles with powerful demons would be more draining to him than remaining within this human form on Earth.

He looked at Sadie, lying peacefully beside him, and thought about the coming battle, recalling that he had been faced with a similar situation just a few weeks ago, before those hitmen had shot Jordan Weaver dead. Then, he had prepared himself to face Satan, though in reflection, he knew that had he not been shot, had he actually faced Satan as he'd intended, he would not be lying here next to Sadie. He just hadn't been powerful enough then.

Now, he felt as though nothing and nobody could stop him. Sadie stirred, and he considered the fact that he was using some of his energy to keep her asleep, energy that he couldn't afford to waste. He withdrew his power, and Sadie's eyes flickered then opened. For a second, she frowned, confused, then her mouth cracked into a smile.

"Jordan," she said softly.

"It's okay," he told her. "Everything's gonna be okay now." But it wasn't, he told himself. He would have to leave Sadie again soon, when he faced Satan in battle. And from that battle, he might not return. There were no guarantees, and it would be unfair of him to give any to Sadie. He couldn't leave her without warning her of the dangers that lay ahead.

"I thought ..." Sadie ran a hand over her face. "I thought I'd dreamt it all."

"No, you weren't dreaming," he told her, stroking her cheek. "And everything's gonna be just fine."

"I'm so glad that it never happened," she said.

Jordan smiled, and it was sincere — inside, however, Kobold felt like a fraud. If he should lose the greatest battle Hell had known in more than two millennia, he would be destroyed.

But if he should win ...

Kobold wondered about that for a moment, because nobody had given him any options should he be victorious. Reizend, the angel, had merely instructed him that he had to destroy Satan. David, the first ever devil, had informed him that it was his destiny to face Satan, to overthrow him, and to become the devil himself. But that wasn't what Kobold wanted.

He looked at Sadie.

And the smile disappeared from his face as a chill spread through Jordan Weaver's body, every hair standing on end, every nerve ending bristling. Human reaction to his demonic senses. There was a presence — a presence that was nearby. The presence was pure evil. And there was only one thing that should've given off such an aura.

The devil himself.

Kobold sat up. He had to get out of here. If Satan was after him, if Satan had dared to venture out of Hell to pursue him, the lives of any humans who got in his way would be insignificant. In fact, any humans who saw him would *have* to be destroyed.

And that included Sadie.

She sat up, concerned. "Jordan?" she asked, putting a hand on his shoulder.

"I have to go," he said, getting out of bed and pulling on his clothes. "I'm sorry."

"Where?" Sadie asked him.

"I can't say," he replied, tugging his trousers on. "But it's not safe for you if I stay here."

"Jordan, you're scaring me. I thought you said this was all over."

"I thought it was," he lied. "I thought you wouldn't become affected."

"Jordan, what the hell is going on?" Sadie pleaded.

But Kobold wasn't listening. He bent over her and kissed her. Then he fished in his pocket for something that David had given him. A crucifix, fashioned out of pure, unsullied gold, straight from the bowels of Hell. He handed it over to her. "Take this," he said.

Sadie frowned as she inspected it. "Jordan, what's this for?"

"Protection," he told her.

"Protection? Jordan, you gave me one of these before. I'm not religious."

"You don't have to be," he said to her. "That crucifix is one of the most valuable pieces of jewellery you will ever come across, not just because of what it is worth, but because of what it can do for you. Keep it with you at all times."

"Why?"

"It will ward off evil."

Sadie blinked. "Ward off evil?"

"Sadie, please, don't think about it, just listen to what I'm saying," Kobold said. "This is perhaps one of the most important things you will ever have to listen to in your life."

"But you're talking about hitmen and guns, aren't you?" Sadie held up the crucifix. "What good is this? I mean, I'm not religious, and I'm certainly not superstitious."

"Do you trust me, Sadie?" Sadie seemed to consider that for a few moments. "Let me rephrase that do you think I would ever let any harm come to you?" Once again, Sadie considered this, and Kobold began to panic. The presence was getting closer— evil, like nothing he'd ever sensed before.

He had to leave this place.

Finally, Sadie nodded her head. "I know you'd always look after me. I believe that, yes."

"Good, then listen to what I'm saying," he told her. "That crucifix is special. It isn't like something you'd get from some jewellers, and it's far more powerful than anything you'd find in a church. It *will* protect you, Sadie, from the men who are after me."

"But what about you?"

It was a question he couldn't answer. He kissed her again.

"I love you, Sadie."

Sadie didn't respond at first, and he looked at her unblinking face. "Jordan, I want to know what this is all about!"

"I can't tell you," he said with a pained expression. "At least, not yet. Listen, Sadie, I have to go." And with that, he rushed for the door, throwing it open and stepping out into the corridor. He looked both ways, then went for the stairs, taking them three at a time. He could've left Jordan Weaver's body and materialized practically anywhere, but that would leave the body catatonic and vulnerable. He had to get Jordan's body to safety.

But there was one more thing he had to do.

He had to shield Sadie.

It would take up a lot of his energy, but he couldn't leave her exposed. Satan might deliberately kill her just to spite Kobold, and he wasn't sure that the crucifix would be any help against the devil, in spite of what David might have told him. As he rushed from the building to his new BMW, parked alongside Sadie's Volvo, he turned back and held out a hand. Immediately, the apartment block was swathed in a dark red veil, which no demonic creature could see — no demonic creature other than Kobold. The veil prevented any demon from using their powers to locate individuals within it. He also cast a similar veil over himself.

Usually, he thought as he climbed behind the wheel of the car, such a task required such monumental energy resources that most demons were sapped of their power after a few minutes. Kobold was counting on himself having enough in reserve for him to hide Jordan Weaver's body and return to Hell, where he could summon Satan for the ultimate battle, luring him from Earth.

He fired up the engine and revved loudly, screaming out of the car park and narrowly avoiding a Ford Focus coming in. The car sounded its horn, but Kobold wasn't listening. He had to move quickly. It wasn't *his* life that depended on his speed, but Sadie's, and if anything should happen to her he'd never forgive himself.

Never.

Saddington cursed under his breath at the other driver as he pulled into the car park. Bloody yuppies, or whatever the hell they wanted to he called nowadays, driving their expensive pieces of German shit. He was still cursing under his breath as he parked the Focus alongside the Volvo belonging to Sadie Bartholomew. Switching off the engine, he glanced up to the window of her flat and let out a sigh.

How was he going to tackle this conversation?

It was going to be a tricky one.

He took a drag from his cigarette, then flipped open the ashtray and stubbed it out.

However he approached this, it was going to be difficult. First there was the good news – the dead hitmen. But then there was the subject of her dead boyfriend's missing corpse. And the additional recent development regarding the death of a drug dealer — a death that her dead boyfriend had only just been implicated in.

All of these things were out of his jurisdiction, but he felt some responsibility to Sadie, especially after all she'd been through over the last few weeks. What his superiors would say about his apparent waste of police resources, he didn't like to think, but he wasn't prepared to let some other officer, without the necessary softly-softly skills, take over. Sadie needed careful handling, otherwise they were likely to end up with a suicide case on their hands.

And Saddington didn't want to be responsible for that.

He looked up at the window again, and then climbed out of the car.

Sadie was holding the crucifix when her buzzer sounded, and she jumped to her feet, startled, but hopeful that it was Jordan, coming back to her. As she ran to the intercom, she wondered why he had to leave again, and in such a hurry. What was so important that he had to lie to her? What the hell did he do for a living anyway?

"Yeah?"

The voice that spoke to her was familiar, but it wasn't Jordan's. "Miss Bartholomew? This is Chief Superintendent Saddington, Scotland Yard. I'd like a word with you please".

"Listen, it's late," Sadie said, though she considered what Jordan had said to her only minutes earlier, about it not being safe for her as well as him, and she really wanted this police officer in her apartment. "Is it important?" she added.

"It is, yes."

"Okay, come on up," she said, buzzing the detective in.

He was knocking at her door within a couple of minutes, and Sadie placed the crucifix inside the pocket of her knee-length dressing gown, ever mindful of the fact that she wore only a pair of panties underneath. She pulled the dressing gown together, and ensured that nothing was on show, and then she opened the door, letting the detective inside.

She took him into the front room and offered him a seat. He sat upright in one of the armchairs, and she sat on the sofa.

"How can I help you?" she asked him.

"I thought you'd like to know," the chief superintendent said. "The hitmen ... well, they no longer present a threat to you or your sister."

Sadie nodded Jordan had already told her that. What the hell had gone on? She decided to ask. "Why's that?"

"Well, you'll hear about it on the news," Saddington said. "There was a gun battle a few hours ago, and two men were shot dead."

"The hitmen?"

"Yes."

"Who were they shot by?"

"Armed police officers," Saddington replied.

"British police?"

Saddington frowned. "Of course," he said. But that meant nothing, because the intelligence services all worked with each other — it would be easy to create the illusion of a state-sanctioned murder being carried out by the legitimate law enforcement officers. And she'd aroused Saddington's suspicions for no good reason. She cursed inwardly. "Why do you ask?"

"Curiosity," Sadie answered, shrugging her shoulders indifferently. "So, these hitmen are dead — how do you know that there won't be more?"

"I don't," Saddington said bluntly. "It may be that you and your sister will require protection for the rest of your lives. Unless, of course, your father's secret accounts are located."

"My father had no secret accounts that I know about," Sadie snapped. Of course, she couldn't know, because her father never discussed such things with her. But these police officers just wouldn't listen to her.

Saddington nodded. "I understand that you might not have been privy to your father's financial business, Miss Bartholomew, but you must understand that locating that missing money is paramount. And if it is all seized by the police and the US Federal Bureau of Investigation, then the Mafia will lose interest, because they will be unable to recoup their losses."

"I know nothing."

Saddington nodded again. "There was one other thing."

Sadie raised an eyebrow. "Yes?"

The police officer seemed a little unsure, took a deep breath then said, "Jordan Weaver's body has gone missing from the mortuary."

Of course it had, Sadie thought that's because he isn't dead. But surely they weren't kicking up a stink about this. Surely that could be hidden by the relevant authorities, by Jordan's superiors. Sadie frowned, and shook her head. "Missing?"

"I know this must be painful for you."

"Did somebody steal it?" Sadie was intrigued as to how this one had been explained away.

"We're working on the theory that Jordan Weaver may've had a brother — perhaps even an identical twin. Did he ever mention such a thing to you?"

Sadie shook her head. "As far as I know, he was an only child."

Saddington pulled out his notebook. "What exactly can you tell us about him?"

"Not a lot," Sadie replied quickly. "We hadn't known each other long."

"He was American?"

"I believe so."

"You believe so?"

"Look, what is this?" Sadie snapped. She tried to sound distressed, but it wouldn't come — after all, Jordan wasn't dead, was he? Jordan was alive and well, and in fact had been the man responsible for the deaths of the hitmen.

And yet ...

Some of the pieces didn't fit. Weren't these the same hitmen who had supposedly killed him more than a fortnight ago? Why had his death been faked?

Saddington asked, "What did he do for a living?"

"I have no idea," Sadie responded. "He never said."

"And you didn't ask?"

"I asked," Sadie said. "But he never gave me an answer."

Saddington sighed, then said, "A serious allegation has been made against Jordan Weaver."

"Considering he's dead, I don't think that's gonna make a whole lot of difference, is it?" Sadie snapped — then she realized she sounded too flippant. Unfortunately she couldn't rectify that now. Luckily, Saddington seemed unperturbed.

"It concerns your sister's recent mishap."

At that, Sadie's senses sharpened. "What do you mean?"

"She denies taking any drugs, you support her with that denial," Saddington went on. "And I have to say, in the light of recent evidence, it would appear as though her drink had been spiked, as has been suggested."

"You're not suggesting Jordan had anything—"

Saddington raised a hand. "The night of your sister's overdose, a local pusher was found dead in a nightclub toilet in the town. He'd been injected with a massive quantity of pure heroin. My colleagues have been investigating the death as a murder and earlier today, fresh evidence came to light."

"What fresh evidence?" Sadie wanted to know. She was trembling now. This was far too much information for her to digest. And it was all negative information. She didn't want to think of Jordan gunning down hitmen like some cold-blooded killer. And she certainly didn't want to consider the possibility that he had something to do with the murder of a drug pusher, no matter what the reasoning behind it.

"An enhancement of the security footage shows a man matching Jordan Weaver's description entering the toilet just after the murder victim."

"This is bullshit!"

"The murder victim was on the guest list of the party where your sister's overdose took place," Saddington. "He'd conveniently disappeared by the time the police arrived. Additionally, fingerprints found on the syringe would appear to match those of Jordan Weaver's."

Sadie shook her head. "This isn't possible."

"Why not?"

"Jordan's no killer."

Saddington shrugged his shoulders. "Well, as you said earlier. Miss Bartholomew, it doesn't matter anymore, does it? We're just clearing up the loose ends to a murder — well, I'm not, it's not even my case. To be honest, I don't know how I got dragged into this, but there you go."

Sadie looked down at the clock — it was after three o'clock, and she was tired.

Saddington stood up. "I'll go," he said. "I think I've taken up enough of your time as it is."

"The missing body?" Sadie enquired.

"Well, it will have to be investigated," the policeman said, "and I'm sure the investigating officers will want to question you, but I'm also sure you've got nothing to hide. I'll see myself out." Sadie got to her feet and followed him to the door. "I'm sorry you've been hit with all this."

"None of it is your fault," Sadie said graciously. "Well, the fact I'm living here, in this flat, instead of my parents mansion ..." She shook her head. "No, that was down to my father. He instigated it. You're just following it through."

"I am sorry," Saddington said sincerely.

"Thanks," Sadie said — but she didn't add that apologies didn't bring back dead people, or right wrongs — particularly when that apology came from somebody who was just going to walk out of your life and never see you again. Those kinds of apologies came cheap, because they didn't have to be backed up with anything.

As Saddington went for the door, somebody knocked on it loudly.

Sadie's heart pounded — nobody had sounded the buzzer. Either this was another of the building's residents, or else Jordan was back.

"Rather late for a caller, isn't it?" Saddington said. He looked at Sadie, and clearly saw the anxiety on her face. He misread it entirely. "I'm here with you," he said. "You're safe, I promise you." He went to open the door.

"Wait," Sadie said quietly. "Let me look through the peephole."

Saddington moved to let her look, and she pressed her face against the door. She didn't know what she was going to do if the person on the other side was Jordan. She could hardly warn him.

She needn't have worried – not about that, anyway.

The person on the other side of the door, standing in the corridor, was a large man, young, no more than thirty, with a head that was bald save for a short Mohican, and a handsome face that wore a fearsome expression. The eyes, dark, almost totally black, seemed to look straight at her, as though they could see her.

Sadie drew back and shuddered.

"Who is it?" Saddington asked her with a frown.

"I don't know," she answered. "I've never seen him before in my life." She looked at Saddington and found herself asking, "Are you sure all those hitmen were killed?"

At that, Saddington reached in his pocket. Sadie was expecting him to pull out some kind of semiautomatic pistol, not the cellphone that he did. Her heart sank. Trust her to be alone in an apartment with a madman at her front door, and only an unarmed cop for company.

"Gerry, this is Saddington," the chief superintendent said into his phone. "I need you to get somebody over to ..." He paused, took the phone from his ear and looked at the display. "Damn. It cut off."

"Try my phone," Sadie said, pointing to the telephone in the hallway.

The stranger knocked again, and then the front door opened.

"Jesus," Sadie hissed, backing away as the stranger stepped inside and closed the door behind him.

"Excuse me," Saddington said, putting himself between her and the stranger's considerable bulk. "What do you think you're doing, barging in here?"

"And you would be?" the stranger asked in a growling voice that seemed to shake the whole corridor.

"I think it's you who should be answering questions," Saddington snapped. "Now, I advise you to turn around and leave, right this minute—"

The stranger raised a hand and pointed a finger at Saddington's lips. "Hush!" His eyes moved from the police officer to Sadie. "Where is he?"

"Who?" Sadie asked.

"Kobold," the stranger growled. "I know he's put a veil over this building. Did he think that it could fool me?" The stranger looked beyond

Sadie. "Did you think that, Kobold?" he shouted. "Did you think that you could fool Ubel, Lord of the Corrupted?"

Saddington grabbed the stranger, Ubel, as he made a move for Sadie.

"Fool!" Ubel turned and lashed out with a fist. No, not a fist, Sadie corrected herself. The man's palm was flat, face down. It caught the police officer in the chest, and with a sickening crack, plunged inside up to the wrist. Saddington bellowed in pain, and gripped the man's arm, trying desperately to pull it away and out of the bloody hole in his chest. Sadie could only watch in disbelief as Saddington was raised from the ground, his feet dangling inches in the air.

Clutching a hand to her mouth to stifle a scream, she darted past the two of them as the stranger threw Saddington aside. The police officer slammed into the wall of the hallway and slid to the floor, blood pouring from the hole in his chest, his eyes wide open, but glassy, his mouth agog.

As she reached the door to the apartment, Sadie's eyes shifted to Ubel, and she realized with horror and an abject terror that almost made her collapse there and then that he was clutching Saddington's heart in the palm of his hand, blood dripping from it as he squeezed it gently. He raised his hand to his mouth, and Sadie turned away as he took a bite from the precious organ.

She almost retched as she wrenched her keys from the lock of the door and ran from the flat and towards the exit at the rear of the building, pushing open the doors and clambering out onto the fire escape. Her bare feet slapped painfully on the stippled metalwork as she made her way down to ground level and the car park.

Reaching her Volvo, she found the key on the ring and pointed it towards the car. The alarm blipped once and the doors unlocked, allowing her access. The car felt cool and reassuringly comforting as she slipped inside, slamming the door shut behind her and flicking the lock. The central locking system took care of her security, but she wasn't fool enough to think that if somebody wanted to get in, they couldn't. She had to get away, away from that freak inside her apartment. Fumbling with the keys, she eventually managed to slot the correct one into the ignition.

Then the side window shattered with a bang, and Sadie twisted her head, finding herself staring into the blood-spattered face of the stranger,

Ubel. He scowled and grabbed her around the throat.

"Imbecile," he snapped. "Did you really think that you could escape?"

Sadie screamed and fought with the stranger, trying desperately to wrestle his arm away from her, but it was no good. He was far too strong. She could feel herself drifting into unconsciousness.

"Where is he? Where is Kobold?"

Sadie felt light-headed, and wondered who the hell Kobold was, and why did this stranger, this maniac, think that she knew where he was? But the name Kobold – it was vaguely familiar to her. Where had she heard it before? Then she remembered. Jodie had spoken about someone called Kobold, a demon, when she'd regained consciousness in the hospital.

An image of Jordan flashed into her mind, and she recalled the last words he'd said to her. The crucifix he'd given her would protect her from the men who were after him. Was this man, this Ubel, was he one of the men after Jordan? If that was the case, then that would mean that Jordan was Kobold.

Even though she was slipping away, she still thought that what she was planning to do next was absurd, but she knew that she was going to die anyway. What harm could it do to rely on superstition and religion? She fumbled with the pocket of her dressing gown, ever mindful of the fact that she had mere seconds to live.

With renewed determination, she found her pocket, dipped her hand inside, and brought out the crucifix, bringing it to bear in the general direction of the man who was killing her.

Almost instantly, his grip on her throat loosened, then was gone completely.

Sadie, gasping for air, finally turned her head sideways, and saw Ubel staggering backwards, holding his hands in front of his eyes. He was growling in pain, and dropped to his knees, clutching his head.

Still unable to breathe properly, Sadie fired up the ignition and floored the accelerator, slipping the car into gear and dropping the clutch at the same time. The Volvo fishtailed out of the car park, and Sadie caught a glimpse of the stranger in her rear-view mirror, as he hauled himself to his feet.

She didn't slow down for the next ten minutes, the Volvo barrelling through the streets as she drove in no particular direction. She just wanted to get away from the apartment, from the corpse of a police officer who had been understanding towards her, from the murderous stranger, from the terrifying and hurtful memories.

Eventually, she pulled into a lay-by and left the engine running as her mind replayed the events of the last half an hour, from Jordan leaving her, to Saddington arriving, to Ubel breaking into her apartment. She felt the hot pain around her throat, and tried to see the trauma in the mirror, but it was too dark, even with the interior light on, to see the full extent of any damage. She tried to speak, just to test whether it were possible, but her voice was hoarse and unintelligible.

She pondered her next move.

And she made up her mind where she had to go to next.

41

The hospital car park was empty as Sadie arrived, and she pulled up in a space nearest the building's well-illuminated entrance. She looked around, and her eyes fell upon a familiar car parked in the shadows right on the other side. A BMW – Jordan's BMW.

So Jordan was here? What the hell was he doing here? Did that mean that Jodie was in danger?

She threw open the Volvo's door and stepped onto the tarmac, which was cold beneath her feet. She was aware of the fact that she wasn't appropriately dressed to be walking the streets, but this was a hospital, and was sure to be full of patients wearing little more than dressing gowns. All the same, she felt uncomfortable as she walked up to the building, and quickly decided that it probably wasn't wise to use the main entrance. She walked around the side of the building, looking for another way in. She came across three different fire exits, but no other way into the building.

Cursing, she gripped her throat again, and tried to soothe away the pain. At least the stranger couldn't possibly have followed her here, which meant that she was safe now unless she had a reason to fear Jordan. Who was that stranger, and why was he after Jordan? And why did he call Jordan by another name? What was the significance of the name, Kobold?

Jordan had always kept his history a secret, had told her nothing at all about what he did for a living. His answers to her questions amounted to little more than a knowing smirk and a sideways tap of the nose, as though she shouldn't be asking. But she loved Jordan, she wanted to spend the rest of her life with him — she had to know everything there was to know about him.

She looked up to see the nurses' quarters a hundred feet away, dozens of small bedsits where those without families could reside close to their place of work, unable to escape from either the harsh realities of the hospital or their fellow workers. And there, hanging on a washing line, were clothes, left out overnight, probably because the owner couldn't be bothered to get them in after a long shift at the hospital.

With clothes, she could enter the hospital.

She yanked a blouse from the line and a pair of jeans, both of which were a reasonable fit, though the blouse was somewhat crumpled. She had nothing on her feet, but recalled that she had a pair of trainers in the boot of her car, so she ran across the grass between the nurses' accommodation and the hospital in her stolen clothes and retrieved the footwear from the Volvo.

Half a minute later, and with Jordan's crucifix around her neck, she was entering the hospital, where she was quickly stopped by a security officer.

"I'm sorry, Miss, but casualty entrance is around the back of the hospital," he said.

"I don't need casualty," Sadie said, feeling her throat and realizing that it certainly looked as though she did. "I'm here to visit my sister."

"Visiting time is over, I'm afraid," the security officer told her.

"My sister is very sick," Sadie said. "I have to see her."

The security officer paused for a second, then turned to his computer's monitor. "What's her name?"

"Jodie Bartholomew," Sadie said.

"What ward is she on?"

"Three G," Sadie said, adding their home address for good measure.

The security guard seemed satisfied, and clearly didn't want to question her as to the nature of her sister's illness — he was aware of the rules governing patients with terminal illnesses, in that the usual rules governing visiting times did not apply, and he didn't want to embarrass either himself or Sadie.

"You know the way?"

"Of course," Sadie replied.

"You know," the guard said as she made her way past the reception desk, "you really should take a trip to casualty and get your neck seen to. It looks nasty."

"Yeah," Sadie said, stroking her throat. She couldn't think of anything else to say, so she just said, "Thanks".

The corridors were deserted and gloomily lit as she made her way to Ward 3G, and the couple of nurses that she did see didn't seem particularly interested in her, or where she was going at such an unearthly hour. They probably saw her neck wound and figured that she was an inpatient, and that she was simply returning to her bed after visiting the toilet.

Ward 3G was a small room with just four beds, two of which were unoccupied. Jodie was in one and an old woman close to death was in the other. Sadie stepped into the room to find Jordan and a woman standing over Jodie's bed. Her sister was asleep, and her two visitors were staring at one another.

As she stepped up to the bed, Sadie recognized the young woman. She'd seen her before with Jordan – one of Jordan's work colleagues, Mira. That was as much information as either of them had been prepared to give away.

Jordan turned to her, but didn't seem surprised to see her.

"Sadie," he said quietly.

"What's going on here?" Sadie asked quietly.

"What happened to you?" Jordan asked her, but it was apparent that he had a pretty good idea. All the same, his expression showed that he was enraged that somebody had dared to hurt her.

"Somebody came looking for Kobold," Sadie told him through clenched teeth. "He killed a police detective who was visiting me, and then he tried to kill me."

Immediately, Jordan threw his arms around her and gathered her up, but it didn't make her feel as good as it usually did. She didn't feel safe, she didn't feel comforted, she didn't feel relaxed. She pulled away.

"What's going on?" she asked. "And what's your friend doing here?"

Mira smiled uncomfortably. "You have nothing to fear from me."

"Oh, I don't doubt that for a minute," snapped Sadie. "The face of an angel and the body of a goddess, and you're here, fucking about with my boyfriend, while some goddamn bastard's trying to fucking throttle me! And that bastard was looking for you, Jordan!"

"I'm sorry," Jordan said. "I thought I had it covered."

"You know what, fuck you!" Sadie hissed and turned to leave, but Jordan stopped her.

"We need to talk," he said.

"Fuck you, Jordan," Sadie snapped. "You wanna know why? Because you never tell me the fucking truth!"

"It's time for the truth," Jordan admitted. "Let's go somewhere and talk about it."

Sadie looked at Mira, then at her sister. "Why are you here? Is this bastard coming here? Is Jodie in danger as well?"

"I'll look after her," Mira promised.

Sadie smirked and shook her head. "You didn't see him." she said. "You'd last about five seconds."

"You got away."

"Barely," Sadie said, "and I didn't have anyone else to save."

"Jodie will be fine," Jordan promised her, tugging lightly on her arm.

"Why should I believe you?"

Mira smiled, and Sadie instantly felt warm inside. "Because I would never lie to you," she said. "And I promise you that Jodie will not be harmed by this man."

She allowed Jordan to lead her away, and they left by a fire exit, making their way across the car park to Jordan's BMW. Once inside, Jordan turned to her.

"Tell me what happened," he said.

"I thought it was time for you to tell the truth."

"I will," he assured her. "I need to know what happened to you. You look like you got pretty badly hurt."

"Yeah, I did," Sadie said. "But not as bad as the cop who came to visit me."

"What cop?"

"He said things about you, Jordan."

"What kinda things?"

"Like you walked out of the morgue." Sadie said. "He wanted to know if you had a twin brother."

"Now, you know I haven't."

"I don't, Jordan, because I know next to fucking nothing about you!"

"What else did he say?"

"He said you had something to do with the death of the drug pusher who put Jodie in hospital."

Jordan looked away, seeming to peer out across the car park.

"Did you?"

"Did I what?"

"Have something to do with his death?"

"Sadie."

"The truth, Jordan."

"Some people deserve everything they get, Sadie," Jordan told her.

"So you killed him?"

"I expedited his final passing into Hell."

"Jordan, this isn't some goddamn biblical crusade!"

Jordan turned and looked at her. "This is exactly what it is." He reached forward and took hold of the crucifix. "How did this policeman die? And how did you escape?"

"The stranger killed him."

"How?"

"He just ..." Sadie paused. She was motioning with her hand, the same kind of motion Ubel had used to kill Saddington. "He ripped his heart out," she finally said, realizing how absurd it had to sound. "Ripped it right out of his chest."

Jordan nodded, still fingering the crucifix. "And you? How did you escape?"

"I ran out when he was killing the police officer."

"He didn't chase you?"

"He did, yeah, but ..."

"But what?"

"The crucifix," Sadie muttered.

"The crucifix saved you?"

"It doesn't seem possible," Sadie said quietly. "And yet ... there was no other way."

"Sadie, that man, that killer, he wasn't human."

"You're saying he was a vampire?" Sadie scoffed uncertainly.

"Bullshit."

"He was a demon," Jordan said, letting go of the crucifix. "And not just any demon. He was one of the Corrupted, powerful demons who have escaped from Hell, and who wreak havoc on humanity."

"This is insane."

"Did he have a name?"

"Ubel," Sadie replied. She looked at Jordan. "You really believe in this religious bullshit?"

Jordan looked out of the windscreen again. "Ubel is the most powerful of all the Corrupted. He is the Corrupted equivalent of the devil. Some say he is more powerful than Satan himself."

"Jordan, talk sense."

"You wanted the truth, Sadie," Jordan said, "and this is what I'm giving you."

"You're talking about demons and the devil, Jordan! How can I believe that?"

"You said yourself, how Ubel killed this police officer," Jordan said. He gripped her wrist and slammed her hand against his chest. "Feel that – feel the ribs? How hard do you reckon you'd have to punch to break your way through that? Do you reckon you could? Do you reckon you could plunge your fingertips through my chest, through my ribcage, through my sternum? You reckon you could do that without breaking your fingers? You think that's possible? It would take even the most skilled pathologist at least two minutes with the proper tools to take out somebody's heart. Even if you weren't too concerned with the mess you made, you're looking at needing a blade of some sort, a hammer and a goddamn chisel, and a lot of strength. How is that possible, Sadie? Ask yourself."

Sadie blinked. "You really do believe this, don't you?"

"Yes, I do."

"What are you? Some kind of Vatican demon hunter?"

Jordan smiled and shook his head. "No, Sadie. I'm a demon as well."

42

"You wanted to know all about me," Jordan went on. "So here it is."

Sadie was almost too stunned to listen. She was certainly too stunned to respond. There was a pause as Jordan looked at her, and then he went on with his story.

"I'm a demon. I come from Hell, to where I was condemned four hundred years ago," he said. "I was hanged for a crime I committed. Punished by man. Man, who does not have the right to punish."

"Jordan," Sadie said, finally finding her voice. "I wanted the truth."

"This is the truth, Sadie," Jordan told her. "How do you think a man who's had his brains blown out can possibly come back to life."

"You said that was all a fake, that it never really happened."

"It happened," Jordan said miserably. "It was me who was the fake. I still am."

"What do you mean?"

"I'm not human, Sadie," Jordan said. "This body, this mortal human form, it's something that I threw together, like a tailor of human flesh."

Sadie shuddered in disgust. "But we made love."

"Inside, I am a demon," Jordan said, "but I have no greater desire other than to be human — completely and utterly, so that I can hold you as a human."

"Jordan, we made love," Sadie said again. "My God, you're not human. It's like I had sex with a fucking animal!"

"It wasn't like that."

"So what is this body of yours?" Sadie said, shaking her head. This just couldn't be happening. It couldn't be true. There weren't any such things as demons — it was all religious mumbo jumbo, dreamt up by preachers wanting to frighten their flocks of loyal followers. "Is this body alive?"

"It's alive," Jordan assured her. "Just as yours is. The only difference between you and I are our souls. You have the mortal soul of a human. I have the immortal soul of a demon."

"A demon? But demons are evil."

"Demons merely punish the evil, Sadie," Jordan corrected her. "Demons are not themselves intrinsically evil."

"Try telling that to the police officer your friend killed."

"Ubel is not my friend," Jordan said. "And he is no demon like me. Ubel is one of the Corrupted, as I've already said to you. Ubel is as evil as any monster humanity creates."

"God, you expect me to believe this?"

"It will be difficult for you," Jordan conceded, "but it's all true. I am a demon, and I have been tasked to punish those who sin."

"And you sinned? To be sent to Hell, you must've sinned."

"My wife committed adultery," Jordan said. "I found her and her lover having sex in our bed. I'd already had a good idea what was going on. I had a scythe with me ... I did what came natural to any man caught in a similar situation."

"You killed your wife?"

"And her lover," Jordan confessed. "I committed a double murder. I had no defence, other than it being a crime of passion. Today, that would probably earn me twenty years in prison. Three hundred years ago, the penalty was death. I was hanged, and I fell to Hell, where I remained in purgatory for over a hundred years, before my sins were forgiven, before I became a demon."

"Kobold?"

"That's my name in Hell," Jordan said. He reached out and touched her, but she shrugged him off. "I am not evil, Sadie. I could never kill anyone in cold blood — unless their soul is already condemned to Hell."

"The drug pusher?"

"And the two hitmen," Jordan said. "They all deserved to die."

"You were killing people who hurt me?"

"Directly or indirectly," Jordan said. "In all three cases, you were affected indirectly. The pusher put your sister in hospital. Who knows how many other innocent children would've suffered at his hands. And the hitmen, they killed the man you loved — they were trying to kill you. They planned to do it during the taxi journey home from Martin Walsh's apartment?"

"You were following me?"

"I was looking out for you," Jordan said solemnly.

"Then you saw ..." Sadie paused. "Martin and Holly?"

"I didn't harm them," Jordan assured her. "I merely planted a seed of doubt into Martin Walsh's mind."

"What seed of doubt?"

"Action and reaction," Jordan said. "Cause and effect. Promiscuity and AIDS."

"You told Martin he had AIDS?"

"I visited him as a demon," Jordan said. "I told him that his girlfriend had contracted AIDS from a casual lover. He reacted accordingly."

Sadie went cold. "What happened?"

"He killed her," Jordan said. "She is in Hell. He will join her after serving his time in prison."

"Jordan, this isn't real," Sadie said softly. "Don't you see that? You're just ... you're just deluding yourself."

Jordan shook his head. "You cannot ignore the evidence, Sadie. You cannot do that."

"My God," Sadie said, feeling her throat again. "My God. This is fucking unreal!" She didn't really know how to react. And yet, as Jordan had said, however illogical it was, there could be no other explanation. "I have slept with a demon."

"I want nothing more than to be human, Sadie," he told her again, stroking her cheek. "I love you, like I've never loved anyone before in my life. I'm prepared to give up my immortality and my birthright to be human again, to spend my life with you."

"Your birthright?"

"I am to be crowned the new devil," Jordan said.

Sadie's jaw dropped involuntarily. "Jordan, this is getting more and more absurd. I'm having trouble dealing with it."

"Then what do you suggest we do?"

It wasn't an ultimatum. But that's what it seemed like. Sadie looked at the hospital, where Jodie lay asleep with a woman watching over her. "And Mira?"

"Reizend? She's an angel," Jordan said. "She will protect Jodie."

Sadie closed her eyes. "You know, right now, I'm wishing that I'd never met you."

"I can understand that."

"I don't believe what you're telling me, but there just doesn't seem to be any other rational explanation, so I'm just gonna have to go along with it for now. But this is way too fucking crazy to comprehend, Jordan. Christ! Why couldn't my life just be simple?"

"Sadie, I don't wanna rush you," Jordan said quietly. "I know this is a lot for you to come to terms with, but we have to leave here."

"What?"

"Ubel. He will be after me. We have to go to the safest place possible."

"And where might that be?"

"A religious building," Jordan said. "Somewhere he would be afraid of entering."

"A church?"

"A cathedral," Jordan said.

"But what about you?"

"What about me?"

"If this Ubel can't enter because he's afraid, surely the same thing must apply to you."

Jordan smiled. "Ubel is evil, Sadie. He is one of the Corrupted. I am a demon, yes, but in spite of what your religious leaders and fanatics would have you believe, I am simply an angel who dresses in red. I am one of God's servants. A religious artefact, a place of worship, a religious leader — these things hold no fear for me."

"And you're sure Jodie will be okay?"

"Reizend will look after her," Jordan assured her. "If needs be, she will give up her life for Jodie."

"But surely she's immortal," scoffed Sadie, partially believing that this was all some elaborate cover story for something more believable, and far more sinister.

"Demons and angels have the power to destroy one another," Jordan said, firing up the BMW's engine, adding ominously, "and there is no life after the afterlife."

And there was something very terrifying about Jordan's last comment, something that sent a shiver running up Sadie's spine, as he slipped the car into gear and left the hospital car park.

43

Ubel was still weak when he finally arrived at the hospital, his powers dwindled by the confrontation with the girl and the crucifix. The thing that concerned him the most about the confrontation was just how drained it had left him. She was just a girl after all – and all she'd had as a weapon was a crucifix. It had appeared to be nothing more than a simple gold cross, with no religious significance whatsoever. But the effect it had had upon Ubel was so extreme that there had to be more to it than that. It was apparent that Kobold had in some way brought up a crucifix from Hell, undoubtedly forged by David himself– the only being in Hell capable of such a task – and therefore it carried with it the power of Heaven and God.

How long the effect would last was the pertinent question. The power of such items was not eternal like demons and angels, they were drained with each use. And Ubel was certain that he had received much of the force contained within that religious trinket with its first exposure. Anything that remained would be little more than a residual amount. One more assault on the human woman, and she would be totally unprotected.

But first, he had to find her – no, he reminded himself, finding her wasn't the most important thing. He had to ensure that he had recovered sufficiently, because if he was exposed to that crucifix again without the proper preparation, he might find himself being totally destroyed by its power, or at the very least, being flung back to Hell, to a place where he no longer belonged, where he could be torn apart by even the most inexperienced of imps hoping to make a name for themselves.

Ubel looked around him as the sulphuric smoke dispersed, blown by a brisk wind across a wide expanse of grass surrounding the hospital. He was still in his demonic form, his crimson head totally bald, save for the thin strip of hair, his horns gnarled, long, unkempt and pitted, his face handsome yet frightening. If he should be seen this way, it would only cause trouble for himself and the legions of Corrupted demons that roamed the planet seeking out human souls to sacrifice in order to rejuvenate their constantly draining powers.

He stepped closer to the wall of the hospital and looked around him. The car park was deserted, save for a handful of vehicles. A row of buildings on the other side of the field was sporadically dotted with lights, but it was doubtful that anybody there had seen him arrive. He felt weak, and knew that in order to sustain a human form, it would require of him great reserves of energy — something he could not afford to give up, not with the battle that he was due to fight.

The method of approach that would require the minimum of energy was for him to adopt the form of a shadow, a state of being that meant only other supernatural forces could see him. Whilst in such a condition, the powers he did possess would be diminished slightly, but then so would those of any opposition. Besides, he wasn't looking for a battle – not here, not yet. He could sense that Kobold was not present, and neither was that bitch of a human the fool had fallen in love with. There was no veil over the hospital, and he could easily sense the presence of the sister of the woman — and also something else.

Something that made him frown.

It had been a long time since he'd felt such a presence.

And as he entered the room where the sister was being held, he found himself staring into the eyes of an angel.

Ubel stared at the creature for some considerable time, digesting her appearance, considering her powers, while she presumably did likewise. She was standing to the side of a bed on which slept the sister. One of the three other beds in this large room held a sleeping female, and Ubel looked carefully at her. It was not unheard of for a demon or indeed an angel to disguise themselves as a human, and with special abilities, allow themselves to go unnoticed by others.

He had learned a long time ago that there was no such thing as being too cautious.

The angel broke the silence. "You should leave this place. You have no right being here."

"Who are you to tell me that?" Ubel snapped.

"I represent everything that is virtuous," the angel said. "In me are vested the powers of God Himself."

"I have no respect for your god," Ubel said dismissively.

"You have no respect for the devil neither," the angel said, sitting down on the edge of the bed. "You have no place on this Earth — you have no place on any celestial plane. You are a bastardization of everything that is good and righteous."

"Your judgements do not impress me, angel," Ubel said with a smirk. "I exist only to please myself. The feelings and thoughts of everything else count for nothing."

"Which is why you have no home."

Ubel scowled. He could not afford to be bogged down in an argument with this angel. He had to find the one called Kobold, and he had to destroy him.

"What business have you in being here?"

"What business have you?" Ubel retorted.

The angel looked down at the young woman lying in the bed. "I am here to protect her from the likes of you."

"As if you could protect her from me," the demon scoffed. "I could destroy you merely by raising a hand in your direction."

"You could try," the angel said — it wasn't a challenge. Her face adopted a serious expression. "As you are one of the Corrupted, your powers, crude though they are, would certainly be impressive. But God Himself has channelled His own powers down through me. You might get lucky ... but you would certainly use up every ounce of strength that you possess, leaving you with nothing in reserve with which to do battle with Kobold. That *is* why you are here, isn't it?"

Ubel wasn't shocked at the angel's apparent knowledge. He smiled. "You may be right," he admitted graciously. "But I can live to fight another day, and it would be worth it, delaying the battle with Kobold, just to witness you being ripped apart as I destroy your soul."

"The battle with Kobold cannot wait," the angel said. "In fact, as far as you're concerned, it may already be too late."

Ubel frowned. "What are you talking about?"

"How much did Satan tell you of Kobold?"

"No more than I was not already aware of."

"You're nothing more than Satan's lackey," the angel said with a snort. "He's not expecting you to succeed, you know."

"What would you know?"

"I know how this battle's going to turn out," the angel said confidently. "And believe me, you aren't the victor."

"I fear Kobold no more than I fear a blunt knife I would use to clean the dirt from under my fingernails."

"Then you are a fool."

Those words hung in the air, unheard by the humans that seemed to be all around them.

Ubel scowled once more. "I should destroy you right where you sit, for your insolence alone."

"You are no match for Satan," the angel said, "and Satan is no match for Kobold. Of that, you should be well aware. And you should heed that advice. Go back to wherever your kind belongs, but stay away from this girl, stay away from her sister, and stay away from Kobold."

"I heed no one's advice, angel," Ubel snapped. "And it is not for you to tell me what to do."

"But we both know what you'll do, don't we?" the angel said with a smirk. "You're going to leave this place, hunt down Kobold, and attempt to destroy him."

"What makes you so sure that I won't destroy you first?"

"Because you're not a fool," the angel said. "Satan would not choose a fool to do his dirty work for him. I'm guessing that of all the Corrupted, you are the most powerful. Without any doubt."

Ubel looked at the angel carefully. She appeared to him in celestial form. Her face was pale, her hair light, her gown white and flowing. She was so bright, she positively glowed. But there were no wings. Angels didn't need wings — that was simply a myth, invented by religious leaders, possibly fooled into believing that as some demons had wings, so some angels also possessed them. But the winged demons used their bat-like appendages to terrify their hapless victims – angels did not need to terrify anybody, and they certainly didn't require wings to get around.

No, this angel looked perfectly innocuous, but Ubel was no fool. Many demons, mostly the Corrupted, made the mistake of thinking that angels were harmless, that they could easily be destroyed like so much of God's cannon fodder. But angels were powerful, and their ranking system was far more complex than celestial creatures from Hell – imps, succubi and incubi, demons and wing demons – three ranks, and their appearance betrayed that rank. Angels, on the other hand, had the ability to disguise their heavenly appearance. This angel before him could be an archangel, merely the next rank up, or she could be a seraph, the highest of all the angels, the purest of all, the most powerful of all.

After all, hadn't she told him at the start of their conversation that God's powers had been vested in her. Ubel was powerful, but a seraph?

Seraphs were as powerful as the devil.

Ubel scowled. "You should consider yourself fortunate," he said.

"Because you're not going to destroy me?"

"There will be another time," he promised her, raising a hand and pointing it at the girl in the bed. "But before I leave, you will do one thing for me. You will tell me where Kobold and the human bitch are."

The angel smiled. "I don't think so."

"I could destroy her without using up any of my energy," he said. "And you couldn't stop me."

"Then do it," the angel challenged him.

Ubel paused for a moment. This angel was demonstrating such confidence, that for once in his existence, he felt uncertainty. He couldn't remember ever being alive — that was an eternity ago, and right now, hundreds of years after his death, the circumstances surrounding it seemed so inconsequential. But he was sure that at the time, he perhaps felt uncertainty, maybe doubt, or even fear. But never, since he had been demonized, had he experienced such feelings.

The angel was smiling, and her whole appearance was completely non-menacing.

To a human, able to see her for what she really was, she would be a comforting sight, in spite of her totally alien physiognomy, something that they could never fear. She represented all that was good and heavenly, all that was righteous and kind. She would never harm them, or allow them to come to harm.

And because of that, to Ubel she was a threat.

"You see, don't you?" she asked him.

"See what?"

"The goodness of God Himself within me," the angel said. "You see it, and you fear it. Like a human, you have fear, the one human trait that no demon desires, and you feel it."

"I fear nothing," Ubel spat — though he knew that he didn't sound entirely sure of that.

"You fear me, because you know that I could stop you harming this girl," the angel went on. "More than that, you fear me, because you know that I could destroy you where you stand now." The expression on the angel's face darkened. "And if I, a mere angel, can destroy you, consider how easily Kobold will dispose of you."

"You are not a mere angel." Ubel said, lowering his hand. "That I can see — any fool can see that."

"Then what am I?"

"A seraph."

"A seraph? Am I really?"

"Only one of the highest of all the angels would dare to oppose me," Ubel said. "I am Lord of the Corrupted, and angels and archangels quiver and drop to their knees before me."

"That may be true — and you are very perceptive. But how do you know that I am not bluffing?"

"Because angels do not play with the lives of humans," Ubel said, looking at the girl in the bed. "Should I call your bluff and destroy that girl, it would be as though by your hand instead of mine. So you must know that you have the power to stop me."

The angel smiled broadly. "A regular detective."

"There will be time to deal with you later," Ubel promised. "When Hell is turned over completely to Satan, when you and your kind are banished from its gates, when the laws laid down by your god are cast aside into the fiery pits where they belong ... that is when I shall deal with you personally."

"That will never happen," the angel said. "For certain, there will be a battle in Hell, the likes of which has not been seen in two millennia, but you will not be around to witness it. The spirit of the devil is strong within Kobold, and with each Earthly second that passes, it grows stronger. Before this night is over, Ubel, Lord of the Corrupted, you will be no more."

Ubel backed away.

Already, he was receiving signals in the back of his mind, like sirens calling a sailor to his doom on the rocks. It was as though he knew precisely where he was going, exactly where Kobold and the human were heading, and that he also knew that there he would face great danger. And yet, he couldn't stop himself from wanting to go there.

"It is my destiny," he said. "I am the chosen one."

The angel shook her head as Ubel closed his eyes.

"Kobold is the chosen one," she said. "You are merely a fool."

44

The BMW screeched to a halt beneath the shadows of a huge building that appeared far more frightening in the light of the moon than it would have looked in the light of the sun. Sadie looked up at its gnarled buttresses, supporting thick, tall walls, a vaulted stone ceiling, and a lead roof and she found herself shuddering involuntarily.

It had been a night full of real shocks. Jordan's miraculous return from the dead, the murder of the police detective by a seemingly unstoppable killer, Jordan's 'confession' — it had all been almost too much for her. Stories of demons and angels, of Jordan not being human, of him having been hanged hundreds of years ago for the brutal murder of his wife and her lover.

She turned and looked at Jordan as he switched off the engine and cast his eyes up at the windows of the cathedral, taking in the vision of them catching the light from the moon. He didn't seem like a killer — he didn't seem like he could possibly be a demon, whose job it was to spirit away those less-deserving mortals and punish them for all eternity.

He looked like a man, a normal human being. Strong, yes, unusually handsome, certainly, but nevertheless, human.

Could she really believe all that he had been telling her?

If she did believe him, if he was telling the truth, then she was mixed up in some dangerous battle between Heaven and Hell, good and evil, something which was way beyond her bounds of understanding, and which all common-sense told her she should run away from. But if Jordan wasn't telling the truth, if there something more mysterious, yet ultimately more believable, to all this, then she was mixed up in something that was equally as dangerous, and which would probably get her killed a whole lot more quickly.

Commonsense was also telling her that Jordan was telling the truth, that he was a demon, that the woman at the hospital, Mira or Reizend, or whatever the hell she was called, was actually an angel, and that she was going to watch over Jodie as she lay in that bed, protecting her from the evil demon that was chasing after Jordan ... Kobold.

She rubbed her face, as though she could wash this all away.

"This is fucking unbelievable, Jordan," she finally said. "You know that, don't you?"

"I never wanted to hurt you," he said to her. "I never meant to fall in love."

"Then why did you?"

Jordan didn't answer straightaway. "I don't know. I can't say. I wish I could, because then this would all be a lot easier to understand." He paused, then turned to face her. "I wish I'd never fallen in love with you."

"I wish I could say that I'm glad you did," Sadie said, somewhat bitterly.

"I wish that I'd had the courage to stay away from you, after those gangsters shot me dead."

Sadie felt a stinging sensation in her nose and her eyes, and she brushed away a tear. "Why couldn't things be easier? Why couldn't this relationship just have been normal? Why does everything that happens to me have to be so fucked up?"

"It's not you."

"It is me. My mom and dad, Jodie, now you ... it's all fucked up."

"No, it's all down to me."

"Because you're a demon? You didn't make my dad break the law, you didn't pump Jodie full of goddamned shit."

"I punished your father," Jordan said.

It was like a slap in the face, bringing her to her senses more than any physical blow could.

"You ... my mom and dad? That was you?"

"I'm sorry."

"My God," Sadie muttered quietly. "My God. I don't believe it."

"I'm sorry, Sadie."

"You killed my mom and dad?"

"I didn't kill them, Sadie. Your father killed himself. He had to be taken. It wasn't something that I had a say in. He was a criminal and his time had come."

"What about my mother? My fucking mother, you bastard!"

"Your mother ..." Jordan looked at her. She could see the tears in his eyes. Here he was, a demon, a thief of souls, and he was weeping. "In every conflict, there are innocent casualties."

"My mother was an innocent casualty?"

"Her suffering is over, Sadie."

"Fuck you!"

"She had cancer," Jordan said. Once more. Sadie felt the supernatural blow to her face. "She didn't know it, not then. It would've killed her within six months. Cancer of the ovaries ... already advanced. Within a month, it would've spread to her liver, then to her lungs a month later. More secondary tumours on her brain within four months. Your mother, Sadie, was going to die. The last few weeks ... they would've been terrible, for you and for Jodie."

"You're making this up."

"I'm not," Jordan assured her. "You know when some drunk driver wipes out an innocent driver coming the other way? Well, there has to be a reason why that innocent driver is chosen over some other innocent driver, doesn't there? It's destiny, Sadie. It's something that *we* can see. *We* know what's inside a person, *we* know how they're going to react to future events, how those around them are going to react, and so we choose them over someone else. And then sometimes fate dictates that there isn't anyone around at that time and in that place, and so the drunk driver hits a tree. It's all fate, Sadie, and fate is something that cannot be controlled. Your mother died in an instant, and her thoughts were of you and Jodie. She's in a better place, and she's seen what her future would've been. You know, in a way, it's all in a person's own mind what they'd prefer."

Sadie looked at Jordan.

"How about you?" he asked her. "If you had cancer, if you were going to die a slow, painful death, lingering and hurting not only yourself but your family ... wouldn't you choose an easier way?"

"I'd rather die quickly."

"Your mother was taken sooner than she may've liked, but in her mind, she knew that she'd choose dying in an instant, painlessly, rather than being struck down by a terminal illness."

"Why does God allow disease and death?"

"Where we go after death is governed by how we live our lives," Jordan said. "And as for disease and illness ... who knows? Maybe it was God's way of taking out the evil members of society. Right at the beginning, at the birth of mankind. Only disease spreads. Maybe God didn't see that as a possibility, that innocent people would be caught in the crossfire. He's not flawless, in spite of what all of the religious people would have you think."

"You make it sound so real."

"That's because it is."

Sadie looked at Jordan. "Will you be leaving me?"

"Soon. I have to go. We, each of us, have a destiny. This is mine. I hope I come back to you, but I can't promise it."

Sadie kissed Jordan lightly on the lips. "I love you. I know I shouldn't, I know that my mind is telling me this is all wrong, but I love you."

"You don't know how happy it makes me feel to hear you say that," he said. "Because I love you so much. It's you who's made me feel human again."

They kissed again, more passionately, and Sadie began to explore his body with her hands, because perhaps this would be the last time ever. She pushed the thought of Jordan as a demon from her mind, and thought only of him as a human, as a handsome man, a fantastic lover, with the body of an athlete. A body her fingers were now running over, as his fingers danced across the back of her head, the top of her spine, tracing a route down to the bottom of her stolen blouse.

"I love you" Jordan said. "I want you to know that."

"I know you do," Sadie said. "And I love you too. You'll never know how much."

"Believe me, I do," Jordan said. "You're still here sitting with me, aren't you? That shows a lot of determination, a hell of a lot of dedication. And you'll never know how much that means to me. I want you to know that whatever happens, I'll never stop thinking about you."

Sadie smiled nervously.

"Nothing's gonna happen, Jordan."

Jordan smiled. "Sadie, you have to understand. I'm about to fight the most powerful being in Hell. I can't guarantee that I'll be victorious."

"You don't have to do that."

"I do," Jordan said. "If there was a way I could avoid it, then believe me I would. But this is my destiny, and I cannot run away. Even if I wanted to. A demon can live on Earth one of two ways. He can join the Corrupted – the demon, Ubel, who pursued you, who even now is tracking us down, he is one of the Corrupted. In fact, he is the most powerful of all the Corrupted. And it is the Corrupted who take innocent people, snatch children and lovers in their sleep. They are pure evil. And I'm not."

"What's the other way? You said there were two ways."

"I turn my back on evil, and I never return to Hell," Jordan said. "Eventually, my powers become drained to such a point that I can never return to Hell. Then I become one of the Ensnared. I become as vulnerable as any mortal. I become, in essence, human."

"Isn't that what you want?" Sadie asked.

"I become helpless, yes," Jordan admitted. "And I have the Jäger chasing after me. The Jäger cannot permit any demon to reside on Earth, for it threatens the whole balance of society. What if a demon should be captured by scientists, his body investigated? The very fabric upon which we – you, *humanity* – base your existence becomes corrupted. The Jäger would hunt me down and destroy me. And for a demon, there is no second chance in Heaven or Hell. For a demon, destruction is final."

Sadie shook her head. "What do we do?"

"We go inside that cathedral."

"Can you do that?" Sadie asked. That didn't make sense.

"That cathedral has been desecrated, like almost every church on Earth," Jordan said. "When you charge people to pass through the doors, when you sell gifts and trinkets in close proximity to the altar, when you charge people to enter, you bastardize what should be a religious sanctuary. God asks for no wealth from those who worship Him. He asks only that we do not allow greed to overcome us. This place of worship has become a den of greed, staffed by men and women who wear the smocks of a priest, but who worship God less than they worship the wealth, comfort and security that their position provides them with. For a truly safe place to hide, we'd need a monastery, but there are none nearby. And we have little time."

"So what protection can this place offer us?" Sadie asked. She couldn't see the point in coming here if that demon could enter this building as easily as Jordan had suggested they could.

"The altar," Jordan said. "That is the one place that hasn't become corrupted. You can hide there."

"What about you?"

"I won't need to hide," Jordan said. "The time has come for me to face up to my destiny."

And he opened the car door.

"Come on," he said to her. "We don't have much time."

And those words struck an ominous chord of terror on Sadie's heartstrings.

45

Getting into the cathedral was far easier than Sadie would've thought, though she suspected that was probably down to Jordan and his 'demonic' powers. Once inside, she found herself being swallowed up by an eerie darkness, the ceiling invisible far overhead, and faint light coming in from the windows down one side of the nave. Ahead, she could see the eastern window, its stained glass illuminated by the light from a street lamp outside. But she could barely see the length of the nave in front of her, or the pillars that supported the heavy stone ceiling, nor indeed the rows of seats that were surely almost full during Evensong.

Jordan turned to her, his face nothing more than a smudge in the darkness.

"Come on," he said. "We have to get to the altar."

"And what about you?" she asked, afraid of the answer.

"I have to go someplace else," he replied, taking hold of her hand. "But I'll have to leave this body here."

"That doesn't make sense."

"Right now, Sadie, this body isn't me," Jordan explained. "It's something I created. It's like a suit. And I can leave it at any time."

"So what will happen to it?"

"It? The body?" Sadie nodded, though she was aware that Jordan couldn't see it. Nevertheless, he responded. "It will sit there, before you, as though deep in thought."

"Will it be safe? If this demon, this Ubel, if he comes here, will your body be safe?"

"I cannot get close to the altar, Sadie, because that will drain my power," Jordan said. "Even though I'm not evil, it still has an effect on me, because it's wrong for demons to be here. And I need every ounce of strength if I am to survive. So that means that this body will remain vulnerable. Ubel can and surely will attempt to destroy it. But I can rebuild it."

"How about if I drag the body to the altar once you've left?" Sadie asked. "It would be safe then."

"I have to return to it sometime, Sadie," Jordan said. "And this battle with Satan ..." He paused. "If I survive. I may be too weak to overcome the power of the altar. It may destroy me."

"I'm scared, Jordan," Sadie said. Jordan hugged her.

"Me too," he said. "And believe me, when a demon gets scared ..." He paused. "That wasn't the right thing to say, was it?"

"It certainly didn't inspire any confidence, Jordan," Sadie said. Jordan began to lead her up the nave, their footsteps echoing eerily on a tiled floor that was hundreds of years old. It was as though they were being followed by a dozen other people, each of them walking at the same speed, with the same reluctance. Finally, they reached the end of the nave, and Sadie felt her eyes being drawn upwards, where shafts of light cascaded in through the tall, narrow windows of the central tower, barely illuminating the tower's ceiling, none of it falling down below the walls of the tower.

Ahead, Sadie could see the choir, and beyond that, the altar, sealed off from the public by ropes which is was forbidden to cross, visited only by the religious leaders, untainted by the modern cancer of commercialism that was rife in the rest of the building. And Jordan was leading her, practically pulling her, towards the altar.

As they got close, he slowed, and almost stumbled, and it took all of Sadie's strength to keep him on his feet.

"Jordan, what's wrong?" she asked him anxiously, panicked by his apparent loss of mobility.

"The altar," Jordan said, his voice coming out in breathless gasps. "It's more powerful than I'd envisaged." He turned to her, and his face was strangely illuminated. "I can't go any further. It must be because I'm destined to be the devil."

And then Sadie realized what the glowing was.

Lights were coming on in the cathedral.

She spun her head around, looking up the north transept, where a figure was approaching. At that moment, Jordan dropped to his knees and looked up at her.

"The altar," he said. "You have to go to the altar."

"Jordan," Sadie hissed. "Somebody's coming!"

But Jordan wasn't listening. He clutched his sides. "I have to go, Sadie," he said. "I can't afford to remain here any longer." Sadie dropped down beside him and ran a hand through his hair.

"You're leaving?"

"I have to."

"But you're not strong enough."

"It's just this place," Jordan assured her. "In this mortal body, I cannot cope with the power of the altar. If I were in my demonic form, its effect wouldn't be so pronounced. But this is draining me."

"Jordan, I don't want to lose you," Sadie said, kissing him. She was aware of the footsteps that were drawing closer. "Please don't leave me."

"I have to," Jordan said. He looked into her eyes. "I love you."

"I love you too," Sadie said quickly.

And then Jordan's body went limp in her arms, his eyes wide open, staring, yet unseeing, glazed over like those of a corpse.

"No, Jordan, don't do this!" Sadie hissed. "Come on!"

"What is the meaning of this?" a voice demanded to know.

Sadie turned to face the stranger, trying to tell herself that Jordan wasn't dead, that the body was still breathing, still living, waiting for Jordan's soul to return.

The stranger was tall, slightly overweight, wearing black, with a white collar — a priest, most likely the dean of the cathedral. Around his neck was a crucifix, and it reminded Sadie that she still had the one Jordan had given her.

"What on earth do you think you're doing here?" the dean asked.

"Please, you have to help me," Sadie said. She couldn't think of anything else to do. Ubel, the demon, was after her and Jordan, and this was the only safe place for them to hide out. She couldn't allow this religious fanatic to throw them out – or worse, to call the police.

Then she remembered all that Jordan had told her, about Heaven and Hell, and realized that perhaps men and women like this dean weren't so fanatical after all. They'd got it right all along.

Sadie stared into the man's face, and wondered whether he actually believed in God, or whether there was a doubt at the back of his mind.

"What's wrong?" the dean asked as he approached. "Is he hurt?"

"He just collapsed."

"I should be calling the police," the dean said, pulling out a mobile phone. "Now I find myself calling for an ambulance."

"You don't understand!" Sadie shouted. "We have to get to the altar!"

"What?"

"It's the only safe place!"

"Safe?" the dean asked, a bewildered expression on his face. "From what?"

Sadie hopped to her feet, leaving Jordan lying on the ancient tiled floor of the cathedral. "There is a demon chasing us," she said, well aware that she sounded insane. "He knows where we are, and he's coming right after us. The only safe place in this building is the altar."

The dean didn't say anything for a few moments.

Then he raised the phone. "We'll get this all sorted out in a moment," he said, about to punch in a number.

"Don't!" Sadie said. "If you call the police or an ambulance, we will all die."

The dean smiled patronizingly, as though dealing with someone who wasn't entirely sane. "My dear, we are all safe here. This is a house of God."

"You don't understand!" Sadie shouted again. "My God, don't you get it? This place has been defiled! The only safe place in this building is that altar! Now, we both have to go there if we're to be saved."

"Saved? From what?"

"The demon, for fuck's sake!"

The dean smiled again. "My dear, there are no demons."

And it was at that precise moment that the west end of the cathedral was illuminated by a brilliant flare of light, and the stench of sulphur washed up the length of the nave. Both Sadie and the dean looked at the burning arc, until first the flames and then the smoke dissipated, leaving behind a tall figure, clad only in a loincloth, his flesh a deep crimson in colour, his legs those of a goat. Horns sprouted from his head, but Sadie recognized him all the same.

"Shit," she muttered under her breath.

Ubel laughed loudly.

"There are no demons!" he shouted victoriously, mimicking the dean, waving his outstretched arms at the ceiling. "There are no demons!" he shouted again, looking skywards.

His gaze fell upon the dean, and with a soft growl, he spoke.

"Then what the fuck am I?"

46

It was obvious that the dean had never expected to see a demon in his lifetime. And from the expression of horror and astonishment on his face, he probably never expected to see anything like it when he died. He backed away a couple of steps, and then shot a look in Sadie's direction.

"Believe me now?" Sadie found herself asking.

"Is this some practical joke?" the dean said.

"Do I look like I'm laughing?"

"This cannot be," the dean muttered in desperation. "This just cannot be. Demons just don't exist. They're a figment of one's imagination. They're nothing more than ..." He struggled to find the word. "... symbols, dreamed up by the same people who dreamed up angels."

"I would've thought you of all people would've known, this is for real," Sadie snapped. "Now, forget the fucking theologizing — let's get to the altar!"

"Of course," the dean said, stepping over to Jordan's prone body. "Give me a hand."

"Forget that!" Sadie snapped. "He doesn't need our help!"

The dean looked up at Sadie, disturbed. "He isn't dead!"

"He's a demon too," Sadie told him bluntly, though it hurt her to speak like that about the man she loved.

Instantly, the dean backed off, almost stumbling into her in the process. Rather ungallantly, Sadie made no effort to catch him, but fortunately for the dean, he didn't fall flat on his back. All the same, by the time he'd fully regained his posture, Sadie was already on her way to the altar. She pushed the ropes, knocking over the steel poles holding them in place, and diving onto the base of the altar. The dean was close behind, scrambling up close to the very centre of the religious universe as far as he was concerned.

Then both of them looked down the nave to where Ubel was walking.

Walking slowly, inexorably, towards them, a smile on his face. "That won't save you!" he said. "You can hide there like frightened lambs if you so desire, if it makes you feel better, but it will not save you."

"He's bluffing," Sadie whispered to the dean.

"What if he's not?" the dean asked in a panic.

"Do you believe in God?"

The dean frowned as he looked at her. "Of course!" he pronounced indignantly.

"Then start praying, because we're gonna need all the help we can get," Sadie said, pulling out the crucifix Jordan had given her. The dean shot her a bewildered look, and then lifted up his own cross. "He is evil," she told him. "And he can be kept at bay."

"This is all too much," the dean groaned. "This is all too much!"

"We can't give up!" Sadie shouted at him. "We are safe, just so long as we stay here" She looked down the nave, which although had no direct lighting, was illuminated by an eerie red glow that seemed to reflect off the walls and pillars. The demon was getting closer, almost at the central tower, the dissection of the two bars that made up the cross shape of the cathedral.

He was smiling.

"This will all be too easy," he said confidently. "You really think that your religious trinkets can stop me? I am evil incarnate! I can never be stopped, not by a mere mortal!" Sadie raised the crucifix higher, and she could hear the dean muttering under his breath.

"Our Father, who art in Heaven, hallowed be thy name ..."

The demon paused beneath the central tower as he broke out in paroxysms of laughter, throwing his head backwards with a loud bellow.

"I love it!" he shouted. "I love it! The power. Oh, the power! Fucking Jesus freaks!"

His head dropped, and his eyes locked onto Sadie's. "Think you're safe there, do you?" he asked seriously.

"Fuck you!"

"Oh?" The demon resumed walking, this time his gait slow and exaggerated, like a catwalk model in slow-motion. "Believe me, you don't know how much I'd like that. You really have no idea." He reached the rope boundary that separated the altar from the rest of the cathedral. "You do think that you're safe in there, don't you?"

"I don't see you coming in to get us," Sadie said. Beside her, the dean completed the Lord's Prayer, and raised his head, a look of abject horror on his face as he stared at the demon at close proximity. "Why don't you just leave?"

"My dear, I have an eternity in which to claim your soul," the demon said. "And I will claim it, of that you are assured."

"Well, we're not moving," Sadie said defiantly.

"What about the morning?" the dean asked softly. He looked at Sadie. "When the cathedral is open? What happens then?" He looked at the demon, then back at Sadie.

"I know what you're thinking, you God-bothering, moronic piece of flotsam," the demon said. "When those people, those tourists, those who have bastardized this place of worship, who have turned it into the very marketplace Jesus Christ Himself wished to destroy, when they come into this building, this hollowed-out hunk of stone that is no more a religious sanctuary than a public toilet full of human excrement, there will be a massacre the like of which has never before been witnessed." The demon smiled as he looked at Sadie. "And you shall be responsible, because you wouldn't sacrifice yourself. Think of all the lives you could save, but for your selfishness, your own vain attempt at survival, at delaying the inevitable."

Sadie's heart sank. The demon was making his side of the argument sound so rational, as though it were the only way. But it wasn't the only way, because wherever Jordan had disappeared to, he was coming back.

Her eyes dropped to Jordan's unmoving body.

And the demon twisted his head to look in the same direction.

He stepped over to the body and lifted it up by the throat, staring into unseeing eyes. "A useless item of clothing unworthy of a demon," he said scathingly. "In this disguise, a demon becomes weak, ineffective, a virtual mortal. A waste of good power." And with a scowl, he hurled Jordan's body down the nave.

Sadie watched as Jordan's limbs flew out at bizarre, unnatural angles, like the pathetic dummies in cheap movies, falling from tall buildings, no natural, coordinated flailing, no attempt to cling vainly to thin air. It was like a doll being tossed aside by a petulant child.

A living corpse.

And Sadie blinked as with a bloodcurdling crunch it slammed into the wall beneath the huge west window, and slithered clumsily to the floor, where it landed with a sickening thud.

The demon turned back to Sadie.

"Kobold will shortly be destroyed," he said. "If it hasn't already happened. That wasn't part of the plan, and I don't suppose for a moment that Satan is going to be too happy. But Kobold is no match for Satan." He stepped back up to the rope boundary. "That is a shame, because I was looking forward to destroying him myself. But then, we don't all get what we want, do we?"

"If the object of your pursuit is going to be destroyed, why are you here?" Sadie asked, keeping one hand on the table of the altar, and the crucifix in the other. "What's the point in terrorizing us?"

Ubel laughed again. "For sport, my dear," he said. "I'm sure Kobold has explained everything to you, how he is a *good* demon, carrying out God's work — the work of a fucking sewage pipe cleaner, washing away other people's shit and piss and used condoms and tampons — and that I am a *bad* demon, one of the Corrupted, condemned forever to spend eternity on the run from the Jäger on this sordid cesspit, fashioned from one of God's own stools. Well, my human lovely, what else can I do to pass the time, but kill for sport? I watch couples in love, see their caresses, their soulful kisses, their tender lovemaking, the pleasure they give to one another. And I rip that apart by diverting their concentration so that they drive their car into the path of an oncoming bus. I see a mother kissing her child and tucking that child into bed at night — and I suck the very life from that child while it sleeps. I damage aircraft, trains, nuclear power plants — all so that myriad human lives can be snuffed out in an instant." Ubel cocked his head on one side. "I kill for sport, for fun, or just for the hell of it. And it's about time I killed again."

"You're a monster!" Sadie shouted.

"Yes," Ubel said with a laugh. "I rather think that I am."

"This cannot be allowed to go on!" the dean said, getting to his feet.

"Wait! What the fuck are you going to do?" The dean stepped to the side of the altar. "Wait! For Christ's sake don't step out of the ropes!" The dean bent down beside the table and then stood upright. In his hands was a large bowl. "What's that?"

"This?" the dean asked, struggling as he returned to the front of the altar. He looked Ubel up and down, and then tossed the bowl at him, "This is Holy water!" he shouted as the liquid engulfed Ubel. The demon instantly dropped to his knees, clutching at his face as though he'd been burned by acid. He was bellowing in agony and flames seemed to erupt from his body, burning orange and red, and licking round every inch of crimson flesh. "He has to be destroyed!" the dean proclaimed, diving over the ropes, the crucifix in his hand.

At that moment, the demon rose to his feet, towering over the dean, his arms outstretched, like Christ on a cross. He frowned as he looked down at the dean, his body burning brightly, reminding Sadie of the monk who'd set fire to himself as a protest at the Vietnam war. But whereas that monk had rocked himself as he burned in agony, the demon seemed to be enjoying his fate.

The dean raised the crucifix, but the demon simply snatched it from him and raised it to his mouth, swallowing it whole. Then he gripped the dean by the throat with one hand and lifted him in the air.

"Did you really think *that* would destroy me?"

The dean fought with the hand that gripped his throat, but it was clenched too tightly. He was gasping for air as the fingers of the demon squeezed his windpipe, pinching at his vagus nerve at the same time.

"Holy water is painful, yes," the demon admitted. "But it pales in comparison to the fires of Hell. And though I no longer reside there, I carry those fires deep within me, and can call upon them at any time. Call it my defensive spray if you like. I choose to call it my *eau de toilette.*" He pulled the dean closer to him, and then opened his mouth wide, revealing a set of sharp canines and huge incisors.

And then he bit off the dean's face, ripping the flesh and muscle from his skull to the accompaniment of a moist tearing sound. He chewed on the face as the dean struggled violently, kicking out legs and lashing out fists, but to no avail. The dean was screaming through a mouth that no longer had lips, that was little more than a skeleton's jaw, wide open because no muscle remained to hold it place.

The demon allowed the dean to struggle for a few more seconds, blood spraying from what was a massive and certainly mortal wound, before he ended the suffering by biting off the top of his head.

Sadie turned her head away, but couldn't block out the noises, the sound of crunching bone being chewed by impossibly strong teeth.

When she looked back at the demon, she saw that the dean's decapitated body had been cast aside, and that Ubel's eyes were now locked on her.

"You are safe," he said. "For the time being. But there is no creation of mortal man than can stop me. And I can destroy any human within the blinking of an eye. I can make it quick, if needs be, so I have no fear of being overwhelmed. And I can wait here for as long as it takes."

And with that, Ubel sat down on the floor, and folded his arms.

Sadie, kneeling beside the altar, shuddered once more.

This time, she didn't stop.

47

When Kobold materialized in Hell, the throng of a hundred thousand voices instantly filled his ears and he became disorientated as he staggered through the huge doorway leading into the devil's chambers, overwhelmed by the sheer volume and noise and the sudden change of his surroundings, from the calm tranquillity of the deserted cathedral to the crushing oppression of the nether world.

No longer in human form, he had become a demon, but was unlike any other demon in Hell. Huge, more powerful, his chest and arms muscular, sweat dripping from crimson flesh, his goat-like legs thick and covered in wiry hair. A thick tail whipped behind him, and Kobold knew that he had the strength within that appendage alone to smite down any demon foolish enough to approach him. As he regained his composure and stood upright, flexing his muscles, he found himself in an arena of sorts, the ground stony and rocky, the ceiling high overhead, almost out of sight, but with hundreds of long stalactites dripping downwards; and the walls ...

The walls were lined with literally thousands of demonic beings – imps, demons, winged demons, incubi and succubi, each of them jeering, their myriad voices a mighty roar that would've overwhelmed the ears of a lesser being. But Kobold was more than up to the challenge, and he gazed around this gathered multitude, staring some of those he saw in the eyes until they looked away. Winged demons swooped down from their perches, almost kicking him in the head as they flew past. But Kobold didn't flinch.

He was here to face the devil.

His initial confusion over, these pale imitations didn't frighten him.

As if to prove a point, when one of the demons swooped within his reach, he lashed out with a fist, striking the demon in the belly and sending him crashing to the rocky ground. Then, with the wave of a hand, he sent a bolt of flame towards the demon. The demon, burning in a hot hellish fire, screamed in agony and tried to douse the flames.

Kobold smiled, and watched as water poured down from high overhead, swallowing up the demon and putting out the fire. The steaming demon rolled across the ground and scurried back to the safety of the wall, losing himself amongst the thousands of creatures there.

In his place stood Satan.

Hands on his hips, he was an impressive sight, but Kobold knew that Satan was no longer larger than he — perhaps more experienced, but no more powerful.

"These are all my demons," Satan said quietly, holding out his arms expressively and turning in a circle to look at the assembled throng. "Each and every single one of them!" The demons roared in approval, and Satan turned to face Kobold, scowling as he spoke. "I take what you did to my child as a personal affront."

"That pathetic excuse for a winged demon?" Kobold scoffed. "If you consider such pitiful individuals to be your children, Satan, then your time is certainly at an end."

"You came here, Kobold, to do battle with me," Satan said. "That was a mistake. One that I will certainly give you time to regret – when this battle is over, I will give you but a second in which to repent your final lapse of judgement. And then you will learn what it is like, perhaps only for a nanosecond, not to exist. You should be privileged, Kobold, for not even God Himself knows what it is like not to exist."

"Talk is cheap, Satan," Kobold said, noticing that none of the other demons present were making a sound— all were listening to the first stage of the battle. The battle of words. Kobold clenched his fists and felt his biceps pumping up. "You broke the laws governing Heaven and Hell. You allowed the Corrupted to enter this sacred place. You even despatched the most powerful member of that sect to destroy me, because deep down, you know that you are too weak to destroy me yourself. Your time is over. It is time for fresh blood."

"There will be blood shed here in this chamber," Satan admitted, nodding his head. "But it shall be your blood."

Kobold smiled. He was beginning to enjoy this – a battle of wits with Satan. Soon to be followed by a battle of strength, a fight to the death for the ultimate prize. For the victor, all of Hell and the ultimate power trip. For the vanquished – ultimate and final destruction.

Kobold flexed his fists.

And then was thrown backwards into the throng of demons as Satan delivered the first blow, a blow that knocked all of the wind from out of him. But he quickly recovered, hauling himself to his feet and tossing aside a handful of imps, as though they were small pebbles. Demons backed away, clearly fearful at the look of rage on his face. Were he not already of a crimson complexion, he felt as though he might now be blushing.

Satan had made a fool of him by making him appear weak, as though he were not an opponent worthy of any consideration. That, Kobold thought indignantly, was a mistake on Satan's part. He would learn.

Kobold grabbed a demon in each hand and flung them across the chamber towards Satan. *En route*, they caught fire, slamming into the devil with the ferocity of small missiles, exploding upon impact and sending the demons to oblivion. The first casualties of war, collateral damage that still left Satan standing. The devil, arms akimbo, simply threw back his head and laughed heartily, small flames dancing down his chest as he absorbed the power of the explosions.

"Impressive," he said with much sincerity. "But ultimately futile."

Kobold heard a roar coming from overhead and looked up in time to see a huge chunk of the ceiling descending towards him. But he simply closed his eyes, and disintegrated as the jagged boulder tore into the ground where only a split second previously he'd been standing, sending out shards of rock in every direction, natural shrapnel that tore into hundreds of the watching demons, ripping them to shreds, some being destroyed instantly, others falling seriously wounded.

When Kobold opened his eyes, he was right where he intended to be – on the opposite side of the arena, behind Satan, who had his back to him. Raising a hand and summoning up a huge amount of energy, Kobold ripped apart the ground, the tear stretching from just a few feet in front of him, racing across the chamber towards Satan.

The devil, alerted by the rumbling sensation, turned to see the ground between his legs splitting open, and he hopped sideways, rolling over and throwing himself across the chamber far from the rip. He jumped to his feet and looked carefully at Kobold, the realization that he was dealing with somebody who was equally as powerful as him finally appearing on his face.

Kobold clenched his fists and felt the power that had drained from him by the exertion of creating the minor earthquake returning almost instantaneously. Never before had he felt this strong. Hell was feeding him, as it fed only the devil, and he was positively thriving.

Satan puffed out his chest and jabbed a finger in Kobold's direction. "It is time to stop playing like children!" he bellowed. But Kobold knew that it was just talk. Satan now knew that he had met his match, and the both of them knew all that was required to win this battle was simply that extra ounce of strength, that extra watt of power, and the victor would be revealed.

The devil made the next move, and it happened so swiftly that it took Kobold by surprise.

The bolt of lightning caught him full in the face, and threw him over backwards. He hit the ground hard, and skidded along on his back for a few feet, before coming to a rest. Stunned, by the time he'd shook his head and come to his senses, Satan was on top of him, a hand around his throat, and a mighty fist pounding the side of his skull. With each blow, Kobold's head was jolted sideways, and all he could hear was ringing in his ears, and all he could see were stars dancing before his eyes, and even closing them didn't make them disappear.

This was a demonstration of sheer brute force, like two drunken men brawling in the street.

And Kobold was taking the brunt of the punishment.

Satan wasn't giving him time to recover, and even though coherent thoughts weren't exactly at the forefront of Kobold's mind, he still considered the fact that, were he in Satan's shoes, had he managed to make the first move on the devil, then he certainly wouldn't be giving any quarter either.

A cheer went up from the watching crowd, and Kobold opened his eyes long enough to see Satan raising his hand, flexing his fingers as though they were the claws of a tiger. He knew what was coming next. The devil was preparing to rip Kobold's heart out of his chest, the very organ that symbolized the soul of a celestial being. Once that was destroyed ...

Kobold sighed.

He had given it his best shot, and whilst he had thought he would've put up a better fight, might've lasted a few more rounds, he knew that he couldn't have done any more. Looking into Satan's eyes, he could see the victory, knew that Satan could taste it in his mouth, knew that this was the end for him, and probably for mankind too. Decadence would rule, because the Corrupted could run wild on Earth, afflicting their own brand of death upon the innocents, the just and the undeserving.

He would never ever have the chance to be human again, would never be able to see Sadie, to kiss her, to feel her soft flesh against his. He loved her like no human ever could, because he knew that his love was a gift, that he should never have been feeling love for any human, for anything, ever again.

Falling in love with Sadie, it had given him a second chance to live his life, even if his life had been based on a lie. That didn't matter, because he'd experienced love, true love ...

He couldn't ask for more.

He could, he told himself in a brief moment of clarity. He could ask to survive, to be allowed to defeat Satan, to be given the strength to overcome this corrupt devil. But he had done all that was in his power.

What more could he do?

He looked into Satan's face again, and suddenly, the trickery, the deceit, it was all revealed.

Of course.

Of course!

This was a brawl, nothing more. Satan had overcome him physically, had beaten his celestial body until it was of no use to Kobold, because it no longer functioned properly. But Kobold had fooled himself with Satan's help, because when a human is beaten, he gives up, he lies there, accepts defeat, because there is nothing more he can do, because he can no longer defend himself, because his body is useless, powerless.

But Kobold wasn't human.

His body was not required.

He looked deep into Satan's eyes.

And he saw fear replacing the sense of victory.

And whilst there was a clarity within the devil's mind with regards to Kobold's full understanding of the situation, the devil seemed unaware that at that precise moment, a huge chunk of the ceiling was bearing down on the two of them, its velocity increasing along with the volume of the assembled demons and imps, who all seemed to be screaming out a warning to their illustrious leader.

At the last moment, Kobold pushed up with all his strength and the devil fell over backwards, his face now looking up into the huge boulder that was just feet away from impact. At the same time, Kobold dissembled his atoms and reformed more than a hundred feet away.

The boulder missed him, and slammed into Satan with a thunderous crash which shook the entire chamber, causing winged demons to fall from their perches with a terrifying screech, and imps to tumble from their footholds. Smaller boulders and loose rocks were shook from the walls and the ceiling, and these bounced into the ground like huge, lethal hailstones.

Kobold stood upright and felt a swell of power and energy rush through his body. He was metamorphosing into something even more powerful. Like a butterfly emerging from the chrysalis, he was close to the completion of his cycle. Soon, he would emerge as the new devil, the new ruler of Hell, and all of the associated powers and responsibilities would be his to behold.

But first, the old devil had to be completely destroyed.

Kobold walked over to the boulder, where dust and smaller rocks were breaking free and rattling to the ground. The assembled audience was now silent, each and every demon and imp present awaiting the outcome of the most frightening battle in Hell. Most of them had never before witnessed such a battle, and even those who had seen Satan defeat Beelzebub were shocked by the ferocity of this confrontation.

Kobold walked around the boulder, and found Satan, the top half of his body protruding amidst a pool of blood. He knelt down and looked into Satan's face.

"You had your chance, Satan," he said. "You chose trickery and deceit, and that was to be your downfall."

"You have not defeated me yet, Kobold," Satan gasped breathlessly. The sheer force of the impact had totally destroyed Satan's body, and any psychic powers he had were severely diminished. It had been sheer good fortune that had seen Satan's heart, the driving force behind his soul, still intact, just inches from the edge of the boulder. "While I still breathe, I still possess the power to defeat you." And he reached up and grabbed Kobold's shoulder, pulling him towards him. "You made a mistake."

"A mistake? You're pinned beneath this boulder, Satan. You lay there, impotent, worthless, without the strength to move yourself, and you tell me I made a mistake?"

Satan gasped again and coughed up blood. "You do not possess the resolve to destroy me, Kobold. You are not ruthless enough. And you are not worthy of assuming the position of devil. You desire just one thing — to be human. The devil cannot afford to be led astray."

"As you were?"

"I never desired to be human."

"You just desired the power, the ultimate power," Kobold said. "And you paid for it with your life."

"If you cannot give your full devotion to the position, Kobold, then you are deceiving everyone in Hell, and all those in Heaven," the devil said, closing his eyes and coughing up more blood. "The power, Kobold, consumes you. And if you desire only to be human, then you have made a mistake — a terrible mistake."

"How do you work that out?"

"Why did you do battle with me, Kobold? Why do you want to destroy me?"

"Because I am the rightful heir to the throne—"

"You are, yes," Satan agreed, "but that is not why you fought me, is it? You fought me to prevent me from destroying you, from hunting you down, from putting an end to your existence, and sending that bitch human you love to Hell."

"She would never have gone to Hell."

"She fell in love with a demon, Kobold" Satan said with a smirk. His eyes were clouding over now, and his breath was coming out in small sprays of red mist. "She has been damned."

"No!"

"But you shall be the devil now," Satan said. "For whatever selfish reason, her fate is in your hands. But to do that, you have to destroy me. You have to destroy me to save your love — and that does not make you worthy. That makes you as corrupt as me. And you won't do that, will you? Debase yourself in such a way."

Kobold stood up and closed his eyes. Satan was right, of course. He might well have been the rightful heir to the throne, but that was not why he had fought this battle. That was not why he wanted to see Satan destroyed. This had all been for selfish reasons. He wanted to be human, wanted to continue experiencing his love for Sadie.

And for that reason alone, he couldn't destroy Satan.

Which ultimately meant that Satan would recover, and both he and Sadie would be destroyed.

"You are right, of course," he confessed. "I could destroy you right here, right now, without exerting as much energy as would be required of me to destroy an imp. But I cannot do that. My honour will not permit me to use the power within me purely for personal gain. You are weaker than me. Satan, and every demon, every imp, every succubi, every incubi, here in Hell, they can all see that. But you win. You win by default. I cannot assume the position of the devil."

"But I can," a voice behind Kobold said.

Kobold spun around to see Zerstörer, the Jäger he had fought in David's chamber, the demon who had turned, standing with his fists clenched.

"I am worthy," Zerstörer said. "If Satan is permitted to continue ruling over Hell, then the Corrupted will seize power, and Earth and Heaven will be under threat of an apocalypse the likes of which has never before been witnessed. A balance needs to be sought — I can bring that balance to Hell."

Zerstörer dropped to his knees next to Satan.

"You must be destroyed." he said. "In the name of all that is Holy and Righteous."

"No!"

And the ex-Jäger plunged his hand into Satan's chest and ripped out the heart.

The devil stared at it in disbelief and then watched as Zerstörer squeezed it.

It popped like a huge blood blister, showering the three of them in thick, sticky blood.

Satan witnessed that, and then his bloated corpse exploded, sending shards of bone, blood and flesh in every direction. Scores of imps came forward to feed on the scattered remnants of their ruler, many in the vain hope that it would make them strong.

Kobold ignored them, and turned to Zerstörer.

"Thank you," he said.

The Jäger nodded his head. "It had to be done."

"I know," Kobold said. "But I could not do it."

"I understand."

The conversation was stilted, and were he a human, Kobold might've been embarrassed.

"What happens now?" Zerstörer asked.

Kobold watched as behind the Jäger, thousands of demons were coming forward, each of them wanting to meet their new leader, wanting to look into the face of the demon or demons who had destroyed the devil.

"I cannot stay," Kobold said. "I do not belong here any longer."

"I may need your help."

Kobold smiled and shook his head. "You destroyed the devil. You are powerful enough not to need my help."

Zerstörer looked Kobold up and down. "You fought the devil, you all but destroyed him yourself. You have the body of a devil. I have the body of a mere demon."

"You have nothing to fear."

"I am no greater than those demons who are coming forward to accept me as their leader."

"You will be," Kobold assured him, and he closed his eyes.

48

When he opened them again, he found himself surrounded by brilliant white light, with a cloudless and vivid blue sky overhead. Gone was the smell of Hell, the sulphuric stench that he'd grown used to but never liked, and in its place, the scent of flowers, light perfume and cologne, an aroma that inspired happiness and serenity.

He whirled around on the spot, and all around saw hundreds of people floating upwards, as though bursting through the misty floor beneath him, their arms outspread, as though preparing themselves for an eternity of beatitude. Some of them wore wary expressions, as though they still had yet to come to terms with their own mortality, but as they were greeted by angels clothed in white robes, most dropped to their knees and wept tears of joy.

He heard a child shout behind him, and spun around to see a small crowd of toddlers running across a meadow no more than a hundred yards away. The meadow seemed to stretch for miles, and Kobold could just make out what he presumed were the Gates of Heaven somewhere in the distance, golden and glittering. Overhead, angels fluttered like butterflies, some of them childlike in appearance. The younger ones dropped down amongst the toddlers, and each accepted a child into its care, showing them the way to the Gates and everlasting happiness.

Kobold felt a tear well up in his eye as he imagined those young children dying. Each of them had looked healthy, but heavenly appearances hid the horrors that befell humans on Earth. The youngest of the children was perhaps eighteen months. He could not possibly comprehend the future, the past, or what had happened to him, how he'd ended up here. Soon, he would want to know where his mother was, would beg for her to cuddle him, to reassure him. Later, he'd want to play with his father, and no amount of coaxing from the angels would change that.

Would these children remain so youthful for all of eternity, or would they grow?

A voice he recognized answered. "They will grow," she said.

Kobold turned around to face Reizend. "And when do they stop growing?"

"Whenever they like," Reizend said. She walked up to him, her blond hair flowing in a gentle breeze behind her. She wore white, as did all the angels, and her gown billowed out as she took each step, revealing the refined shape of her body.

"What happens when their parents come to Heaven?"

"Finding your loved ones isn't easy," Reizend said as she stood beside him. She too watched the children being led to the Gates. "I still haven't found my family. There are billions — quadrillions upon quadrillions — of people in Heaven, as there are in Hell. But then, we each of us have an eternity. Who knows. Maybe I'll stumble across my parents, my brother — maybe I won't."

"But won't they get lonely?"

Reizend held his hand. "The loneliness doesn't last an eternity, Kobold. And there is love here in Heaven. True love. There isn't any need for jealousy, for hurt feelings, because everyone here is a friend. Those children, they may miss their parents. But there are millions of other people who can be like a mother or a father to them."

Kobold turned to Reizend. "You know. I'd like to know more about this place. I'd like to know everything there is to know."

"Maybe one day you will."

"Relationships?"

"For example, with Sadie?"

"Do people have relationships?"

"Sexual relationships?" Reizend smirked. "There is no need for physical love here, Kobold. This isn't Earth, these people are not humans. They – I – do not desire physical love. We are friends to one another, that is all. Physical love leads to jealousy, leads to misunderstandings and hurt feelings. You don't get thrown into Hell for cheating on your husband or wife but here in Heaven, that opportunity never arises. If we allowed people to fall in love ... it would corrupt Heaven. Take for example the young woman whose husband dies. She remarries fifteen, twenty years later. And then her and her new husband die. Who should she spend all of eternity with here in Heaven. Who has the right to her feelings and her love?"

"It must take some adjusting to."

"It does," Reizend said. "A few years. But that is but the blinking of an eye to those who have eternity to look forward to. Believe me, you soon forget about love and carnal desire. You realize that it isn't important, not here in Heaven,"

"To some, this would be more like Hell."

Reizend laughed. "I guess so."

Kobold looked at the smiling faces surrounding him, at the expressions of wonderment, disbelief and relief, and he realized that this was so very much different from Hell, so very much different from Earth even. He turned back to Reizend. "We spend years looking for partner, for someone to fall in love with, and then, when we die ... we have to forget them?"

"We never forget."

"It seems so harsh," Kobold said. "It makes how we live our lives on Earth so pointless."

"It makes our time on Earth more precious," Reizend said quickly. "It is but the blinking of an eye. There are souls here who are almost as old as mankind itself. Do you realize how long eternity is?"

"It is never-ending," Kobold remarked. "That is all I can say."

"But you can never comprehend that," Reizend said. "Like some people just cannot comprehend death — the disbelievers, those who may well end up breaking through the grounds of Heaven like fresh flowers, and have their well-meaning theories disproved."

"I should look forward to being here," Kobold said. "Though my destiny probably lies beneath us."

"That chapter still has to be written," Reizend said. "In Hell, you proved yourself. Your selfless act did not go unnoticed. You were prepared to sacrifice yourself, even though it contradicted every law written by God." Kobold frowned. "You were the rightful heir. And in refusing to destroy

Satan, you most surely condemned Sadie to death. But you considered the options, and you made the right decision."

"Sadie would've ended up in Heaven, wouldn't she?" Kobold wanted to know. "There was a moment there, when Satan suggested she was condemned for sleeping with a demon."

"Satan was a liar,' Kobold," Reizend said, squeezing his hand. "And you made the right decision. But your destiny may well lie in Hell. Until you have cast aside your powers, you remain the devil."

"That is not what I desire."

"You desire to be human?"

"More than anything."

"But what about Sadie?"

"What about her?"

"Left to the mercy of Ubel the Corrupted."

Kobold's eyes widened, and for a moment, he considered closing them and sending himself back to that cathedral. With the power of the devil inside him, he could surely defeat Ubel.

Instead, he stood firm.

"It's all about sacrifice, isn't it?"

Reizend nodded her head.

"If I become corrupted, then so does Sadie."

"But Ubel will kill her, as he has already killed so many who have stood in his way."

"And she will end up in Heaven?" Kobold asked. He wanted that guarantee. Reizend nodded her head. "Then I must face a future without her — as a human."

"You're prepared to spend the next forty or fity years mourning the death of a woman you love, when all along you had within you the power to save her?"

Kobold felt the tears streaming down his face. "It breaks my heart, more so because I only yearn to be human, because I love Sadie, but I cannot use my powers for selfish reasons. I cannot allow myself to become corrupted, because in doing so, Sadie will end up tainted."

Another voice spoke. "Is it wrong, Kobold, to save an innocent from the clutches of a corrupt, evil demon?" Kobold looked around and tried to find the source of this voice, but Reizend held him tightly so he couldn't move from the spot. "Is that a selfish act?"

Kobold didn't know what to say — he had a good idea who was talking to him, and felt the urge to drop to his knees, but Reizend held him upright. "I ... I don't know what ..."

"Your destiny is in your hands, Kobold, your future. Sadie's future, the future of her sister," the voice said. "What do you truly desire?"

"I desire to be human," Kobold said blandly. "To spend the rest of my life with Sadie."

"Then tomorrow, you shall be human," the voice assured him. "But tonight, you have a task to complete. You have very little time remaining."

Kobold turned to Reizend. "Then I must save Sadie."

The angel nodded her head. "You have our blessing," she said.

49

Sadie shivered almost uncontrollably as she hugged her legs to herself, and watched the faint light creeping along the nave, the rising sun sending shafts of light through the tall windows, casting long shadows that could have hidden all manner of monsters. But it wasn't those child-like, invisible, non-existent monsters she was concerned with.

It was the monster who paced around the altar which had her fullest attention, a monster she couldn't shake from her mind, because he was real, and because his threats were real.

Occasionally, he would make a lunge for her, but it was just pretence. He knew that he would never break through the protective barrier that the altar provided, just as Sadie knew. All the same, she was still petrified. What if he was simply toying with her? After all, the Holy Water the Dean had thrown upon the demon had had little effect. In fact, the demon had simply appeared to relish the sensation of burning. What if this was all a charade? What if he killed the first few visitors to arrive, and then dived onto the altar and attacked her as viciously as he'd attacked the Dean?

She shook that thought aside.

No, that wasn't possible.

Jordan had told her that the altar was too powerful an icon. And she believed what Jordan told her. She had to believe him now, because in spite of her initial doubts when he'd told her the truth, she could see that it all made sense now. She could see that he had been a demon — was still a demon — and that before her now stood another demon.

Ubel paused, and knelt down before the altar, almost as though he were mocking a priest or a religious visitor. He crossed himself, and seemed to enjoy the pain it caused. Laughing, he looked Sadie in the eyes and ran a hand through his Mohican haircut.

"I can make it quick," he promised her. "I can rip out your heart in an instant. You wouldn't even feel the pain. And one as righteous as you ... well, you'd be on your way to Heaven even before I'd had time to consume your flesh."

Sadie felt a wave of hopeless overcome her.

"Your resolve ... it's wilting, isn't it? You know what's going to happen when the visitors start to arrive. That front door — it's unlocked. I can snatch aside every single person, every man, woman, child and baby to come in through that door. Snatch them aside, and rip them asunder." Ubel smiled. "And it would all be on your head, because you weren't prepared to make the final sacrifice. Think of the honour, of the kudos. You would be revered as a saint in Heaven. You would instantly become an angel. Does that hold any attraction for you?"

Sadie didn't answer.

"On the other hand ... if you permit me to slaughter possibly hundreds of innocent people — and believe me, that would be possible — you may be condemned to Hell. Do you know what that's like, Sadie? Do you have any comprehension of what it's like to spend an eternity being tortured?"

Again, Sadie didn't stayed silent.

Then there was a fantastic explosion of light, as though a nuclear device had been set off, and Sadie looked away, fearful that her eyes would burn in their sockets. A loud roar filled the cathedral, echoing up the nave, reverberating off the walls, shaking the centuries old glass, and it was quickly followed by a rush of air that almost blew Sadie over backwards.

She watched as Ubel struggled to his feet and turned around, as the light subsided, leaving in its place a being that looked just like him.

No, Sadie corrected herself. This being, this demon, was crimson in colour and possessed the goatish legs and cloven hooves, but that was where the similarity ended.

For this demon had Jordan's face.

Sadie let out a gasp.

He had been victorious.

As this new demon walked up the nave, holding out his hands,

Sadie took in every intricacy of his body; the taut muscles of his chest and arms, the long claws at the ends of his fingers, two horns, five inches in length, tapering to fine, razor-sharp tips. The gait of this demon was crooked, but that came from having to walk with inhuman legs, and she could imagine this beast resting between her own limbs, writhing in ecstasy.

She shuddered at the thought.

Ubel cast her a withering look and then smiled.

"So, the mighty Kobold, back from the dead," he said quietly. "He lives to fight another day" Then he looked at Kobold. "Or did you shy away from your battle with Satan? Is this human more important to you than your destiny?"

Kobold paused.

He was now twenty feet from Ubel, and Sadie could see how massive he was. Ubel came no higher than Kobold's chest.

Ubel took a couple of steps back, reaching the ropes guarding the altar.

"Satan has been destroyed," Kobold said. "And I played my part without even breaking into a sweat. You, Ubel, pale into insignificance in comparison."

Ubel threw out his arms. "I am the Lord of the Corrupted! And this, devil, is my domain! It is your powers that are insignificant, for this environment is alien, is hostile to you!"

Kobold laughed. "I think you're forgetting, Ubel. Earth is familiar to me. I have fought many battles here, and recently. And I thrive on destroying corrupt demons."

"Your battle with Satan means nothing to me, devil," Ubel hissed. "Satan's powers were weak. I shall destroy you, and I shall use your body to destroy and corrupt this altar. And once this altar is corrupted, I shall take your human, rape her useless form, and devour her flesh. That is the destiny for you and this bitch."

Kobold smiled, pointed a finger at Ubel.

And Ubel was flung backwards into the altar.

Flames rose up, and Sadie scrambled to the side, as they engulfed the demon's body.

Ubel screamed and staggered forwards, crashing to the ground a few feet from the altar, where the flames were quickly doused by his body's own defence system. He crawled forward and pulled himself to his knees, looking up at Kobold, who stood before him, arms akimbo.

"You see," the new devil said. "You are nothing to me. I could destroy you in the blinking of an eye, and possibly without expending as much effort. You are welcome to try to defeat me, Ubel, but you will merely be prolonging the agony. And agony it shall be."

Ubel, however, seemed to believe that he could still fight this mighty demon.

He made a grab for Kobold's legs, but Kobold simply side-stepped and stamped a cloven hoof down on Ubel's back, leaving a bloody imprint where the hoof broke the flesh. Then he reached down and plucked Ubel from the ground, holding him by the flesh of his chest.

"You are not worthy of wearing a demon's skin," he said. "It will be a pleasure to strip it from you."

"No," Ubel said quietly, as though he didn't want anybody to hear him.

"What?"

"No."

"No?"

"Do not destroy me," Ubel said meekly.

"You dare to beg for your life? You wear the skin of a demon, and yet you beg for mercy like a pathetic human murderer?"

Sadie watched as Ubel began to whimper. "Please. I was led astray by Satan. It's not my fault." Kobold tossed the weeping demon to the floor in disgust. "It's not my fault!"

"Do you know what powers the devil has?" Kobold asked. "As well as the usual demonic abilities, I have a number of skills unique to the devil. One of those skills is the ability to read the greatest fears of every creature around me. Not just human fears, but those of demons also. And I know, Ubel, what your greatest fear is."

Ubel shook his head. "Please don't kill me!"

"If I killed you, Ubel, you'd be dead in an instant, and what possible pleasure, what sense of vengeance for terrorizing the person I love could I derive from that?" Kobold knelt down before the scorched Ubel and smiled.

"You enjoy being one of the Corrupted, don't you? You enjoy the power. Shit, you're the *Lord of the Corrupted,* aren't you? You could destroy practically everything on this planet, should you so desire. You wouldn't, because you're not insane, because once everything is gone, you won't have fear and death to feed off, will you? But you are powerful. Very, very powerful. Not as powerful as me, admittedly, but you are a demon to be feared, for sure."

Ubel couldn't see where this was leading. And neither could Sadie. That was the man she loved, kneeling before a fallen demon, threatening that demon with powers that she could never have dreamt of.

The man she loved?

Kobold said, "Another ability unique to the devil. I can strip away your demonic powers. Ordinarily, it takes a lot of strength, and I should say that you will put up a fight — an admirable fight, certainly, but a fight from which I shall surely emerge victorious."

"Strip me of my powers?"

"Make you human again, Ubel," Kobold said with a grin. "Mortal." He looked across to where the corpse of the Dean lay. "With your fingerprints all over this crime scene."

"And yours," Ubel sneered. "And hers!"

Kobold nodded. "Of course, you're right." He let out a sigh. "But I can resolve that. But you ... I think I shall have to make do with simply seeing you in human form, afraid of your surroundings, penniless, with no background, no wealth to fall back on. Homeless, with no chance of ever redeeming yourself. And when your miserable human life finally comes to an end ... well, maybe I'll see you back in Hell."

"You can't do that," Ubel said. "I will fight you—to the death."

"You have two choices, Ubel," Kobold said, getting to his feet. "Become human, or be destroyed. I think you know there is no other outcome."

Ubel frowned. "I shall fight," he insisted.

"You know, earlier I said that ordinarily it required a lot of strength to strip you of your powers," Kobold said. "But that wasn't the full story. Ordinarily, it does. But faced with a choice, much like that which I just gave you, the fate of a demon is in his own hands."

"What do you mean?"

"I offered you a choice — become human or be destroyed," Kobold said. "You said aloud that you would fight. That wasn't an option. And your mind ... well, we both know what your mind said to you, don't we? Your mind said that you would rather be human, that you couldn't face destruction. You could not face not existing." Kobold began to laugh.

"What? No!"

Sadie watched as Ubel's body was bathed in a fiery glow. He screamed as though in agony, but then she realized that he wasn't in pain — he just didn't want to face the future that was being offered to him.

When the glow subsided, a naked man lay on the floor where Ubel had been sitting.

His body was moderately toned, but scratched and bruised. His hair was short, but the Mohican strip was still there, lying limply on his scalp rather than erect. His face was that of a forty-year-old, unshaven, pockmarked. His skin was pale and filthy.

Pulling himself to his knees, he looked up at Kobold with fearful eyes, and then glanced across to where Sadie sat.

Sadie knew that she should've been feeling pity.

Instead, she felt nothing.

As the sound of the man's weeping filled her ears, she closed her eyes, and wished that she was someplace else, and that she'd never seen Jordan as this demon, this hateful, vengeful creature, full of bloodlust and hatred.

50

When she opened her eyes, she wasn't in the cathedral any more. Blinking, she sat up in the bed and looked down at herself. She was naked, and her body was bathed in a light coating of perspiration. As the cool air from the open window hit her, she felt chilled and pulled the quilt up to cover herself.

Her mind was attempting to run through the events of the last few hours, but nothing coherent was coming out. None of it made sense.

It had felt like just a moment ago, she'd been sitting by the altar, clutching it as though her life depended upon it – and in a way, it had. But here she was, in her own bedroom, in her own bed, with the early morning light coming in through the crack in the curtains, and nothing made sense anymore.

She climbed out of bed and grabbed her dressing gown from the chair next to the bed, pulling it tight around herself. Wasn't this the dressing gown she'd worn when she'd been chased from the flat?

She clutched a hand to her mouth.

"Fuck," she muttered. The police detective, Saddington, who had been murdered by the demon, Ubel. He was still in her hallway, evidence pointing to a crime she hadn't committed and could never hope to explain.

What the hell was she going to do about it, she wondered as she stood next to the bedroom door? There was blood and rotting flesh on the other side, and she had to face it, because she couldn't stay locked in this room for the rest of her life.

All kinds of ridiculous notions entered her head – she could call the police, say that she had heard a man being murdered in her house. She could stay in her bedroom until the police arrived – the front door wasn't locked, because she'd just bolted out leaving the demon behind, and it was a sure bet that he hadn't taken the time to close the door behind him.

But then, how had she got back here, from the cathedral? From the cathedral that was miles away? Who had brought her back? Had they locked the door behind themselves? Had they cleaned up the blood, and the half-eaten corpse?

Suddenly, she felt queasy.

But there were so many questions that needed answers.

And she could only begin to find those answers when she looked beyond her bedroom door.

Gingerly, she gripped the door handle and twisted. The door popped out of its latch, and creaked noisily as it opened. Pulling it all the way ajar, Sadie took a deep breath and peered out into the hallway.

There was nothing there.

The hallway was as it had been before Detective Superintendent Saddington had been butchered by the demon, the walls immaculately papered, the carpet unblemished, not even a spot of blood in sight.

Warily, she stepped out of her bedroom and looked up and down the hallway.

Nothing.

"What the fuck?" she muttered softly.

The bedroom door opposite opened, and Sadie jumped back into her own room, her heart throbbing violently in her chest. She almost fell over, her legs turning to jelly.

Jodie was standing before her, wearing her night-shirt and pair of socks. Her long hair was unkempt, but other than that, she appeared perfectly healthy.

"What are you doing here?" Sadie hissed.

"Uh," Jodie frowned and looked up. "I live here, dumb-ass."

"Yeah, but ..." Sadie paused. Her sister should've been in hospital; off the danger list, sure, but still in hospital. What was she doing here, at home, sleeping in her own bed? They hadn't brought her home last night.

"Yeah, but what?"

Sadie shook her head. This was getting too weird. "Nothing," she said. Better not to say anything at all until she knew for certain that what had happened to her last night wasn't just some crazy dream. Maybe everything that had happened in the last few weeks hadn't really happened at all.

"Are you okay?" Jodie asked her.

"Fine," Sadie said. "You?"

"I'm getting better," Jodie said, turning to go to the kitchen. Sadie closed her eyes. So, perhaps the drug thing, the stay in hospital, that hadn't been part of the dream. Maybe she'd skipped a day. Maybe Jodie had come out, and she couldn't remember it. It was strange, she had to admit, but it was possible.

More to the point, it was the only feasible explanation.

"What do you want for breakfast?" Jodie asked as she entered the kitchen.

"Uh, I dunno," Sadie said. "Maybe I'll get something later."

She looked at her watch — it was eight in the morning.

And yet, moments ago, it had seemed like it was only four or five o'clock.

What was happening here?

The telephone started to ring, startling Sadie.

She made her way to the lounge and grabbed the receiver.

"Hello?"

"Sadie, it's Billy," an excited voice on the other end said. "Did you check your post this morning? I mean, I suppose this has gone out to all of us! Man, it's incredible!"

"What is?" Sadie asked, sounding unsuitably underwhelmed. But then, today wasn't exactly starting in a sensible way.

"They love us! Fuck! This is a three album, three-year deal!"

Sadie clicked. "The band?"

"Of course the fucking band! Jesus, they want us to go down there this week, sign the contracts! I mean, Christ, we should get legal advice, but this is a four-hundred grand deal! That's a hundred grand each! You'd better check your post, Sadie!"

"I don't believe it," Sadie mumbled. What the hell else could happen on this strange morning. She looked up as Jodie entered the room. "Listen, I'll call you back." She put down the handset. "Jodie, I've got a bizarre question for you. I mean, humour me on this one, right, but just when did you get out?"

"Huh?"

"Out of hospital," Sadie said. "When did you get out of hospital?"

Jodie gave a look as though Sadie were insane, then said, "Yesterday. You and Jordan came and collected me. Man, I was glad to get out ... Sadie, what's wrong with you? You going nuts?"

Sadie shook her head, a manic grin on her face. "Well, I guess I must be because ..." She paused. It probably wasn't a good idea to give her version of yesterday to her little sister. "Forget it. I'm gonna go see what post we've got." She stood up and went to the hallway.

"Better put some clothes on then," Jodie suggested.

Five minutes later, and wearing jeans and a wrinkled sweatshirt, Sadie made her way down to the mail boxes, slipping the key into their slot and taking out the post. There was the usual amount of junk mail, and three letters.

The first was a council tax demand. She didn't even bother opening it, because she knew what it was. No other reason for the district council to be writing to her. Goddamn Brits and their ridiculous taxes. The second was official looking, quite bulky, and on closer inspection had a Metropolitan Police stamp in the corner. Shaking her head, she ripped open the third, which was even bulkier than the second, and a thick sheaf of papers fell into her hands, along with a letter, which she read as she climbed the stairs back to their flat.

It was just as Billy had said – a contract from one of the major record labels. They wanted to sign the band up as quickly as possible. They wanted them in the studio almost immediately.

They'd made it!

She handed the letter to Jodie as she flopped down on the sofa.

"Man, I don't believe it!"

"We're gonna be rich again," Sadie said calmly. "No more slumming it."

Jodie hugged her. "Yeah, but all things considered, it was fun, wasn't it?"

"There were one or two scary moments, but yeah, it was fun," Sadie said. "See, I did tell you we didn't need money to be happy."

"All the same ..." Jodie held up the letter. "You know, I've got my eye on this outfit — Gucci?"

Sadie ruffled her sister's hair. "All in good time, sis, all in good time."

"We should crack open a bottle of champagne!" Jodie said, standing up. "Do we have any?"

"Champagne? We have Coke, that's about the nearest we'll get to it!"

"What's wrong? I mean, you should be happy, Sadie. This is what you've always wanted, isn't it?"

"Yeah," Sadie said but she knew she didn't sound convincing. But how could she? This just didn't make sense. She couldn't remember fetching her sister from the hospital; as far as Jodie was aware, Jordan was dead; and where the hell was that police officer who'd been ripped apart in their hallway?

And what really happened last night?

She held up the envelope from the police.

"What's that?" Jodie asked her.

"I daren't look," Sadie said.

But of course she did.

The letter said that the investigation into her father's business affairs was concluded. They'd discovered the Swiss bank accounts, and there was more than enough in them to cover both the debts and the fines. Which meant that the two properties owned by her parents were being handed back to them.

"But this is great!" Jodie exclaimed.

Sadie nodded her head.

It was great.

It was almost too great.

Almost too good to be true.

She thought about Jordan – Kobold the devil – whatever, whoever he was.

This had to be his doing.

Jordan parked the BMW in the car park and looked up at the flat window— Sadie's bedroom window. She'd be up by now, and she'd be confused. Nothing would add up. The dead policeman, gone; Jodie back home; the events of last night washed away because they couldn't possibly have happened. How could she have been in a cathedral, stalked by a demon, when she'd been asleep all night in her own bed?

But situations and circumstances could be manipulated.

He turned to the woman sitting beside him.

Reizend smiled. "How do you feel?"

"Nervous."

"You sure this is what you want?"

"I want nothing else," Jordan said, taking the bottle of champagne from her.

"You can change your mind, Kobold," Reizend told him. "There's no need to worry for her safety now. Her future is assured."

"And so is mine."

Reizend didn't speak for a few moments.

"Zerstörer will be a good devil," she said. "But you will always be the rightful heir."

"In name only."

"It's refreshing to see someone who isn't tempted by power," Reizend said. "Love is more important to you."

"The money," Jordan said. "Was that appropriate?"

"You assisted the police and the FBI in recovering their lost funds," Reizend said. "That was appropriate. You didn't manipulate the figures, you didn't create money out of thin air."

Jordan shook his head. "All the same ..."

"Sadie and Jodie now have what is rightfully theirs."

"And the record contract?"

"You know that was my handiwork," Reizend said. "I can be persuasive. But those people didn't really need much in the way of persuasion. They were impressed. I merely hurried them along."

"So no rules were broken?"

"Hey, I'm an angel, I don't break rules," Reizend said. "Besides, if any rules had been broken, neither of us would be here."

There was a pause, a long silence.

"Thank you for your help," Jordan said.

"It was my pleasure."

Jordan leant across and kissed Reizend on the cheek.

"It's over now, is it? For me?"

Reizend didn't answer at first. Then she said, "You will always be the devil, Kobold. You will always possess the powers of the devil. They cannot be taken away. You have been granted leave, and what you do in this mortal life will determine the path you take at the end. Do well, and I have no doubt that you will, and you will end up like me."

"A seraph?"

Reizend nodded. "You will always be too powerful to be contained as a mere soul."

"So I still have my powers?"

"You can manipulate people and events," Reizend said. "Should you so desire."

"But I don't."

"If you do, you may become corrupted."

"That's not gonna happen."

"I hope not, Kobold."

"Call me Jordan," Jordan said, climbing out of the BMW. Reizend followed.

"Good luck, Jordan."

And then she turned and walked away.

Jordan made his way to the flat and knocked on the door. Jodie answered.

"Hey," she said. "You'd better get in here. Sadie's acting kinda weird. And she's got loads of good news."

"I think he already knows," Sadie said, stepping into the hallway.

Jordan entered the flat and closed the door behind him. He held up the champagne. "I did hear this rumour that a certain band had created a lot of interest."

"I bet you did" Sadie said raising an eyebrow. Jodie made herself scarce and Jordan followed Sadie into the front room. "So, what's the explanation?" Sadie asked him.

"What do you know?"

"Just what you told me last night and what happened last night.

What I don't understand is all of this?"

"You don't have to," Jordan said, gathering her in his arms. At first, she tried to pull away, and he loosened his grip. Then she fell back into him.

"I love you, Sadie."

"I love you too. But I don't know what you are."

"I'm human."

"Completely human?"

None of us are completely human, Sadie," Jordan said. "We all have our secrets, our quirks. We've all trod down the road that leads to Hell. Some of us jump back over to the other road, the one that leads to Heaven. Some of us continue down the road that leads to Hell. And some of us get there, don't like it, and come back."

"That's what you've done?"

"I've given up everything for you, Sadie," Jordan said.

"Everything?"

"Everything."

"So you're human?"

"I always was human to you, Sadie."

"But you were behind everything that happened here?"

"I put the wheels in motion," Jordan confessed. "I didn't falsify anything. I just expedited it all. And your recording contract ... you have Reizend to thank for that."

"And the policeman and the Dean?"

"They no longer exist," Jordan said sadly. "Nobody will mourn them."

"That's not right."

"It has to be that way, Sadie, because nobody can ever find out the truth, the real truth. The afterlife, and what happens to us all when we get there, has to remain a mystery. It has to rely on faith, rather than absolute knowledge. And so the policeman and the Dean never existed. The slate has been wiped clean. It's time for us to get on with our lives."

Sadie hugged him tightly, and he felt her warmth and her love, and for the first time in hundreds of years, he felt truly human again. Like a real human, not just somebody play-acting.

Then Sadie asked him, "So you're not the devil?"

At first he couldn't answer. He couldn't lie to her — but then, he couldn't tell her the truth, that he wasn't allowed give up his powers, that he would always be the devil, if only in name. If he told her that, she'd never want to see him again. Of that he was certain.

But to lie to her ...

Then he said, with much reluctance ...

EPILOGUE

"... I am not a demon, I am not the devil, I am a human. And that is all I have ever been."

The man stared wild-eyed at the psychiatrist and shook his head. He wasn't going to say it, and the psychiatrist had to admit that he'd known that even before he'd asked him to repeat it.

It had been this way for the last six months, ever since he had been brought to Broadmoor for the brutal murder of three people in one night. The man, his Mohican hair dirty and straggly, and soaked with the blood of his victims, naked and grubby, had been convinced that he was some kind of vengeful angel, a demon, out to punish the evil. In his defence, two of the victims had been about to rape a woman in the graveyard. But the self-proclaimed demon had also killed the would-be rapists' victim.

Insane, totally and utterly insane.

He had, with his bare hands, succeeded in ripping the heads from the shoulders, and had been in the process of devouring what flesh and muscle he could find in the open wounds when the police had turned up. It had taken eight officers to subdue him, and the injuries he'd sustained during his arrest were still evident all this time later. His right arm was crooked, because it had been broken in four places, and even after the doctors had set it, he'd ripped off the plaster with his teeth and pulled the shattered limb in every direction. He was fortunate that the arm hadn't been infected.

A hopeless case.

He'd never be released.

His strength and the sheer depth of his insanity would see to that.

The psychiatrist packed up his things and smiled at the unnamed man, strapped to a bed. He was in solitary confinement, and the psychiatrist couldn't really see a day when he would be allowed to roam free within the grounds with his fellow inmates. On his very first day at Broadmoor, he'd slain one child murderer and had savaged another, holding the killer down as he devoured with relish the man's genitals. The guards had watched from a safe distance, before moving in.

The castrated child killer, who probably wasn't actually insane before he came to Broadmoor was certainly doing a better impression of a lunatic now.

He said goodbye to the 'demon' and left the room, leaving the patient with the television for company.

Ubel couldn't communicate with the humans because they just wouldn't listen to him. In his sparse moments of clarity, he could see why, but reasoning had got him nowhere.

He was here, in this home for the criminally insane, because on that first day, he couldn't adjust to being human. He'd been a demon for as long as he could remember, and he'd acted in the way demons were programmed to act. He'd seen two men raping a woman, and he'd taken their lives, destroying their souls in the process. The woman he'd killed for fun, because that's what the Corrupted did, and he'd sent her soul to whichever branch of the afterlife she deserved.

Except destroying souls and condemning them to Heaven and Hell wasn't something he could do any more. He was no longer a demon, no longer one of the Corrupted.

He was a human.

He could see that now.

And even though he'd tried to communicate with the scores of psychiatrists who'd paid him a visit, they just wouldn't listen. He wasn't going to lie, he wasn't going to say that he'd never been a demon. He had been Ubel, Lord of the Corrupted!

So now he was the unnamed man – for they wouldn't accept Ubel as his name – condemned to spend his life within the walls of this prison, unable to redeem himself.

And it was all the fault of one person.

He looked up at the TV, where a music channel was playing softly.

The face of the woman, singing her song – a face he recognized.

The man who was kissing her in the video – a face he recognized!

"Kobold?" he said with a frown. "Kobold?" But Kobold was human now.

Kobold was no longer the devil!

Excited, Ubel pulled on the restraints.

"Kobold! You have no defence now!"

He ripped away one of the straps.

"Kobold, you are human!" he screamed, laughing like a maniac, as he continued to wrench away at the straps. "Just as I am. You have no power with which to defeat me now! And I shall make you pay for what you did to me!"

He was free now, running over to the wall, where he pulled the TV from its stand.

He shouted right into the face of the man who had sentenced him to this mortal hell.

"I shall kill you, Kobold!"

Hands grabbed him, pulling the TV from him, forcing him to the ground.

"No, you don't understand!" he shouted, looking up at the psychiatrist as the guards held him down. Nobody else spoke. "On the TV! That is Kobold! He was Satan's heir, he is the man who stripped me of my demonic powers!" He felt the needle enter his arm, the sedative squeezed into his vein. "No! Listen, that man on the TV! He is the devil. And he's in human form! I can kill him now! I can make him pay!"

And as the darkness overcame him, he shouted. "Kobold, I shall make you pay! You and that bitch human!"

THE END